W9-CEQ-556

Praise for *The Killing Kind*

'Nobody understands the dark gap between justice
and the law better than Jane Casey'
No.1 bestselling author Val McDermid

'Cool, accomplished, compulsive'
Cara Hunter, author of *The Whole Truth*

'Extremely tense and very gripping with a killer "what if":
your stalker claims to be the only person who can save
you – what if this time he's telling the truth?'
Ruth Ware, author of *One by One*

'An intense, action-packed mystery . . . brilliant'
The Times

'Chilling' *Sunday Times*

'Creepily good' *Daily Mail*

'A compulsive page-turner of the highest order'
Steve Cavanagh, author of *Fifty-Fifty*

'A brilliant, breathless game of cat-and-mouse'
Erin Kelly, author of *He Said/She Said*

'A truly masterly thriller. Fasten your seatbelts,
this is going to be a bumpy read'
Liz Nugent, author of *Our Little Cruelties*

'A tense and well-plotted novel'
Harriet Tyce, author of *Blood Orange*

'Tense, pacy, addictive'
Sarah Vaughan, author of *Little Disasters*

'Jane Casey is one of my favourite writers . . .
so fast, so clever, so compelling'
Dervla McTiernan, author of *The Ruin*

'Brilliantly plotted from start to finish'
Catherine Cooper, author of *The Chalet*

'Twisty and unexpected, with some great surprises'
Ann Cleeves, author of the Vera Stanhope series

'Each twist tightens the screw of fear and distrust'
J. R. Ellis, author of the Yorkshire Murder Mystery series

'Endlessly surprising, impeccably
plotted and hugely satisfying'
Catherine Ryan Howard, author of *The Nothing Man*

'Heart-stopping twists and a seriously satisfying ending'
Sarah Hilary, author of the DI Marnie Rome series

'One of those "just one more page" books'
Susi Holliday, author of *The Last Resort*

'Authentic, tense, thrilling and completely engrossing'
Will Dean, author of *Dark Pines*

'Intricate . . . authentic'
Jane Shemilt, author of *Daughter*

'Will keep you guessing'
Elle Croft, author of *The Guilty Wife*

'Brilliant, satisfying'
Lucy Mangan, author of *Bookworm*

'Breathtakingly brilliant'
Elizabeth Haynes, author of *Into the Darkest Corner*

'A fast-paced thriller'
Jo Spain, author of *Dirty Little Secrets*

'Will keep you up all night'
Sam Blake, author of *The Dark Room*

'Keeps pages flipping and hearts racing'
Lucy Atkins, author of *Magpie Lane*

'Addictive' *Prima*

'Fascinating' *Irish Times*

'Outstandingly good' *Daily Express*

'Near perfect' *Red*

THE
KILLING
KIND

Jane Casey has written eleven crime novels for adults and three for teenagers. A former editor, she is married to a criminal barrister who ensures her writing is realistic and as accurate as possible.

This authenticity has made her novels international best-sellers and critical successes. The Maeve Kerrigan series has been nominated for many awards: in 2015 Jane won the Mary Higgins Clark Award for *The Stranger You Know* and Irish Crime Novel of the Year for *After the Fire*. In 2019, *Cruel Acts* was chosen as Irish Crime Novel of the Year at the Irish Book Awards. It was a *Sunday Times* bestseller.

Born in Dublin, Jane now lives in southwest London with her husband and two children.

@JaneCaseyAuthor

Also by Jane Casey

THE MAEVE KERRIGAN SERIES
The Burning
The Reckoning
The Last Girl
The Stranger You Know
The Kill
After the Fire
Let the Dead Speak
Cruel Acts
The Cutting Place

STANDALONE NOVELS
The Missing

THE
KILLING
KIND

JANE CASEY

HarperCollins*Publishers*

HarperCollins*Publishers* Ltd
1 London Bridge Street,
London SE1 9GF

www.harpercollins.co.uk

HarperCollins*Publishers*
1st Floor, Watermarque Building, Ringsend Road
Dublin 4, Ireland

This paperback edition 2022
1

First published by HarperCollins*Publishers* 2021

Copyright © Jane Casey 2021

Jane Casey asserts the moral right to
be identified as the author of this work

A catalogue record for this book is available from the British Library

ISBN: 978-0-00-840496-3 (PB b-format)
ISBN: 978-0-00-852922-2 (PB b-format US-only)

This novel is entirely a work of fiction.
The names, characters and incidents portrayed in it are
the work of the author's imagination. Any resemblance to
actual persons, living or dead, events or localities is
entirely coincidental.

Typeset in Sabon LT Std by Palimpsest Book Production Ltd,
Falkirk, Stirlingshire

Printed and Bound in the UK using 100% Renewable Electricity
at CPI Group (UK) Ltd

All rights reserved. No part of this publication may be
reproduced, stored in a retrieval system, or transmitted,
in any form or by any means, electronic, mechanical,
photocopying, recording or otherwise, without the prior
permission of the publishers.

MIX
Paper from
responsible sources
FSC™ C007454

This book is produced from independently certified FSC™ paper
to ensure responsible forest management.

For more information visit: www.harpercollins.co.uk/green

For Alison Gleeson

I think about death a lot; it's my job. Specifically, I think about how death happens. About the truth of it, or the lie. About when you can be absolutely certain, and when the edges are blurred, and what gets lost to memory or misunderstanding.

I think about my job, which is to take the facts of a case and arrange them into a story – without elaborating or exaggerating – and how that story must convince the jury to believe my version of events. I am very convincing. I tell a good story.

But I have to think hard about where to start with this story, because the beginning isn't the accident, even though it seemed that way to me. The wolf was already at my heels, planning his next move as I walked, oblivious, through the forest.

He had waited for a long time, and now he was ready.

1

I think about death a lot, but I was not thinking about it the day it came for me. I was too busy running up Ludgate Hill, dodging other people's umbrellas so they didn't shower me with icy October rain when they collided with mine. The rain was a curse for two reasons: I hated having wet feet, and otherwise I would have been hiding behind the biggest sunglasses I owned.

I wasn't just wet: I was late, which was the greatest sin of all for a barrister. My pupilmaster had told me as much on my first day. *You may have to go to court unprepared, sick, hungover, stressed or even wretchedly unhappy, but for God's sake, get there on time.* The whole situation made me furious with myself. I knew better than to cause myself problems for no reason, other than that I'd been up too late the night before.

I didn't go through the smoked-glass revolving door of the Central Criminal Court, also known as the Old Bailey. Instead I hurried across the road to a small café that was thronged with people. A bull-necked bald man was sitting near the back, reading a newspaper. He glanced up and whistled.

'Dear oh dear, Miss Lewis. What happened to you?'

'Late night.' I parked my wheeled bag beside the table and concentrated on folding my umbrella so I didn't have to look him in the eye.

'Not the best preparation for today, was it, Ingrid?' Disapproval rolled through every consonant, lent more weight by his accent which was still pure Glasgow despite thirty years in London. Because he was a solicitor and the reason I was at work at all, I couldn't quite bring myself to make a joke about it.

'I'll be fine.'

'Of course you will.' He grinned. 'I'm only kidding you on. Have a coffee and get your breath back.'

'Can I get you one?'

'White, two sugars.' He went back to his newspaper with a hint of a smile still softening the corners of his mouth and I turned to the counter to order. I quite admired how he'd managed to get me to buy him a coffee. It was a small gesture when Niall Hyde had made it possible for me to pay the rent that month, and the month before. Moreover, I knew what the clerks would say if I annoyed him. What was good for me was good for chambers, and if I made an enemy of one of the most successful defence solicitors around, I would make twenty more among my colleagues.

Barristers had a way of working that was confusing to outsiders, but it was based on centuries of tradition. We were self-employed, independent of one another in theory, but most of us pooled our resources in a set of chambers that was more like a club than a shared office.

6

The downside was that what affected one of us in chambers could affect us all. Each set had clerks who ran the barristers like benign and cocky gang-masters, allocating cases and work as they saw fit. Cross the clerks and I would end up on an endless run of first appearances in magistrates' courts across the south east instead of pursuing the nice little practice that had me at the Bailey on a Monday morning. I had been doing this job for seven years, after a law degree and a year at bar school and another year as a pupil, and I was finally starting to feel I was getting the hang of it. My income still varied wildly and most of the time, if I worked it out, what I earned wasn't close to the minimum wage. But I loved it. It was worthwhile, and challenging, and sometimes even inspiring.

And I liked it when I won.

'What was it, a break-up?'

I pushed his coffee across the table and sat down. 'Yes, but not mine. My best friend's boyfriend of three years walked out on her.'

'Is that right, aye?' Sarcasm coated the words. 'And the solution was red wine?'

'Among other things.'

'Haven't you learned not to mix your drinks?'

'You'd think,' I said ruefully. 'But I really will be okay in court.'

'Of course you will.' He twinkled at me, his eyes bright with amusement. 'Tried hair of the dog?'

'No, and I'm not going to. I'm never drinking again.'

That made him chuckle and we drank our coffee in perfect amity. It was Hyde's routine to head to the café in the mornings and a steady stream of lawyers came to pay court to him. In between interruptions I made sure I knew exactly what Hyde wanted to achieve for his client that morning. It was a pre-trial hearing, completely routine, where a man was going to plead not guilty to attempted murder. A sex game gone wrong, according to him; long minutes of strangulation according to the prosecution, who had the medical evidence of bruises and broken blood vessels to back it up. I'd met him and looked into his wide, honest eyes and heard the ring of sincerity in his voice, and we had evidence from a dating website of his girlfriend's stated sexual preferences that included 'breath play' and bondage. A post-sex argument, a false accusation of violence to get revenge: it happened.

'But did it happen in this case?' my best friend Adele had slurred at two in the morning, and I'd shrugged.

'His story is that it did. The evidence doesn't contradict him.'

'But he *hurt* her.'

'With her consent, he says.'

'You can't know that for sure.'

'The point is that the prosecution can't prove otherwise.'

Adele poured another slug of wine into her glass, spilling some over the side. 'Whoops. I don't know how you can live with yourself, telling lies for these bastards.'

People who weren't barristers worried a lot more about innocent and guilty than we did. We separated ourselves from questions of morality because we had to. Everyone deserved a decent defence or justice couldn't be done. We took the work that was offered to us without demur because that was the cab-rank rule; we generally didn't pick and choose cases that suited our personal tastes or morality. We were professional and polite and did our best, and most of us quickly got used to it. The system worked for everyone or it worked for no one.

'I don't know it's a lie,' I'd said patiently. 'That's up to the jury to decide. I presume he's not guilty unless he actually tells me he did it, at which point I have to advise him to plead guilty. Until then he's entitled to the best defence he can get. If he still gets convicted, then at least I know I tested the prosecution case.'

'And if he did it but you persuade the jury he didn't?'

'Then the prosecution didn't do their job properly and I did.'

'There are times,' Adele said blurrily, 'that you don't sound anything like yourself any more.'

Ouch. 'It's just part of the job,' I said. 'You have to put some distance between yourself and the work or you'd go mad.'

'I don't mean,' Adele said, 'work. I mean . . . everything.' She gestured around her vaguely.

And don't you think I have good reason to be different?

I didn't say it out loud.

'Sick,' Adele pronounced, which I thought was a further comment on me until she flopped over sideways and started heaving.

The Old Bailey was one of the few courts that still had separate robing rooms for male and female counsel, and the female robing room was a safe place in every way. I closed the door behind me and scanned the room for people I knew, recognising a couple of barristers I'd been up against before. A young woman in the corner was one of the pupils from my chambers. At present her face was as white as the sheet of paper that vibrated in her hands.

First-timer nerves, I diagnosed, and smiled at her. She managed a watery sort of smile in return.

I needed to change into court dress myself: it was deeply traditional and not particularly practical. I fastened the starched bands around my neck, then drew a billowing black gown over my staid black suit and white shirt. The finishing touch was the horsehair wig that demanded neat hair underneath it so that all anyone could see was a hint of pale gold under the rough grey curls. I had inherited fair hair from my Danish father, Jens Villemand, along with grey-blue eyes, but my cheekbones, arched eyebrows and surname all belonged to my mother. I had taken her name after they divorced, from a sense of loyalty, and because it made life simpler since I lived with her.

I was concentrating on pinning my hair back in a tight bun, my mouth full of hairpins, when a woman rushed into the robing room, moving fast despite terrifyingly high heels. Belinda Grey, one of the sharpest women I'd ever met, thirty-five and well on her way to a dazzling career. I'd been her junior on a rape trial four years earlier and it had been both terrifying and exhilarating. It was a small world and I ran into her often enough that we were edging towards friendship, though I was always going to hero-worship her. She was whippet-thin and glamorous, with a glossy sheen of wealth and confidence. Her suit was fitted to her body as if it had been made for her, which was actually a possibility. I opted for flats so I could get places quickly, and work clothes that verged on dowdiness they were so plain. I didn't like attracting attention any more. Belinda positively revelled in it.

She was on the phone, as usual.

10

'No, he needs his sports kit for Playball. After school.' A note of irritation. 'The forecast is for the rain to stop by lunchtime so—I did write it on the fridge, actually, Michael, so if you didn't see it—' She broke off to wave at me and mouth *hello*. I smiled back. 'Well, it was there. Yes, it was. Did you even check? Did you—' She looked at her phone and shook her head. 'He's gone. Hung up on me.'

'How is Michael?' I asked.

'Fed up. We're between nannies and he's using up his annual leave being a house husband.'

'And he doesn't like it?'

'He's *terrible* at it. Archie is running rings around him, as only a five-year-old can. And meanwhile the world of advertising seems to be surviving without Michael.'

I grinned. 'Very disappointing.'

'Well, exactly. You'd think they'd pretend to miss him, just to be kind.' She checked her watch. 'Of course I'm supposed to be in two places at once. The judge insisted I had to come along today for this hearing which is mainly so he can give me a bollocking, even though I've got a conference in chambers at eleven. And this *rain*. I'll look like something the cat threw up if it hasn't stopped.'

I knew her chambers – Garter Buildings – was at least a ten-minute walk from the Old Bailey, because it was right opposite mine. 'No umbrella?'

'I couldn't find it before I left.' She rolled her eyes. 'The cleaner quit last week, and good riddance because I'm sure she deliberately broke things when she was pissed off with us, which was all the fucking time. Anyway, the house is total, utter chaos. I'm amazed I managed to find matching shoes.'

I finished stabbing pins into the ball of hair that was

coiled at the back of my neck. 'You can have my umbrella if you like.'

Her eyes lit up for an instant but then she shook her head. 'I couldn't.'

'Take it. I don't have anywhere important to be and my hearing isn't for a while. But if you're wrong about the forecast, I won't be happy.'

'Ingrid, you *star*.' She picked up the umbrella. 'I won't forget this.'

I had no illusions; she would still take every opportunity to kneecap me if we were on opposing sides in a trial. However, it couldn't do any harm to have someone like Belinda Grey on my side. And I liked her, despite her acid tongue and terrifying reputation and staggeringly high turnover of domestic staff.

Belinda had moved on and I turned back to my reflection, checking the details: my hair was smooth and neat. My make-up was enough to make the best of the hollow hangover eyes that had greeted me that morning, but no more than that. My bands were sitting flat, my gown was immaculate, and not too much white shirt was showing. I took a deep breath and let it out slowly. The hearing was straightforward, as I'd said, but there was always a flutter of nervous energy in my stomach before I went into court. You couldn't take anything for granted, and the day you did was the day it would all go wrong.

There was no sign of Belinda or my umbrella when I got back to the robing room, but the rain had stopped. My hearing had gone well and Niall Hyde had been pleased enough to clap me on the shoulder afterwards.

'Good job, lassie. See you soon.'

12

The last traces of my hangover had even disappeared in the glow of satisfaction. There was a definite spring in my step as I bowled out of the court building, or tried to. The elderly security guard was leaning through the door, eyeing the traffic that was nose-to-tail up the street.

'What's going on?'

'Accident down on Ludgate Circus. Pedestrian went under a lorry.'

'Oh dear,' I said inadequately. 'Were they . . .'

'I should think it was fatal. Happened a while ago and the traffic has been like this ever since. Backed up all the way to Holborn and Aldwych, from what I've heard.'

I shuddered. 'I never take a risk with crossing that road.'

'No, you wouldn't want to. Happens every year. Don't expect the rain helped.' He shook his head, his eyes watering. 'Everyone in too much of a hurry these days, that's what it is.'

I nodded, not having much to add to that and being in a hurry myself because I had a case to prepare for the following day. I set off past the stalled traffic, thinking about work as I emerged from Old Bailey onto Ludgate Hill. I spared a glance for the imposing portico of Wren's cathedral, because what was the point of living in London if you couldn't nod to the classical grandeur of St Paul's when you passed it. Then I headed down towards Ludgate Circus at a brisk pace, calculating the detour I would need to make if it was still closed off. There was a crowd of onlookers massed on the pavement. Because of the steep hill, I had a grandstand view of the lorry stopped in the middle of the intersection, and the tent that was propped up against the front of it hiding God knows what. I had prosecuted a death by dangerous driving

13

once, and had learned enough about processing the scene to be able to understand what was going on. There was a cordon manned by grim-faced City of London police that extended around the entire junction and officers in fluorescent jackets were engaged in measuring distances and taking photographs. Circles of spray paint indicated where pieces of evidence had landed across the carriageway. A fatal accident, as the security guard had thought. Someone wouldn't be going home that night. They would never be home again.

Reality was doing a good job of obliterating my good mood. I skirted the cordon, making for Blackfriars where I would be able to cross—

I stopped dead.

A circle of paint had caught my attention, in spite of myself. It was maybe twenty feet in front of the truck, in the middle of the road. It was sprayed around a shoe that had fallen on its side. The patent leather was cloudy with scratches, but it was still recognisably the same shoe that Belinda had been wearing earlier. High heel. Pointed toe.

No mistake.

2

'So you were one of the last people to talk to her before the incident, is that right?'

'I must have been, I think. I can't be certain.' Incident was such a useful word for the police officer to use, I thought. Not an accident, definitively, but not implying it was deliberate either. The City of London officer seemed to be the kind of woman who used words with care. She was maybe fifty, with bright blue eyes and a quiff of greying hair cropped almost to her scalp on the back and sides. It looked as if it would be soft as velvet.

Concentrate.

I swallowed and jammed my hands between my knees, knowing that I was taking every opportunity to distract myself from the conversation because I didn't want to think about poor Belinda and her devastated husband and their small boy who couldn't understand why Mummy wouldn't come home. Two days had passed since her death and I had struggled to put her out of my mind. Now that

I was actually supposed to be thinking about her, I was finding excuses to do anything but.

I think it was my fault. The words stuck in my throat. I couldn't say that out loud. I couldn't even admit it to myself.

The clerks had let me use one of the chambers meeting rooms for my interview with the police officer and it was a neutral, comfortable space, devoid of interest apart from an ancient fireplace on one wall and the leaded bay window that gave away the age of the building. The set of chambers I belonged to was in the Inner Temple, housed in a building that creaked with age and overcrowding. The meeting room was clinically clean and tidy. Most of the other rooms were obscured by the tide of debris that washed around the spaces where barristers worked – old briefs, towering boxes crammed with files, bags, bins for confidential papers, gowns hung on the back of doors, shoes kicked off under desks, the remains of someone's lunch from the previous week, a printer that had ceased to work some months before. It was disgraceful and chaotic, but I preferred it to the cream upholstery and tasteful barley-coloured carpet in the meeting room. My eyes skittered over my surroundings, failing to find anything of interest apart from the keen, focused face opposite mine.

'Would you say you knew her well?' the police officer asked.

'I only worked with her once, but we were friendly.' I swallowed. 'I had dinner at her house once, at the end of the trial.'

Michael, tall and lanky, pouring champagne with a lavish hand in the high-ceilinged house in Richmond that

16

he'd bought for cash after selling his agency. Archie, then a toddler in pyjamas, pink toes like baby shrimp, curling up on his mother's knee and refusing to go to bed even though he could barely hold his head up for tiredness. Belinda laughing, happy because she had won.

'Would you have noticed if she was upset on Monday?'

'Yes.' I thought about it for a moment. 'She was on edge, but she was trying to do a hundred things at once. She was always operating at top speed.'

'But she seemed normal.'

'She was having a bad day,' I said hesitantly. 'But nothing out of the ordinary. I mean, I don't want to give you the wrong impression.'

'Just give me *your* impression.' The officer smiled reassuringly. She was PC Alison Buswell, from the major investigation team in charge of finding out what had led to Belinda's death. The lorry driver would be looking at a charge of dangerous or careless driving, assuming he'd passed the breathalyser at the scene. Dangerous driving carried a heavy sentence. It was a serious case, and even though PC Buswell was looking relaxed I felt she was waiting to pounce on anything I said that might help.

'She didn't seem to me to be suicidal,' I said at last. 'But she was . . . distracted. And in a hurry. She could have been preoccupied when she was crossing the road.' If it was an accident.

'Did she say anything else?'

'That she was going to get a hard time from a judge and she had to be back in her chambers for a con at eleven.' I glanced out of the window involuntarily, across the Temple, to where Garter Buildings stood in a Victorian terrace that had the ordered symmetry of books on a shelf.

17

'Was she upset about the judge?'

'No.'

'Really?'

I shrugged. 'It happens. You're representing everyone involved in the prosecution or defence. If anyone messes up, the judge takes it out on you. No one likes getting in trouble but you learn how to deal with it. You could find out who she was in front of—'

'I've spoken to the judge.' PC Buswell smiled again, this time with a hint of complacency that I suppose she deserved. 'He said they had been able to reach a solution that worked for all parties and he hadn't taken her to task. The other barristers in the case confirmed it. She was in good spirits when she left.'

'Was it still raining?'

'Why do you ask?'

'I was just trying to make sense of what happened to her.' I swallowed. 'She'd forgotten her umbrella and I gave her mine.'

'Ah. Yes, it was raining. She had an umbrella.'

I pictured her walking down the hill, hurrying, head bent, my bright, distinctive umbrella shielding her from the worst of the rain. It would have hidden her face, suggesting to the world that the woman who had hurried into court under that umbrella had come back out again.

'Can I see the CCTV?'

PC Buswell looked surprised but her voice was level when she spoke. 'I don't think that would be appropriate.'

'I want to see what happened.'

'Why?'

'I just . . .' I trailed off. 'These questions are your way of asking me if she could have deliberately walked into

18

the traffic, aren't they? So there's some reason for you to think the driver didn't do anything wrong. You're focusing on her behaviour more than if he'd run a red light. I want to know the circumstances. Was the pavement busy? Was she running, or being careless because she was distracted by something? Is there something about this that makes you question whether it was an accident or deliberate?'

PC Buswell closed her notebook and set her pen down on it with decision. 'All good questions. But they're not questions for you.'

'I know. But—'

'You've been very helpful. You're a good witness, as I would expect. I would also expect you to try to bring your professional experience to bear on this – it's only natural. But the fact is, you're not going to be prosecuting this case if it ever comes to court. You don't need to know anything more about it and I would advise you not to try to find out details that I haven't mentioned to you. It could only be distressing for you to see the CCTV or images from the scene. What happened to her was very traumatic, physically.'

'I understand.' *I can imagine what happens when a pedestrian is struck by an articulated lorry, believe it or not.*

PC Buswell leaned away from the table and folded her arms. 'You weren't all that close, were you? One trial, a few years ago, one dinner at her house. But you seem deeply upset by her death.'

'It's tragic.' My lips felt stiff.

'Of course. But it's not your tragedy, is it?'

Not this time. I kept the words back, because *tragedy* was a bold claim and she would want to know if I could back it up, and I wasn't ready for that.

'This is hard to explain, but I have some concerns that maybe – if it was deliberate – maybe she wasn't the intended target. Maybe it was supposed to be me.'

PC Buswell's eyebrows shot up. 'Why would you think that?'

'The umbrella. I was carrying it on my way into court – it might have made someone think it was me. We were dressed similarly. Someone might have made a mistake.'

'Someone?' She looked baffled. 'Who?'

'I had a client a few years ago who . . . crossed the line. He became a major nuisance.'

'In what way?'

'He bothered me for a while, until he got bored.' *And I've been waiting for him to come back ever since.*

She flipped open her notebook again, with visible reluctance. 'What's his name?'

'John Webster.' I half-expected the walls to cave in, the windows to shatter, but the room was silent apart from PC Buswell's pen moving across the page.

'What did he want – a relationship with you?'

'Not the way you might imagine. He's not motivated by the same things as normal people. Sex doesn't mean all that much to him, as I understand it.' I swallowed. 'He likes fear. He likes manipulating his targets. He was drawn to me because he wanted to see what it would take to break me. I was confident, I suppose, and . . . happy. He saw me as a challenge.'

'And has he been in contact with you recently?'

'He's been in prison. Nothing relating to me. He was convicted of a small fraud – that's how he makes a living, I think, but this time he got caught. He did nine months. His probation officer told me he was out.' I swallowed.

20

'I had a restraining order but it ran out in September.'

'That could be extended. Has he threatened you?'

'Not recently. But—' I broke off. What I wanted to say was that he was always a threat to me, hiding in every shadow and behind every door. But that sounded insane.

'Has he threatened you in the past?'

'Yes.'

'Do you think he's capable of murder?'

I almost laughed. 'I know he is.'

'Do you know where he lives?'

'Not any more.'

'I'll see if I can trace him.'

'His probation officer would be able to find him for you, probably.'

'I'll look into it.' She shut the notebook again.

'And can I see the footage?'

'I don't think it's appropriate. You're asking me to let you see a woman's death, because you loaned her an umbrella and you attracted some unwanted attention once upon a time. It would be an unforgivable invasion of her family's privacy.'

'I understand.' My face was flushed; the police officer hadn't minced her words. 'But you're not treating this as a straightforward accident, are you?'

I wanted her to say no, but she pulled a face. 'I'm not sure. I will admit that a number of things are unclear at present. I'm not satisfied that we have the full story of what happened on Monday.' She leaned towards me again, her eyes fixed on mine. The effect was hypnotic, designed to lull me into a state of calm. 'And until I'm satisfied, I won't give up.'

From: 4102@freeinternetmail.com
To: Durbs, IATL

I thought you said it would be easy. You said we couldn't make a mistake.

From: Durbs@mailmeforfree.com
To: 4102, IATL

It wasn't a mistake.

From: 4102@freeinternetmail.com
To: Durbs, IATL

That wasn't what we were planning, though, was it?

From: Durbs@mailmeforfree.com
To: 4102, IATL

Not what you were planning, maybe. But you don't need to know every detail, do you? It's all the same in the end. You'll get what you want and so will I.

From: 4102@freeinternetmail.com
To: Durbs, IATL

I wouldn't have gone along with it if I'd known. That woman had a child.

From: Durbs@mailmeforfree.com
To: 4102, IATL

Bit late for your conscience to kick in.
Look, don't waste your tears on her. She was just as bad as the others.

From: 4102@freeinternetmail.com
To: Durbs, IATL

I don't like being lied to. And I was promised a different outcome.

From: IATL@internetforyou.com
To: Durbs, 4102

Relax, both of you. Let it play out.
It won't be long now.

2016

3

'Just a few more questions, Miss Seaton.'

I smiled for the benefit of the woman who was trembling in the witness box, and for the jury who were watching me curiously, and for my client in the dock.

You don't need to worry about me. I know what I'm doing.

I did know what I was doing but the truth was that I needed to be very lucky in the next few minutes, or my client was going to be found guilty of stalking under Section 4A of the Protection from Harassment Act 1997. The judge looked as if she was just waiting for an excuse to send him to prison for the maximum ten years. But I was in control.

I didn't need to look over to the dock to know that the defendant was watching me. John Webster had paid close attention to every moment of his trial. The taut, dangerous attention of the true obsessive, according to the prosecution; the wary concentration of the innocent man accused of a horrible crime according to me. What the jury could see for themselves was that he was a man with handsome, regular features and expensive taste in suits, a man who was clearly out of place in the dingy circumstances of Harrow Crown Court, a man who had been unfailingly courteous and pleasant to everyone he encountered in the court building over the first two days of the trial. The sort of man whose attention you would want, not fear.

Emma Seaton was a wreck, in comparison. There was something colourless about her, as if the vitality had drained out of her eyes and hair and skin, leaving her grey and faded. Her lips were chapped and dry. Pale blue had been a poor choice of dress: there were two darker half-moons under her arms, her fear made visible. She looked vulnerable and defeated. I had already got her to admit that she had known my client since school, had been in a relationship with him for years, had dropped out of university to be with him when he was at Oxford . . . that she had followed *him* to the city.

'And how would you describe your relationship at this time?' My words fell into the hush of the courtroom, which always reminded me of the charged silence in a theatre. There weren't many people in the public gallery, but those who were there hung on my every syllable. I was imposing in my wig and gown. I looked the part, I sounded the part, and all I had to do was hope that everyone else knew their lines.

'I was in love with him.' Emma's voice was barely audible. The judge had already reminded her to speak up. 'I would do anything for him. It wasn't a normal relationship exactly – he lost interest in having sex with me quite early on. But I adored him. We broke up a few times. He used it as a way to control me when I refused to do things he wanted me to do. He would dump me to teach me a lesson and I would beg him to take me back.'

'What kind of thing did you do to win his favour?'

'Embarrassing things. Stupid things. I'd steal things and tell lies. Once he told me to go and stand in the middle of the University Parks in my bra and knickers. It was February. I was there for hours, freezing.'

'Why?'

'I don't know. Because he wanted to see if I'd do it, I suppose.'

I frowned. 'Is that the occasion that you were hospitalised in the Olympia Unit at the John Radcliffe hospital? February 2009?'

'I – yes.'

'What is the Olympia Unit?'

'It's a closed ward. A women's mental health ward.'

I didn't look across at the jury but I let her words hang in the air while I turned a page slowly and unnecessarily, as if I was having to search for my next question. It was acting. I knew exactly where I was going with my cross-examination and how I was going to get there.

'And you were sectioned, isn't that right? For your own safety?'

'I was struggling. I wasn't sleeping. I couldn't contact my family. I believed he was watching me all the time. I believed he could even hear my thoughts.' She licked her lips. '*He* did that to me. He *broke* me.'

'Miss Seaton, if you were in a state of mental crisis at the time of that incident, is it possible that you imagined that my client wanted you to take that bizarre course of action by standing in the University Parks, unclothed?'

'No.'

29

'Even though you were suffering from extreme para-noia. Even though, in your own words, you were broken.'

'He made me do it.'

'How long were you in hospital?'

'Two months.'

'Did you receive a diagnosis?'

She mumbled something and Judge Akinye looked at her with the steady stare she favoured when someone had displeased her. 'Please, speak up, Miss Seaton.'

'I was diagnosed as having severe depression.'

'Are you still receiving treatment for this condition?'

'I take Seroquel.'

'What type of medicine is Seroquel?'

Her chin went up, defiant. 'It's an anti-psychotic medication.'

'Have you been taking this medication since 2009?'

'I've had breaks. It's best for me to stay on it.'

'What are the effects on you if you don't take it?'

'I get confused.'

'Do you imagine things?'

'Yes.'

'Hallucinate?'

'Sometimes.'

'Hear voices?'

'Sometimes.'

'Suffer from paranoia?'

'Yes.'

'Harm yourself?'

'Sometimes.' She tugged the sleeves of her dress down over the pale cross-hatching of scars on her wrists.

'So it's very important to take this medication.'

'Yes.'

'When was the last time you had a break from it?'

'Last year.'

'When last year?'

'April.'

'Please remind me, when did you go to the police to accuse my client of stalking you?'

She nodded, a weird half-smile dragging one side of her face down. I realised she was trying not to cry. 'It was at the end of April. But that was nothing to do with the medication and whether I was taking it or not. Pills didn't make him turn up at my house, at my job, telling lies about me.'

In the dock, John Webster shifted his weight to sit up straighter, a move much subtler than a shaking head but a signal to the jury nonetheless. *Don't believe her. She's crazy.*

'Going back to 2009, when you left hospital where did you go?'

'I stayed in Oxford.'

'Where?'

'In John's house. He was living in Jericho in a shared house.'

'You couldn't go home?'

'He wanted me there and I obeyed.' She touched her forehead, wiping beads of sweat off it.

'How long did you stay there?'

'The lease ran out in August.'

'Then what happened?'

'He had made me give him my savings – my inheritance from my grandfather. Twenty thousand pounds.'

She had mentioned that in her examination-in-chief and the jury had reacted to it: that was a lot of money to give anyone, let alone an abusive boyfriend.

'What did he want to do with it?'

'He said he was starting a business and he needed money.'

'Did he ever pay you back?'

'Years later. Plus a bit for interest.' She glowered at him but he met her gaze squarely, his expression unchanging.

'Isn't that what's called an investment?' I asked lightly.

'He took all the money I had and kicked me out. I had nowhere to go. I ended up on the streets, trying to do whatever I could to survive. I stole. I sold everything I had. I sold *myself*.'

'You were a prostitute?'

'Yes.'

'Were you arrested for prostitution?'

'A few times.'

'Went to prison?'

'Once. For theft.'

'Then what?'

'Back on the streets.'

I looked sympathetic, and I was; Emma had been through a lot. 'It sounds like a very difficult time. How did you get back on track?'

'John came and found me. He took me to my parents. I hadn't seen them for two and a half years. I hadn't spoken to them. They thought I was dead.'

'So he saved you?' I turned it into a question. *Have I misunderstood? How does that fit in with your narrative of coercion and terror?*

'He likes to give and he likes to take. The point is that he was in control. Then as soon as I was depending on him again, he left and I didn't see him for years. *Years*.'

'Miss Seaton, you seem to be angry with him for being in your life and not being in your life. Which is it?'

'I – it's hard to explain.'

'Isn't it the case that your problem with my client isn't that he's harassing you, but that he *isn't*?'

'No. Not at all. He's threatened me, he's stolen from me, he's destroyed my life, time and time again, for his own pleasure. He's made me scared to leave the house. I've quit jobs because of him.' She started to lose her composure, her voice wavering. 'I've tried so hard – so hard – and I can't get free of him. And no one has ever listened to me. It made me feel so small and worthless. It made me feel as if no sound comes out when I think I'm talking, that no one can even hear me—' The words had been tumbling out, faster and faster. She cut herself off. Her breathing was loud in the silence that followed.

'Do you have any tattoos?'

The change of tack made her blink.

'One.'

'Where is it?'

'On my arm.'

'Could you show us?'

I had expected her to look worried – panicked, even – but she smiled at me. 'Of course.'

Never ask a question if you don't already know the answer. It was the basic rule of cross-examination, the foundation of a good day in court. You weren't there to get answers. You were there to coax your witness to give the evidence that made your case, or to goad them into saying something that demolished the prosecution's case, depending on which side you were on.

What you didn't want was a witness taking great

33

pleasure in slowly turning back the right sleeve of her dress.

The tattoo was a wolf that stalked down the inside of her forearm, through the scarring from hundreds of razor-blade cuts that looked like long grass around it. She held her arm out so everyone in the court could see it.

'When did you have it done?'

'A couple of months ago.'

'And what does it cover?'

The triumphant smile faded. 'A tattoo that said "Property of John Webster".'

'And when did you get that first tattoo?' Beside me, the prosecutor's pen stopped moving. Ned Eldridge was a good lawyer and he sensed danger.

'When I lived in Oxford.'

'Before your relationship with Mr Webster deteriorated into abuse.'

'Exactly.'

I flipped open a folder. 'During the time you were home-less in 2009 and 2010, you were arrested several times. There's no mention of a tattoo in the police description of you.'

'They must have missed it.'

I looked to Judge Akinye. 'Your Honour, I'd like to show the witness a photograph.'

'Has Mr Eldridge seen this?' the judge enquired.

'No, Your Honour, but I have a copy for him.' I handed it to Ned, who was looking sick. A second copy went to the usher, a flat-footed lady named Babs with an imper-turbable expression. She took it across to the witness box where Emma was waiting.

'Could you describe the image for us, Miss Seaton?' I

handed Babs a sheaf of copies, one for the judge and the rest for the jury.

'It's me and some of my friends.' In the image, Emma was at the centre of a small group. She wore a long-sleeved dress but her right arm was in the air, holding her drink aloft, and her sleeve had slid back. There was a banner in the background reading Happy New Year and one of the women who flanked her wore glittery fake glasses in the shape of the numerals 2015.

'Would you agree, Miss Seaton, that it was taken on the thirty-first of December 2014?'

'Yes.'

'There's no tattoo on your arm, is there?'

'I sometimes cover it up with make-up.'

'The lighting is quite good, isn't it? You can see scarring on your arm. If you'd covered a large tattoo with heavy make-up, wouldn't you have covered the scarring too?'

'I—' She looked past me, behind Ned, where the police officers sat. No help from them or the prosecutor. She was on her own.

'When did you get the tattoo that read "Property of John Webster"?'

Her shoulders sagged. 'Last year.'

'When?'

'I don't remember. March, I think. Yes, March.'

I raised my eyebrows. 'Are you sure? March 2015?'

'Yes.'

'Take your time.'

'I'm sure.'

I flipped through my notes again. 'You went to the police to make an allegation that my client was stalking you on the twenty-third of April last year.'

'Yes.'

'On the second of May, you were at Painted Lady Tattoos in Lewisham, where you received a forearm tattoo.'

'That was the wolf, to cover up the words. A reminder to me that he's a threat.'

'That's another lie, isn't it?' I said it pleasantly. 'Just to be clear and so the jury understands exactly what's going on, we know you've lied several times in the last few minutes about when you commissioned the first tattoo. I'm going to give you one more chance to tell the truth.'

'It was last March, when he came back into my life again.'

'No. It wasn't.' I took out a folder and handed it to the prosecutor, then gave a stack to Babs for the witness, the judge and the jury. She trudged over to pass them out, moving as if her feet hurt. I waited, hiding the simmering impatience that would have made me fidget if I hadn't needed to be professional. 'There are two items in the folder I've given you. They are receipts from Painted Lady Tattoos. The first tattoo is from the second of May. Six weeks later, you returned and had a second tattoo. The receipts are dated. What was the first tattoo?'

Emma Seaton stared at the folder, her face stricken.

She had been so focused on John Webster she hadn't realised he wasn't actually the most dangerous person in the courtroom. That honour went to me.

She was intelligent enough to know that it was time to stop lying.

'The first was the one that said I was his p-property.'

'And the second?'

'It was the wolf.'

'The first tattoo looks bad, doesn't it? That's why you

lied. It looks as if you were still infatuated with a man you can never have, as you have been since the start.'

'No, I—'

'You decided to lie about it because you knew it undermined your case. If you were deathly afraid of my client, to the point that you went to the police about him and made serious allegations against him – allegations that you were scared for your life, that he was torturing you with psychological abuse and intimidation – why on earth would you get his name tattooed on your arm?'

She shook her head, tears streaking her cheeks.

The judge stirred. 'I think we should have a break here.'

The usher sprang into action, removing the jury and Emma Seaton with great efficiency. Those of us who were left behind knew exactly what was going to happen next. In the dock, John Webster was watching me. When I glanced at him, he gave me a slow, appreciative smile.

The judge cleared her throat. 'It's a matter for you, Mr Eldridge, but you might need to take some instructions at this point.'

The prosecutor jumped up. 'I'm minded to agree, Your Honour.'

'It's not a matter for me to suggest how the Crown might choose to proceed,' Judge Akinye said carefully, 'but I'm conscious I'm going to be asked to rule on a submission at the close of your case. Am I not, Miss Lewis?'

I stood as Ned sat down. 'You are indeed, Your Honour.' She nodded. 'I'll rise.'

As the door closed behind her, a murmur rose from the public gallery. Ned Eldridge turned to me. 'Well, that's fucked it.'

'Sorry.' I didn't sound sorry and he knew I didn't mean it.

'I'll be offering no evidence unless the CPS lose their minds and make us wait until half-time.'

'Good decision,' I said supportively.

'The judge is going to throw it out in any case. This just means I get to decide when to call a halt.'

'We all have days like that.' I picked up my papers. 'I'd better go and have a word with my client to let him know what's happening.'

'You should be proud of yourself. You led her right down the garden path. You didn't rush her.' He looked rueful. 'I saw it happening and there was nothing I could do.'

'Never mind. There's always next time.'

If he was anything like me, there would be a part of Ned Eldridge that believed he should have done something to save his case. Losing was part of the job, but winning was always better.

4

Most clients came to court with family and friends for support, but John Webster was alone apart from his solicitor, a middle-aged man who always looked as if he had just remembered an important appointment elsewhere.

'Well done.' The solicitor nodded. 'You did that very nicely indeed.'

'Thank you.' I turned to Webster. 'They'll be dropping the case. The prosecutor just has to get the go-ahead from the CPS to offer no evidence but the judge will throw it out anyway, even if they say no.'

'So I gathered.'

'Well, I'm glad it's good news,' I said, wrongfooted. I hadn't been expecting lavish praise but usually defendants were more upbeat when they managed to avoid a lengthy prison sentence.

'Do you think—' He broke off and shook his head. 'Look, it's none of my business but is someone looking after Em? That was – well, it hurt to watch. I can't imagine how she must be feeling.'

'She'll be looked after.' The officer in the case was a motherly detective constable with decades of experience. She would know the importance of reassuring Emma Seaton that she'd done her best, that it wasn't her fault the case had fallen apart.

'It didn't feel as if it was a fair competition.'

'Well, it wasn't. I knew what I was going to ask her and why, and she didn't. All she could do was tell the truth, which is what the police would have told her in advance – even if it made her look bad. She didn't do that.'

'She sounded convincing. If I hadn't known about the tattoo, we might have been in trouble.'

'There was enough to make the jury doubt her version of events. Lying under oath just made the case impossible to prosecute.'

'They won't charge her with perjury, will they?'

'No, absolutely not. There's no public interest in prosecuting her for it.' I smiled. 'Try not to worry about her.'

'I always do,' he said soberly.

'I think we'll be back in court shortly,' the solicitor said, fidgeting. 'Get this over with.'

Before I could reply, the loudspeakers crackled. 'All parties in the case of Webster return to Court Three.'

'Here we go,' the solicitor said, and steered John Webster back to the dock for the last time that day, before he was set free without a stain on his character.

I moved at a fast clip as I headed down to leave the court building. I'd changed out of my court clothing and taken my hair down, which was essentially like putting on a disguise. Most people saw the wig and the gown and didn't really notice much more. Barristers weren't allowed to give interviews to reporters, so I didn't have to worry about the media, but I was always wary about being accosted. You never knew when an angry family member would take offence at something you had said or done in court.

'Miss Lewis?'

The voice came from behind me. I turned to find John Webster was following me, a little closer than I would have liked.

'Could you do me a favour?'

'I don't think—'

'It's Emma.' His face was pale. 'I need someone to check on her.'

Emma. I had fully intended to say no and continue on my way, but now I hesitated.

'Please.' His eyes were fixed on mine.

'I've got to go.' The words had no force though. I stood my work bag up on its wheels and sighed. 'Where is she?'

I pushed open the door to the bathrooms off the lobby. There was an outer door and an inner door with a space between them, an airlock of sorts. I hesitated before I opened the inner door, steeling myself. *Get on with it.* A waft of stale air and industrial disinfectant made me flinch as I leaned on the door. What was I doing? This wasn't my job.

'Miss Seaton? Emma?'

Silence. So John Webster had been wrong and she wasn't there. I stood in the doorway, chewing my lip with indecision. I could just go back out and tell him he was wrong. But I hadn't really looked, and I felt he would know that. I let the door swing shut behind me.

'Emma?'

I worked my way along the row of dingy cubicles, trying the doors to make sure each stall was empty. The bathroom reeked, the air heavy with stale urine, body odour and a suggestion of cigarette smoke. The final cubicle was locked, even though there were no feet in view when I peeked under the door. 'Emma? Are you in there?'

'Who is it?'

I jumped, although I should have known she was there. 'Ingrid Lewis.'

She gave a long, wavering sniff. 'John's barrister?'

'Yes.'

'The ice bitch.'

I couldn't hold back a smile, in spite of myself. 'I haven't heard that one before.'

'That's what I *called* you in my *head*.' She was angry, I thought, with that childish rage that makes people forget themselves, lash out – anger that makes them want to hurt anyone near them. I took a step back so I wasn't as close to her. Of course she would have chosen the last cubicle in the room . . . I measured the distance to the door.

'Emma, I just wanted to check that you were all right. I'm sure it was a tough day for you but it's done now. You did your best.'

'But you were better.'

'It was easier for me. It's what I do for a living, remember.' I felt exhausted. This was supposed to be neat and tidy: you went to court, you gave your evidence, you were believed or not believed, and you went home. Emma wasn't playing by the rules and it felt uncomfortably close to chaos. Besides, this was really none of my business. 'Look, I'm going to find DC Singh and get her to take you home, okay?'

'How did you know I was in here?'

'Lucky guess.'

'That's a lie.'

Yes, but I'm not under oath. 'I was just concerned,' I said. 'I don't want to drag this out. I'm going now, okay?'

'Wait. I want to talk to you.'

Why? I couldn't think of a single thing she'd want to say to me that I would enjoy hearing. I edged towards the door, wary. This had been a mistake. Why had I agreed to it just because Webster had asked me to? I should have known better. I should have run a mile.

A clatter on the inside of the cubicle door made me flinch. Metal, I thought. Metal on the laminate that was scarred with graffiti and nameless gouges. What kind of metal?

The cubicle door opened and she shuffled forward so I could see her, though she didn't quite come out of the cubicle. Her hair hung around her face in strings. She stared at me for a beat.

'You look different like that. More normal.'

'I'm not in court now.'

'So you don't get to tell me what to do any more. You don't get to ask questions and you don't get to demand that I do anything. You're not in charge here, pissy britches.'

'I prefer ice bitch, if I get a say.'

'You don't.'

43

'Right.' I smiled at her, trying to look unthreatening and friendly. I had been locked in small cells with very angry, very violent prisoners on several occasions, explaining to them that they were going to prison for a long time, but I had never been as scared as I was then. I was a long way out of my depth and the shore wasn't even in sight. I jerked my thumb in the direction of the door. 'You know, I think I'm just going to go and check if DC Singh is in the lobby. I won't be long.'

'I don't want her.' Emma moved out of the cubicle. The whites were showing around her pupils. 'I want *him*.'

'The other officer?' I tried to remember his name as I moved further away from her. Everything in me was screaming that I should turn and run, but if I did, she would come after me, I thought. *Keep her talking.* 'Nash, isn't it?'

'*John*. I want John. And you're going to make him come in here.'

'He won't do what I tell him,' I protested. 'I've got no power over him.'

'He'll come if he thinks you're in danger. And you are in danger, by the way. I don't like you. I don't like you at all. And I hurt the people I don't like.' Something silvery glinted in her hand but it was hidden in the folds of her skirt.

'Emma.' My back collided with the wall behind me. My legs were shaking. I'd seen pictures of defensive injuries from knife attacks – I'd seen the scars . . .

What was I good at? Not fighting, not against someone armed with some kind of blade. But I was better with words than just about anyone I knew.

'Listen to me, Emma. There's no need for you to be like this. John sent me in here because he was worried about

44

you. He's waiting just outside the door. You don't need to persuade him to come in. Will you let me go out and tell him you're waiting for him?'

'He'll come if you scream, I think.'

'Emma—'

'It's better if you really mean it.' She came towards me, her right arm swinging, and I saw the inch-long blade caught between her knuckles, a wedge-shaped knife mounted on a bar, designed to be discreet and deadly. I would have screamed then, but the sound stuck in my throat and all I could manage was a sob that no one could have heard. Blindly I reached out and found the door, and threw myself into the tiny hallway outside, only to find myself in the arms of the young police officer – Adam Nash, that was it – who had already come through the outer door. He shoved me aside and kept moving towards Emma as he yelled for assistance.

'She's got a knife,' I said, and fell to my knees in the horrible little space between the two doors, cringing out of the way as bodies charged past me: DC Singh and two of the court security officers, and a uniformed PC who had been there giving evidence in another case. From inside the bathroom I heard shrieking that was like a noise an animal might make in a trap. I was glad I couldn't see whatever they did to subdue her but it had to hurt: the screaming reached a crescendo that was followed with low, guttural swearing as the officers spoke to her calmly. Then, at last, there was silence. It was somehow worse than the fighting.

The door to the bathroom opened and a dishevelled DC Singh came out. She helped me to my feet and hauled me into the lobby.

'You're all right now. You're safe. Are you injured? Try to calm down. You're okay.'

I hadn't even realised I was crying. I twisted in her grasp. 'Is she all right? Is Emma okay?'

'She's fine.'

'She had a knife.'

'She hasn't got it now.' DC Singh turned me round so she could look at me, her kind face worried, the lines carved deeper on her forehead and around her mouth. 'Are you sure she didn't hurt you?'

'She didn't touch me.' I was staring at the bathroom door. 'Where is she? Can I see her?'

'Better not.'

'What's going to happen to her?'

'She needs to go to hospital.'

'You're not going to arrest her?'

'She's been arrested but she's not going to custody. She needs to be looked after properly.' DC Singh had been patting me down, making sure I wasn't hurt. 'I'll need a statement from you. Do you mind waiting around for a bit? I'll get someone to take it. We just need to get Emma sorted first.'

'That's fine,' I said. 'Of course. I need to ring my boyfriend. But I can wait.'

'Good girl. Just have a seat there.' She disappeared back into the bathroom with a quick, bustling walk, someone who didn't mind taking charge of a situation that had briefly been completely out of control. If DC Nash had been two minutes slower . . . if I had said the wrong thing . . . But I wasn't hurt.

Sitting there in the lobby, I was an object of interest for everyone who was passing in or out of the court. I lost count of the number of times I smiled and told people I was fine. I wasn't fine, not at all, and one proof of that was that it took me a surprisingly long time to register that one person in particular was nowhere to be seen.

'Miss Lewis?' DC Nash stood in front of me. My thoughts were all over the place, floating like dust motes in the air of my mind and I found myself wondering why I thought of him as being young when he was my age, mid-twenties – but there was still something boyish about him. His earnestness, maybe. But he was talking, and I should listen.

'Delia – DC Singh – asked me to tell you to go home. We're waiting for a van to transport Emma and she doesn't want to keep you here any longer.'

'How long has it been?'

'Just over an hour.'

'Really?' I rubbed my forehead. 'I thought it was about ten minutes.'

'Shock is a funny thing.'

'Where did John Webster go?'

'He left.'

'When?'

'When I told him to.'

I looked up at that, in surprise. There was an edge to him all the same – and I thought of him running full tilt into the bathroom even though he couldn't know exactly what was waiting for him there, only that it was bad . . .

If I'd been starting to feel a creeping admiration for him, that evaporated with his next words.

'You know, John Webster is a very dangerous man. That was our best chance to get him locked up. We won't get another.'

'I was doing my job.'

'Yes, you were.' He looked down at me and his eyes were dark with worry. 'I just hope you won't come to regret it.'

2017

5

April

Witness Statement

Criminal Procedure Rules, r 16.2;
Criminal Justice Act 1967, s.9

Statement of: Ingrid LEWIS

Age if under 18 (if over   Occupation: Barrister
insert 'over 18'): Over 18

This statement (consisting of . . . 1 . . . Page(s) each
signed by me) is true to the best of my knowledge and
belief and I make it knowing that, if it is tendered in
evidence, I shall be liable to prosecution if I have

wilfully stated in it, anything which I know to be false, or do not believe to be true.

Signature: ...⌐⌐⌐⌐... Date: [21/04/17]

I am the above-named person and I am making this statement regarding videos that have been uploaded onto YouTube and other social media that make a reference to me, and photographs that have been uploaded to an unknown number of message boards and other internet forums.

In APRIL 2017 I became aware that some videos had been uploaded onto YouTube without my knowledge by a user named 'SHADOW912'. I believe this to be the username of John WEBSTER.

I am aware of WEBSTER because I defended him in a trial that took place in 2016. Following the trial, WEBSTER subjected me to a campaign of harassment by email and text message. Subsequently WEBSTER was arrested twice but released without charge.

I have had no involvement or contact from WEBSTER since the second arrest in February 2017.

On THURSDAY 20 APRIL 2017 I received a phone call from a man who identified himself as JERRY. He refused to give me his last name and I did not recognise his voice. He asked to make an appointment with me for the purposes of procuring sex, explaining that my name, picture and telephone number were listed on a number of sites advertising the services of prostitutes. Following this call, I received seven phone calls from other men in the space of an hour, all with a view to arranging a meeting for sexual purposes. None of them identified themselves to me.

Having searched for my name and image on the internet, I discovered several listings on sites offering sexual services that included my name, age, telephone number and address. I believe they were uploaded by John WEBSTER. They include fictional reviews of services allegedly offered by me, written in degrading and obscene language ('NICE TITS, BIG MOUTH BUT I SLAPPED IT SHUT' and 'LIKES ROUGH TREATMENT, RAPE FANTASIES, NO NEVER MEANS NO'. I believe this is an incitement to sexually assault me and I have real fears for my safety. I immediately requested that the websites remove the relevant listings, which they did. I took screenshots of them before they were removed.

I also found pornographic videos on multiple video-hosting sites titled 'INGRID HARD AT WORK XXX' and 'INGRID LEARNS HER LESSON XXX'. My contact details were listed in the information underneath. The videos depict a fair-haired woman but blur her face. I believe that this woman is supposed to resemble me. I find this extremely upsetting. I requested that these videos be removed.

I believe that WEBSTER has created the above material because of his vindictive nature, as a response to being arrested for harassing me in FEBRUARY 2017. I believe that WEBSTER found a way to harass me via third parties.

After viewing this material, I am very concerned about actions that may be taken by WEBSTER or those he has incited to contact me. I have changed my telephone number. I feel WEBSTER'S behaviour is vindictive and malicious and am concerned that my name and image have been used in such a way that they might be found with a straightforward internet search.

I am willing to support the police investigation and attend court if required. I am making this statement at 1904 hrs on FRIDAY 21st APRIL 2017 at LAVENDER HILL POLICE STATION.

Signature:...

Signature witnessed by: PC 637 WW PALMERSTON

From: Elizabeth.Rowley@metpolice.co.uk
Date: 1 June 2017 at 10:39:51 GMT
To: 'Ingrid Lewis' <IL@3tw.co.uk.cism.net>

SUBJECT: Harassment Statement 21/4/17

Dear Ingrid,

Just to keep you informed, I've conducted a detailed investigation based on the information you provided us in your witness statement. I have been in receipt of user identity information provided by the video-hosting sites and the prostitution websites you listed. I'm afraid that I can't find any link between the username 'SHADOW912' and John Webster. We have tried to trace the person who uploaded the material but their identity was encrypted and so far we have failed to find out anything about them or their location. However, I can reassure you that all the information has been removed now and the websites are aware that you may be the subject of malicious false listings in the future. They have promised to prevent any such listings from being posted. Hopefully this will be the end of this distressing experience.

I have interviewed John Webster myself and despite your earlier experiences with him I'm satisfied that he had nothing to do with this malicious act. He was unaware of any such listings. I no longer consider him a suspect so you can put him out of your mind.

Obviously this means we have no current suspects. If you have any other suggestions as to who might have done this, please let me know as soon as possible. It might be useful for you to keep a record of any further incidents that cause you concern, including the date, time and any information you think might be of use in a police investigation.

In the meantime, please be conscious of your personal

safety and security, as we discussed. If I can be of any further help, please don't hesitate to get in touch.

Kind regards

Liz

Detective Constable Elizabeth Rowley
EMERALD UNIT
Lavender Hill police station
176 Lavender Hill, Battersea, London SW11 1JX

6

June

It was a beautiful morning, at least. I stared out of the window at the quiet street, empty apart from an early jogger on the other side of the road and tiny birds flitting from one tree to the next. No one else seemed to be up, which wasn't surprising. I wouldn't have been up if I hadn't been getting the train to Leicester for a hearing that morning.

Everything looked normal, I told myself. Everything was fine. It was going to be a good day.

The cat stropped himself against my legs, purring, and I reached down to stroke him. 'I know, Geoff. You want feeding. You'll have to wait until I get dressed.'

The email I'd had four days earlier from Liz Rowley kept repeating in my mind. John Webster had persuaded the police he had nothing to do with the website. Maybe he hadn't. Maybe someone else had thought it was funny.

I turned away from the window and headed to the

bathroom to wake myself up with a brisk shower. The morning routine was soothing, requiring no thought as I dressed, applied make-up and did my hair with practised ease. I had shuffled into the bathroom squinting with tiredness and yawning; I strode out of it looking cool and in control, ready for court or just about anything the day might throw at me.

Our bedroom was warm, the blinds glowing with the promise of a hot day ahead. One knocked against the window frame as a breeze caught it. That would probably be the last cool air of the day. Mark lay sprawled across the entire bed, face down, his light brown hair tousled, one arm stretched across the space where I had been as if he had reached for me. We had reduced our bedclothes to a single linen sheet because of the hot weather and it was crumpled around his hips, leaving his bare torso exposed. I yearned to run my hand over the tanned skin of his back, tracing his spine.

No. Concentrate.

Quietly, moving with the care and deft control of a burglar, I scooped up my watch and earrings and my engagement ring from the bedside table. My phone was next and I switched it on to check it quickly: no calls, no messages, nothing untoward.

Should I kiss him goodbye? I didn't want to wake him. I stood with my shoes in my hand, hesitating, and had just made up my mind to leave when he spoke.

'What time is it?'

'Quarter to six.'

'Christ.'

'Go back to sleep.'

He rolled over and prised an eye open, rubbing the

other one with the heel of his hand. 'What time will you be back?'

'I don't know. I'll text you. It should be a short hearing, but you never know.' The sheet had slipped even further. I found my eyes tracking down Mark's torso. *Oh* . . .

His thoughts must have been running along the same lines as mine. His other eye came open and he gave me a look that was by no means sleepy. He sat up on one elbow, stretched out his hand and found my leg, his fingers curling around my thigh, just above the knee. 'Are you in a hurry?'

'I should go.' I didn't move.

'What time is your train?' His hand slid upwards, slowly, and the heat of his touch spread through my entire body.

'I—' I would need to get ready again, to do my hair and my make-up. I really didn't have time. I pulled a face. 'I can't. Later. When I get back.'

He grinned and let himself fall back onto the pillows. 'I can wait. It was worth a try, though.'

'Always.' I kissed him goodbye and went downstairs with Geoffrey running ahead of me, his tail in the air. I felt lucky, and loved, and like it would take very little for me to abandon Leicester in favour of a day in bed with my handsome fiancé.

It was already hot, I discovered when I stepped out onto the doorstep. The milkman had been, and I put the bottles in the hall. The tiled floor was cold, even during a June heatwave; Mark could put the milk in the fridge when he got up in half an hour or so. I walked down the garden path, smelling the jasmine that clustered around the porch of the house next door, and – because it was London – the bitter stink of an urban fox who had left an olfactory calling card on our wall. It wouldn't smell any better as it aged. I would wash it off later with the hose when I watered the front garden, I thought, stepping down off the pavement to cross the road, imagining myself in the cool evening, dressed in shorts and a strappy top instead of this fitted suit, a glass of wine waiting for me in the kitchen, cloudy with condensation—

Something crunched under my feet and I looked down to see broken mirror glass glinting in the road. I glanced back to see where it had come from.

'Oh *no*.'

Mark's car was parked on the street, just outside our house. Parking was a major issue locally because none of us had drives or garages; the houses were Victorian and terraced and the street was relatively narrow, so you parked your car and folded in the wing mirrors and hoped for the best. On this occasion, he must have forgotten to push the roadside mirror in (which wasn't like him) and someone had driven past with enough speed to knock it off (which was absolutely typical). The casing for the mirror dangled against the side of the car, scratched and shattered, as if whatever hit it had been moving fast, and there was a scrape mark the length of the driver's door. He was not going to be pleased to discover his car was damaged, I thought.

With an inward sigh I ran back to the house to break the bad news.

It had promised to be a good day but that was a lie. I'd been late for my train, late for court and then late getting back, landing in the middle of rush hour when I got off my train. The incident with the car mirror was entirely responsible, I thought, battling through the crowds with my bag as my hair stuck to the back of my neck and sweat pooled at the base of my spine. My clothes were clinging to me, clammy now from a day of hacking around in the heat. Mark had been upset, of course, and swore blind that he hadn't left the mirror sticking out. Our conversation attracted the attention of the neighbours who came out of their houses in ones and twos, until there was quite a crowd standing around the car in various states of undress, chatting about other car-related incidents and whether the council should *do* something.

'These things happen in London,' I offered, and Mark looked at me across the group of neighbours with a tiny frown denting his forehead, because he knew as well as I did that these things happened a lot more often if someone was making sure they did.

'Would you watch where you're going?'

I came back to myself to find an elderly gentleman scowling at me, one hand to his shin. The bag I was towing across a crowded concourse was a liability and I needed to be more careful. I apologised, given that I was totally in the wrong, and tried to focus on where I was and what I was doing. The station was far too crowded and all I wanted was to get to the Underground and go home. Some clear space opened up in the crowds in front of me and I darted forward, only to stop as the phone in my pocket began to hum. Unknown number, the screen informed me.

'Hello?' I jammed my hand against my free ear. 'Hello?'

Nothing.

I ended the call and looked at the phone for another second, wondering. They would call back, if it was a police officer or a CPS lawyer or another barrister trying to get hold of me.

There was no reason to think it was John Webster, any more than I should think the car was his work – and yet I did think that.

I spent a lot of the journey home checking over my shoulder.

At twenty past two in the morning, the landline in the house began to ring, startling me out of an uneasy sleep. Mark slid out of bed before I was fully awake and ran downstairs to answer it, swearing all the way. I put the bedside light on and sat up to listen, wary in case it was his parents, or mine – some unexpected disaster that couldn't wait until morning.

'Hello?'

I heard him end the call, and then press a couple of buttons and listen, before he hung up. A cable rattled against the floor and he started back up the stairs again.

'What are you doing? What was it?' I asked as he came into the room.

'I checked. The call was from a withheld number.' He stood by the door, tall and angry, his hair standing up on end. 'I've disconnected the phone, in case.'

In case. He didn't need to say in case of what. In case the next four hours were filled with more silent phone calls, or calls where there was just the sound of breathing, or faint music, or screams, or barking dogs, or any of the thousands of noises that John Webster had played to us the last time he'd tormented us.

'It's him, isn't it.' I was shaking, I discovered, tremors that came from somewhere deep inside me.

'Turn out the light.' He lay back down and turned

towards me, drawing me into his arms in the darkness. 'It might not be. And if it is, we'll deal with it.'

'Mark, I'm scared.'

'I know.' He pressed his forehead against mine. 'But we're together. We'll get through it together.'

The next morning was Saturday. He plugged in the landline while I watched from the kitchen doorway, eating a bowl of cereal.

'There. Although I was thinking maybe we should get rid of the landline. We hardly need it.'

I shrugged, and began to say something, but I was cut off by the high-pitched shrilling of the telephone. I jumped and the bowl seemed to leap out of my hands, spinning through the air to smash on the floor. Milk and cereal splashed the walls and my feet, but I barely felt it.

We stared at one another in silence as the phone rang on and on and on.

The phone rang eighteen times in a row that morning, until Mark yanked the cable out of the wall again with a muttered curse and we had peace. Peace, until a shocked neighbour knocked on the door to tell us – because she thought we should know – that someone had drawn 'something *horrible*' on our wall.

Something horrible proved to be the word 'cunt'. They hadn't drawn it, I discovered, when I tried to wash it off. They had burned it, with a blowtorch, so it scarred the brickwork and couldn't be removed.

Nothing happened on Sunday. No calls. No visits. No criminal damage. Mark researched alarm systems for the house, grimly, and I tried to work on my case for the following day. I spent most of the time gazing into space, flinching whenever there was an unexpected sound.

Two days later I was on the Victoria Line on my way to work, travelling north between Oxford Circus and Warren Street. A hot wind pushed through the carriage from the window at the end, and it blew my hair around my face. I turned towards the front of the carriage so that my hair was blowing behind me instead of into my eyes, and glanced idly through the open window to the carriage in front, where a man was standing by the last door.

John Webster, wearing a black T-shirt and jeans, with a bag slung across his torso. His hair was short, his skin tanned. He looked fit and well and as if he was lost in his own thoughts, tapping a pair of sunglasses against his leg.

I glowered at him, willing him to turn his head, to acknowledge me. I was clenching my fists so hard that later I discovered my nails had left half-moon cuts in my palm. He seemed oblivious to me and I knew he wasn't.

As the train came into Warren Street, I tried to guess what he was planning and where I should go – should I get off? Move carriages? Ask for help?

'Sorry—' A young woman pushed past me and I lost sight of Webster for a second as I moved back, out of her way. When I looked again, there was no sign of him. He wasn't in the other carriage. Panic caught my throat, making it hard to breathe. I rushed to the door and peered out even as the warning bell sounded, but there was no one on the platform.

He had gone.

The doors slid closed and I leaned against the carriage wall, fighting for composure. It was a coincidence, except that John Webster didn't do coincidences. It was nothing you could take to the police. Oddly, although he hadn't tried to talk to me, I felt thoroughly shaken. The phone calls were annoying; the car was expensive to fix but ultimately just a car. This was different. He had followed me without my knowledge. He had proved he could get close to me.

For the first time I felt truly unsafe.

'Ingrid . . .' Martin Holdsworth QC was a large, confident man, terrifying as an opponent, avuncular and kind as my head of chambers. He was red-faced and cheerful, prone to opening a bottle or two of wine on a Friday afternoon and throwing an impromptu party in his room in chambers.

What he wasn't, as a rule, was diffident, which made it very surprising that he was standing in the doorway of my (shared) room, holding an open cardboard box, looking as if he really wished he was somewhere else.

'What can I do for you, Martin?'

'This came for you.' He held the box delicately in his shovel-like hands, touching it with the tips of his fingers. 'It was addressed to me, which I'm afraid I really don't understand as I certainly wouldn't buy anything from this particular – ah – *vendor*. So I opened it and – well, your name is on the invoice and so I *assume* . . .'

'What is it?' I stood up and moved towards him.

'Well, I don't really . . .'

It was very unlike Martin to be lost for words, and his face had turned a worrying shade of puce. He pushed the box into my arms awkwardly, and muttered something as he hurried away. For such a big man he was capable of moving quickly.

'What the hell did you buy?' Henry – one of the other barristers who shared my room – came to stand beside my desk as I opened the box. 'I've never seen Martin in such a— oh.'

The invoice lay on top of the items in the box: Love! Sex! Fun! It proclaimed across the top, along with Martin's name, the address of chambers and my name as the purchaser. I lifted it out.

'Oh shit.' Henry leaned in so he could see better. 'Oh that is *nasty*. What is that, twelve inches?'

A large dildo lay in the bottom of the box, along with a leather harness and a pair of handcuffs. I stared at them, feeling sick. 'Clearly I didn't order these.'

'Clearly,' Henry said sarcastically, reaching in to pick up a bottle I hadn't noticed. 'Lube. Well, that's considerate. Mark is a lucky guy.'

I snatched it out of his hand and threw it into the box, folding the lid so I didn't have to look at it any longer. 'I didn't buy these things! And if I had, why would I have them delivered to my *fucking* head of chambers, Henry?'

He looked bemused. 'You're really upset, aren't you?'

'Of course I am.'

'Look.' His voice softened. 'It's clearly someone's idea of a joke. You can explain that to Martin. Don't fall for that oh-gosh-oh-no routine of his – he tells the filthiest jokes I've ever heard and he's been in the game long enough to deal with thousands of sex cases. This is nothing. In fact, I bet he was in on it.'

'I doubt it,' I said. I was staring at the invoice in my

hand, my horror fading as the wheels of my brain began to turn. 'I think I know exactly who did this. But I think he just made a mistake.'

'What was that?'

'The invoice has a credit card number on it.' I fanned myself with the paper. 'I'm going to show it to the police. Maybe they'll believe me now.'

7

September

No Jail Term for Harassment of Lawyer

A man who conducted a campaign of harassment against the barrister who once represented him has been given a suspended sentence at Southwark Crown Court. John Webster, 29, pleaded guilty to sending a series of threatening texts and emails over several months to Ingrid Lewis, a 28-year-old barrister from London.

The court was told that Miss Lewis had represented John Webster in 2016, when he was acquitted of stalking a young woman. Following the trial, Webster sent Miss Lewis unwanted gifts and messages, including over eighty text messages sent in a single weekend. He admitted registering her on sex worker sites, resulting in nuisance phone calls and messages.

Webster's barrister, Dan Knowles, said the defendant had been affected by stress and depression after the trial and became temporarily obsessed with Miss Lewis. 'He is very sorry for his actions and his main concern is Miss Lewis's mental and physical well-being. This behaviour was out of character and he is ashamed of himself.'

Webster had been acquitted of seven other charges at his trial last month, including criminal damage and harassment.

Judge Harold Grey told the defendant that he was a clever and talented individual with a bright future ahead of him and didn't deserve a custodial sentence for his behaviour. The judge described it as 'a moment of madness', and sentenced Webster to a six-month suspended sentence and 100 hours of community service.

He also made him the subject of a restraining order not to go within 200 metres of Miss Lewis or contact her in any way. The judge made the order to run for the next two years, until September 2019.

October

Log of Incidents taken from Ingrid Lewis's notes

2.10.17	16.07	Silent phone call	Call from an unknown number to my mobile phone
2.10.17	16.09	Silent phone call	Call from an unknown number to my mobile phone
2.10.17	16.20	Silent phone call	Call from an unknown number to my mobile phone

2.10.17	16.23	Silent phone call	Call from an unknown number to my mobile phone
2.10.17	16.31	Silent phone call	Call from an unknown number to my mobile phone
2.10.17	16.33	Silent phone call	Call from an unknown number to my mobile phone
2.10.17	16.35	Silent phone call	Call from an unknown number to my mobile after which I turned my phone off
3.10.17	06.05	Silent phone call	Call from an unknown number as soon as I turned my phone on
10.10.17	08.15	JW breached conditions of restraining order	Saw JW in the same Underground carriage (Central Line travelling east).

			He made no make contact with me, and got off at Bank station, the first station after I noticed him.
15.10.17	Exact time unknown 01.00 – 05.00	Damage to car	Rear windscreen smashed outside the house
17.10.17	09.03	Silent phone call	Call from an unknown number to my mobile as soon as Mark left the house
18.10.17	14.24	Silent phone call	Call from an unknown number to my mobile as soon as Mark left the house
19.10.17	?02.00	Criminal damage to CCTV cameras	CCTV cameras installed outside house on 19.6.17 were smashed

21.10.17	?03.00	Criminal damage to CCTV cameras	Replacement CCTV cameras smashed
24.10.17	06.28	JW breached conditions of restraining order	Saw JW while waiting for a platform announcement at Euston station. He walked past me carrying what seemed to be an empty bag.
26.10.17	13.42	JW breached conditions of restraining order	At Aylesbury Crown Court for work, went to a café for lunch, JW came in and ordered a coffee

27.10.17	21.00 approx	Handbag stolen	Handbag stolen while at dinner in Ecarté on the South Bank, sitting outside. Had to change locks, cancel card, wipe mobile phone. *Possibly not JW.*

8

November

'*No one* goes to Venice in November.' Mark grinned at
me and leaned over to clink his champagne flute against
mine.

'No one,' I agreed. It was what his mother Diana had
wailed down the phone at him when he told her he was
taking me away for a few days, as a surprise, and it had
made us laugh from the moment he told me about it in
the taxi on the way to the airport until now, when we
were sitting on a terrace overlooking the slow green water
of the Grand Canal. 'Although there do seem to be a few
tourists around.'

'Can't have everything.'

'No.' I wriggled my shoulder blades against the back
of the chair. 'This is amazing. I can't believe you did this.
I can't believe this *hotel*.'

He set his glass down carefully. 'It's worth it to see you
looking happy again.'

'Is it?' I said wistfully. 'I feel as if you had to spend a lot of money to cheer me up.'

'No point in having it if you can't spend it.'

That was true, but one of the things I loved about Mark was that he didn't feel the need to spend money; he could be just as happy in a tent as the rain pelted down, or the tiny Greek cottage with an outside shower and no electricity that we'd rented the previous year for our holidays.

'And I know you love Venice, so . . .'

It was true; I did love Venice. I had been there before but it was his first time. We had spent the last two days walking the narrow streets that ended abruptly in water just when you thought you knew where you were going. It was misty in the mornings, murky and grey and cold enough that we had to dive into tiny cafés and restaurants at regular intervals to warm up. Around every corner lurked a church filled with priceless art, or a gallery selling fantastically intricate glass that was as light and insubstantial as a bubble.

The hotel was a former palazzo, not far from the famous Gritti but smaller and more intimate. Our room had a four-poster bed and a view of the Grand Canal. I was more or less in heaven.

'I'm not going to want to go back, you know.'

'It would be hard to get tired of this,' Mark agreed. 'But you'd hate having to walk everywhere all the time.'

'There are vaporetti.'

'There are.' Mark had flatly refused to go for a gondola ride, despite the concierge's blandishments, but he'd taken to the water buses that the locals used to get around. He didn't want to see the tourist version of Venice; he wanted the real thing. With great difficulty I had dragged him to St Mark's Square that morning for a photograph (for his mother) and then persuaded him into the basilica itself. He trudged through the tour groups (even in November) with a martyred expression, right up until the moment when we saw the four bronze Roman sculptures known as the Triumphal Quadriga, the horses that had once stamped the air high above the square.

'I thought you'd like them,' I whispered. 'Petrarch did too, back in the fourteenth century. The Venetians liked them so much they stole them from Constantinople, and then Napoleon nicked them and took them to Paris. But they came back here in the end.'

Instead of answering me he took my hand, and we stood there paying homage for half an hour as the tides of tourists washed around them. It was spellbinding, all of it.

'Signor Orpen?' The concierge was at Mark's elbow, holding an envelope. 'There is a letter for you.'

'Thank you.' Mark waited for him to leave before he opened the letter. 'This has to be from Mum. No one else knows we're here.'

I watched his face as he read it, his expression changing from mild exasperation to a kind of stillness that made my heart begin to race. 'What is it?'

'Nothing.' He folded it over and shoved it in his pocket. 'Nothing that need worry you.'

'Was it from him?'

'Ingrid. Leave it.' He glanced at me but he didn't meet my eyes. 'It was nothing.'

Easier to pretend to believe him than to argue. I knocked back the rest of my champagne and flipped open the guidebook, because when it came to travel, peering at a mobile phone didn't have quite the same romance as an actual book you could mark up. 'So tomorrow is a tour of the islands in the lagoon – Murano, Burano and Torcello.'

'Murano is the lace one, isn't it,' Mark said absently.

'No, that's Burano. Murano is glass.'

'Right.'

I carried on talking about the trip the following day, rambling about what we would see and what time we had to be ready, as if Mark's mouth wasn't thin with tension, and the whole evening ruined.

In other circumstances the tour of the islands would have been the high point of our trip. As it was, we dragged ourselves through it, admiring the colourful buildings jammed tightly together along the canals, commenting on the artists' work politely, and wandering through the vineyards on flat, ancient little Torcello. We pushed lunch around our plates at the restaurant we'd been recommended to try near the Ponte del Diavolo. I read the myth about the bridge in my guidebook and decided to keep it to myself: we had both had enough of death and the devil. Even the sight of Venice's domes and campaniles, silvery under the failing daylight as the boat took us back, wasn't enough to shake Mark's bleak mood. Mine matched his exactly. We had barely talked all day, both of us preoccupied. I didn't know what the letter had said, but I could imagine it was nothing good, and I knew I wasn't imagining the way Mark kept checking over his shoulder. The narrow calles and unexpected little squares had lost their magic. The city felt threatening in a way that jolted me – dark and gloomy, with an undertone of rot in the salt-scented air. The damp had soaked into my bones that day, and I couldn't get warm. Mark held my hand as we walked, but tentatively, as if it was a dead and fragile thing.

'We'll be home tomorrow,' I said, attempting to sound positive as we walked into the reception of the hotel. The concierge saw us. Instead of rushing forward as he usually did, he melted into the room behind his desk. Surely he couldn't be avoiding us, though, I thought. It was probably that he knew we were leaving so his opportunities to book concerts and tours for us were at an end. 'I think I'll be glad to get back after all.'

'Look, Ingrid—' Mark began, and the receptionist looked up. She was a cheerful twenty-something, but this evening she seemed cold. For once her smile was not in evidence.

'Ah, Mr Orpen, Miss Lewis. There was a message for you.' She reached up for a folded sheet of paper that was in the pigeonhole for our room. 'Here you are.'

Mark took it from her. 'Was this delivered to the hotel?'

'It was a phone message.' She looked down at her blotter. 'He read it out and I wrote it down. He insisted that I write down exactly what he said. He made me read it back twice.'

'Thank you.' Mark glanced at it and swore under his breath. I reached over and twitched it out of his hand before he could stop me. 'Ingrid, don't read it.'

The receptionist's handwriting was, I discovered, remarkably clear, and I managed to read the entire message before Mark took hold of my shoulders.

'Leave it. You don't need to know what it says.'

Mark
Ingrid is cheating on you
she has been with hundreds of men
she is a slag if you have any sense you'll dump her
she has chlamydia and you should get an aids test
she doesn't give a fuck about you
or anyone else

'Is that what was in the letter yesterday?' I asked, barely able to form the words. My face felt stiff from shock. 'Was it that?'

Mark nodded. 'I didn't want to tell you.'

'But you should. You shouldn't keep these things to yourself. We have to deal with them together. You said that.' I turned to the receptionist. 'It's all lies. There's a man who is harassing us – the man on the phone. He's trying to embarrass us. He's trying to ruin our holiday here.' *And my life.*

'Do you still want to keep your dinner reservation, Mr Orpen?' the receptionist asked, peering at her computer screen so she didn't have to look at us.

I turned away.

'I think,' Mark said evenly, 'we've lost our appetites.'

The journey back was a nightmare of delays thanks to fog and an air traffic controllers' strike in France. We got back to the house at two in the morning, six hours late, yawning and shivering with cold. The house was icy and I put the central heating on.

'I know it's late and we should go to bed,' I said, as Mark came into the kitchen, 'but it's too cold and I'm too keyed up.' I was filling the kettle. 'I thought I'd make a cup of tea.'

'There's no milk.'

'Herbal tea, then.'

'Mm.' He was going through the post. 'Ingrid, there's a note here.'

Every muscle in my body tensed. 'From him?'

'From the police.' He was frowning. 'Judith next door heard noises here the other day. Officers attended but there was no sign of a break-in and the premises were secure.'

'The alarm didn't go off.'

'No. It didn't.'

'Poor Judith,' I said. 'I sometimes wonder if she's getting a bit Alzheimer-y.'

'Yeah, you're right. It's probably nothing.' Mark rubbed his hands. 'That tea would be good, actually. I swear I can see my breath in here.'

'No problem.' I busied myself with finding him a mug and a teabag, and neither of us admitted – then – that we knew very well Judith was sharp as a tack, and if she said she'd heard something, she had heard something.

I knew John Webster had been in our house.

I just didn't know why.

Transcript of 999 call made by Mark Orpen at 22.23 on 30 November 2017

Operator: Hello, fire service.

Mark Orpen: My fucking house is on fire. I don't believe this.

Op: Calm down, sir. Please, just calm down. What's the address?

MO: 17 Henryson Road. That bastard. That fucking *bastard*.

Op: Sir, if you can just listen, was that seventeen, one seven, Henryson Road.

MO: Yes, yes.

Op: And what town are you in?

MO: London, you— London. In Battersea. Can you send someone quickly please? The whole place is going up.

Op: And are you in the house, sir?

MO: No, I've just got back. I'm on the pavement outside. [sound of breaking glass]

Op: You're on the pavement outside. Right. Is there anyone else in the house?

MO: No, my fiancée is at the cinema. Oh my God. Oh God. [muffled sobbing]

Op: Listen to me, sir, you need to calm down. We are on our way.

MO: The whole top of the house is on fire. The roof. Everything. Oh God, the neighbours. What if it spreads?

Op: We'll take care of that, sir, don't worry. You could knock on their doors to alert them if they're not aware.

MO: Someone else is doing that. There are people here. Lots of people. I don't know where they've all come from.

Op: What's your name, sir?

MO: Mark.

Op: I'm Suzanne, Mark. Just stay on the line with me.

MO: Okay.

Op: And just to check, you are out of the property and there's no one else in there to your knowledge.

MO: It's empty, I think. If Ingrid is still out [inaudible] Oh God, what if she came back early?

Op: We're on our way to you now, Mark. You should be able to hear the sirens.

MO: I just need to [inaudible]

Op: Mark? Mark, please stay outside.

MO: [inaudible, sounds of coughing]

Op: Mark, do not go into the house. Please, just wait for us. We are two minutes away.

MO: [coughing] I can't . . . breathe . . .

Op: Mark? Mark, can you hear me?

Op: Mark?

[sounds of sirens getting closer]

Op: Mark, are you there?

Op: Mark?

2019

9

I decided to go home after PC Buswell left. I was unlikely to do any good at work in my current state of mind, which was as close to panic as I'd been for years. The police officer hadn't reassured me; I felt worse, if anything, after our conversation. I was all too familiar with trying to tell police officers about John Webster and the 'unwanted attention' PC Buswell had dismissed so easily. No one took you seriously until you were dead, and by then – from your point of view, anyway – it was too late.

Chambers hummed with late-afternoon energy as barristers drifted back from court before heading home, or going out for the evening, or settling down to prepare for the next day. Not everyone came back after court, but those who did tended to have anecdotes to share.

'—the jury went out on *Monday*, and then today, they send a note to the judge asking if they can find him not guilty if they don't think he'll do it again. I mean, *Christ*—'

'—waited four hours for them to produce my client and then they admitted she hadn't been put in the van this morning and they couldn't actually transport her today which meant the whole hearing was pointless—'

'That nightmare of a trial's gone off to a date I can't do, which is typical. I bet he'll plead on the first day, after all that.'

'Whose cheese is in the fridge downstairs? Barney? It reeks. It smells as if it was made with milk from the cows of hell. If you're going to eat that kind of thing don't inflict it on the rest of us.'

The door to my room swung open to reveal the most junior of the clerks, a boy barely out of his teens called Jordan. 'Miss Lewis, are you here for the drinks this evening?'

I had forgotten that there were drinks. 'Who are we having?'

'Shepperton Woodson, miss.'

They were a large solicitors' firm and got good work, and large firms were a vanishing breed these days of slashed Legal Aid budgets. I should go, and I knew I should go. The thought of making light legal chit-chat for a couple of hours was utterly impossible.

'I've got a lot of work on. I'm going to have to skip it this time.'

'Right you are, miss.' He hopped off to the clerks' room to take me off the list, and I sat at my desk with my hands clasped together between my knees, trying to stop shivering.

What if Webster was back?

What if he had decided that toying with me wasn't enough fun any more?

What if he had decided the best way to mark the end of his fascination with me was to remove me from the world altogether? It wouldn't be the first time he'd resorted to that as a way of solving a problem.

I didn't want to be John Webster's problem, but then I'd never been given much of a choice about it.

I trudged out of chambers and through the narrow alleys and squares of the Temple, my head down so I didn't have to make conversation with anyone I knew. The bus stop was swarming with people in a chaotic, unmanageable queue. I had to wait twenty minutes for a bus that had enough space for me and my work bag. I heaved it into the luggage rack by the driver with some relief.

Even though the bus was slow and crowded I preferred it to the Underground when I wasn't in a hurry. For one thing, I liked to see where I was going. For another, being underground made me feel trapped. You could always get off a bus and lose yourself in a side street or a crowd. When you were stuck in a tunnel, there was nowhere to go. I looked at the faces of everyone who got on the bus after me, and I recognised none of them.

As the bus swayed in jerky increments towards King's Cross I ran through what I'd learned from what the police officer had told me. Something was bothering her, clearly, and she was too good an investigator to let it go. That didn't mean it was anything for *me* to worry about. People died in accidents all the time. In a city of eight million people it was remarkable that there weren't more road deaths.

Fear hummed at the edges of my brain like a half-forgotten tune I never wanted to hear again. *What if . . . what if . . .*

If the driver hadn't done anything wrong, my logical mind asserted, then Belinda had to be at fault. She wasn't the sort of person to take her own life, I thought, without really knowing if that was true. But if she had been unhappy, she had hidden it well. And besides, I knew she had been in a hurry. Those lights took an age to change. She might have thought it was possible to dart through the traffic, if cars were queuing across the junction.

I wished I could see the footage. Then I would know.

'Excuse me, love. Excuse me.'

A large woman edged past me, laden with groceries in string bags that seemed close to breaking point. I tried to make myself smaller and was rewarded with a smile that faded as she took in the grim expression on my face. A little too late I managed a kind of smile in return.

Pull yourself together.

It was an accident.

I'm not satisfied that we have the full story of what happened on Monday, PC Buswell murmured in my head.

She was in a hurry and stepped into the road without looking.

The rain wouldn't have helped, or the umbrella she was holding in front of her eyes.

My umbrella.

But accidents happened.

I hopped off the bus at King's Cross on a tide of commuters and walked away from the station, trundling my bag through busy streets towards the canal, looking back now and then as a reflex. The sound of pneumatic drills tore the air, the noise coming from the building sites that seemed to be a perennial feature of where I lived. There were times I regretted renting a flat in such a buzzing area, even though it was much improved from the bleak old days ten or fifteen years ago when the area had been on the fringes of respectable London life. It had been a byword for criminality. Gentrification had transformed it, or ruined it, depending on your perspective. I could certainly have rented a more conventional and practical place than the converted industrial building I called home, but it was my gift to myself after a couple of anonymous modern one-bedroom flats that had promised to be nothing except safe and secure. The day I realised I was slowly killing off everything that made me who I was, just to exist, was the day I found my current home. Left to my own devices I'd choose character over comfort every time, so that's what I did.

Besides, it had a really big gate.

Cheered by the thought of it, I picked up my pace. Ahead of me the pavement ran under scaffolding, the path reduced to a narrow track lined with plywood on both sides. It was unlit, but only thirty metres or so in length, and I could see it was empty. I was a few paces in before I felt the old, prickling nausea rising from my stomach: claustrophobia, unreasonable and unignorable. I hesitated and looked behind me again. No one appeared in the rectangle of daylight at the nearer end of the tunnel. I could turn and go out again, cross the road and walk in the open air, and no one need know I was being a coward, and irrational, and stupid . . .

If you start giving in to how you feel, where does it end? What else are you going to give up?

I squared my shoulders and started walking again, faster now, each step echoing weirdly as the sound bounced off the plywood hoarding. It was disorientating, but I was halfway through so I'd be out before I knew it, and all I had to do was keep moving . . .

91

'*Ingrid.*'

It was a yell, and I couldn't tell where it had come from. I wasn't even sure I'd heard it or if I'd imagined someone saying my name. I whipped around and peered behind me, trying to work out if there was anyone there – but it could have come from anywhere, across the road, or nowhere if I'd made it up—

A clatter overhead made my head snap up. The clatter became a jangle, a rattle of something metal plummeting down towards the ground, gathering speed, banging off scaffolding planks and poles as it fell. It smashed into the pavement just outside the tunnel, exactly where I would have been if I hadn't stopped.

In the second after the impact, there was absolute silence. Then people began to appear from nowhere, drawn to the near-tragedy like iron filings rushing towards a magnet.

'Oh my God—' A pair of young women, clutching one another, on the edge of hysterics. 'It's a bit of scaffolding, look.'

It was a large metal coupling piece, I saw, the kind used to link several scaffolding poles together.

'That's just fallen down from up there somewhere. That could have killed someone.' A cab driver with a beer belly, who had pulled in on double-yellow lines to comment.

'I saw it happen, I literally saw it.'

'They just leave those bits lying around. Gust of wind and there you are. Dangerous, that's what it is.'

I moved through the gathering crowd until I was out of the immediate area beside the scaffolding, then looked up, shading my eyes. I couldn't see anyone moving around, but the building had been gutted and the windows were frameless voids. Anyone could have stepped inside, out of sight. I imagined them picking their way through empty rooms. They could be feet away from me, on the other side of the wall.

'Is there someone up there?' a dark-haired man asked me, but a woman in a thin blouse replied before I could.

'No one's working there today. It's been closed for a week or so. I work just across the road.'

'Right.' The man stood beside me, squinting up at the building: a stocky man with a round head, and there was nothing remarkable about him except that he was noticeably out of breath, as if he'd run as fast as he could to be by my side.

I'd never seen him before, but I would know him again, I thought, and edged away from him into the gathering crowd.

'Was anyone hurt?'

'Call the police,' the cab driver said firmly.

'An ambulance. Did someone call an ambulance?'

'No one's hurt though, are they? Just lucky. Lucky timing.'

A murmur of agreement, tinged with something like disappointment. They had crowded around the entrance to the tunnel. The dark-haired man glanced at me casually. I took another step back.

What if the person had been calling my name to make me move faster?

What if it had been Webster, ushering me into harm's way?

Or someone working with him?

'Are you all right?'

I came to myself to realise that the last question was directed at me. A kindly woman was blinking at me from behind thick glasses that made her eyes look tiny. I'd have guessed she was a regular at the British Library down the road even without the canvas book bag that was weighing down one shoulder.

'I'm fine.'

'You were awfully close to it.'

'Not that close, really. It was just an accident.'

When I turned away from her, the dark-haired man had disappeared. He had vanished as suddenly as he had arrived.

I walked away, feeling irrationally guilty about leaving the scene before the police arrived, if they bothered to turn up. But I hadn't seen anything. The only thing I could say for sure was that if I'd kept walking the way I'd been going, I would have been right underneath the scaffolding when it fell.

10

I took the long route to get back to the flat, changing direction more or less at random, my head full of John Webster and how he had inserted himself into my life three years earlier and what dark roads that had taken me down. I was tired, almost to the point of tears, by the time I trailed up to the big gate, put in the code and let myself into the courtyard that was surrounded by eight flats. They had been converted from canal-side factory units a few years earlier with minimal attention to niceties like insulation. My flat was tucked in one corner, on the upper level, with a metal staircase leading to the front door.

It's a human trait to want to find significance in random events, I reminded myself – an order, a pattern. Shapes in clouds and faces in wood grain and secrets in the tea leaves. Pareidolia: that was why I saw a threat in Belinda's death, and in the scaffolding incident. I knew violence all too well, and I expected it to follow me like my own shadow, but that didn't mean anything.

I was fine.

Nothing had happened to me.

I let myself in to my flat and switched on the lights, looking around to see everything was as I had left it. The flat was essentially a single large space with a bathroom attached. There was a sofa with a sleeping platform over it rather than a proper bedroom, and a table with three chairs, and not much else.

Five minutes after getting home I had changed into jeans and a disreputable sweatshirt, coaxed the heating into life, poured myself a large glass of wine and peered into the fridge to decide what I was going to cook for dinner. If I behaved as if everything was normal, everything would be normal.

But a black feeling sat on my shoulders. It got heavier and heavier as the light faded outside.

Ridiculous, I told myself.

I had checked and double-checked that the door was locked, as were the flat's only two proper windows. They overlooked the courtyard, which itself was behind the large and heavy gate. I was safe; the only thing that could threaten me was my own imagination.

I looked at my phone.

Leave it. The scaffolding could have been a coincidence. *Someone called your name.*

Or I imagined it.

Maybe you did, said the worried little voice inside my head, *or maybe you didn't. And Belinda is definitely dead.*

I could go back and forth on it all night, but until I made this phone call I wouldn't get any peace.

It took me a minute of scrolling through my contacts to track down the number I had for DC Adam Nash, thirty seconds to leave him an incoherent voicemail message, and three hours for him to call me back. By that time I had decided he hadn't meant it when he told me to phone him if I ever needed to. I was lying wide-eyed in the dark, convinced that the thudding of my heart was footsteps on the stairs to my front door. Sleep was as remote as the stars, and when my phone vibrated next to my ear I answered it on the first ring.

'Ingrid Lewis.'

'It's Adam Nash.' His voice was instantly familiar, even though it was a long time since we'd last spoken. Serious, unhurried, measured. 'Sorry I'm so late getting back to you. I had my phone off. I was in interview.'

'No, it's fine.' I sat up and put the bedside light on. 'I'm just glad you called. I wasn't sure you would remember—'

'I remember.'

'Right.' I put a hand to my forehead. Why did I feel like crying? Because I had found someone who might understand how I was feeling – someone who could tell me if I was going mad or not. When Webster turned his attention to me, after the trial where I'd represented him, there had been a trial, and publicity. Nash had contacted me after he was convicted, to offer his assistance if I ever needed it. Adam Nash was a little bit obsessed with John Webster, I thought, and I appreciated it in a way that was the exact opposite to how I felt about Webster's obsession with me. For him, Webster was the one who'd got away.

'The thing is – well, I'm not sure if you could understand what I said in my message.'

'Parts of it,' he said carefully, and I almost laughed: I hadn't been at my most eloquent. 'Maybe you could start at the beginning.'

I stumbled through what had happened to Belinda and how I felt I wasn't getting the full story from the police who were investigating it. 'And then I was going home and I thought someone said my name – and then some scaffolding fell down, right in front of me.'

'Scaffolding.' He sounded dubious and I swallowed, hard.

'A piece of scaffolding. A coupling piece. The big metal things that hold the poles in place. I was walking underneath and – stopped. And it fell just where I should have been.'

'Lucky.'

'Very.'

'And you think it wasn't an accident.'

'No.' I hesitated. 'I don't know.'

'Is it the usual route you take from work?'

'Yes.'

'At your usual time?'

'Yes.'

A tiny silence. Then, in a voice carefully scrubbed of judgement, Nash said, 'We talked about changing routines, didn't we?'

You can't change your routine all the time, I thought. There aren't infinite ways you can move through the world if you have a fixed point A where you live and a fixed point B where you work.

'I try to vary it,' was what I ended up saying. It sounded lame, even to me.

'What street was this scaffolding on?'

'Field Lane, near the station.'

'And what was the address?'

'I haven't a clue,' I said truthfully. 'I don't know who

put up the scaffolding either, and I'm not all that keen to go back and check.'

'I can find out.' I could hear him tapping on a computer. It was the middle of the night; he'd have been justified in telling me to call him back the next day or not at all, but he was completely focused on what I was telling him. I should have found that reassuring, but in some ways I'd have preferred him to dismiss me and my fears instead of taking them seriously.

I don't want to have to do this again.

Any witnesses?' Adam asked.

'Loads, but I didn't get their names.'

'Emergency services respond?'

'Not while I was there. No one was hurt.'

'And you didn't see anyone acting suspiciously. You just heard someone say your name.'

'Maybe.' I bit my lip. 'I was thinking about him. You know how it is. I might have imagined it.'

No need to specify who I meant when I said *him*.

'Could he have been following you from work?'

'He could, I suppose.'

'How did you get to King's Cross?' He listened as I described my journey home. 'Did you use your Oyster card to pay your fare?'

'My bank card.'

'Give me the number. I can use that to trace which bus it was and get BTP to check the CCTV on board so we can see if he was on it, or nearby.'

'You think it's him, then.'

'Don't you?' His voice softened. 'Isn't that why you called me?'

'Yes. It is.'

'I'm not surprised he's back. I knew this would happen.'

I didn't say anything. I had known it too, after all. I'd just hoped Adam Nash would say I was wrong.

I had an early start in the morning, going up to Luton to cover a bail application for someone else. Glamorous it wasn't, but it was work. I got dressed in the suit and shirt I'd laid out the previous night, and from habit double-checked that I had my gown and my wig tin – a battered black and gold oval tin with a hinged lid and my initials stencilled on the top – as well as my laptop, charger and the papers I needed to work on. I looked around the flat before I left to check that everything was as it should be, which was reasonable and the sort of thing anyone normal might do.

You do realise, my counsellor had said in what turned out to be our final session, *that consciously avoiding the behaviours connected with surviving trauma doesn't mean that you haven't experienced trauma, or that it hasn't had a long-term effect on you.*

I know that.

I think you don't like being the victim. You're used to being in a position of power in court, in control. You don't like being the one on the other side for a change.

No one wants to see themselves as a victim, I had said, and she had smiled.

You're bright enough to control your actions, but you can't outthink your feelings. One day they will overwhelm you.

I think, I had said, *I've got as much as I can out of counselling.*

We're not finished though.

You might not be, but I am.

I hadn't liked that counsellor, and she hadn't liked me. She'd thought I was arrogant. What I hadn't allowed her to know – what I couldn't even say – was that my fear was as loud and all-consuming as a blast furnace, and keeping the door closed to it was essential for my survival.

So I didn't take elaborate steps to check whether anyone had broken into my home, and I didn't open all the drawers and cupboards ten times a day or catalogue the contents of my underwear drawer, but I wanted to.

I let myself out of the flat and locked the door before heading down the stairs, treading as softly as I could because it was still early.

I was glad to have work to think about, having spent all night worrying about John Webster. Nash had agreed to meet me to talk it over when I got back from Luton, which should be mid-afternoon. I wasn't sure how he could help but at least it felt as if I was doing *something* to take control – although how you could take control of a situation when you weren't even sure what that situation *was*—

'Hi.'

I was halfway across the courtyard, skirting the rectangular pond at the centre of it, and I hadn't noticed that anyone else was there. A woman, sitting on a bench in a shaft of morning sunshine. Steam twisted upwards from the mug she held in both hands. She was my age, with a round, friendly face that looked freshly scrubbed. Her hair was damp and she had plaited it into two fat ropes.

'Sorry. Did I give you a fright?'

'Not really.'

101

'I'm your new neighbour.' She gave me an awkward little wave, still smiling. 'Helen. Just moved in a week ago.'

'Congratulations. I'm Ingrid.'

'I live downstairs from you.' She dimpled. 'Don't worry. I don't listen to loud music or have lots of parties.'

'Me neither.'

'It's nice, here. The garden.'

I looked around. 'Yes, it is. It's one of the reasons I moved here.'

'I suppose it won't get much sun later in the year.'

'I've never really noticed.' I hesitated. 'Sorry, I don't mean to be rude, but I'm on my way to work, so—'

'Of course! Sorry! I don't want to delay you.'

I started to walk away.

'Are you a stewardess?'

'Excuse me?'

She was looking at my bag. 'Are you a stewardess? I've seen you coming and going with the bag, so I wondered.'

'No.' I moved towards the gate with decision, and this time she let me go. It wasn't the most friendly way of ending the conversation, I thought, as I let myself out, but I felt uneasy about Helen. She was trying far too hard. No one ever sat in the courtyard to enjoy the morning sunshine – not that early in the day, when it was cold enough for me to need gloves. If she lived downstairs from me, she could have heard me getting ready. She could have come out to intercept me.

What did she want?

Paranoia, my old friend. I hadn't missed it.

11

I'd arranged to meet Adam near his office. It was in Vauxhall, he'd told me, and he'd given me directions to a café nearby that turned out to be small, with steamed-up windows and bright murals on the walls. I got there early and spent half an hour jumping every time the door opened. I recognised him straight away when he walked in: medium height, medium build, brownish hair, brown eyes, two years older than when I'd seen him last. The shock of relief hummed through me at the sight of him, along with a quick, private feeling of surprise that he was better looking than I'd remembered. His eyes went to me, then dropped to the tea I was nursing. He raised a hand in greeting. 'Can I get you anything?'

I shook my head and he went to the counter to order. I watched him talking to the morose woman who had served me. I couldn't hear what he said but she laughed and tucked her hair behind her ear, flushed and suddenly pretty, which spoke volumes about the general standard of her clientele because while Adam Nash was acceptable, looks-wise, the jury was still out on his personality. I'd never got to know him well. He was reserved and extremely professional, and I hadn't been in a very good frame of mind the last time we'd had anything to do with one another, given that my entire life had been collapsing around my ears.

What a good thing that wasn't happening again.

'I'll bring it over,' the woman said to him at last. She had made me wait at the counter for mine.

He came to sit opposite me, unsmiling now, serious to the bone.

'Miss Lewis.'

'Ingrid,' I said quickly. I couldn't bear this conversation if he was going to Miss-Lewis me throughout. 'I'm pretty sure we should be on first-name terms by now.'

He considered that for a moment. He was assessing me in much the same way I'd scrutinised him when he was ordering his tea. Maybe I looked different too, two years on. I tucked some hair behind my ear, suddenly self-conscious.

'How are you?' he asked, as if he really wanted to know.

'Tired. I – I didn't sleep well last night.' *If by* not well *you mean* not at all.

'I haven't had a chance to look into this other barrister's death. What can you tell me about it?'

Straight down to business. What else had I expected? Comfort? I dug in my bag for a newspaper clipping I'd kept that had described Belinda's death in fairly comprehensive and accurate detail. He read it with absolute concentration, giving it his full attention while I tried not to watch him. The woman behind the counter was staring at us, curious, and I caught her eye without meaning to. I smiled; she didn't.

'Has anything else happened since we spoke?'

I dragged myself back to pay attention to Adam. 'No.'

'No one following you?'

'I don't think so.'

'Have you been checking?'

'Now and then. When I remember.'

'You are taking this seriously, I hope.'

'I'm taking it as seriously as I ever do.'

He looked at me as if I was completely insane. 'You know John Webster is dangerous.'

It was as if Webster had pulled up a chair and sat down at our table. He would be enjoying this conversation so much if he knew it was happening.

'I know exactly what he's capable of. But when he started harassing me after the trial where I represented him, I realised there was nothing I could do to stop him. He's not scared of the police and he doesn't listen to reason. I decided I wasn't going to give him any kind of power over me. He thrives on fear and I didn't want him to enjoy mine.'

'When we spoke last night you sounded terrified.'

I felt the blood warm my face. 'That's why I'm here. I wouldn't have called you—' I broke off as the woman appeared at our table with a cup of tea that she placed in front of him reverently. His came with a biscuit on the saucer. Mine had not.

'Thanks, Marta.' He smiled at her, then turned back to me, his face reverting to solemn as if he'd flicked a switch. 'You were saying.'

'I was saying I wouldn't have contacted you if I hadn't been worried.'

'About Webster.'

'It just feels like a step up from what he did before.' I stirred my tea. 'He set out to destroy my life but he didn't seem to want to end it.'

'Why now? What triggered this, if it is him?'

'Webster's just come out of prison. You know he got convicted of fraud. He tried to persuade the wrong old lady to fund his lifestyle and her family got to hear about it. Unfortunately he'd only taken a couple of grand off her so the sentence was light.'

He nodded. 'He wasn't in prison for long but any time behind bars is better than nothing.'

'Not if he spent that time dwelling on all the things he hadn't had a chance to do when he was free. Not if he was making plans that he's now putting into action. And the restraining order I had expired in September. There's nothing to stop him from following me again.'

Instead of answering me, Adam Nash pulled a face.

'You don't believe me, do you?' I looked away and blinked, hard. I didn't want to sob in front of him. 'You think I'm making it all up.'

'What happened to your friend, and the scaffolding – it's not necessarily connected with Webster, is it?'

'She wasn't really my friend. We worked together once. I knew her to say hello to, and I remembered her husband's name – but we weren't close. I gave her my umbrella so she wouldn't get wet, and I can't shake the thought that it was what killed her.' This time, I held his gaze. 'The last time John Webster was causing trouble for me, someone else died, horribly. It's a pretty huge coincidence if the two things aren't connected, isn't it?'

Adam cleared his throat, suddenly awkward. 'Look, this

is a difficult question to ask – but are you sure he's the only person who might want to harm you?'

'This might surprise you, but I don't have that many completely insane stalkers.'

'Really?' The look on my face must have answered his question because he held up his hands defensively. 'I'm only asking because your job involves hanging out with the kind of criminals most ordinary people try to avoid.'

'But they don't want to hurt me. I'm on their side, remember. I'm there to help them. They want me to do my job and then they forget about me, whether I win or lose. I'm just part of the process.' I shook my head. 'Webster is the only one who's ever bothered me afterwards.'

His gaze fell to my hands, checking for rings. 'Have you got a boyfriend?'

'Not at the moment. No one serious since Mark.' Instantly I wished I hadn't said his name. *Don't think about him. Not now.* Quickly, to distract Adam, I said, 'How about you? Seeing anyone?'

He looked tired rather than amused. 'The reason I ask is because if you had a new partner that might have prompted him to act.'

'Does he need a reason?'

'I've been keeping an eye on him. He's seemed to be on his best behaviour since the incidents involving you.'

'You know about everything that happened.' I was turning my teaspoon over and over.

'I've read the file.' His eyes were steady.

'It turned my life upside down and inside out. I've moved house three times. I should have been married by now—' I broke off, horrified to find my voice cracking with emotion again. I got myself under control and finished off

107

with, 'And Webster was never, ever punished for that part of it.'

'There wasn't enough evidence to charge him with anything in 2017.'

'Yes, I remember.' I swallowed the knot in my throat and managed to smile. 'Don't waste your time looking for something I've done that might have provoked him. You know as well as I do, this is how he works. He goes quiet, and just when you think you're safe, he reminds you he's still out there.'

'What do you want me to do?'

'I'd like you to talk to Alison Buswell. She's a City of London officer on the team that's investigating Belinda's death. I want you to tell her about John Webster because I think she might take it seriously if it comes from another police officer. I just sound crazy when I try to tell people about him.'

'Anything else?' He was writing her name down.

'I want to see the CCTV of Belinda's death.'

He blew out a lungful of air. 'Why?'

'In case I see something Alison Buswell missed. I'm more likely to recognise John Webster than she is.'

'I'd be able to pick him out of a crowd, I'm fairly sure.'

'You probably would, but I still want to see it myself.'

'Why?'

I shrugged. 'It's not every day you get to watch yourself die.'

I was trying to sound tough and objective, like a professional in the criminal justice system who had seen a thing or two instead of coming across as a panicky victim, but it made Adam blink. 'You've changed.'

'In what way?'

108

'You weren't cynical before.'

I felt his words hit home. 'Maybe I just hid it better.'

He shook his head. 'No.'

'The last two years would be enough to make anyone cynical.'

'I didn't think you were like that.'

I took a deep breath. 'I'm not – not really. I'm trying not to overreact here. I don't think it's funny, if that helps. Belinda is dead, and it's because of me.'

'You think he killed her because he assumed it was you under the umbrella.'

'I think it's possible. I think he's capable of it, don't you?'

'Without a doubt. But if he did kill her, it's not your fault. It's his.'

I gave him a crooked smile. 'That's not what you said when I got him acquitted.'

He was nice enough to look embarrassed, but I didn't see why. After all, he'd been absolutely right.

12

Three days after I met Adam I went to a party, mainly because I didn't want to go. It was that stubborn streak that had made me refuse to submit when John Webster set out to scare me before. No matter how he threatened me, I was going to live my normal life even if it killed me.

But it might just do that.

It was very inconvenient to have Adam Nash's quiet, ironic voice echoing through my mind, I thought, and the memory of his dark eyes, soft with concern as he said goodbye.

I put on my reddest lipstick so that at least I looked brave, even if I didn't feel it, and dug out a pair of heels, which I regretted as soon as I'd been standing around in them for twenty minutes.

The party was to celebrate two new members of chambers, one a QC who had moved from a set in Birmingham, one a pupil who had been taken on. It was a long-standing tradition that it was their responsibility to buy the champagne for everyone else to drink, and drink it we did. The room where the party was held rang with loud voices and guffawing laughter. The QC – a tall woman with curling hair and a fearsome reputation – was in her element. The ex-pupil's face was flushed, his tie at half-mast. He'd had a couple of months to get used to the idea of being a tenant – his name was already painted on the board outside the front door – but he still looked as if he couldn't believe his luck.

'Were we ever so young?' Karen Odili murmured in my ear and I grinned.

'I doubt it. He makes me feel a hundred years old.'

'The first-six pupils are worse. They're *children*.' She gestured with her glass and I looked across to where two of them stood by the door, trying not to yearn too obviously.

'Do you remember what that was like? Wondering if it would ever be you or if you were going to have to find somewhere else to do a third six?'

'Vaguely.' She grinned. 'Of course I do. It's the pits. A year-long job interview.'

The third pupil slipped into the room, looking as if she wanted to be ignored. She was the girl who had been at the Old Bailey the day Belinda died.

'Did you hear about Belinda Grey?' Karen asked, echoing my thoughts.

'Yes. I spoke to her just before it happened.'

'Not that.' Karen dropped her voice so no one else could hear. 'Apparently she was having an affair with her head of chambers and she got pregnant. She got rid of it but he dumped her anyway. She was devastated.'

The champagne I was holding suddenly smelled revolting. I set the glass on a nearby shelf with some care. 'Absolute rubbish. Where did you hear that?'

'I was in a trial with a guy from Garter Buildings. He told me. It was common knowledge apparently.' She shrugged. 'They all think she killed herself.'

'People always say that kind of thing once someone isn't around to defend themselves. And she once told me she was as likely to clean someone else's kitchen as sleep with their husbands.' *Why make extra work for myself*, she had added with a wicked smile. I couldn't believe that sharp-edged tongue was silenced forever. 'It's just gossip. No one can think why she would have wanted to kill herself so they're making it up.'

Karen looked mildly offended. 'Sorry. I didn't realise you were such close friends.'

'We weren't close, but I met her husband once, and her little boy. They seemed like the perfect family. I can't believe she would have chosen to die when she had so much to live for.'

'People with kids kill themselves too, Ingrid. All the time. Motherhood doesn't make you some sort of super-woman who can rise above depression, believe me.' Karen had two adorable girls herself.

'I know that. But—' I stopped. I couldn't reveal my suspicions about Belinda's death without telling her about John Webster, and that was the last thing I wanted to talk about. 'Don't mind me, Karen. I'm not in a great mood tonight for some reason. Tired, I think.'

'Drink more.' She raised her eyebrows at a waiter who hurried over with a bottle. 'That'll perk you up.'

I retrieved my glass and allowed the waiter to fill it, but I didn't actually drink from it. I stood around for another forty minutes chatting to people, laughing when everyone else did, but my heart wasn't in it. As soon as

I could, I slipped away, giving the party up as a total failure.

I stopped for a moment on the steps to survey the Temple, which was deserted. It had rained while I was inside and the air was cold. My breath clouded before me. The cars parked under the great old trees had misted up too, their windows opaque. Nothing stirred and after a few deep breaths of the raw air I made my way down the steps and walked through the car park. I glanced up at Garter Buildings where one or two lights still shone. Had Belinda been having an affair? Possibly, but I couldn't see her dying for it. I shivered and turned away, picking up my pace as a car door closed softly behind me. Getting run over in the car park would round off my evening nicely. My steps echoed as I passed under the archway to Church Court, which was restricted to pedestrians and unutterably ancient.

In the cloisters by the Temple Church a trick of the acoustics doubled my steps, the echoes sounding exactly as if someone was walking behind me. I stopped and looked back, remembering Adam's warning to me to be on my guard. Nothing moved. No one stepped into view. I felt uneasy and didn't know why.

Pump Court, narrow and graceful, the trees fluttering their last leaves against the night sky. Brick Court, open, larger, busier as a rule, deserted now. From habit I started to walk towards Fountain Court with its tall water feature before I recalled that the gate would be closed and locked at this hour. Instead I turned to go back up narrow, cobbled Middle Temple Lane towards the Strand. Something made a noise behind me: the sole of a shoe grating on stone, an echo to it as if it came from under one of the arches that led to other parts of the Temple. I looked back, my eyes wide, straining to see anyone lurking in the shadows. My heart thumped, drowning out all other sounds. Below the level of logic, of common sense, I was afraid, as animals are when they know they are being hunted. Someone was watching me – someone who wished me harm.

A man stepped out of an archway some distance away from me. He was a silhouette, but something about the set of his shoulders and the shape of his head was familiar. Recognition made my heart hammer in my chest: the man from the scaffolding accident, who had run to my side and then disappeared.

Had he called my name as the scaffolding piece fell? To warn me or to make sure I was in the right place?

Don't wait. Don't think. Go.

I ran up the lane towards the heavy black gate that separated the hush of the Temple from the traffic outside. The buildings crowded in around it, with one hanging right over the top. It cast a shadow that seemed darker than coal. I was hurrying, gasping for breath, aware of being alone apart from the man behind me, aware that I would be the easiest of targets . . .

I was twenty feet away when something moved against the darkness of the gate and became human. He turned his face towards me and stepped forward with a measured, long stride, into the light.

I stopped where I was, my feet rooted to the ground. I couldn't run. I couldn't scream.

Behind me, footsteps echoed. Moving in the wrong direction, away from us. Come back, I thought helplessly, whoever you are. Come and save me.

'It's all right.' He was staring past me, frowning. 'There was someone following you but I think they've gone. I must have scared them off.' His voice was just the same: clipped, precise, totally distinctive.

John Webster, in person, stepping out of my nightmares to stand in my way.

He glanced back at me and whatever he saw in my face must have amused him because he grinned. 'That's what I do, isn't it, Ingrid? Scare people?'

He hadn't changed, I thought dully. He would never change.

'What are you doing here?'

'Just trying to help.' He moved a step closer to me. 'I wonder what would have happened if I hadn't been here.'

A clatter at the gate took the place of my answer. The wicket swung open and a group of young barristers piled in, all talking at the tops of their voices, happy-drunk and giddy.

'No because I'm sure I left it—'

'As usual.'

'Have you checked? Have you checked, because this has happened before, hasn't it?'

'It's always in your handbag,' a deep-voiced, tall man offered. 'Every time.'

'Oh God, it's not, Faraz. It can't be.' The young woman crouched and started rummaging through her handbag as the others milled around aimlessly between me and John Webster. There were eight of them altogether: three women, five men. Webster's eyes were fixed on mine, as if the other people didn't exist for him. They seemed oblivious to him too, I clenched my jaw to stop myself from screaming a warning: *this man is more dangerous than you can possibly know.*

'I can't believe we had to walk all the way back here. Why didn't someone make her check her bag before we left El Vino's?'

'Because she said she'd looked.'

'She always says she's looked.'

'Here it is!' She held up a wallet, flushed with triumph. 'It was in my bag! Amazing! I thought it was on my desk!'

A groan rose from the party, as one. 'Come on. We'll be in time for last orders if we hurry.'

Without making a conscious decision about it, I fell into step between two of the larger men and moved towards the gate, past Webster. I didn't look at him as we swept through the wicket and out onto the pavement, where I walked away with my host of drunken, chatty bodyguards until the first black cab appeared with its amber light on. I hailed it and hopped in as the young men crowded around to compete for the honour of closing the door and said goodnight. The engine roared throatily as the driver took off towards Trafalgar Square. I sat back, trembling, and called Adam Nash to leave another message on his voicemail.

Not a wild fear. Not my imagination.

John Webster was back.

From: IATL@internetforyou.com
To: Durbs, 4102

It's all going according to plan.

From: Durbs@mailmeforfree.com
To: 4102, IATL

Are you sure? Because I thought we were going to bring this to a conclusion. She got away.

From: IATL@internetforyou.com
To: Durbs, 4102

Maybe you didn't understand the plan, then.

From: Durbs@mailmeforfree.com
To: 4102, IATL

Maybe I didn't. I thought we all wanted the same thing.

From: 4102@freeinternetmail.com
To: Durbs, IATL

So did I.

From: IATL@internetforyou.com
To: Durbs, 4102

Now is not the time to start arguing amongst ourselves, not when we're almost there.

You both wanted to punish her. I've seen her up close and trust me, she's terrified. The police aren't going to listen to her and she knows it. She's got nowhere to hide.

From: 4102@freeinternetmail.com
To: Durbs, IATL

I suppose you're the expert.

From: IATL@internetforyou.com
To: Durbs, 4102

I know her better than she knows herself.

This is only going to get worse for her and I'll be there, watching her suffer.

13

Adam Nash wasn't always good company, but I was glad of his presence by my side in the small, stuffy room tucked into a corner of PC Buswell's office in Wood Street police station in the heart of the City. There was nothing in the room but two chairs in front of a computer. It was actually a good thing that John Webster had reappeared the previous week, because it had made all the difference for Adam when he was persuading PC Buswell to change her mind about letting me see the CCTV. From the look on her face, though, she wasn't happy about it.

She gestured at the chairs, unsmiling.

'You can sit there. It won't take you long to watch it through. The footage lasts about fourteen minutes. I've booked the room for an hour so you can take a closer look at any of it that seems useful.'

'Where's the footage from?' Adam asked.

'Dashboard camera on the lorry and a black cab that was coming the other way, traffic cameras on the intersection, two cameras mounted on buildings that front on to

Ludgate Circus and a helmet camera a cyclist was wearing. It's raw footage but it's all good quality.' She hesitated. 'I'd watch it with the sound off, unless you particularly want to hear what happened. There's audio from the cyclist's footage. Belinda doesn't make a sound, but—'

'I don't think we need to hear it,' Adam said, with a glance in my direction. I shook my head.

'What are you looking for?' PC Buswell asked.

'Someone I recognise,' I said.

'This John Webster.' She folded her arms. 'What's he like?'

What a question. I did my best. 'The first time you meet him, you like him. Then you realise he doesn't have emotions like a normal person but he's brilliant at manipulating people. He lives off other people – he finds lonely and vulnerable people with houses and money, and he moves in on them. I think he's capable of anything.'

'Like what?' She was looking sceptical and I couldn't decide where to start.

'He burned down her house.'

That hadn't been the worst of it, I thought. 'He was a nuisance at first. Then he was dangerous. Someone died.'

'Someone?' Adam was clearly about to explain what had happened but the look on my face stopped him. PC Buswell did not need to know all the details and I certainly didn't want to hear them again.

PC Buswell nodded, still confused. 'Why was Webster interested in you?'

'I defended him on a charge of harassment and got the case dropped. I was tough on the woman who'd accused him during my cross-examination.' I swallowed. 'I . . . destroyed her along with the case. He felt it wasn't a fair

120

fight, so he engineered a situation where I was alone with his accuser, to give her a chance to do the same to me. I didn't know it but he was measuring me against her. Whoever won was worthy of his attention, he'd decided.'

'And you won.'

'I was rescued.' Emma Seaton came at me, the blade flashing, more real than the two police officers in front of me. I blinked the image away. 'He decided that was enough. She was too pathetic for him to bother with any more. He wanted to break me instead.'

'What happened to her?'

'Nothing good.' It was Adam who answered, his voice harsh. 'Also, Webster has inherited money on three separate occasions from people not related to him.'

'Did he kill them?'

'Not as far as we know. But anything's possible. They died when it was convenient for him.'

'I haven't seen him since last week in the Temple, but I can't think it was a coincidence that he turned up again.' I'd spent the intervening days on the edge of terror in case I turned a corner and found him waiting for me.

'And what did he do, exactly?'

'He scared someone away. Someone who was following me.' I was shivering. 'I mean, I assume he set it up. It's the kind of thing he'd do. He'd enjoy me being grateful, because he knows it's the last thing I'd want. It's all part of how he operates. He likes to destroy his victims. I've disappointed him because I haven't quite reached my breaking point yet.'

'Right.' To her credit, PC Buswell revised her opinion of him, and me, without any further demurring. 'I can see why he's on your list of suspects.'

'He won't necessarily be on the footage. He could have been there, or he could have sent someone else to do it.' My mouth was Sahara-dry. 'He can persuade most people to do what he wants – even terrible things. He doesn't usually make mistakes. I'm surprised that he confused Belinda with me, if that's what happened. That's another reason I want to look at the footage. I want to see what he – or whoever pushed her – saw.'

'If she was pushed.'

'So it's not clear from the footage?' Adam asked.

'You'll have to watch it for yourself. There are two schools of thought here about what happened.' She didn't say which version she believed.

'Thank you for this,' I said impulsively.

'Don't thank me yet. It's disturbing, as I said.'

I wanted to point out that I wasn't as innocent as most civilians – that I'd spent plenty of time watching people die on camera since I'd been a barrister, frame by bloody frame – but she had a point. This was someone I knew. And if I was right, it had been supposed to be me.

'Ready?' She waited for me to nod, then typed a password and the screen filled with a paused colour image of Ludgate Circus taken from the top of Fleet Street, facing towards Ludgate Hill. She pressed play. 'Belinda Grey should be visible on the left of the screen in about three seconds.'

Three . . . two . . . one . . . a red umbrella bobbed into shot, moving fast. From that angle, I could only see Belinda's feet and lower legs. She hurried down the hill, dodging slow-moving tourists trudging up towards St Paul's.

'She was in a hurry,' Adam observed. 'And you walk

quickly, as a rule. He'd have been expecting someone moving fast.'

'She was thinner than me. Her skirt was shorter. And I don't wear heels like that.'

'In the rain that would have been easy to overlook.'

I nodded, my heart in my mouth. There was something awful about the inevitability of it. No way to warn her, to steer her away from the edge of the pavement. I was clenching all of my muscles, I realised, clinging to the edge of my chair, and I forced myself to relax my hands, and breathe deeply, and focus on what I needed to see.

'Lots of people waiting at the pedestrian lights,' Adam said as the red umbrella reached the bottom of the hill and joined the group. They disappeared behind buses and lorries as the traffic flowed past them.

'Those lights take ages to change.' My voice didn't sound like my own. I cleared my throat. 'She would have wanted to get across quickly once they changed. She would have wanted to be at the edge of the pavement.'

'That's exactly what happens.' PC Buswell leaned over and paused the footage as the umbrella moved forward through the crowd. 'We've managed to trace about half of these people – we did an appeal on social media and there are yellow boards at the scene looking for witnesses. There are ten people we haven't identified yet. I doubt we'll find all of them if they were tourists.'

'Did any of the witnesses you traced see anything strange?' I asked.

'Apparently not. But there was a bit of jostling, according to this lady here.' Her pen circled a woman who was beside Belinda. 'Nothing out of the ordinary at a busy junction, she said. In her opinion, Belinda slipped.'

123

'That's possible.' Adam glanced at me. 'He could be taking advantage of a genuine accident to scare you. It's a way in for him. You're already off balance. All he needs to do is give you a push.'

'That had occurred to me. It's why I wanted to see the footage for myself.'

'This is just before the incident,' PC Buswell said quietly. 'Are you ready for me to go on?'

I nodded. She pressed play and the stream of vehicles going down towards Blackfriars Bridge resumed its progress. A white lorry appeared on the left of the image and time seemed to slow down as it slewed to a stop halfway across the junction, where I had seen it. The lorry was between the camera and where Belinda had been standing, mercifully, but as people rushed to help or turned away there was no mistaking what had happened.

'The rain was heavy at that point in the morning,' PC Buswell said. 'Visibility wasn't great. You'll see it on the driver's dash cam but he had almost no chance to react.'

'Any issues with him?' Adam asked.

'Nothing. Clean licence, passed the breathalyser at the scene, cooperated fully. He wasn't speeding. He did what he could.'

'Poor man,' I said, meaning it. The screen went black and then flickered into full colour again, from the Ludgate Hill side of the road, and we watched the end of Belinda's life once more, in silence this time. Every new vantage point revealed some new detail of her death – that she had collided with the front of the lorry and slid under the wheels, that the stupid umbrella had caught in the grille, that she had been sprawling forward off balance when she came off the pavement, not stepping down to cross the road. The best view – or the worst, depending on how you felt about watching a woman die – was the cyclist's camera, because he had been coming up along-side the lorry and was a few feet away from the place where it happened. At long last the screen went black for the last time and PC Buswell moved round to face us.

'Well? Seen enough?'

'Not quite.' At some point as the tape played I had moved from shock to the objective concentration I brought to bear on my cases. I checked the notes I'd scribbled. 'Five minutes and forty-two seconds in, there's a shot of the crowd on the pavement from behind. I want to have another look.'

PC Buswell compressed her mouth as if she was phys-ically holding back what she wanted to say, but she went back to the point I'd specified, which showed Belinda moving forward through the group and others joining it behind her.

'Pause it.' I leaned in, my attention focused on the back of the group of pedestrians reacting to her death. 'Can you go on one frame at a time?'

'It's not ideal for image quality,' PC Buswell warned me.

'Doesn't matter.'

The images hitched past, blurring and splintering into pixels and snow but occasionally clear enough to see the group bunch together before it fell apart. I watched a couple moving back, the woman turning to her partner and burying her head in his chest. Beside them, an elderly man seemed to be standing on tiptoe, trying to see the road and Belinda's body. He raised his arms and I saw the rectangle of a phone screen as he filmed or took

125

pictures. People being people, I thought, and frowned as one person detached themselves from the rest of the group and moved away to the right, out of sight. The figure was hunched over so it was hard to gauge the height, and there was a blanket over the head and shoulders.

'Who's that?'

'A homeless person. He was sitting outside a shop on the corner, begging.'

'Have you got hold of him?' Adam asked.

'Not so far. A lot of them don't want to have anything to do with us, as you know.'

'The homeless charities might be able to help,' I said. 'They generally have a better chance than the police of getting street people to trust them.'

PC Buswell looked irritated. 'Yes, if I want another statement where someone tells me it was raining and they didn't see what happened, I'll definitely spend a few hours trying to track down someone without a proper description or name.'

Adam frowned, and said nothing. He would have spent the time on it, I thought, even if he thought it might be a dead end.

'Did any of the other people you traced from that group mention him?' I asked.

'One of the tourists did. She was Dutch. She said he smelled terrible and she was trying to avoid standing too close to him. She was worried he would try to steal from her handbag or pick her husband's pocket, and that distracted her from what happened to Belinda.'

'Can we watch it at the proper speed?' I asked.

On screen the homeless man stood behind Belinda. The blanket muffled his movements as well as disguising him

– it was impossible to see what position he had adopted or whether his arms were moving.

'Why did he come forward then? He had a good pitch there on the corner, and it was only going to get busier around lunchtime when the offices emptied out.'

'Why did the tramp cross the road?' Adam said quietly and I glared.

'Watch what happens after Belinda falls. He moves to the back of the group as everyone else crowds forward, apart from this couple who are comforting one another. Human nature would make you look but he's edging away because he knows what's happened. And then once he's sure everyone's attention is fixed on the road he turns and moves away.'

'Do you think it's Webster?'

I looked at Adam. 'What do you think? He doesn't move like him.' John Webster was athletic and moved with a kind of springy energy; this man's progress was slowed by a limp that drew one shoulder down.

'That could be part of a disguise.' Adam ran that section of the tape again, concentrating on the screen. At last he shrugged. 'I'd be lying if I said I was sure that was Webster, but the limp wouldn't put me off. If we're looking for a guy with a limp we're less likely to think of him.'

'He's heading up towards Holborn.' PC Buswell flipped open a notebook. 'I'll try to trace him on camera.'

'You won't find him. He'll disappear on you.' I looked at Adam. 'That's right, isn't it? He just melts away.'

Adam nodded soberly. 'If it's Webster.'

'Of course it's him.' I pushed my hair back from my face with shaking hands. 'Webster must have realised that he could get away with anything if he was dressed as a street person. No one wants to look at them, do they? No one makes eye contact in case they ask for money. He could cover his face and behave as oddly as he liked and no one would think it was strange. He was basically invisible. He could sit on the street corner and wait until he saw her and saw his opportunity.' I pointed at the screen. 'That's John Webster and you're never, ever going to manage to pin it on him.'

14

The following Saturday morning I woke up early feeling edgy and out of sorts. Too much time sitting around worrying, I diagnosed, plus nerves about whether I was ready for the trial I was starting on Monday. I prescribed myself a long swim followed by brunch with Adele. Later I might fit in a trip to Borough Market to buy something strange and exotic to cook for dinner. Normal, normal, normal, except that the edges of my day were shadowy with fear. I was trying to hide from it – and from Webster – without admitting to myself that it was a factor in my decision-making. But the pool was near my flat, and there would be safety in numbers at brunch, and I could get home before dark if I was cooking for myself. What I wanted to do just happened to correspond with what I had to do, I told myself, and knew it for a lie.

It was a beautiful day, clear and bright, and I jogged down the steps from my flat. A voice greeted me warmly.

'Going to the gym?' My new neighbour was planting

herbs in hand-painted pots, and had paused, trowel in hand, to talk to me.

'How did you guess?'

'Which gym do you go to?'

'Why do you ask? Are you thinking of joining one?'

Helen shrugged. She was comfortably built rather than athletic, but that didn't mean she wasn't a gym bunny. 'I need to do a bit more exercise. This area is quite busy. I used to run, but I'm not sure I want to start again with all the traffic.'

'I'm not sure I can recommend mine.' Not least because I don't want to see my over-friendly new neighbour when I'm there, I thought. But I knew it wasn't kind, and the hurt in Helen's eyes, quickly hidden, made me feel awful. 'Look, I'll pick up a leaflet for you when I'm there.'

She clasped her hands under her chin. 'Thank you! That would be wonderful.'

It's just a leaflet, not the Koh-I-Noor.

'Bye, Helen.' I closed the gate behind me and went on my way, shaking my head.

I spent a happy hour in the swimming pool, taking pleasure in being faster than the splashy men who hogged the lanes. In the water, with my cap and goggles, I was anonymous and unobserved. I cut through the water like a fish, pushing myself harder and harder as my limbs tired, losing myself in pure physical exertion. After I got out of the pool and changed, I set off down the street, and had gone quite some distance before I remembered the leaflet. Because I was being nice I doubled back to get it, but I did it with very bad grace.

*

130

Brunch involved bottomless mimosas, Adele and two other friends I hadn't seen for ages. Adele had fully intended to spend her time holding forth about her ex and their break-up, which I had already heard more than once, so I was relieved that Ciara and Eve were there. Then it transpired that Eve had just got engaged to her boyfriend of five months and Ciara had bought a flat since I'd last seen her. I spent a lot of brunch trying to catch the waiter's eye for a refill of our drinks as Adele and I were out-adulted at every conversational turn.

'And what about you, Ingrid?' Ciara, having finally run out of things to say about bathroom fittings, turned her attention to me. 'What's going on with you?'

'Nothing much.' Except for the person who is maybe trying to kill me, as usual. I pushed Webster back out of my mind. 'Work is fine. I'm doing a robbery next week.'

'That always sounds so funny,' Eve said, wrinkling her nose. 'Like you're actually planning to commit a robbery.'

I smiled politely. If she thought that was weird, she should hear barristers talking about their cases, since the convention was that you spoke as if you and the client were one. *I've admitted stealing a hundred grand from my employer . . . You're on CCTV punching him in the face . . . My story is that she provoked me . . .*

'Are you seeing anyone?' Ciara asked.

I shook my head. 'No one.'

'Come on, Ingrid. You really need to start dating again. Forget about Mark.'

His name made me freeze in the middle of picking up my glass. Ciara looked embarrassed.

'Sorry. I didn't mean to upset you. But . . . maybe it's time to move on.'

131

'Easy for you to say.' I said it with a smile to hide that I really meant it: of course they'd had romantic ups and downs but they'd never moved from happiness through fear to total desolation the way I had.

'You need to meet someone.' Eve tilted her head to one side, deeply sympathetic. 'You deserve someone nice in your life.'

'I think so too,' I said flippantly.

'I thought Paul was nice, but then he turned out to be a *wanker*.'

As Adele finally took control of the conversation and began enumerating Paul's many shortcomings, I drained my glass.

Inevitably, brunch modulated into a shopping trip that took up most of the rest of the day, ending up with sickly-sweet cocktails in a hotel on Park Lane. I postponed Borough Market, with regret, and settled for picking up some shopping on the way home. Day-drinking had left me listless and headache-y, and I found myself craving comfort food. Brunch had been a long time and many shops ago. I loaded my basket with the ingredients for lamb ragú with pappardelle: solid, peasant cooking full of flavour and life.

When I reached the gate I put in the code warily, checking that Helen was nowhere to be seen before I committed myself to the courtyard. I was carrying a huge bunch of blush-coloured roses and eucalyptus leaves that Adele had insisted on buying for me, my handbag and an overloaded bag-for-life from the supermarket that was failing to live up to its name. I hurried up to my door and juggled bags and flowers while I tried to fit the key into the lock. As I stepped inside, my phone started to ring. A frantic pat-down told me it wasn't in my jeans or my coat. I dumped everything on to the table and the grocery bag split along one seam, shedding its contents. A tin of chopped tomatoes rolled off the edge of the table and I caught the mince as it tried to follow suit.

'Piss off,' I said to everything, and got to my phone in time for it to stop ringing. No number displayed. No message.

'And you too.' I threw my phone onto the sofa in disgust, and stopped, unsure of myself.

Something was wrong. Something had changed.

I turned my head slowly, cautiously, trying to make sense of the feeling I had. It was the same fear I'd had in the Temple; it made no sense to be scared, but I was. The air was still and there wasn't a sound except for the familiar scratches and thumps from the pigeons that roosted on the roof tiles.

How had I left the place? Neat. Tidy. I had shed a lot of possessions over the past few years, some of it the natural attrition that comes from moving frequently, some of it lost from my old life, thanks to John Webster. I had come to like living with enough of everything rather than a surplus, the minimum instead of clutter. I looked around at the table, the chairs neatly tucked underneath it, the sofa. There wasn't a cushion out of place or a wrinkle in the rug. The bathroom door stood open, the shower curtain hanging in folds that matched my memory of how I'd drawn it out of my way, my hairbrush balanced precariously on the edge of the sink where I'd left it. The kitchen then: breakfast things on the draining board stacked the way I stacked them, chopping boards leaning against the wall.

What had made me edgy? A smell? A sound?

Slowly, reluctantly, I climbed up the ladder to look at the bed.

It looked untouched, the covers smooth, the pillows as plump as I liked. But it wasn't quite right, somehow. I reached out for a handful of the duvet and drew it off the bed.

Up near the pillows – just about where my heart would be when I lay down to sleep – there was a smear of something reddish brown.

Blood.

I dropped the duvet and took a few steps back, my eyes fixed on it, my heart hammering as if the mark were the threat, and not whoever had put it on my bed.

15

Adam came back down the ladder and looked across to where I stood in the corner, my arms tightly folded. 'Tell me again about what happened when you came home. You didn't notice anything was wrong.'

'I was distracted. My phone rang.'

'Who was it?'

'They hung up. Unknown number. I came in, I put everything down on the table, I went for my phone. And then the bag split and my shopping went everywhere.'

'So you didn't realise at first that anything had changed in here. What made you think there was something to find?'

I shook my head.

'You must have had some reason to check the place over.'

'I must have, but I don't know what it was. Instinct, I suppose.'

'And there's no chance the mark could have been on the sheet already.'

'Of course it wasn't. I would have noticed it when I was making the bed this morning.'

'Would you?'

'Yes.' No equivocation. I knew how I'd left it. I clenched my jaw to stop my teeth from chattering.

Adam was looking at the shopping that was spread across the table. I hadn't even got around to picking up the tin that had rolled onto the floor.

It was strange, him being in my home, looking at my things. He was wearing a heavy navy jumper, jeans and a North Face jacket that he hadn't taken off yet; he looked like nothing except an off-duty police officer.

I was aware that he wasn't officially responsible for my safety, and that I should report the incidents to my local police station, but the thought of starting to explain everything again was impossible, too huge to contemplate. Besides, Adam had pointed out it would take hours for the local response officers to come round, if they came that night at all.

'I'll come right now and do a report for them,' he had said on the phone, and there was something reassuring about how matter-of-fact he sounded.

'But if you're busy . . . and it's not even your job . . .'

'I want to.' And that had been that.

On the other hand, he had been in the flat for mere minutes and I was already wishing I hadn't involved him. He was asking the kind of questions that implied he didn't believe me.

'How long were you out today?'

'All day.'

'Tell me where you went and what you did.'

I cleared my throat. 'Um – I went out at a quarter to

136

eight this morning. I went to the gym. Then I came back. I got changed. Did my make-up and my hair.'

'And nothing was different.'

'No.'

'Could anyone have been here while you were here?'

'No.'

'Did you lock the door when you came back? Could they have got in and hidden while you were here?'

I gestured at the flat. 'You can see for yourself, there's nowhere to hide. He must have broken in.'

Adam went across to examine the door. 'No damage. No broken glass.'

'So what?'

'Nothing.' He turned to look at me, surprise on his face. 'Just a comment.'

'I thought – I wasn't sure if you believed me.'

'You know as well as I do, it's not about whether I believe you.' His voice was gentle, for once, and his kindness brought a lump to my throat. 'It's about evidence and being able to prove something happened.'

'The blood in my bed is evidence.'

He didn't answer me straight away. 'It's something. I think we should get it tested. Find out if it matches any particular person that we have in the system. You'll need to give a DNA sample so they can rule you out.'

'It's not my blood, Adam. I would know if it was my blood, don't you think?'

'Just to rule it out.'

'To rule out the idea that I'm crazy and paranoid. To head off the belief I would set this up just to get attention or to frame John Webster or something.'

'I don't think you would. But—'

'But what?'

Without asking, he moved over to the kitchen and filled the kettle. 'Where's the tea?'

'In the cupboard in front of you.'

'I want to protect you from that accusation, that's all.' He had his back to me, and I wished I could see his face.

'What I think,' I said carefully, 'is that someone wants me to be scared. I think someone wants me to be making a huge fuss about all of this – Belinda, and the scaffolding accident. I think I've been taking it all too well. I haven't been panicked enough. So they're raising the stakes by breaking in here and showing me I'm not safe anywhere.'

'You could be right. But then, John Webster isn't exactly subtle, is he?'

'I would be much more subtle if I was making it up.'

That got an ironic eyebrow-raise; signs of a sense of humour at last. 'No one thinks you're making it up.'

'What about PC Buswell?'

'Alison? I don't know what she thinks.'

That wasn't as reassuring as he might have intended it to be.

'Has she made any progress with finding the man from the video?' I asked.

'No one recognises him. They've been asking the homeless charities about him, as you suggested. He just seems to have disappeared.' Adam took his phone out of his pocket. 'Look, do you mind if I give her a quick call to let her know I'm here, and why? I want to keep her in the loop.'

'On a Saturday night?'

He gave me a sweet smile that I found disarming. 'You know we're never really off duty.'

'I suppose not, or you wouldn't be here.'

He looked as if he was about to say something but instead he went out, pulling the door closed behind him. I could hear his voice, low and pleasant, but not the words. Those I had to imagine.

Yes, I'm with her . . . I don't think it's anything to worry about . . . Maybe a bit of exaggeration to get us to listen to her. That's a real concern for her . . . No, no evidence of a break-in. Yes, that's what I thought.

Why did I assume they didn't believe me?

Because I'd been here before. Police officers liked tangible evidence of serious crimes. The slow and steady chipping away at my safety, at my peace of mind, wasn't the sort of thing that stood up in court, and that was what mattered.

When he came back I was pouring the boiling water into the mugs.

'Sit down,' he said. 'I'll finish it. You like it strong, don't you?'

'How did you know that?'

There was something in my voice that made him turn around from the kitchen to look at me. 'When we met last week you were drinking proper builders' tea.'

I collapsed onto the sofa. 'Sorry. I'm a bit jumpy when people know things about me.'

'I'm not surprised.' He went back to opening drawers, finding the milk, his movements deft.

'What did PC Buswell say?'

'She'll make a note on the file. She's happy to leave it to me to take a statement from you. I said I'd give you some advice and stay until you were happy for me to go.'

'Did you?'

That made him turn around again. 'Unless you want me to go?'

'No. No, I don't. I'm glad you're here.'

'I'm glad I am too.'

'So what's the advice?'

'You could do with replacing the lock on your front door. The one on the gate outside is decent but I could unlock the one on your door with a card in about three seconds.' He set the mug in front of me and I leaned forward to gather it up, the heat warming my chilled fingers. I was trembling so much that the tea almost slopped over the side. Adam put his hand on mine to support it, and that made me jump.

'Steady. You'll spill it.'

'Thanks. I don't know why I'm shaking. I'm so cold.'

'I'm not surprised. It's freezing in here.'

I put a hand out to the radiator and discovered it was lukewarm. 'The heat's gone off. It doesn't do much good when it's on. I love this place but it's Baltic. Bare bricks and floorboards don't keep the heat in.'

'What do you do in really cold weather?'

'Stay with my boyfriend,' I said over my shoulder as I leaned into the boiler cupboard, coaxing it into life.

There was a silence. Then, 'I thought you said you didn't have one.'

'I don't. Last year I acquired one for the winter months to avoid hypothermia. I haven't got around to it this year yet.' The boiler began to hum and I turned back to discover he was looking amused. 'What?'

'Nothing. Do you want me to check your security in general? See if you need to make any other improvements?'

'You just want to have a nose around.' He started to

protest and I waved a hand at him. 'Go ahead. It won't take you long.'

He moved around the flat as I leaned against the warming radiator and drank my tea and wondered what he made of the way I lived. The windows passed inspection, the door got a firm headshake and a reproachful look in my direction as he waggled the lock.

'Did you find anything to worry you in there?' I asked when he emerged from the bathroom.

'You need a window lock on the skylight. I can recommend a good locksmith for that and the door.' He was inspecting the bookshelves beside the kitchen.

'Do you think the books are dangerous?'

He twisted to look at me, sheepish. 'No. I was just curious.'

'At least you're honest about it.' Almost human, in fact. It made me feel I could be straight with him. 'The blood is the sort of thing John Webster would do.'

'It's his style. That doesn't mean it's him.'

'Who else would it be?'

'I understand why you don't want to think there could be someone else out there who wishes you harm, but—'

'There isn't. I keep telling you.'

'No ex-boyfriends? Someone you turned down? Someone who resented being used for their central heating?'

'That was a joke.'

'I was joking too.' He shoved his hands into his pockets, obviously ill at ease.

The untidiness of the flat suddenly seemed intolerable. I roamed around the room, putting away the shopping, finding a vase for the flowers. 'I don't know why this is so hard for people to understand. John Webster likes to torment me. He takes his chances when he can. Have you spoken to him about this?'

'Not personally.'

'Has anyone?'

'I don't know.' Adam winced. 'It's not my case, Ingrid. I'm not entitled to go and ask questions. PC Buswell—'

'Wants to wind up her investigation. She doesn't want to get drawn into this. It's nothing to do with her remit.' I picked up a blanket and folded it, snapping the ends together. 'No police officers ever want to investigate this kind of crime. They have to take endless trouble over tiny misdemeanours that take up a huge amount of police time but then all of those misdemeanours don't add up to a decent charge. And then the victim ends up dead, so the officer who was dealing with the case gets in trouble. I don't blame you for not wanting to get involved – I don't want to be involved either. I just don't have a choice about it.' I stopped because the prickling sensation in my sinuses was a precursor to uncontrollable sobbing.

'I didn't say I don't want to be involved.' He came across the room and took the blanket out of my hands, laying it down on the sofa. He put his hands on my arms, just above the elbows, and held me gently. It was surprisingly intimate, I found, and I felt myself blushing. 'I could walk out of here now if you want me to go. But I wouldn't be here if I didn't want to be.'

'Then why won't you believe me when I tell you it's Webster?'

'I don't want to make any assumptions. I don't *know* it's him yet, and neither do you. I think it's him, don't get me wrong, but I have to keep an open mind until there's some definite evidence.' He looked down at me, his eyes bright. 'This could be it, Ingrid. This could be what gets him locked up for a decent stretch.'

'So what should I do?'

He dropped his hands, back to being the perfect police officer again. 'Take precautions. Improve your security. Be aware of people around you.'

'I do most of that anyway.'

'Get better at it.'

I rolled my eyes. 'Yes, sir.'

'And don't trust anyone new who comes into your life. He's good at recruiting people to do his work for him. Don't let strangers in, don't talk to anyone you don't know, don't agree to any meetings or appointments that you haven't arranged yourself.'

'Anything else?'

'Try to live your life.'

I laughed in spite of myself. 'While I still can? Great advice, thanks.'

He shook his head. 'It's all I've got.'

16

In the interests of getting on with living my life, I went out the next day to what was supposed to be a quiet little Sunday-evening engagement party in Clapham. The groom was a university friend, Harry, and his bride was a steel butterfly named Vicky. I had reckoned without her desire to make sure everyone she knew was aware she had coerced Harry into making a commitment. There must have been two hundred people at the party, which was in a gastropub that looked out on Clapham Common. I stared out of the window at the autumn leaves in the fading light, and wished I hadn't come. Shadows gathered under the trees, suggesting lurking figures. The Halloween decorations were up everywhere. I couldn't for the life of me see why anyone actively sought the thrill of being scared. Forget pumpkins and skeletons and fake cobwebs: John Webster was far more frightening because he was unstoppable, implacable, determined, ruthless.

Take precautions. Improve your security. Be aware of people around you.

I squared my shoulders and turned back to face the room, pinning a smile to my face. I had already caught up with a few people I hadn't seen for years and I knew there were other friends at the party, but finding anyone in the throng was likely to be difficult. Vicky was everywhere, showing off her engagement ring – a vast diamond solitaire flanked with ruby shoulders – like a dog giving the paw. I had already smiled at it politely even though I thought it looked like a bloodshot eye. Harry was on his way to getting very drunk with his rugby pals, his tie askew, the condemned-man vibe too sincere to be a joke.

'Don't lose this!' The woman next to me was holding up a silver bracelet. I put a hand to my wrist automatically, even though I knew the bracelet couldn't belong to anyone else. It had been a gift from my father, proper modernist Danish silver: a slithering chain of geometric shapes like very small razor blades.

'Thanks. It must have fallen off.'

'I saw it slip off your wrist when you were hugging that big guy.' She smiled at me, dimples appearing in her cheeks. She was very pretty, with curling dark hair and a knockout figure.

'Jonesy. I was at university with him. He's always the tallest person in the room.'

I took the bracelet from her and examined the catch, testing it and discovering it didn't need much pressure to give way. The safety catch was a delicate loop of metal that went around a tiny stud. I must have knocked it out of place without noticing. I put the bracelet on again and folded the safety catch across carefully.

'That should hold it. I probably need to get it fixed.'

'How do you think she did it?'

145

I looked at her, surprised. 'Did what?'

'Nabbed him.' She was staring at Harry.

'Oh – pregnancy scare, I should think. Or she made his mother tell him to ask her.'

The woman giggled. 'Have you met his mother?'

'A few times. She can make Harry do anything.'

'I never met her.' The woman drained her drink and set the glass down on the bar. 'But then I wasn't supposed to exist.'

'You weren't?'

'I was Harry's bit on the side.'

'I think most of the women here have been Harry's bit on the side at one time or another.'

'Even you?'

'Mmm, no.' I liked to think it was because I had enough self-esteem to avoid being one of the endless string of girls who had fallen into bed with him and fallen out again immediately afterwards. The truth was that the attraction had never been strong enough on either side to change the rules of our comfortable friendship.

'I've forgotten your name.'

That would be because I hadn't told her my name. Since she was having a certain amount of trouble focusing already, I didn't say that. 'It's Ingrid.'

'Ingrid-from-uni?'

I nodded. 'That sounds like me.'

'Vicky *hates* you.'

'I got that impression. But she has no reason to hate me. I never even went out with Harry. We were just friends.'

'That's the point, I think. She thinks you're "unfinished business".' She mimed big loopy quotation marks in the air.

'Harry has about a hundred girls who are unfinished business and I really don't think I'm one of them,' I said drily. 'But I see most of them are here tonight, so maybe Vicky doesn't agree with me. She wants to make sure everyone knows the score – not that I was tempted to sleep with him anyway.'

'I was.' She had managed to grab another drink from a passing waiter and was in the process of downing it. She surfaced to say, 'I was tempted and I did. I mean, I was in love with him.'

'When was this?'

'For the last seven months.'

I processed that. 'He's been being unfaithful to Vicky?'

She nodded mournfully. 'I'm their neighbour. I'm friends with Vicky. She didn't tell me about their engagement, though, which makes me wonder if she knew about us all along.'

'When did you and Harry break up?'

'Well, we haven't really. I saw him last night. He gave me my invitation to this party and told me he couldn't see me for a while but he'd call me when he got back from honeymoon.'

'Christ almighty, Harry.' I was genuinely shocked. 'He wasn't that bad at university. So much for learning and growing.'

'Do you know what the worst thing is?' Her eyes were suddenly swimming with tears. 'I worked out why he chose me to be his other woman.'

'Because he liked you?'

'Because of my name.' She sniffed. 'Guess what it is.'

I shook my head.

'It's Vicki-with-an-i.' The tears spilled over and ran down

her face. 'So he didn't even have to remember who he was with. He'd never slip up.'

Vicki-with-an-i turned out to be an excellent wing man once she'd dried her eyes. She introduced me to the people she knew and I introduced her to the ones I knew and we worked our way through the bar, trying to find her a Harry-replacement to mend her heart. Harry drank steadily, watching her with a hangdog air. I fetched up beside him at one point.

'Why didn't you propose to Vicki instead of Vicky? Did you get confused?'

'Don't.'

'Didn't you do this name trick before? With two Lucys?'

He brightened. 'No, but there was one term when I had three Fionas on the go. One was at home, two at uni.'

'You're a disgrace, Harry.'

'I know. I can't help it.'

'Everything okay here?' Vicky-the-fiancée stretched up to kiss Harry's cheek, taking his arm firmly before she turned to glower at me. 'Did you see my beautiful ring?'

'I *did*,' I cooed. '*Beautiful.*'

'Did Harry tell you about the wedding?'

'No, actually, he—'

'We're going to Sardinia to get married. Family and *really* close friends only.' She paused, savouring the moment. 'I'm afraid we won't be able to invite you.'

'Never mind,' I said. 'I got food poisoning once in Sardinia. My memories of it are mainly toilet-related and I'm not sure I'm ready to go back.'

Harry laughed. Vicky-the-fiancée did not.

'I should go and get myself another drink.'

148

'The free bar is about to run out,' Vicky spat. 'You'd better hurry.'

'I'll run.'

All things considered I was quite glad Harry had had the full use of his balls while he had the chance. From now on they were clearly going to be kept in Vicky's pocket.

At the bar I found the second Victoria in Harry's life. She had lined up two drinks and was gulping a third.

'Do you want to get out of here?'

She nodded. 'This place is grim. It's full of stockbrokers and currency traders.'

'Where do you want to go? It's Sunday night. I'm not sure anywhere is going to be jumping.'

She grabbed her bag. 'We'll find somewhere and make it a party.'

Somehow, we managed to acquire one Ella, one Charles, a Dave and two Sarahs on our way out, despite the fact that Dave appeared to be a stockbroker and I had my doubts about one of the Sarahs. Someone needed to get money out; someone else needed to buy cigarettes. Dave ordered an Uber and Vicki snatched his phone to cancel it while we argued about where to go. Someone else ordered two Ubers, and then Charles flagged down a black cab. Somehow, we ended up in a tiny Italian restaurant in Chelsea where we shared thin, brittle pizzas loaded with mozzarella while drinking carafe after carafe of wine. At one in the morning Charles confessed to being a trader in the City and picked up the bill for all of us, along with Vicki's telephone number.

'But I'm not going home with you,' she purred in his ear. She was unsteady on her feet, which meant that he had to put his arm around her to support her. 'Even though I want to go home with you. I'm going home with Ingrid. Because she's my friend.'

'Of course,' Charles said lovingly. 'Let's get you a cab.'

'Don't you want to go to *your* home?' I asked her. I wasn't very keen to have an unexpected houseguest, especially someone I'd never met before. I didn't think Vicki could possibly be anything to do with John Webster but that was the awful thing – I couldn't know for sure.

She blinked up at me, trying hard to focus. 'I want to shout at Harry. If I go home, I'm not going to be able to stop myself, you know?'

I did know. And I was lukewarm about Vicky-the-fiancée but a drunken revelation of Harry's infidelity was no way to end the evening of your engagement party.

There was a part of me that welcomed the company too. I hadn't slept well the night before, after Adam left.

'I don't have a spare room. You'll be sleeping on the sofa.'

'I can sleep anywhere,' Vicki promised, and proved it by falling asleep with her head on my knee as soon as the taxi started moving. I watched London-by-night flashing past the windows: minicab offices and chicken shops and mopeds delivering takeaways, homeless people bundled into doorways, swaggering drunks, scuttling junkies, limousines and police cars and ambulances and students and cleaners, dead-eyed with exhaustion, dragging themselves from one job to the next. I had been out of my usual territory, in a part of the city I rarely visited any more, with people who had nothing to do with my usual life. I had been able to forget about Webster, most of the time. Now I felt the fear clamp down on me like a large

150

hand closing around my throat as the taxi manoeuvred through the narrow canal-side street to my address. It was a topsy-turvy world when the familiar was frightening.

But at least I had tiny, bubbly Vicki for protection. I shook her awake, and she slid off the back seat to lie in the footwell, mumbling something about school.

The taxi driver helped me to get her into the courtyard where she collapsed on a bench.

'Mm'okay. I want to look at the *stars*.' She threw an arm up and gestured vaguely.

'I think it's too cloudy for stars.' To the taxi driver I said hopefully, 'There's just one flight of stairs to my flat.'

'I've got to go.'

'Thanks anyway. We'll manage.' He'd gone, leaving us standing in the courtyard. 'Probably.'

Vicki was fumbling with something.

'What are you doing?'

'Cigarette before we go inside,' she mumbled, and I twitched it out of her mouth before she could light the filter.

'Wrong end. Do you even smoke?'

'When I'm drunk.' She started to paw at the packet again. 'I borrowed these from Sarah. No – I think it was Sarah. Other Sarah. Fuck, why does everyone have the same name?'

'I don't think smoking is a good idea.'

'Mmph.' She was waving the lighter dangerously close to her hair, the flame streaming out like a flag.

'Look, let me light it for you.'

'You're so *kind*. I'm so glad I met you. You're my nicest friend, Ingrid.'

'Course I am.' I turned away, cupping the flame to shield it from the breeze that was whispering through the reeds

151

in the pond. I felt completely sober now, despite the vast quantities I'd had to drink. The end of the cigarette ignited with a soft fizzle of crisping tobacco and I blew out a cloud of smoke before turning back to discover that Vicki had curled into a ball and gone to sleep again.

'Brilliant.' I shook her knee. 'Vicki. Hey, Vicki.'

Nothing.

'What's going on?' The voice came from behind me.

Shock punched a hole through the pit of my stomach. I whipped around, frightened and angry with it. The anger came out uppermost. 'Why are you creeping up on me?'

Helen's eyes widened. 'I'm not. I was asleep and then I heard a commotion out here.'

I looked at her, taking in the messy hair and the pyjamas with a hoodie thrown over the top and the fluffy slippers with rabbit ears. She was jumping from foot to foot, her arms tightly folded across her chest, obviously freezing. She looked as if she'd just woken up.

'Is everything okay?'

'My friend's asleep. I'm just trying to wake her up so I can get her into my flat. That's all. No emergency.'

'She seems pretty out of it.' She frowned. 'Are you *smoking*? I didn't think you smoked.'

'I don't. It wasn't mine. I was holding it for her.' I bent down to stub it out on the pavement and she squeaked.

'Don't throw it in the pond! There are frogs in there and little fish. It would be bad for them.'

'I wasn't going to,' I said, with dignity. 'Now if you'll excuse me—'

Helen bent down to Vicki. 'Wake up. *Hey*. Wake up.'

Vicki mumbled something and opened her eyes for a moment.

'She's out of it.'

'What's her name?'

'Vicki,' I said sullenly.

'Come on, Vicki. You can't sleep out here.' Helen had a particularly penetrating voice. Vicki, who had been dead to the world, blinked.

'What is it?'

'You need to walk up the stairs. We can't carry you.'

Vicki got to her feet. She was swaying, and her knees looked as if they were in danger of buckling at any moment, but she was upright.

'Come on,' Helen said. 'Before we all die of hypothermia.'

She set off for the stairs, hauling Vicki with her. I followed, wary in case Vicki slipped back down and collided with me.

'Give me your keys,' Helen ordered.

I handed them over obediently and she unlocked the new lock, fitted that very day. Inside, she steered Vicki over to the sofa where she made her lie down and pushed her onto her side with a couple of cushions behind her back.

'That should stop her from rolling over. She's absolutely smashed though. You'll need to check on her if you hear her being sick during the night.'

'Are you a nurse?'

Helen looked surprised. 'No – I have first-aid training.'

'Well, I'm impressed.' I was, too.

'I'm going back to bed,' Helen said. She was still shivering as she headed for the door. 'She'll need a blanket. Make it two. Why is it so cold in here?'

'The boiler is a dick.'

'You should get it serviced.'

'Yes,' I said, and shut the door softly in her face.

17

I woke up when my alarm went off with a thumping head and a tongue made of felt. I'd been fairly restrained, or so I'd thought, but over the course of the whole evening I had managed to drink a lot, and it had added up to a stinking hangover.

I got ready in double-quick time despite having to chisel off the previous night's mascara; not having breakfast helped. My face was white, my eyes red-rimmed. I gagged twice while brushing my teeth. I was too old for carousing on a school night, and too responsible. But it had been worth it to escape my fears. I'd slept solidly, exhausted and comforted by the occasional snore that drifted up from the sofa.

When I was ready to leave, Vicki was still fast asleep. She was bundled in the spare duvet like a caterpillar in a cocoon. I left her a note with my phone number and instructions to make herself at home. Across the bottom of the page I wrote:

And do not ring Harry! He doesn't deserve you.

If she felt the way she *should* after our night out, she would be incapable of ringing anyone.

I was relatively relaxed about work that day. I had a ten o'clock hearing to deal with a breach of probation where the defendant, my client, was looking at being resentenced to a prison term. He was well used to prison – another six months would make no great difference to him, the solicitor had suggested to the clerks. And it was at Isleworth, so I didn't have to make a long and expensive journey outside London. I dragged myself and my work bag across town, early enough to miss out on the worst of the traffic, and in time to get a coffee from the little shop at the station before I arrived at court. Food was still out of the question.

What I found when I got to court, naturally, bore no relation to what the clerks had passed on. Rather than being calm and philosophical about a custodial sentence, Ronnie Gilmore was outraged. He was wiry and tall, well above average height, with very short hair. Smudgy tattoos spiralled across his hands and over the collar of his shirt. There was something intimidating about the way he carried himself, something that made people on edge around him, from the security staff to the woman who gave him a cup of tea in the court canteen. He had convictions for a long list of offences from when he was a teenager to the present day – small-scale stuff such as shoplifting and assaults, some criminal damage, driving without a licence or insurance. He would never be a master criminal, but equally he would never stop breaking the law when it suited him.

'They said I behaved aggressively,' he snapped, leaning in to eyeball me at close range. 'They said I was rude and uncooperative. It's bollocks. They just want to get me locked up because they know it will piss me off. They've got a grudge against me.'

'Right.' If this was how he dealt with me, when I was on his side, the probation officers might have a point. 'And why would they think it would piss you off?'

'Because my missus is having a baby in four months and I promised her I would be there this time.' He jerked his head away from me, blinking hard, trying to hide the tears that were brimming in his eyes.

I softened. Suddenly his agitation made a lot more sense. 'That is a very good reason for not wanting to return to custody and I'll put it to the judge.'

'I can't let Karen down. You've got to get me out of this.'

I truly wanted to do my best for Ronnie and his partner and their unborn child. What that meant, however, was that I needed to turn the short, businesslike hearing into a mini trial. I would need to cross-examine the probation officers about their allegations, since we were contesting them. I would need to put Ronnie himself on the stand. I would need to come up with a persuasive speech about why the judge should offer him the benefit of the doubt rather than the probation staff.

That meant getting him to give me a version of events that was as uncontroversial as possible, and didn't include wild allegations of bias and a grudge against him and how he had been framed. Accusations like that would go down extremely badly with any judge, let alone the one who was waiting for us. He had a reputation for being tough and I didn't know if I could persuade him to take a lenient view in the circumstances.

The headache I'd been nursing all day escalated a notch. It was going to be a fight.

This is why you love the job.

If the day had gone as I expected, I should have been finished at work by eleven – half past at the latest. As it was, between one thing and another, the judge gave his ruling at a quarter to four. I hadn't held out much hope – the witnesses from the probation service had been earnest, calm and experienced. I had managed to get them to agree that there was a possibility of a misunderstanding in their interactions with my client, and that was as far as I'd got. Ronnie himself had played a blinder, sitting bolt upright, eyes wide with shocked innocence, explaining how he had raised his voice but not from any wish to threaten anyone, because he sincerely appreciated the work the probation service did on his behalf and the early-release programme that meant he was serving half of his sentence on licence. If I'd had a jury to impress, I had no doubt they would have been convinced, but the judge was another matter. He was relatively young, which meant nothing – the idea that all judges were old and out of touch was a stereotype and anyway the younger ones could be much harder on defendants. For the first half of his judgement I thought we were sunk. He went through every allegation that the prosecution had made against Ronnie, in detail, and pointed out Ronnie hadn't actually denied any of it.

'But I am reminded of the purpose of a custodial sentence. In the criminal justice system we seek to improve society, not to punish unfairly. If it is safe and right for Mr Gilmore to continue his community order, then that is what should happen. It is the outcome most likely to encourage him to turn away from criminal activity and to put his family first.'

If you believed in miracles. I didn't want to be cynical about Ronnie and his chances of going straight, but I fully expected to see him again.

The judge's face grew stern. 'However, I do not want to put anyone – especially a member of the probation service – at risk. Mr Gilmore is familiar with the terms of his sentence and the behaviour expected of him. If it becomes necessary to return to court to discuss any breach whatsoever of his conditions, I trust he will be prepared to expect a very different outcome, Miss Lewis.'

I jumped up. 'I'm sure he will, Your Honour.'

The judge's face became fractionally kinder for a moment. 'And we do, of course, wish him the very best.'

It was half past four by the time I got away from a delighted Ronnie and his solicitor, who promised to send me some decent trials she had coming up. I was dog-tired and the rush hour I'd hoped to miss was starting. I wanted to go home, cook something easy, have a bath and go to bed. But as I walked to the station, my phone hummed. Adam's name flashed on the screen.

'Hello?' I stopped and jammed my hand against my other ear to block out the sound of the traffic roaring past. 'Adam? I can barely hear you.'

'Can you meet me near my office?'

'When?'

'Soon as possible. I've got something to tell you.'

I couldn't hear his voice well enough to guess whether it was good news or bad. It seemed wisest to assume the worst.

18

'Sorry for dragging you all the way down to Vauxhall.' Adam was standing on the street, waiting for me. From the look on his face now that I could see him, I'd been right not to anticipate good news. 'I didn't want to talk about this in the office. I'm not officially working on the case and I thought my boss might start asking questions.'

'And I thought it was just an excuse to see me.' He looked startled and a little embarrassed. I'd been joking but from his expression I might have got closer to the truth than I'd intended. 'Never mind. What did you want to tell me?'

'They tested the blood.'

'Was it Webster's?'

'It wasn't human blood. The lab report said it was from uncooked beef.'

'Okay. So . . . what? I don't prepare food on my bed. It still shouldn't have been there.'

'So in that case it looks more like a prank than anything.'

I felt a wave of cold nausea sweep up from my stomach;

159

when was the last time I'd eaten? 'It's a warning and you know it.'

'There's no evidence it's him, Ingrid. I need evidence to take it further, you know that.'

'What kind of evidence do you want? My blood on his hands?'

'Ingrid, please. I don't want you to come to any harm. But this isn't going to get us any further towards the ultimate goal of putting John Webster behind bars. That's what we both want. This accident has brought him out from under his rock. It's an opportunity for him to bother you, and an opportunity for us to catch him.'

I was stuck on his choice of words. 'What do you mean by *accident*?'

'Alison's been looking at the footage again with her colleagues.' He ran a hand over the back of his head, ill at ease. 'It looks like an accident. You saw what you wanted to see.'

'I definitely didn't want to see Belinda being murdered.'

'No, but you went in with the assumption that she had been, in your place.'

'I didn't imagine the blood. Someone was in my flat.' I felt as if the ground was sliding under my feet. 'Don't you think that's serious?'

'You've improved your security. It shouldn't happen again, if it ever did.'

'What do you mean, "if it ever did"?'

'We talked about it, Alison and I.' He was choosing his words with care. 'We know you want to get John Webster out of the way. You can't really live your life when he's out there, can you? So maybe you felt you had to make sure we connected Belinda's death with Webster.'

I was starting to feel angry and it stung like the blood flowing back into a numb limb. 'You think I staged it.'

'That's one possibility.'

'I didn't make up seeing Webster the other night in the Temple. And I haven't lied to you. Did your pal Alison ask you to put me off? Did she tell you I was wasting their time?'

'No. That's not what – I just thought—' He lifted a hand as if he was going to touch my arm but then dropped it to his side again. 'The trouble is it's easy to get caught up in fear. You have every reason to be scared when things like this happen – God, anyone with your experiences would be on edge most of the time. These things you've found – you're right, it could be Webster. But if it is him, you need to hope he gives himself away. You might need to *encourage* him instead of running away from him.'

'That sounds incredibly dangerous,' I said shakily.

'It could be.' He grimaced. 'I know it's not fair to ask you to do this but if it gets rid of him for good you could save a lot of people from experiencing what you've endured. And it would be a nice way to get revenge, wouldn't it? Poetic justice. He'd hate for you to be the one who got him locked up.'

'What do you want me to do?'

'I don't know. It depends on what Webster does next.' He lifted his shoulders, helpless. 'All I can say is that I'll try to keep you safe, if you're prepared to take the risk.'

'And Belinda?'

'At the inquest her death will be ruled an accident, unless we have anything to contradict that. But Alison doesn't hold out much hope at this stage. She's under pressure to end her investigation.'

161

The injustice of it made my jaw tighten. 'So I'm bait.'

'I don't like that word. We will get him, Ingrid—'

'—but the evidence doesn't add up. Yet.'

'This could be the end of it.'

There would be no end, I thought, while Webster was still out there. No end, and no help. No way out of the trap I'd wandered into. It was lonely, being Webster's target, as if I was an outcast animal limping after the herd while the predator kept me in sight.

I managed to smile at Adam, who was looking worried. 'I can't complain, can I? You warned me about him.'

'I tried.'

'You've been very kind, Adam. I appreciate it.'

'You don't need to thank me.' He sighed. 'Just think about it, all right? Let me know what you want to do. If you want to book a one-way ticket to Djibouti, I completely understand.'

I laughed at that. 'I'll bear that in mind. But I think I'm just going to go home.' It would have to be the Underground, but at least the Victoria Line was quick and direct.

'I'll see you to your door.'

'You don't have to do that.'

'No, but I'd like to.'

There was a train at the platform when we got there and once it set off there was no possibility of conversation. It rattled over the rails, the brakes whining with tooth-gritting shrillness. A warm wind gusted through the carriage and pulled strands of my hair loose to blow around my face. There were no free seats. Adam stood opposite me, his eyes watchful as he considered our fellow travellers. Never off duty, I thought. Never quite relaxed.

At Oxford Circus, the carriage filled up and Adam

moved to stand in front of me. The crowd pressed us closer together, his face inches from mine. He was looking away from me so I was free to study him without being observed: long eyelashes, a vertical scar on his cheek from some childhood injury, the bow of his top lip, the hollow at the base of his throat.

I had made him blush earlier.

It would be very inappropriate for me to develop feelings for Adam Nash.

King's Cross came too quickly for me, for once, and we spilled out onto the platform along with a hundred other commuters. Adam walked beside me, escorting me through the endless tiled corridors filled with scurrying travellers until we reached what passed for fresh air, on the open space in front of the station.

'Thanks, but you don't need to come with me from here.'

'I'd like to.'

'You must have somewhere else to be.'

He shook his head. 'No plans.'

'Can I at least buy you a drink to thank you for your time?' I asked impulsively. 'There's a nice bar near my place. If you don't have anything else to do, I mean.'

He hesitated. 'Okay. I'd like that.'

'Come on. It's not far.'

The bar was a moody, high-ceilinged place lit with great dusty chandeliers. There was a moment of pure awkwardness after I bought the drinks. I went silent, for once, tongue-tied because what the hell were we supposed to talk about, if not John Webster and Belinda and my fear?

Adam put down his glass. 'Okay. We each ask each other five questions. They can't be about work, or the last week.'

'You first.'

'What did you want to be when you were seven?'

'Ballet dancer. What about you?'

'Police officer.'

'Consistent.'

'That's me. Four questions left.'

I reeled. 'That doesn't count as a question!'

'You asked, I answered. My turn.'

We bickered gently through the next round of drinks and I found myself laughing a lot. He was at ease in a way I hadn't seen before, leaning back in his seat, watching me lazily, picking up on my jokes and throwing them back to me. The awkwardness was gone. It was fun, and normal, as if we were any other couple on what might become a date. Webster wouldn't dare to bother me when Adam was there, but that wasn't the only reason I liked him being around.

'Okay.' He was on the second-last question, his eyes bright with amusement. 'This has to be a good one.'

'I'm waiting.'

'Cats or dogs? I see you as a cat person.'

I felt the smile stiffen on my face. It was as if the lights had dimmed for a moment, as if my hearing had dulled too. The air in the bar was stifling, I realised. I had to get out.

'What's wrong? Ingrid?'

I picked up my bag and pushed my way to the door.

'Ingrid?' Adam was behind me. 'What's the matter?'

'I had a cat,' I said. It was cold on the street but my shirt was sticking to my back. 'I had a cat that I loved. His name was Geoffrey. He was grey and he liked to sleep on my feet and when he wanted me to wake up he would put his paw on my mouth and purr.'

'Okay.' I could tell Adam still didn't know how he'd triggered my reaction.

'He was one of the only things I had left after the fire.' I swallowed. 'He was out, you see, when the house burned. I found him two days later in a neighbour's garden, in shock. He was such a comfort to me.'

'What happened?'

'I came home from work one day and I couldn't find him. I was living in a flat and he wasn't allowed to go out. I looked everywhere. Under the bed, the sofa. In the wardrobe.' Tears were streaking my face.

'Where was he?'

'The freezer.' I half-laughed, half-sobbed. 'I don't know what made me look in there. I was too late, obviously. He was dead. And Webster sent me a card the next day. It said, "Now you only have me."'

By mutual agreement, we ended our evening at that point. Adam came with me to the courtyard gate and watched me unlock it.

'I said the wrong thing.'

'You didn't know. It just brought everything back.'

'I don't like upsetting you.'

'It's fine.' I sniffled. 'Maybe we could try this again another time, though.'

He nodded and said goodnight, his hands in his pockets, a good metre between us.

Not how I had thought the evening would end. I had ruined it for both of us.

Helen's door was closed, her curtains open so I could see her lights were off. I would have to thank her for coming to my rescue the night before. Flowers maybe –

but was that too much? I didn't want to encourage her . . . I fumbled with the unfamiliar new lock because it was stiff and awkward and I missed the old one, quite frankly, even though it had been practically an open door.

The flat was in darkness and I reached back to switch on the lights. Once again I had the feeling that something was wrong. Different.

But of course Vicki had been there after I left. I flicked the switch, only for nothing to happen.

'First the boiler, now the fuse box. Typical.' I stepped forward, fiddling with my phone to switch on the torch. My foot skidded on something that had spilled on the floor and I almost fell. I steadied myself on the table, peering down at liquid that glistened unpleasantly in the light of my phone.

A dark, dragging smear stretched away into the darkness.

I took two steps to my right to find the bathroom light switch and flicked it on. This time a shaft of light cut a lopsided rectangle out of the blackness, framing the blood that was in pools and splashes and smears from the sofa to the corner of the room, as if someone had crawled across it, bleeding all the while. My torch followed the trail to where it stopped.

'Oh my God. Vicki?' I dropped everything I was holding except my phone and ran to the corner, to the huddled body wedged between the TV and the wall, where she had tried to hide. Her head was bent to her knees, her hair hanging down in glossy curls where it wasn't stiff with dried blood. I touched the back of her hand and it was cold – too cold, even allowing for the flat's chill. Gently, I pushed her head back so I could see her face.

Sightless half-closed eyes, pearly teeth gleaming in the light from my phone, blue lips, no sign of life.

It would be difficult to report it to the police, I thought, with that weird half-logic of shock. I didn't even know her last name.

The boiler switched itself on with a click and I leapt to my feet, fear and horror surging over me.

They would have to believe me now. I had been right about Webster all along.

19

The woman who died in my flat was Victoria Joy Granger, aged 26, known as Vicki to her friends. She was a part-time actress and part-time nanny and part-time bar worker and occasional temp. She liked spending time with friends and dancing and cycling around London on an old-fashioned bike with a basket. She cooked vegetarian food for preference but she ate steak in restaurants. She had almost a thousand followers on Instagram, three hundred-odd Facebook friends, no time for Twitter. She took selfies every day – yawning in the morning, gym progress shots, standing perilously on the side of the bath to snap her outfit in the mirror, almost naked in a tiny thong while looking over her shoulder with a cheeky smile, on holidays, at Christmas, at parties, alone. She had a brother who lived in Australia, and parents in Wiltshire, and a half-share in a neighbour's cat, and at least one secret lover.

She woke up in my flat on Monday around lunchtime and made herself a cup of tea and an omelette, using the eggs in my fridge and my favourite pan. She had a shower with the rose-scented oil I bought in bulk, then borrowed a jumper to put over her party dress. She took the spare key I'd left so she could lock up and walked from my flat to St Pancras station where she bought a coffee, a scented candle, a thank-you card and a box of rainbow-tinted macarons from the stall near the Eurostar arrivals. She tried on two pairs of shoes and a coat, and almost bought a red lipstick but decided against it, then ordered an almond croissant in a café but only ate half of it. She borrowed a pen in the bookshop and wrote the thank-you card standing up, by the till (*Ingrid, thank you so much for taking me home with you! I'm sorry I ate your eggs. Think of me when you light the candle. Vx*). Then she walked back through Granary Square and along the canal. The sun was shining and the sky was a clear, clear blue.

She died in my flat between four o'clock and six o'clock that afternoon while I was talking to Adam, oblivious. Her killer stabbed her a total of forty-two times, including defence wounds to her forearms and hands where she had tried to ward off the blade, and deep wounds to her chest and abdomen. The tendons in three of her fingers were cut. Her aorta was severed. She bled to death.

No one heard anything.

No one saw anything.

She should never have been there.

She only went back to leave me the card, and the candle, and the box of macarons.

Of course, at first I didn't know any of this; no one did. The information came to me in dribs and drabs – a conversation here, a pathologist's report there over the next few weeks. I gathered it together and turned it into the story of Vicki's last few hours, just as I would have if I'd been presenting the case to a jury. What happened first, after I called the police on that terrible night, was that a couple of response officers turned up to make sure I wasn't a fantasist or an attention-seeker. They came through the gate and across the courtyard, massive in stab vests and high-vis jackets, not hurrying even when they saw me standing at the foot of the stairs.

'She's up there. On the left,' I said, huddled inside my coat, and one of them jogged up the steps while the other stopped in front of me to begin taking my details.

Yes, my name was Ingrid Lewis.

Yes, this was my address.

Yes, I had called the police.

Yes, as soon as I found the body.

No, I hadn't seen anyone coming or going.

Yes, I was renting the flat.

Yes, I'd known Vicki was there.

No, I didn't know her full name.

'I know where she lives,' I said. 'Not the actual address, but I can get it for you. She's a neighbour of a friend of mine.'

I could ring Harry and ask him—

I'd have to tell Harry what had happened.

I crouched down with my head between my knees and waited for the wave of sickness to pass.

The flat ceased to be my property from the moment the police arrived. It was a crime scene now, not my home. People arrived in twos and threes, all of them business-like and focused. I was irrelevant, except that I was asked to tell my story over and over again. The other residents

170

of the flats were allowed to come and go with the permission of the police officers guarding the scene, but there was nowhere for me to be. At one stage I turned and saw Helen peeking out from behind her curtains, her face a pale moon against the darkness behind her. I raised a hand to acknowledge her, but dropped it as she snapped the curtains shut. If the situation had been reversed, would I have let her come and sit in my flat and drink cups of tea while the police went about their work? I thought I might, actually, and the tiny betrayal stung more than I would have expected.

It couldn't have been as much as an hour since I'd called the police when the murder investigation team arrived. That was a grand name for two women in sensible boots and trouser suits. One conferred with the duty inspector, then came over to me.

'You're the person who called us?'

'Yes, I'm Ingrid Lewis.'

'I'm Jennifer Gold. I'm a DS with the murder investigation team who have been tasked with this case.' She was mid-thirties and wore not a scrap of make-up on her strong features. Her hair was plaited and pinned into a bun, but in a careless way that suggested she just wanted to get it out of her way while she worked. There was a white stain on the lapel of her jacket where something had splashed and had not been cleaned away. I'd met that type of police officer before: obsessed with work, to the exclusion of everything else. 'We're going to need to take you to the nick to interview you properly.'

I nodded, shivering. 'At this stage, I just want to go somewhere I can get warm.'

'I'm sure you do.' She turned away and spoke to her

colleague, DC Akram, who took me to their car. I sat in the back seat, still trembling despite the heater she thoughtfully switched on for me, and waited for the detectives to finish their work at the scene.

As I thawed my brain started to work again. An interview at the police station, about a murder that happened in my flat.

When DS Gold and DC Akram came back to the car, I waited for them to get in before I asked, 'Am I a suspect?'

A look passed between them.

'What makes you say that?' Jennifer Gold asked, her voice casual.

'I think I should tell you what I do for a living.'

To be fair to them, as soon as they heard I was a barrister, the atmosphere in the car changed.

'We need to interview you on video because you're a Sig Wit,' Jennifer said.

'A what?'

'Sorry. Significant witness.' She looked amused. 'That bit of jargon hasn't made it to counsel, then.'

'Not to me.' I hesitated; I didn't want to ruin the friendly mood. 'Am I a suspect?' I asked again.

Another glance, this one like an electrical current flowing between two poles.

'Not at the moment,' Jennifer said evenly.

But that could change, I thought.

It was a good thing I'd spent the evening in the company of a police officer, all things considered. Adam Nash would make a decent alibi, if nothing else.

The heating was turned up to the maximum at the station and the detectives stripped off their jackets with practised speed as soon as we reached the interview room. I knew the room was hot and airless, but I still couldn't seem to get warm.

'That's the shock,' DC Akram said. 'Can I get you a cup of tea? Some water?'

'Water, please.' I turned to Jennifer Gold. 'How long am I going to be here?'

'A little while.' She raised her eyebrows. 'Do you have somewhere else to go?'

'No.' I really didn't. My flat was going to be out of bounds for days, if not weeks. I had no idea where I was going to stay.

I shoved my own worries out of my mind and concentrated on the police officers' questions when the interview started: all the questions I'd answered at the scene and then some.

'So you didn't know her before last night?'

'No.'

'And you let her stay in your flat?' DC Akram asked, incredulous.

'It seemed like the right thing to do. She was quite drunk by the end of the evening, and she didn't want to go home.'

'Why not?' Jennifer Gold reminded me of a hunting falcon: nothing of interest escaped her.

'It's complicated,' I said, knowing that wouldn't be enough.

'Go on.'

'She had . . . feelings for my friend who was hosting the engagement party, who lives next door to her. She was worried about giving herself away.'

'Feelings,' Jennifer repeated.

173

'I don't know any details,' I said quickly. I felt as if I was betraying Vicki, and Harry. 'You'd need to speak to him. But – get him on his own. I don't think he'll want to talk in front of his fiancée.'

DC Akram made a note. 'What else?'

What else? I knew so little about Vicki.

What I did know was that it wasn't the first violent death that had befallen someone near me, and that the detectives needed to know that. Once again, I had to try to convince police officers to take me seriously – to treat me as a potential victim rather than a witness, or even a suspect.

Once again I had the feeling that someone I liked had died, and that it should have been me. I told them about Belinda, stumbling through the story while their eyebrows edged upwards in polite bafflement.

When I had finished, I was absolutely exhausted.

'Can I go now?'

'We still have a few more questions.' Jennifer Gold was writing a note to herself slowly, concentrating.

'I've told you everything I know.'

'We just need to go through it all again.' She looked up with a smile that didn't reach her eyes. 'After all, it's not the first time someone's died in your home, is it?'

From: 4102@freeinternetmail.com
To: Durbs, IATL

What happened this time? What's the excuse?

From: Durbs@mailmeforfree.com
To: 4102, IATL

Calm down. It's not a problem. She's terrified which is what we wanted.

From: 4102@freeinternetmail.com
To: Durbs, IATL

I think it's a pretty big fucking problem, actually. I really do. I think we should pull the plug. You went and poked a tiger and it bit someone. You can't be surprised.

From: IATL@internetforyou.com
To: Durbs, 4102

Keep your nerve. It's not exactly what we intended but that doesn't mean it's a sign to stop. We're almost there.

From: 4102@freeinternetmail.com
To: Durbs, IATL

If anyone else gets hurt though, I'm dropping out. It's too much.

From: Durbs@mailmeforfree.com
To: 4102, IATL

Anyone but her, you mean.

From: 4102@freeinternetmail.com
To: Durbs, IATL

Anyone but her.

20

Three weeks later, I waited in the dark for a bus at Aldwych, shivering in a cold wind that threw stinging grit into my face and made my eyes water. I pulled my scarf up to cover my mouth, tucking my chin down to my chest. It had been a long day in court and I ached as if I was coming down with the flu. I hadn't been getting a lot of rest. I had been staying with Adele in her heroically untidy one-bedroom flat in Ealing, sleeping on the world's most uncomfortable sofa-bed, but I couldn't ignore her hints about when I might leave. The despicable Paul had returned a few days previously and that was finally enough to drive me out.

I had phoned Jennifer Gold often enough for updates that she sounded resigned when she answered now: no news. No suspect. Nothing to link John Webster to Vicki, or her violent death. No one had seen anyone coming or going. No one had heard anything. All of my neighbours had been out, or listening to loud music. Even the omni-present Helen had been elsewhere.

I had asked the landlord if I could break my lease and leave my flat, but he had refused. I could see his point; renting it again was going to be a nightmare given that it was a crime scene. The bloodstains had been cleaned away but you couldn't clean away the faint disquieting hum of violence. Part of me wished I could just leave it and everything I owned and walk away, but I couldn't afford it, and I couldn't stay with Adele forever, and I couldn't let Vicki's death fade out of memory until I could prove who had killed her.

This trip was so that I could see what needed to be done before I moved in again, if anything. In addition to cleaning the place and repainting the walls, the landlord had installed a new, cheap alarm system that I didn't trust at all. Alarms meant nothing to John Webster. There was no way to keep him out, if he wanted to get in.

When it arrived, the bus was almost empty. I went upstairs and automatically sat at the front, because everyone knew that was the best seat and it was never free. The route from Aldwych was a straight line up to the Euston Road, and clogged with traffic as usual. The familiar streets lulled me into a waking doze as each one gave way to the next: Kingsway, Holborn, Southampton Row . . . Harsh strip lighting made it easier to see what was inside the bus than the outside world, and I found myself staring at my reflection in the window in front of me, with rows of seats behind. The reinforced window glass gave me a double outline, blurring the detail of my features. It looked almost as if someone was sitting in the seat behind me, their movements mirroring mine as the bus hit potholes and bumps in the road on its slow, halting journey. I leaned to my right to rest my head on the glass, and one layer of my reflection did the same. The other stayed where it was.

Pure instinct made me leap to my feet, or try to: as soon as I moved, the scarf around my neck tightened. My field of vision narrowed, darkness rushing in on either side. I clawed at the scarf, desperate for air, pinned in my seat.

'Don't fight, don't run, don't scream.' Webster's breath was warm in my ear, his voice low. 'Got it?'

I made some sort of sound that he took as assent, and the pressure on my neck eased. I dragged the scarf off completely as panic overwhelmed me: he was *here*, right behind me, and there was no way to call for help . . .

'You're hard to get hold of, Ingrid. I don't like getting the bus.'

I coughed.

'Sorry about your neck, but you do lash out when you're surprised, don't you? Or run away.' A new note entered his voice, one I hadn't heard before. 'And we need to talk.'

'About what?'

'I think you know.' Irritation sharpened his words. 'Look at me, Ingrid. Don't be rude.'

I turned, slowly. Everything had that heightened reality of a disaster, each second lasting an eternity. The empty seats stretched behind him. We could have been the only people in the entire world. I looked at him properly, noting that he had lost some weight that he hadn't needed to shed: his cheekbones were more defined than before and his hair looked dishevelled.

'You've been talking about me to the wrong people.'

Understanding dawned. 'The police came to see you.'

He inclined his head. 'At your request.'

'I didn't ask them to interview you.'

'You told them I broke into your home and murdered a girl.'

'Did you?'

He looked amused. 'Of course not. You know that, don't you? They told you I had an alibi.'

'I don't believe your alibi for a second,' I said, trembling.

'It happens to be true.'

'The very fact you say that makes me sure it's a lie.'

'How unpleasant, Ingrid.' He leaned forward. 'There are easier ways to get my attention, if you missed me.'

'I didn't. I don't want your attention. I've never wanted it.'

A commotion on the stairs became two teenagers in massive parkas, laughing and shoving each other. Webster turned his head and looked at them, and whatever they saw on his face stopped them in their tracks.

'Go away.'

London teenagers didn't scare easily, as a rule. This pair shrank into themselves and scuttled back down the stairs, suddenly silent. The distraction gave me a chance to collect myself, to remember that this was an opportunity – at least, Adam had said it might be. I couldn't waste it.

He looked past me, out at the street. 'This is your stop, isn't it?'

'No. Nowhere near.'

'Come on, Ingrid. You know you can't lie to me.'

'Don't do that.'

'What?'

'Pretend you know everything about me. It's a con. Almost everything you say is a bluff.'

He stood up. 'Most people never work that out. You see, Ingrid? I knew you were special. Now let's go.'

180

I found myself moving in front of him down the narrow stairs to the lower deck and stepping out of the central doors, because I had no choice.

He drew my arm through his as he reached the pavement a split second after me. I made one attempt to pull free, but his grip was firm enough to bruise.

'Shall we walk and talk? I'm afraid we'll find some trouble for ourselves if we stand here, since we're so close to King's Cross. Haven't you ever noticed how train stations attract exactly the wrong sort of people?'

'I'm starting to.'

He smirked. 'It must have been a nice break for you to have a change of scene. I would have thought it was worse to have to deal with the Central Line every morning, but what do I know?'

I tried to free myself again and failed. The fear was like lightning running through me. He'd known where I was. He'd been watching me when I was in Adele's flat.

'Don't make a scene,' he murmured. 'There's really no need.'

'What do you want, John?'

'Why did you tell the police I tried to kill you? Why did you tell them I killed the girl?'

'Didn't you?'

He shook his head, his face sombre.

For a moment, I doubted myself. Then I remembered that was his great gift: convincing you that black was white. I got a grip on myself. 'I think you tried to kill me, John, but you killed Belinda instead, and then Vicki surprised you when you were in my flat so you killed her. Now you're just trying to cover up because you took too much of a risk and you're scared you'll get caught.'

'I'm not scared of anything.' Again I had the impression he was being honest. *Remember you can't trust him.* 'I'm a little bit concerned for you, though, Ingrid. It looks as if you've run across someone who genuinely wishes you harm. Don't you think you should try to find out who they are?'

'Not if it's you.'

'But it's not. And whatever about Belinda, this other girl's murder feels personal. There's a real anger to it, isn't there? Maybe frustration that it wasn't you. Maybe they did to her what they'd planned to do to you.'

'No one wants to hurt me except you.'

'I don't want to hurt you. You've always been wrong about that.' He tilted his head to one side. 'I just want to understand you.'

'By taking me apart, like a clock.'

'If necessary.' He sniffed. 'You should make a list of everyone you've ever annoyed. All the people who hate you.'

'Again, I'm not aware of anyone who feels that way about me.'

'No?' He looked amused. 'Think about it though, for me. And you don't have to worry any more. I'm going to help you.'

'*Help* me?' I laughed, a cracked and horrible sound. 'You must be joking.'

'Don't be tedious, Ingrid. You need me.'

'The police—'

'Are useless. We know that. That's why I have to get involved. I'm your best resource. Forget the police, Ingrid. They're five steps behind and bound by the law. If you want someone to save you, you need someone like me.'

'I'll never need you.'

'That's not what your phone message said.'

'What are you talking about?'

'You called me.'

'I certainly did not.'

He dug in his coat pocket for his phone, flicked to voicemail and held it up. 'Listen.'

'John, I need to talk to you. I need your help.' The voice was high, frantic. 'Please. I'm sorry, but I'm scared. Come and find me.'

It was like stepping into ice-cold water: the shock of it drove the breath from my lungs. John Webster lied all the time, but on this occasion, he was telling the truth.

It was my voice.

And I had no recollection whatsoever of making the call.

'That can't be me. I didn't call you.' I stared into his eyes. They were as hollow as a predator's, hungry with the desire to destroy me, and nothing else. 'How could I call you? I don't even have your number.'

For the first time, a little assurance drained out of him. 'You don't.'

'I never have.' A thought struck me that seemed, in that moment, hilarious, and I felt myself start to smile. 'You always hid your number when you phoned me. You must remember that. All those heavy-breathing calls were from a withheld number. I could never call you back.'

He frowned at me, not used to being laughed at. I should have known he would strike back, and hard. 'So then the question is who has the skills to fake a phone call from you? Who could record your voice and cut it together so it sounded like you begging for help?'

The wind swirled around my throat like an invisible hand, plucking at my hair, chilling my skin. I felt my smile fade.

'Don't tell me you forgot about poor old Mark, the love of your life, who was so good with sound recording he had his own bloody studio.'

Mark.

'He's in Canada.'

Webster's eyes narrowed. 'Is that what he told you?'

'That's where he is. He lives there now. Permanently.'

He leaned in, dropping his voice to a whisper. 'He's back, beautiful. Didn't you know?'

No was the obvious answer. I shut my eyes for a second, gathering my strength. 'Why should he tell me he was back? We're not in touch.'

'I suggest you remedy that straight away and find out if he was responsible for this.' He waggled his phone at me before he slipped it into his pocket.

'Where does he live?'

'Are you asking me for help?' Webster took hold of my chin, twisting my face up so he could look at me. 'I'll help you, if you ask nicely.'

I shook my head, beyond speech.

'The time will come, Ingrid, when you will beg me to help you and you'll promise me anything I like in exchange. Until then, you're on your own.' His words were clipped, his mouth tight. Usually he controlled his emotions; this was unusual. 'I'll be sorry when you're dead, but do remember, it will be entirely your own fault.'

He let go of me and moved away into the crowds without a backwards glance. I stood where he had left me, still trembling long after he was out of sight.

21

It may have been news to me that my ex-fiancé was back in England, but my mother knew all about it.

'Of course he is. He came back three . . . no, four months ago.'

'How did you know?' I felt the frustration start to tingle in my joints. 'More to the point, why didn't you tell me?'

'Oh, you know . . .' she drifted away from the phone and I heard her fiddling with the oven. Baking was her passion and an endless source of distraction.

'*MUM.*'

'I'm here, darling. There's no need to shout.'

'How did you find out about Mark being back?'

'His mother rang me, of course. Diana knew I would like to know.'

'And what about me?'

'Well, no one thought you would be particularly interested, after what happened.'

My frustration heated to scalding rage; I swallowed hard before I spoke again. 'Oh, did you discuss it?'

'Not in great detail.' She sounded placid, because she was: I had inherited my temper from my father. You'd never find two more different people and I'd never been able to work out why they'd married, or why after ten years they had calmly admitted their mistake and split up. Neither of them had had much money to spend on me when I was growing up, but they were both loving and supportive. I had been happy despite the divorce.

A terrible suspicion occurred to me. 'Have you seen Mark?'

'Yes, I met him for lunch.'

'You did *what*?'

'Well, you know I always liked him. I met him and Diana – oh, it must have been in September. He was just finding his feet again. Julius was diagnosed with Parkinson's and I suppose Mark wanted to be there for his father.'

'That's awful. Poor Julius.' I was fond of the man who had been supposed to be my father-in-law, a sweet-natured former accountant with a slow smile and a dry sense of humour. 'How is he?'

'The medication is much better these days than it used to be, so I think it's being managed. Between you and me, I think Mark was looking for a reason to come back to England.'

'Oh?'

'He didn't settle well in Canada. He didn't like the weather, he said.'

Is he single? I suppressed that question because it was far too loaded and found myself saying, 'Did he ask about me?'

'I'm sure he did.'

'You can't remember?'

'You know how Diana talks. Most of the time we were just listening to her go on and on about her neighbours and their bloody dog.'

I felt a pang. I had lost touch with the Orpens without time for much regret, in the maelstrom of fear and loss that life had become after Mark left me, but I felt guilty about it and I missed them. Diana and I had nothing at all in common except Mark, but somehow we got on well.

'Anyway, why are you asking about Mark?' Mum sounded much less distracted all of a sudden, which made me wary.

'No reason. Someone told me he was back.'

'I see.' She waited.

'Yes, I do want his number.'

'Ah, I was wondering.'

'Not because I want to get back together with him.'

'Of course not.' She found the number and read it out in her clear, measured way and I scrawled it in the back of one of my trial notebooks.

'And don't ring Diana and tell her I asked for it.'

'You're no fun.' I could hear her smiling.

'She'll take it the wrong way, and you know it.'

'What is the right way to take it?'

'Sorry, this line is terrible,' I said. 'You're breaking up. I can barely hear you. But thank you . . .'

The following Friday, I moved back into my flat, and the next morning, after approximately five minutes of sleep spread thinly over seven hours, I started cleaning. I knew it had been cleaned properly and professionally after Vicki's body was removed and the police had released the crime scene – I knew there were no stains or smudges of fingerprint powder, and the grime from strangers' shoes was in my mind rather than on my floor, but I cleaned anyway. Then I took the longest, hottest shower the boiler could manage, and tried on three different versions of weekend casual until I settled on the right combination of jeans and a heavyweight cardigan with a delicate lace-trimmed camisole underneath. I dried my hair so it hung in silky waves, then changed my mind and knotted it on top of my head, then tried half up, half down, then gave up on the whole thing and tied it back in a ponytail. No make-up. I looked fine. Mark had seen me without make-up often enough.

I looked at my reflection one more time: purple shadows under my eyes and the pallor from lack of sleep made me look a hundred years old.

Bugger.

I was halfway through applying a third layer of concealer, looking like the sort of prey animal that pins its hopes on camouflage to stay alive, when I heard footsteps on the stairs followed by a knock on my door. Someone must have let him in through the outer gate; it happened all the time in spite of dire warnings from the management. I'd been counting on at least thirty seconds of warning before he arrived.

'No no no no no,' I muttered, swiping at my face, and, brightly, 'Just coming!'

I was smiling brilliantly when I pulled the door open. 'Mark.'

'Ingrid.' He matched my tone exactly – a little too calm, a little too practised. He was sombre, as if he had come to attend a funeral. I felt myself blushing. Well, no need to worry about looking pale.

'Come in.'

He stepped over the threshold and stopped, looking around. 'Wow.'

'Do you like it?'

Silence. That would be a no.

'It's a bit different,' he said at last.

I was knotting my fingers nervously, which was ridiculous: his opinion didn't matter any more. While he was staring at the stark walls and makeshift kitchen in undisguised horror I examined him, reminding myself of the details I'd forgotten. He had worn his hair long enough that you could see the curl in it. Now he kept it short, cropped so it showed off the shape of his head. He was a tall man, broad in the chest and athletic, and that hadn't changed. If anything he looked as if he'd put muscle on since the last time I'd seen him. He looked serious – almost grim, in fact – but he was the sort of person whose face lit up when he smiled.

He was not smiling currently.

'It's very you, isn't it?'

'What does that mean?' I asked, and regretted it, because it couldn't really mean anything good. 'Never mind. Cup of tea?'

'Thanks.'

I was aware of his eyes on me as I walked over to the kitchen and filled the kettle; his turn to assess the woman he'd last seen two years ago. I tried not to mind.

'I was surprised to hear from you.' A dragging sound told me he had pulled out a chair at the table. Well, I hadn't wanted to snuggle up with him on the sofa either.

'I was surprised too. I only just heard you were back. I thought you'd moved to Canada for good.'

189

'I thought I had. But plans change.'

'What are you doing about work? Are you setting up another studio?'

'No. Moving countries twice wasn't great, financially speaking. I'm working for a friend while I get myself sorted out.'

He was the sort of person who made money easily; things always worked out for him. He would be fine in the end, I thought.

'I'm sorry about your dad.'

'He's doing all right. Better than I expected.'

'Good.' I turned around to look at him and was startled by déjà vu: he had always sat back at an angle from a table like that, with one elbow propped on the tabletop and his legs stretched out.

'What is it?'

'Nothing. Just – it's good to see you.'

He raised his eyebrows. Surprised was the nice way of describing his demeanour, but sceptical was closer. 'Why am I here, Ingrid?'

'Here, specifically? Because I didn't want to have to worry about being watched while we talked.'

Now he looked wary. 'Why?'

'Some weird things have been happening.' I busied myself with the kettle that was hissing and juddering as it came to the boil.

'What kind of things?'

One thing that I had learned from my job was how to lay out facts in an orderly and clear way. My professional training came to my aid now as I poured the tea and sat down opposite him. I described what had been happening, from Belinda's death to Vicki's murder to the appearance of John Webster on the bus behind me. Mark listened in silence, except to ask one or two brief questions. When I had finished, he ran his finger over the handle of his mug thoughtfully. Then he looked back at me.

'How can you stay here?'

'I can't afford to move.'

'But that girl died here, in this room.'

'It's awful. I'll never feel the same about it. I wish she'd gone home with someone else.' I shrugged, helpless. 'I have to stay, so I'll stay.'

He nodded. Then he asked, 'So why am *I* here, Ingrid?'

'John Webster had a recording of me. A voicemail. I asked him for help in it.' I folded my arms defensively. 'You know I would never have called him.'

'So?'

'So I didn't remember doing it – I thought I was going mad. But when I said that, Webster suggested that someone might have spliced it together to lure him into making contact with me.'

'Sounds like a lot of work. Why would anyone want Webster to be interested in you again?'

'I don't know.'

'Can't the police get rid of him?'

'They're trying.'

'Not hard enough.' He drank some tea and pulled a face because it was tepid by now. 'Still not seeing why I'm here, Ingrid.'

'Webster was the one who told me you were back.'

He looked up at that, surprised, and I felt a tiny thrill run through my body as his eyes met mine. 'How did he know?'

'I assume he's been keeping an eye on you. Which is

more than I have. I can't believe you didn't tell me you'd come home.'

He chose to focus on what I'd said first. 'Why does John Webster want to have anything to do with me? He's already destroyed everything I cared about.'

'Everything?' I said, when I could speak.

'You heard what I said.' His moss-green eyes could look soft, but now they were hard, like stone. 'What I hear in this story, Ingrid, is a typical set-up. John Webster is up to his usual tricks and you're falling for it again. I'm not going to join you this time.'

'You are the only person I know with the skills to fake a voice recording,' I said stubbornly. 'It's literally your job. Webster even said that. He said I should ask you.'

'Oh, you're taking suggestions from him now? Good to know.' He was pale. I recognised the expression on his face and felt tired; we'd been here before and it hadn't gone well. There had been a time when he could make me laugh without even trying, when I could show him something and know how he would react to it, when he was my first thought every morning and my last every night. This person was the stranger who had stalked through my life after the fire, cold and withdrawn, until we had finally broken up. 'You need to be careful, Ingrid. He'll hook you and reel you in and you won't even know it until it's too late. You shouldn't need me to tell you not to trust him, unless you've turned stupid.'

'I preferred you when you lived in Canada,' I said, trying one last time to make a joke, as if his laughter would prove there was still an ember of something between us that might flare back into life.

He flinched. 'I'm only here because you invited me.'

'I know. Sorry.' I'd managed to hurt his feelings, which was strange; there had been a time that I would have celebrated it but that had changed. Maybe *I* had changed.

As if he'd been following my thoughts, he shook his head. 'I didn't invite the girl to our house. I didn't know she was there.'

The girl.

He couldn't even say her name.

Poor little Flora Pole, twenty-three and in her first real job as the receptionist at Mark's recording studio, with a tattoo on her shoulder and a nose piercing and an occasional coke habit, who had thought herself a bad girl when she was just young and careless and well brought up.

'Flora was in our bedroom, Mark.'

'I don't know why.' He got to his feet and ran a hand over his head as if he could wipe the memories away. 'I've tried and tried to understand it, Ingrid. I came back and the house was on fire. I wanted to get in to make sure you were safe. The flames and the smoke were too strong. I wound up with smoke inhalation, in the back of an ambulance, and that's when the police told me they'd found a body.'

'I remember,' I said. He was shaking. I got up and crossed the room to be near him. I wanted to comfort him, and it wasn't my place any more, so I settled for standing close enough to touch him without actually doing it.

'Do you remember when you turned up?'

I would never forget it: the horror of seeing our lives burning like a bonfire, and the crowds of onlookers, and how Mark had wept, and grabbed me, and held me so tightly I could barely breathe, and the smell of smoke in his hair and on his skin . . .

'If I had known Flora was in the house, in our bedroom,' Mark said, his voice level, 'I would have known she was the woman who died in the fire. I would never have thought it was you.'

'I know, but—'

He went on as if I hadn't spoken. 'Sometimes when I think about it, I'm sure you didn't know she was there. Sometimes I think it wouldn't have mattered if you had known.'

My voice was unsteady. 'John Webster set our house on fire.'

'At whose request?' He smiled, not kindly. 'This isn't the first time you've asked for his help, is it? He helped you out with a little bit of arson because you'd got jealous for no reason.'

'I didn't ask him to do that. I didn't even know about you and Flora until after the fire.'

'Because there was nothing to know!' His voice had risen. 'For God's sake, Ingrid, why won't you listen?'

'I know you think I'm gullible, but I'd have to be a fool to believe you,' I said coldly.

'I'm going to go.' He gathered up his jacket and phone. 'Just so you know, I didn't fake any recordings. I have better things to do.'

He stalked out and I gave a sigh of relief as his footsteps echoed on the stairs outside my door. I picked up his mug and then almost dropped it as someone knocked on the door, a jaunty little *tap-tap-ti-tap-tap*.

'Well, hello!' Helen was beaming when I answered the door. 'When did you come back?'

194

'Yesterday.'

'Sorry about what happened.'

'Thank you.' I waited, but she didn't say anything else. 'Was that it?'

'Oh, yes, sorry! I almost forgot. I was wondering if you had any baking powder I could borrow.'

'Baking powder?' It was probably hysteria that was making me want to laugh, but there was such a sharp contrast between Mark's anger and Helen's determined cheerfulness. 'I think I have some. What are you making?'

'Oh.' She looked floored for a second, as if she hadn't thought about it. 'Just a cake. A sponge cake.'

'Lovely,' I said politely, and handed her the container of baking powder. I was pretty sure the baking powder was just an excuse, and her next question proved it.

'Who was it who dropped by just now? Was that your boyfriend?'

'My ex.'

'Oh.' She hesitated, pretending to read the label on the baking powder. 'I heard him shouting.'

'I haven't seen him for a while. We had a lot to discuss.'

'If you ever need help,' Helen said, her face earnest, 'give me a knock.'

I won't. I didn't say it out loud because I didn't want to be rude, but Helen was not what I needed.

No, there was only one person who could help me now.

22

'I know I told you to encourage John Webster, but you can't possibly think of inviting him here. It's far too dangerous.' Adam shook his head, horrified. 'I want him to incriminate himself so we can lock him up. I don't want you inviting him into your life.'

For the second time in a single weekend, I was explaining myself to a man in my own flat. This time it was Adam Nash. I couldn't help comparing him to Mark, who had thawed from icy politeness to pure rage. Adam was quiet but forceful, concerned for my well-being and solidly on my side. He was the kind of man who kept all of his feelings under control. He would smother them as if they were a rolling grenade and absorb any damage they did, in silence. Now he was pale, his jaw tight with tension. 'It's you I'm thinking of. You can't take that kind of risk.'

'I don't have any choice. He's literally the expert on stalking, Adam. If he isn't the one who's targeting me – and he swears he's not – I can't think of anyone who would be better at working out who is.' I pulled the collar of my huge jumper up so I could bury my chin in it. The temptation to hide inside it was almost overwhelming. 'I want to see how he behaves when he's here. I want to know if he's been here before.'

'It's dangerous.'

'Of course. That's why you're here.' I was shivering: Adam was voicing my own doubts with unerring accuracy. 'Don't lose sight of the fact that someone's trying to kill me. Vicki was killed here. Maybe he did it, and maybe it was someone else. If it wasn't him, I think he can help me find out who it was. If it was him, maybe he'll give himself away. Either way, this is important.'

'You're playing into his hands, Ingrid.'

'If John wanted to kill me, he'd have done it years ago. It would be easy for him. He'd have strangled me on the bus the other night with my own scarf, or stabbed me when he saw me in the Temple. He's had every opportunity to do it since Belinda died.'

'What about Vicki?'

I curled up on the sofa, trying not to look at the shadowy corner where she had fled in vain, and died. 'The one thing we both know about John Webster is that he's brilliant at talking his way out of trouble. If she'd come back and found him here sharpening a knife, wearing a T-shirt with Murderer written on it, he'd have charmed the socks off her. She'd have walked away completely unharmed.'

'Like Flora Pole?'

'That was different.' I folded my arms, hugging myself. 'He made a mistake that time.'

'I don't think it was a mistake.'

'What then?'

'It was a good way to prove that Mark was cheating on me. Webster would view Flora as an acceptable level of collateral damage.'

'What about you?'

'I was devastated that she died. Why she was in my house was irrelevant.'

Smiling at me when I popped in to visit Mark, making conversation about what we were planning for the weekend and where we were going on holidays. Ludicrous clothes and make-up, in contrast to me with my uptight suits and white shirts. A little bird with bright plumage, fragile and flawed. I'd liked her, and she'd been sleeping with Mark all the time. But Mark should never have touched her – he should never have wanted to. I blamed him, not her. I'd fallen for Mark; why shouldn't she?

Someone knocked on the door: I hadn't heard anyone approaching and from Adam's reaction, neither had he. Even as I watched, his muscles tightened, his body stiffening in pure hostility. 'He's here.'

'Good. Right on time.' I walked across to the door with what I hoped looked like confidence and opened it. Light fell out, illuminating Webster, casting his face into sharp relief. He took his time about moving forward – savouring the moment, if I had to guess. I had the fleeting desire to slam the door in his face and lock it, to run and hide, even though I had invited him there. The way he moved reminded me of an animal hunting, slow and deliberate, containing its speed until the moment when it would make its move. A wolf, like the one that had prowled up Emma Seaton's arm.

My fingers slipped on the handle, slick with sweat; no one had told my fight-or-flight reflexes that he wasn't a threat, even if I was trying to convince myself that was the case.

'Ingrid.'

'Come in.'

He crossed the threshold and stopped, looking around slowly. It reminded me of the way Mark had stood there, but Webster's face was alight with pleasure, not disapproval.

'Yes. Of course.'

'What's that supposed to mean?'

'A space you can see at a glance. You got tired of checking every room in your home over and over again, and trying to remember if anything was different – wondering if you were imagining that someone had been there. You'd spent long enough thinking you heard a noise down the hall and steeling yourself to investigate. You wanted somewhere you could check before you were shut inside with whatever lurked behind a door. Sensible girl.'

'I liked the high ceilings,' I snapped, refusing to admit that he was right, that he'd seen something I hadn't even realised myself. He laughed at me, and moved inside so I could shut the door. I turned to find that he had stopped again. This time his attention was focused on Adam.

'What's he doing here?'

'Personal protection.' Adam had folded his arms and his expression was openly hostile.

'You're not required.'

'Ingrid wants me here.'

'Ingrid wants *me* here,' Webster said childishly.

'She called me first,' Adam replied, descending to his level without missing a beat.

'I don't really want either of you here ruining my Sunday night,' I said, irritated. 'I have a speech to write for tomorrow and I need to iron a shirt. I could do without this, especially if there's going to be a pissing competition before you begin.'

'I just want to make it clear,' Adam said, as if I hadn't spoken, 'I don't trust you, even if Ingrid does. I've got my eye on you, Webster, and I'm not going to rest until you're behind bars where you belong.'

'Boring,' Webster said, which was a little unfair but at least succinct.

I clapped my hands to get their attention. 'Okay. Well, do your thing.'

Webster raised his eyebrows. 'What do you want to know? How he's been getting in?'

'I've advised Ingrid on her security already,' Adam said stiffly. 'She's made a few changes as a result.'

'I noticed the lock was new.' Webster was standing very still, his head tilted back, considering the space. 'That would slow me down for a minute. Two, possibly, if I was out of practice. But if I wanted to pick that lock, Ingrid, I would make sure I had practised with a similar model until I got it right, and then I'd practise until I couldn't get it wrong. All in all, it wouldn't hold me up for long.'

'Great. Thanks. I feel so reassured now.'

'We want to keep you alive, don't we?' Webster smirked at me. 'I'm not going to give you the idea you're safe when you're not. You should be on edge. Two deaths are too many.'

'That might be the only thing we agree on,' Adam said heavily. 'What else?'

'Give me a minute.' He prowled around the flat, leaning

in to inspect my belongings. I watched him, noting that he hadn't tried to take his coat off. This visit was strictly business. His hands remained clasped behind his back and I hoped they would stay there. The one advantage of the last few weeks was that there had been so many people in my home that I'd stripped away almost everything personal already. It was as close to a neutral space as it had ever been.

He moved deliberately, choosing where he stepped, tasting the air like a snake.

'What are you looking for?' Adam asked eventually.

'Shhh.' He held up a finger. 'Not yet.'

'This is ridiculous. I—' Adam caught my eye and subsided.

He lingered at the top of the stairs, staring at my bed, but he didn't go any further – there was nothing to see on the sleeping platform anyway. I would change the sheets after he was gone, I thought, and use the longest cycle my washing machine had to offer. Even if he didn't touch anything, his gaze made me feel as if he'd tipped grease all over everything. He paused for a moment in the kitchen, eyeing the metal strip where I had kept my knives. It was empty now.

'Did the police take your knives?'

'Yes.'

'Have they found the weapon that killed your little friend, then?'

'No. I don't know. One of them was missing.' The sharpest, with a worn black handle that fitted into my palm as if it was made for me. 'They took the others in case he touched them.'

'Interesting.'

'Why?' The question burst out of Adam as if he couldn't contain it.

'If someone came here to kill Ingrid, they weren't exactly prepared, that's all.'

'You would have brought your own knife, I imagine,' I said. He laughed but he didn't deny it.

He leaned forward and worked his way along the kitchen counter, inspecting everything. 'You haven't been eating much, have you? You look thin.'

'I've been eating.'

'Not toast, though.'

I wanted to lie, but what was the point? 'How did you know?'

He waggled his eyebrows at me, like a terrible magician preparing to do a trick. 'Watch this.' With one swift movement he picked up the toaster and turned it upside down. A cascade of crumbs fell out, all over the counter and the floor.

'Was that necessary?' Adam was looking even more annoyed, if that was possible.

As an answer, Webster shook the toaster again. This time, something metal slithered out and landed in a small, shining pile on the counter.

'My bracelet!' I started towards it but checked; I did not want to get so close to Webster, even with Adam there for back-up.

Webster eyed me. 'When did you lose it?'

'I don't know. The clasp was wonky. The last time I know I had it was the night before Vicki died, at the engagement party. But how did it get in there?'

'Who knows? A mystery.' Webster set the toaster the right way up, at the exact angle I preferred. 'Maybe you dropped it in there when you got back. Or your little friend found it and put it there for safekeeping. It's a good thing you were off carbs.'

He spent quite a long time reading the spines of the books on my shelves, until I was ready to scream. The bathroom got a very cursory glance though. I stood with my arms folded, hating every minute of him being in my home. He came back and stood in front of me to make his report.

'I like it, Ingrid. It has character, like you.'

I unclenched my jaw to say, 'That's not why you're here.'

'All right.' He looked amused. 'Well, there are three things you need to remove, assuming you don't want to be spied on.'

'You found something?' My stomach plummeted as if I'd missed a step.

'There's a double socket in the kitchen that doesn't match any of the other sockets in the flat. Different shape, different switches. It works fine – it's wired in, all right. But it's also an audio transmitter. If it's the kind I think, it's got a chip like a SIM card in it. You can call in from anywhere in the world and listen to whatever fascinating conversations are going on in here, including this one.'

'Are you sure?' Adam demanded.

Webster nodded. 'Go on. Get your screwdriver out and check. It's the one on the right. I know you've got some sort of penknife in your pocket. You're that sort.'

Adam looked furious but he slid a Swiss Army knife out of his pocket and weighed it in his hand. Curiosity had won out over the desire to prove Webster wrong, which was why he was a good police officer and a better person than me.

'What else?' I asked. My mouth had gone dry.

'You've got two dictionaries over there on your shelves. One of them isn't a dictionary. It's a camera that's focused on the front door, at a guess. It's up on the top shelf.'

'A camera,' I repeated, aghast.

'Don't worry. Unless you make a habit of answering the door in the nude, it won't have caught you at an unfortunate moment. It would be filming the wall behind the door if the door isn't open. Purely functional. Someone wants to see who's coming and going. Maybe they want to know when you leave and get back.'

'Christ.' Adam had pulled the socket off the wall. He showed me the back of it and the green electronic circuit board with a SIM card mounted on it. 'He was right.'

'Anything else?' I asked bitterly.

'I'd check out the smoke alarm.'

'It works.' I knew that all too well; I set it off about once a week by cooking too aggressively.

'They do. Doesn't mean they don't have a recording device built in. The ceiling in here must be what – twelve feet? You'll need a good ladder. Unless the copper has one up his sleeve – no? Ah well. You can sort it out tomorrow.'

'How did the police miss these devices? They were all over this place after Vicki died.'

He shrugged. 'They weren't looking for listening devices, or the devices weren't here. But if you're wondering how someone put together that recording of you asking for my help, collecting audio from your phone calls would work.'

'But I never sound like that on the phone. I—' I broke off, remembering how I'd called Adam's voicemail and

204

sobbed at him after the scaffolding accident. From the way he was looking at me, he was thinking the same thing. 'There must have been something recording me for ages. Weeks.'

'Or longer,' Webster agreed.

'And whoever has been recording me must have recorded Vicki's murder.'

'That's also a possibility. Or they killed her themselves. Did you ask Mark about the recording?'

'I did.'

'And?'

'He got angry with me. He said he wouldn't waste his time on something like that.'

Webster looked amused. 'He gets angry easily, doesn't he?'

'You bring out the worst in him.'

'He has good reason to dislike you.' Adam sounded grim. 'You ruined his life.'

'He ruined his own life.' Webster jerked a thumb at me. 'He could have had *her* if he'd behaved himself. No one forced him to fall cock first onto his receptionist.'

'*John*. That's enough.' I might as well not have bothered.

'Whoever set fire to his house – and I'm not saying it was me so don't take this as a confession – they did Ingrid a favour by showing her what Mark was really like, so she didn't waste any more time on him.'

'You destroyed everything Ingrid owned. And as if that wasn't enough, you came after her *cat*. You're a monster.' Adam had gone white with rage.

'Oh, she told you about the cat. Your relationship is a lot further advanced than I thought.' Webster smirked. 'Did she tell you the cat was dying?'

'I don't see what that has to do with it,' Adam said, but uncertainly.

'It had cancer. It was in pain. It needed to be put to sleep but Ingrid couldn't bring herself to do it. She was terribly sad, you see, after Mark left her and all of her belongings were destroyed by fire, or smoke damage, or water. She had nothing left. You couldn't expect her to take a decision like that herself.'

'You killed the cat.'

'A vet killed the cat. I put it in her freezer so she could decide how she wanted to bury it.'

'You didn't want me to have anything to love,' I said. 'You wanted to take away everything I cared about.'

'What a terrible interpretation of a kind act.' He looked at me across the room and it had much the same effect on me as if he had touched the cold steel of a blade to my throat. 'I will admit that I enjoyed taking him on his final journey. But just so you know, his death was quite peaceful.'

'Fuck off, John.'

He smiled. 'I notice you don't have any pets these days.'

'I think you should leave now.'

'I think that's a good idea.' Adam started moving towards him and Webster held up his hands.

'I'm going. But I should thank you, Ingrid. It's been a fascinating visit. Far more interesting than I anticipated.'

'Just go,' I said. 'Please.'

Slightly to my surprise, he went, pausing only to test the lock on his way out the door. He closed it behind him and I let out a long breath. The relief made me shaky.

'I hope that was worth it,' Adam said. He slid the SIM card from the fake socket into an envelope. 'I'll get this looked at. See if we can find out who put it in your wall.'

'Thanks.'

He hesitated. 'You need to be very careful around John Webster, Ingrid.'

'I think I know that by now, thank you.'

'No.' He was looking at me with compassion and a hint of doubt. 'You're starting to trust him. And that's the one thing you should never do.'

23

The following Wednesday, I made my way to a church hall behind Euston station, in two minds about whether I wanted to be there at all. I'd picked up a leaflet from a local café the previous morning on my way to work, when I was buying coffee as a substitute for breakfast. I'd discovered my fridge was empty the night before but the shop was a ten-minute walk. It would be the height of stupidity to offer myself up to whoever wanted me dead for the sake of a meal, I'd decided, and then lay awake cursing myself for being a coward instead.

The leaflet was a cheerful yellow with a row of silhouetted figures punching and kicking along the top and bottom.

Self-Defence Classes!
Learn to defend yourself
Get fit and have fun!
WOMEN ONLY
Drop in – No Need to Book

£10 per session/10 sessions for £80
7pm
Wear comfortable clothing and trainers!
Experienced Female Instructors!
No equipment or experience required.

I wasn't convinced that there was a lot of point in a self-defence class; it would have done nothing to help Belinda as she plunged into the path of a lorry, and I knew Vicki had fought hard for her life. The words of the pathologist's report I'd nagged out of Jennifer Gold kept repeating in my mind: *defence wounds to her forearms and hands . . . deep wounds to her chest and abdomen. The tendons in three of her fingers were cut . . .* I had no illusion that I could do any better. But it was something to do instead of hiding in my flat, waiting for the next attack.

I dressed in leggings and a sweatshirt and my big parka, and set out into the dark and drizzling night. Belinda was on my mind, but it was Vicki who haunted me. Pure chance that she'd been in my flat, pure chance that she'd answered the door instead of me.

It should have been me.

London was full of surprises and the church was no exception. It wasn't a heavy, pillared affair as I'd expected but a 1960s building that seemed to have sunk into the ground under the weight of its drum-shaped nave. There was no sign of a hall though. After wandering around it for a bit I realised the church hall was actually underneath the church itself. I made my way down the steps and stopped at the door to read the notices pinned to it, playing for time. I could still double back, I reminded myself. No one knew I was supposed to be there; I hadn't needed to book. In the meantime, the handwritten notices gave me something to look at. Do-gooders fed the homeless every day from the kitchen at one end of the room, but a glance through the glass set into the door confirmed it was shuttered now. There was a drop-in play session twice a week for carers and toddlers. A further notice informed me that Monday nights were devoted to Irish Dancing, Tuesdays to English Language Lessons, Wednesdays to Self-Defence and Thursdays to Swing Classes. Would I, I wondered, prefer to put myself through this self-defence class or swing-dancing? Given my lack of coordination, I would probably be at more risk of hurting myself at the dance lessons.

Two women came down the stairs behind me, chatting and laughing. They were large, cosy women, cheerful and loud, mid-twenties and full of confidence.

'All right, love? Going in?'

'Is this where the self-defence classes are?' I asked.

'That's the one. Come on. It's fun. They don't bite.' The first woman put a hand on the door, pausing to examine her heavily detailed manicure. 'That jewel's gone, look. Fell right off. What's the point in that?'

'I told you it wasn't worth the extra,' her friend said.

'I'm going back in to complain.'

'You should. You should get your money back for that.'

'I will.'

Assertiveness didn't seem to be a problem for either of them; if this was what the class could do for you, I was signing up for ten sessions immediately.

The aggrieved woman shoved the door open and a gust of air greeted me that was familiar from every other parish hall I'd ever been in: equal parts mince, dust and holiness. The room itself had institutional cream walls that were in need of a paint, a sprung wooden floor and pavement-level windows just under the ceiling. Pedestrians hurried past, visible from the ankles down.

'Hi, Cookie. Hi, June.' A tiny woman with cropped fair hair was dragging mats off a stack in the corner. She was pure muscle and no nonsense in a favourite-gym-teacher kind of way: discreet stud earrings, no make-up, the tanned skin of the outdoors athlete and a smile with double dimples like inverted commas around it. 'Give me a hand, girls.'

The two women pushed past me and took charge of the mats, giggling and shoving each other around. The blonde woman dusted off her hands on the seat of her tracksuit bottoms and turned to me. 'We haven't seen you here before, have we?'

'First time.'

'You're very welcome. I'm Kate.'

'Ingrid.'

She turned her back to the others who were starting to arrive and dropped her voice to a murmur that couldn't be overheard. 'Any particular reason for wanting to be here?'

'Not really,' I lied.

'Any issue with having a male instructor?'

'Er . . . no. But I thought – the leaflet said it was all women?'

'I usually teach this class with my friend Tara, but she's away this week so I've asked a mate of mine to come along and stand in for her. He's really just here so we can beat him up.' Her eyes tracked over my shoulder and she grinned, the skin around her eyes fanning into creases. 'I was just saying, Ben, you've come along so we can practise our moves on you, haven't you?'

'It's a pleasure.'

I turned, pushing my hood back, and found myself staring at the dark-haired man from the scaffolding accident – the man who I thought had followed me through the Temple. My whole body jerked in shock.

To give him credit, he looked as horrified as me. He froze in the act of lowering his kit bag from his shoulder.

'Do you two know each other?' Kate was looking from him to me.

'No,' I said blankly. 'Not really. We met once.'

'Sort of. You were pretty shaken, as I recall. Not what I'd call a proper meeting.'

I nodded.

'Can I have a word, Kate?' He took her by the elbow, guiding her as far away from me as possible. He was speaking rapidly and earnestly as she listened, and nodded, and shook her head once.

He looked awfully like the man I'd seen in the Temple – the man John Webster had scared away – but I couldn't be sure. I couldn't be sure of *anything*.

If I was a predator, I might volunteer with scared women. I might find out more about them than they realised. I might gain their trust.

I could leave, it occurred to me. No one would come after me if I just walked out; there would be no repercussions.

I tore my eyes away from him to find that Cookie and June had ground to a halt in their mat-laying, the better to stare at him.

'He's all right,' Cookie pronounced.

'Too short for me.'

'You're so picky.'

'Well, you have to be, don't you? Or what's the point?' The two of them cackled happily.

From the expression on Ben's face he hadn't been expecting to see me any more than I had expected to see him. If he'd been following me, he'd have known I was there. And I didn't *know* he had been in the Temple. Paranoia could convince me he was dangerous when there was no evidence at all to prove it.

I occupied myself by shoving a tenner into the tin by the door and draping my coat over a chair.

Whatever he was talking to Kate about, they came to an agreement. He settled himself in the corner on a plastic chair, concentrating on his phone rather than the class. I felt myself relax a fraction. I had been afraid of being watched, I realised, but he couldn't have looked less interested. Kate looked around at the twenty or so women who had gathered since I arrived – all ages and races and sizes. She clapped her hands.

'Right. Most of you have been here before, I think. Any first-timers?'

A pale, wan girl put her hand up tentatively, and I waved too.

'You'll get the hang of it quickly enough. Let's get ourselves warmed up and focused. Spread out, please. Give yourselves some room to swing your arms.'

The chatting died down as we sorted ourselves out and began to copy her in a series of stretches and exercises. I had found a place near the back of the room where I could see most of the class failing to keep time with Kate.

213

Coordination was an issue for most of the participants, and flexibility. I started to feel better about my skill level. Kate was endlessly encouraging and missed nothing, barking at me to look where I was punching instead of staring into space. She came and stood behind me with her hands on my hips and swung me into the move.

'The punch comes up from your feet, not your shoulder. Turn into it. Use your hips and abs to power it.'

I felt the difference immediately, and said so.

She nodded. 'That's it. You're a quick learner.'

She gave us moves to practise in pairs, such as dragging our hands out of an assailant's grasp by drawing them in and down instead of pushing away. It was surprisingly effective. 'Use their own force against them! They'll be pressing inwards to control you so go with it. Assume they're stronger than you – don't test your strength against them because you'll just get tired.'

Kate's emphasis was strongly on getting free and running away but she had a few aggressive moves too. I liked the hammer strike, driving the side of a fist into the attacker. 'Better if you have keys in your hand! You'll see people recommend putting the keys between your fingers but that's fiddly – bunch the keys in your fist and you won't drop them. And make some noise. Get used to shouting. When you're afraid, your vocal cords tighten up and you'll find it harder to get a deep breath, so you won't be able to shout as easily. The more noise you make, the more likely it is that you'll attract attention. Attackers don't like noise.'

Vicki hadn't made a sound, according to my neighbours.

All around me, the women were yelling and shouting, but I couldn't join in. Neither could the wan girl, who had sought me out so we could trade pretend punches and kicks. Her name was Laura, she whispered shyly, and she was there to get more confidence. She seemed even less prepared than me for physical exertion; she had come straight from work in neat trousers and a cardigan, with suede loafers instead of trainers.

'Why are you here?' she asked.

'It seemed like a good idea at the time.' I pushed my hair back with my wrist, unsticking it from my forehead. 'God, it's warm in here.'

'Boiling.'

'Let's take a break,' Kate called, and I joined a queue for cups of tepid tap water.

'Get your drinks and take a seat around the edge of the room,' Kate said. 'Ben, your time has come.'

He jumped up, swinging his arms and stretching as he bounced around. Kate watched him with her arms folded. 'Ben is a nice guy, but tonight he's going to be a violent and threatening attacker.'

'Ooooh,' the class chorused, as if this was a pantomime. I said nothing.

'So where are we going to hit him?' she asked.

'Eyes,' a tiny Asian woman called.

'Throat!'

'Get him in the balls,' Cookie suggested. The watching women giggled.

'And the nose.' Kate mimed a heel palm strike to the centre of Ben's face and he threw his head back oblig-ingly, staggering away from her. 'He goes back, you turn and run. Don't waste your time trying to kick him or injure him further. Make space and go. A kick to the groin is a good move but you'll probably be off balance

215

when you deliver it. If you miss and he grabs your foot' – she kicked out and he twisted to catch it on his thigh, his fingers trapping her ankle at the same time – 'you end up in this situation,' Kate finished. 'Can I have my foot back?'

I expected him to drop it instantly, and I think Kate did too, but he lifted it instead until she was hopping to keep her balance. His face was a sneer, suddenly, and we went quiet because it was a reminder that even Kate wasn't quite a match for his physical dominance.

'See? There isn't a lot I can do. He's out of reach so I can't punch or shove him.' She used him as leverage for a jump and kicked him hard in the chest with her free foot. He let go as she turned in the air and landed, springing away as we cheered.

'Ow.' He rubbed the middle of his torso.

'I asked nicely first.'

Go, Kate.

'It's all right for you to do that kind of stuntwoman move, but I wouldn't be able.' The comment came from a grandmotherly woman with tight iron-grey curls.

'I don't suggest you ladies try that now, but if you keep coming to class, who knows what you might achieve.' She grinned, well aware that what she had just done was showing off. 'The main point to remember is that you don't want to offer your opponent any advantage at all, so don't be aggressive unless you need to be. Defend yourself and give yourself a chance to get away.' Kate turned her back on Ben. 'Right. Try to pick me up.'

He pounced on her, wrapping his arms around her in a bear hug, and she bent forward. Suddenly his size wasn't an advantage, I saw, as he almost overbalanced. She threw an elbow that caught him just under the jaw, and slammed her fist back, stopping just short of his crotch.

'Oof.' He slid his hand in between her fist and his tracksuit bottoms and moved her hand away with great care. 'That was a close one.'

'If I'd made contact, I'd have taken his mind off whatever he was planning to do. And now,' Kate addressed the class, 'if someone grabs you by the wrists from behind . . .'

Ben did as he was told and Kate swivelled on the spot. He got a shoulder in the chest followed by an elbow in the stomach and a knee that made contact with his forehead with an audible thud. He fell back, sprawling on the ground. 'I give up.'

'We haven't even started.' Kate grabbed his hand and pulled him back up. 'There are no quitters here and that includes you, Ben.'

She beckoned to the nearest student, a competent-looking woman in her forties. 'Let's try you out. See what you've learned.'

One by one, the class went up and grappled with him as Kate shouted instructions and advice. I stood by the wall, watching with increasing unease. I did not want Ben to touch me, I realised.

'Ingrid!' Kate beckoned. 'You're up.'

I hesitated. Ben smiled at me.

'Come on. All over in a minute.'

'I bet that's what you say to all the girls,' Cookie drawled and there was a general shout of laughter. He grinned at her, then looked back at me and the smile faded from his face, leaving his eyes first.

I stepped forward.

'Okay. Ben is going to grab you from behind.' Kate steadied me, her eyes locked on mine. 'Remember what you've learned. Create space, move away.'

I barely heard her over the thumping of my heart. The space between my shoulder blades tingled in anticipation of the moment when I would be caught, and held, and have to fight my way out. *Three . . . two . . .*

And Kate nodded at me, smiling . . .

'I can't do this.' I half-turned and shoved Ben away from me before he could make contact. He stepped back smartly, concern now uppermost on his face. With speed that was as much from embarrassment as fear, I bolted towards the door, grabbing my parka on the way out.

'Ingrid—' The door slammed behind me, cutting off Kate's voice and the class's sympathetic murmuring. I hurled myself up the steps and onto the street, where I headed in the opposite direction from home. The drizzle had turned to rain, heavy and cold. I ran through it, letting it drench my hair and run down my face.

24

'It's not a lot to go on.' I could hear from his voice that Adam was frowning. Doubt and mistrust vibrated through the silence after he spoke. I bit my lip, holding back what I really wanted to say.

Can't you just do what I ask, for once?

'I mean, that's part of the problem, isn't it? I don't know anything about him. I saw him after the scaffolding nearly fell on me, and then at the self-defence class. What if he's involved?'

'A coincidence? They do happen. If he lives or works near you, it's not all that strange for him to turn up at this class.'

'I don't think it is a coincidence, actually.' I sounded sharp, on edge. It wasn't all that unusual to have irate phone conversations at court but I caught an enquiring look from a small round grey-haired barrister who had come into the previously deserted robing room. I turned away to face the window, staring out at the view of a hideous office block that was the best Reading Crown

Court could offer. I lowered my voice. 'He made contact with me the same week Belinda died, and I've seen him at least once and possibly twice since then. I'm just asking you to find out what you can about him so I can be reassured.'

'You could probably find out whatever you need to know from Google.'

'I can't,' I said, summoning up extra patience from somewhere deep within me, 'because I don't know his last name or anything else about him. I did try, but all I've got is his first name and the fact that he helped out with a self-defence course in a church hall. I know you have access to more information than I do so please, could you just see if there's a CRB check on file for him?'

'I could get in trouble.'

I closed my eyes. DS Gold had refused to help too. I was surrounded by police officers and none of them would help me. 'I could die, Adam.'

'Ingrid . . .'

'You know it's true.'

'I just don't see why you've got agitated about him.' The voice of reason.

'I've seen him on the street, more than once, and then he was at this class, I told you.' I didn't want to mention the Temple because I wasn't sure about it. I wasn't sure about *anything*.

'Would he have known you were going to be there?'

'I don't think so. It was a drop-in thing. Casual.' I rubbed my forehead with the heel of my hand.

'Okay. How did he react when he saw you?'

'Honestly, he seemed shocked. I thought he didn't want

me to be there. But that could have been what he wanted me to think.'

'Where was this class? They'd have his details on file, so you can find out his last name from them.'

'I don't think that's going to work. The woman who was teaching said he was a friend who was helping out. I had the impression it was kind of an informal arrangement.'

'That's frustrating,' Adam observed. Understatement of the year.

'What if he's the one who put the devices in my flat? What if he was the one listening to me?'

'Ingrid, that is a massive leap.'

I stared out of the window at the ugly office and wished I worked there, putting in my hours from nine to five and going home to an ordinary, quiet little life that didn't involve being around sociopaths. 'Look, I have to go, Adam. Can I count on you to find out what you can about this Ben?'

'I'll see what I can do.' He hesitated. 'If you want any tips on self-defence, you know I can show you a couple of things.'

'I'll bear that in mind.'

I used the ten minutes left before my hearing to look up the number for the church, phone them, and run into the implacable obstacle of the lady who worked in the office.

'No, I cannot give you Kate's phone number. I wouldn't give people's numbers out to someone who calls up asking. You could be anyone.'

I had explained exactly who I was, but she was right. I balled my hand into a fist and punched the window lightly. 'Well, that's completely understandable. Could you give her my number and ask her to call me?'

She lacked charm but the church lady was efficiency personified. My phone rang as soon as I switched it back on after my hearing and I recognised Kate's clear voice.

'Máire at the church told me you were looking for me. How are you today?'

'I'm okay. First of all, I wanted to apologise for running out like that last night.'

'That happens more often than you'd think. It's not easy to get through a whole class when it's your first time. I hope you'll come back next time.'

'I'd like that. It was a great class.' I gathered my courage. 'The other reason I wanted to talk to you was because I wanted to ask you something in confidence.'

'Go for it.'

'It's about Ben.'

'Ben?' She sounded surprised. 'What do you want to know?'

'Well, you said he was a friend. How well do you know him?'

'Fairly well.' A note of wariness had entered her voice. 'Why?'

'Look, I have my reasons for wanting to find out more about him. I can't really put it into words for you. All I can say is that there's something about him that bothers me. It's probably very unfair of me but I'm on edge at the moment and he's not helping.'

'Okay,' she said slowly. 'Well, I'm not going to tell you to ignore your instincts, Ingrid. That would go against everything I was trying to teach you last night. If there's something that bothers you about him, I'm not going to argue with you. But for me, personally, I don't see him as a threat, and I've never heard that from anyone else who knows him. I wouldn't have asked him to help out with the class last night if I'd had any concerns.'

'And you asked him to come along? He didn't ask you?'

'I asked him. At the last minute, too.'

I felt very slightly reassured by that. Maybe he hadn't been feigning his surprise after all. 'How do you know him, Kate?'

'He's a friend of a friend.'

'Do you know his last name?'

'Um . . .' she was thinking about it. 'No. I suppose I don't.'

'Do you know where he works?'

'No.' Kate groaned at herself. 'I'm sorry, I'm not being much help, am I? I know you're scared, Ingrid. I can see it in you. I don't know why, but I'm sure you have your reasons.'

'I am scared,' I admitted. 'All the time.'

'Come back to class,' Kate said. 'Let me help you. And keep listening to your instincts. They'll tell you who to trust and who to avoid.'

There wasn't much point in having instincts, I mused, if you were going to ignore them completely. I leaned on the river wall beside Hungerford Bridge and watched the reflection of the lights rippling in the inky water. It was a busy Saturday night and the restaurants of the South Bank were thronged, with long, good-tempered queues stretching outside them. People strolled up and down the paved promenade that ran along by the river, holding hands, or jogged past with intent faces, or stopped to laugh at the street entertainers that were performing for their pleasure. Across the water St Paul's held its own among the spiky skyscrapers of the City, floating on the skyline like a bubble. A breeze made something rattle over my head and I glanced up to see fairy lights swinging in the bare branches. They twinkled prettily but they did nothing to lift my spirits.

'Ingrid.'

I jumped, one hand to my chest, and glowered at the man standing beside me.

'Christ. There's no need to sneak up on me.'

'I didn't sneak. You weren't paying attention.'

'I was looking at the view.'

Webster turned his back to the river as if the very idea of the view offended him, burying his hands in his pockets. 'This doesn't strike me as your sort of place, Ingrid. Much too busy and noisy.'

'You're right about that. I didn't want to meet you anywhere I like spending time.'

He winced. 'Bitchy.'

'You can't be surprised.'

'Don't you know that's why I like you, Ingrid? You're always surprising.'

'Let's not bother with that tonight.' I hugged myself. 'What have you got for me?'

'Nothing.'

'*Nothing?* But you said—'

'I said I'd found out something interesting about this Ben. And that's what's interesting. I haven't been able to find a trace of his existence under the name I got from the church lady, Ben Sampson. Incidentally, she was a sweetheart, not a dragon. I had her purring at me.'

'Well, that's your thing, isn't it? Old ladies. They love you, and then you inherit their estate when they tragically die of natural causes.'

He pulled a face. 'I make them happy, Ingrid. Their last months on earth are wonderful instead of isolated and miserable. Isn't that something to prize?'

'One day, someone will catch you for it.'

'Catch me for what? You said it yourself, when they die it's of natural causes. They're lonely people who want to make a connection and are grateful for the happiness I can give them, unlike you.' He banged his hand on the wall. 'Look, we're not here to talk about me. We're here because of *Ben*.'

'Why do you say it like that?'

'Because I'm willing to bet it's not his real name.' He shrugged. 'There's nothing there. Nothing to tell you. For the last few years Ben Sampson wasn't spending money and he wasn't travelling and he wasn't anywhere I could find him. And if I can't find you, you're hiding somewhere very hard to reach indeed.'

'Could he have been in prison?'

'That's a possibility.' Webster nodded. 'I'd thought of that. I did speak to a couple of people, but I couldn't trace him. If he was there, I could easily have missed him.'

'Right,' I said blankly.

'The other possibility is that he's not who he says he is.'

'Speaking from experience?'

'Always.' He grinned lazily. 'That's why I'm here, isn't it?'

'You're here because I had no one else to ask.'

'What about Adam?'

'He said no.'

Webster looked pained, his smile evaporating. 'You asked him first.'

'Of course. If you have a tame police officer, you make use of them.'

'Is that the only reason?' He nudged me lightly with his elbow and I drew back, repelled by him. 'I think you like Detective Constable Nash. I think you're starting to like him quite a lot.'

'Leave him alone, John. I don't need to worry about his safety when I should be concentrating on my own.'

'I won't touch him.' He was looking away from me though, and I didn't trust him at all. God, I would have to warn Adam to be careful, and tell him why, and the thought of *that* conversation brought heat to my cheeks.

'This Ben.' Webster was suddenly serious. 'Be careful around him, Ingrid.'

'You of all people don't get to say that.'

'I know, it's ironic. But I mean it.' For once I thought Webster was being sincere, and that was unusual enough to make me listen. 'People with no background are usually hiding something.'

'Why would you, of all people, want to save me when you put so much effort into destroying me?'

'I've only ever tried to help you, Ingrid.' He smiled at me. 'It was my way of saying thank you for all you did for me. You were better off without Mark. I think you know that now.'

The lights of the South Bank blurred and dipped as tears flooded into my eyes, for Mark, and for all I had lost. I turned and walked away from him, threading a path through the crowds, and I didn't look back.

25

Throughout all of this I was still working, in part because it was practically impossible to take time off at short notice, and in part because I wanted to. My best and only weapon against constant, crippling fear was defiance. Besides, these were my cases. I didn't want to give them to anyone else.

When I was in court, I was safe, and I could concentrate on just doing my job. On the way home, I remembered to be scared. When I had to use the Underground I got in the habit of standing with my back to the tiled walls of the platforms, letting the crowds surge onto the train before I moved forward to board. I had never been a fan of waiting with my toes touching the yellow line but now I hung back, eyeing my fellow travellers with more than ordinary big-city suspicion. Train stations were as bad: big, windy platforms made me feel exposed. Every time a fast train charged through without stopping I felt a shudder of fear. One quick nudge and I could be under the wheels. I was glad when hearings were over early, allowing me to travel at quieter times, avoiding rush hour and the dark. I knew that fear was having an effect on me despite my best efforts, but stubbornly, blindly, I kept doing what I had to do.

It was Tuesday lunchtime when I made a post-court trip into chambers to drop off some files and check my desk. The day was cold and bright and the buildings in central London looked like cardboard cut-outs stuck against the dark blue of the clear sky. If I didn't dawdle in chambers, I could be back in the flat before sunset, I thought, checking my watch for the hundredth time. Sunset was at four in the afternoon on these short December days, and getting earlier all the time. At home I would be locked away again, safe – but at what cost to my sanity? I had to avoid thinking of it as a prison, I reminded myself – it was where I was safest, especially now that I'd invested in a deadbolt to back up the new lock. The handyman had also replaced the smoke alarm, bemused to be asked to do it when it was working perfectly. I hadn't explained. The flat was as secure and private as I could make it, and it was the only safe place I had.

Before I ducked in through the gate that led to Inner Temple Lane, I twisted to inspect the pedestrians who had been walking behind me on Fleet Street. Blank, uninterested faces. No one I recognised. The knot in my stomach eased a fraction, so that – for a moment – I almost felt normal.

But I would be afraid for the rest of my life unless I found out who was behind Belinda and Vicki's deaths. It was like my job. I won or I lost.

I couldn't allow myself to lose.

The narrow lane wound down towards the square outside Temple Church, one of my favourite places in London. One side of the square was the back of Inner Temple Hall; another was a colonnade that had been stolen wholesale from Italian classic architecture. The third side was occupied by the venerable Temple Church that crouched there like a dozing round-headed cat, self-contained and inscrutable. It was usually busy with tourists trying to come to terms with its tremendous antiquity – and in fairness, even I struggled to imagine what life could have been like in 1185 when it was originally founded. Today a wooden sign outside advised that the church was closed to visitors because of a memorial service. I glanced through the open door as I passed and saw a barrister I knew quite well standing just inside the church. His face was grim as he looked around him; he must be there to pay his respects, I thought. It occurred to me with a chill of fear that the memorial service might be for someone I knew.

I sidled past the sign and stepped into the church. The thunder of the organ drowned out the sound of conversation, but the pews were packed: dark coats shoulder to shoulder all the way to the altar. At the front of the church, a woman in a very well-cut black dress was standing with two men who looked as if they were in their early twenties, all three with grave faces. The family, I deduced.

My barrister friend was still standing where I'd seen him first.

'Peter.' I murmured it but he jumped. He was the sort of tall, thin man who lived in a constant state of anxiety; he was five years older than me and had looked as if he was fifty ever since I'd known him.

'Ingrid! Haven't seen you in ages.'

'I've been busy. What are you doing here? Whose memorial is it?'

'Judge Canterville.'

'Ron Canterville? The one who sat at Guildford?'

'That's the one.'

'He *died*?'

Peter nodded. 'A couple of months ago.'

Judge Canterville had been young for a judge – in his mid-fifties – and fit. The last time I'd seen him, he had been sporting a fine tan from a skiing trip to Canada. I turned to look at the family. Now that I knew who their father was, I could see that both of his sons resembled him. They had the same square jaw and prominent nose. 'What happened? Was he ill?'

'Accident,' Peter whispered, and winced as someone in the nearest pew turned to glare.

I nudged him and pointed to the side of the church where there were seats more or less behind a pillar. He darted over to them, relieved to be out of sight. I followed more slowly, scanning the nave for anyone I knew, out of habit. There were plenty of familiar faces in the congregation. As barristers we spent our lives shuttling around from one court to another, opposing one another, and there weren't all that many of us; it was quite normal to see the same people over and over again. At a glance I saw a handful of former opponents, bar-school acquaintances, a QC who interviewed me for a pupillage I did not in fact get, several judges and a few people from my own chambers, including Karen Odili. No one jarring; no one out of place. It was safe to pay my respects.

I sat beside Peter, who seemed more relaxed now we

were tucked away. The organist spiralled through a succession of flourishes, outdoing Elgar in a way that was very helpful for those of us who wanted to chat.

'You were saying it was an accident,' I prompted.

'He was out jogging very early on a Sunday morning near his house. Apparently he was training for the marathon, so he had gone out before dawn. He fell down a slope. Cracked his skull on a tree.'

'Where was this?'

'Oxshott Woods. Have you ever been there?'

I shook my head.

'Where he fell was pretty dense woodland. They didn't find him straight away.'

'I had no idea,' I said blankly. 'I always liked him.'

Peter nodded. 'Big loss to the judiciary. He could be scary but he was generally fair.'

'He was nice to me. Mind you, that was the only time I was in front of him for a trial and I had a leader so I didn't have to worry too much about him being scary . . .'

I trailed off, horrified. At the same moment the organist began to play a different piece that heralded the arrival of the choir, and the start of the service. They processed in past us, solemn in their cassocks, the choir boys with faces as angelic as their voices. The music soared, filling the vaulted ceiling over my head as I stood up automatically along with the rest of the congregation. I wasn't really hearing any of it.

What had I just said?

'We have come together in this church to give thanks for the life of His Honour Judge Ronald Canterville,' the vicar intoned. 'We join our prayers with those of all who miss him and who mourn for him.'

I bowed my head as the fine words of the service echoed around me, half-hearing the familiar phrases *(. . . I am the Resurrection and the Life . . .)* while my mind raced *(. . . neither death, nor life, nor angels, nor principalities, nor powers, nor things present, nor things to come . . .)* because although Judge Canterville's death could have been an accident *(. . . blessed are the dead . . .)* there was a chance that it was nothing of the kind.

(. . . deliver us from evil . . .)

The trial I had done in front of Judge Canterville was the trial that Belinda and I had done together. The trial we had won.

Belinda.

The judge.

Vicki, in my place.

Someone was picking us off, one by one.

Someone who made John Webster look as innocent as one of the choir boys in the Temple Church.

From: Durbs@mailmeforfree.com
To: 4102, IATL

She was at the service. I saw her there.

From: 4102@freeinternetmail.com
To: Durbs, IATL

How did she look?

From: Durbs@mailmeforfree.com
To: 4102, IATL

Terrible ☺

From: 4102@freeinternetmail.com
To: Durbs, IATL

Good.

From: Durbs@mailmeforfree.com
To: 4102, IATL

Do you think she's worked it out yet?

From: IATL@internetforyou.com
To: Durbs, 4102

If she hasn't she will.

Don't underestimate her.

From: Durbs@mailmeforfree.com
To: 4102, IATL

Yes, sir!

26

In ordinary circumstances I would never have wanted to meet Hugh Hardwick for a drink. There were solicitors I got on with as friends and solicitors I viewed purely as a means to the end of getting work, and Hugh was in the second category. He was tall and thin, with hawkish good looks, but the puffy bags under his eyes made him look mildly dissolute. He had a perpetually jaded expression that was an accurate reflection of his personality. I knew lots of women thought him attractive, that he was good at his job, and that his clients found his aggression and cynicism to be reassuring, but I didn't enjoy his company and I worried that he was well aware of that. Still, he had agreed to see me once he was finished in court, and I found him waiting for me in the Viaduct Tavern near the Old Bailey. I felt my stress levels rise as I stepped into the ornate pub, shaking the rain off my coat, and saw him hunched over a pint like a heron by a pond. I would have preferred to get there first.

The Viaduct was a classic Victorian drinkery, gilded and embossed to within an inch of its life, with a bar as solid as an altar and small booths around the walls. That was why I had chosen it. I wanted as much privacy as I could get for this conversation.

I hurried across to the booth where he was sitting. He looked up at the sound of my heels on the worn wooden floorboards, and treated me to a heavy-lidded glower.

'Sorry I'm late,' I said, knowing I wasn't.

'I was early.' He gestured across the table. 'You know Niall Hyde, don't you?'

Fuck. I hadn't noticed the big Scottish solicitor was there, leaning back in the corner of the booth. He raised a shovel of a hand in a salute.

'Good to see you, Ingrid. How are things?'

'Fine.' I said it a shade too brightly and he laughed.

'Don't worry. I'm not staying. If you want a private word with Hugh here' – he broke off to wink – 'I'm not going to get in the way.'

Niall was a huge gossip and if I looked as if I wanted to get rid of him, he would be even more intrigued.

'Not at all,' I said briskly. 'Can I get you both a drink?'

'Another of these please.' Hugh looked past me and waved his glass at the barman, who set about pulling him a pint of bitter.

'Nothing for me, thanks, Ingrid. I'm supposed to be cutting down.' Niall looked ruefully at the empty pint glass in front of him, the inside lacy with froth. 'Easy for the doctor to tell you to stop but you need to unwind, don't you?'

'They try to ban everything that's fun.' Hugh tipped the remainder of his pint down his throat.

'Anyway, I can't stay.' Niall began to heave himself along the bench. 'I do need to get home. I won't play gooseberry.'

'It's work-related,' I said thinly.

Hugh looked pained and not a little bored, though I couldn't tell if it was because of Niall's heavy banter, or what I'd said, or just because that was his default setting. Why couldn't it have been Niall I needed to talk to? It would have been so much easier.

I went to the bar to order a glass of wine for myself and pay for Hugh's pint. The barman had been staring out at the street, waiting for customers. The bar was still quiet, the post-work crowd not yet unleashed. Court finished a long time before everyone else's working day ended, and it was something I'd counted on so I could talk to Hugh in peace.

Niall barrelled out of the pub with a cheerful wave to me and I wondered what he and Hugh had talked about before I arrived. The legal world wasn't exactly on message about equality and sexism. There was also the fact, I recalled, that Hugh had just been divorced for the third time. Suspicion and embarrassment prickled my skin like heat rash. As if I would swoop in as soon as he was technically single . . . As if I would even be *interested* . . . He was far too old for me and he and Niall should both know that . . . I straightened my back and reached for court-level composure. I was here because it was important to warn Hugh, and to find out what he knew at the same time, and if I incurred a little embarrassment along the way, that was the price I had to pay.

'So what's this thing you can't talk about over the phone?' Hugh asked as soon as I returned with the drinks.

He had taken Niall's place in the booth, leaving me to perch on the stool on the other side of the small table.

'Do you remember Guy Lanesbury?'

His eyes went opaque for a moment as he thought about it. 'The student.'

'That's the one.'

'When was that?'

'Four years ago.' I gulped some wine and managed not to wince as it scoured the surface of my tongue. 'I was the junior.'

'The joys of privately paid work.' He frowned at his pint as if it displeased him. 'I can't remember now why we needed a junior for a three-day trial.'

'There was a lot of disclosure to work through. Phone records and emails and text messages. Social media posts.'

The frown cleared. 'That's right. You did a good job, I remember. The jury didn't take long to acquit him, quite rightly in my view. If you want a reference—'

'That's not why I'm here.'

His eyebrows went up again – really, he had a most expressive face, I thought, and maybe that was part of his charm. 'Do go on.'

'My leader on that trial was Belinda Grey.'

'Ah, poor Belinda.'

'You know what happened to her.'

He shrugged. 'Of course. It was a dreadful shock. I knew her well. She was a favourite of mine. Always prepared, never slapdash, good with clients and families.'

'She was an excellent barrister. A good example.'

He adjusted the coaster under his glass, not looking at me. 'And you are interested in taking on some of her work?'

'No. No, that's not it. Not at all.' My face was hot; he really had a low opinion of me. Moreover, he was busy assuming I didn't have anything important to say. Well, persuading people to listen to me was my actual job. I leaned forward, my elbows on the table, and said, 'Have you noticed anything weird in the last couple of months?'

'Define weird.'

'Have you had any accidents? Or come close to having an accident? Have you felt as if you were being followed?'

He looked surprised and then, to my despair, amused. 'Ingrid, I don't think—'

'I was in the Old Bailey the day that Belinda died. I don't think that what happened to her was an accident.'

Hugh took a moment before he answered, tapping out a rhythm on the small table with his long fingers. He had beautiful hands, straight out of a Renaissance portrait. 'What do the police think?'

'I don't know,' I said. 'They were inclined to agree with me, but then they changed their minds. Her death was ruled to be accidental at the inquest. I think everyone thought I was paranoid.'

Hugh took a long, slow swallow from his glass to avoid making any kind of comment but I could read his thoughts quite clearly: *I'm inclined to think the same.*

'The police had wound up the investigation into Belinda's death, and then someone broke into my flat and killed a friend of mine. She wasn't supposed to be there.' I remembered Webster's comment on the empty knife rack. 'It might have been a spur-of-the-moment thing. They panicked. Or they might have been planning to kill me, just like they killed Belinda. I mean, I thought that maybe Belinda had been killed in my place because she had my umbrella and it was pouring rain and you know, we all look alike in our court suits, don't we? And I've had my share of problems with a client stalking me. But then Vicki died, and then I saw about Judge Canterville, and I realised what the connection was—' I was aware that my words had been getting faster and faster, tumbling out. I managed to stop myself as Hugh held up a hand.

'Hold on. I'm lost. How does Ron Canterville fit into this?'

'Guy Lanesbury's trial. He was the judge – he sat at Isleworth before he moved to Guildford full-time. Belinda was my leader, defending Guy. You were the solicitor. Two of us are dead, one of us is terrified. So I want to know if anything has happened to you.'

He shook his head. 'Go back to the beginning, please. I'm not following.'

With an effort, and with the help of another gulp of the oily, harsh-edged wine, I went back to the beginning and led Hugh through what had happened over the previous weeks as if he was a particularly thick juror. He listened with intense concentration, probing at the weak points of the story, pushing me for evidence that there was anything sinister going on – anything beyond a series of tragic coincidences.

'I can't prove it,' I said at last. 'If I had proof of what was going on, I would know who had done it. As it is, I'm watching the street behind you in case I can spot a threat. I'm scared, all the time.'

'I'm not surprised.'

'You're not?' I felt jolted that he believed me. I would almost have preferred a pat on the head for making up stories. But Hugh looked serious.

'I'll pay more attention to what's going on around me, I promise.'

'You think it's worth being worried.'

'Of course.' He frowned. 'That Lanesbury case. I know we won, but it was unpleasant, wasn't it?'

'At times,' I admitted.

'It's possible that the verdict didn't satisfy everyone.'

'I'm sure it didn't.' I took a deep breath. 'That's why I have a favour to ask.'

'How can I help?'

'Names. I don't have a detailed record of that case. I didn't keep my notes – Belinda did. I can't ask her widower if he'd mind digging through her papers. I know you'll have records.'

'Of what?'

'The case. The people who were involved in it. Witnesses. Police. The families.' I glanced up with a start as the door swung open and a couple came in, laughing. They looked as if they didn't have a worry between them. 'I don't know what I'm looking for, Hugh. If it is connected with Guy's trial, I should probably warn him and his family that someone is picking us off one by one.'

He was watching me. 'And if it's not?'

'Then I have to keep looking.'

27

IN THE CROWN COURT
AT ISLEWORTH

No. T20165344/T20164512

36 Ridgeway Road
Isleworth
London

6 APRIL 2015

Before: THE HONOURABLE MR JUSTICE CANTERVILLE

REGINA

-V-

GUY LANESBURY

MISS S ALLEN appeared on behalf of the
prosecution

MISS B GREY QC leading MISS I LEWIS appeared on behalf of the defendant, GUY LANESBURY

THE EVIDENCE OF LISA MULLER

LISA MULLER, SWORN
Examined in chief by MISS ALLEN by video link

Q. Please tell the court your full name.
A. Lisa Vivian Muller.

Q. Thank you very much. Now, I want to ask you about last year, and the events of the night of 17 October. What did you do that night?
A. I went out with a group of friends.

Q. And why did you go out?
A. To celebrate my nineteenth birthday.

Q. I see. And how many were in this group?
A. There were eight of us. The booking in the restaurant was for eight.

Q. And what restaurant was that?
A. A little Cambodian place near the British Museum. I don't remember the name. It was tiny.

Q. And who was there? Friends of yours?
A. Yes. Other students. There were four other girls and three guys.

Q. And you knew them all well?

A. Pretty well. One of the guys was someone's boyfriend from home and I didn't know him.

Q. What did you do after dinner?

A. We went to a couple of pubs. Three, I think.

Q. Were you drinking alcohol?

MR JUSTICE CANTERVILLE: You need to say yes or no, Miss Muller, rather than nodding or shaking your head.

A. Yes, then.

MISS ALLEN: Did you have a lot to drink?

A. I think so. I don't know how much. People were buying drinks for me. Lining them up. I don't drink that much usually. I got sick in the third pub. We had to leave.

Q. Where did you go then?

A. Someone got us into one of the UCL student bars. We stayed there for a bit, until it closed. Then we went and had some more food. Kebabs.

Q. Did you eat anything?

A. I had a Diet Coke.

Q. Did you buy it yourself?

A. No. He bought it for me.

Q. Who is 'he'?
A. Guy.

Q. The defendant, Guy Lanesbury.
A. Yes.

Q. And what happened then?
A. We went back to Guy's flat.

Q. Mr Lanesbury.
A. Yes.

Q. Who went to Mr Lanesbury's flat? All of you
who had gone to dinner?
A. No. There were five of us. Me and Guy, and
my best friends Umi and Tess, and someone
called Robert who I didn't know that well.
I think he was a friend of Guy's.

Q. What happened at the flat?
A. We had a couple of drinks. Robert wanted
to skin up and Guy wouldn't let him. He
ended up throwing him out.

Q. Mr Lanesbury, the defendant, threw Robert
out.
A. Yes. And then Umi was falling asleep so
Tess took her home.

Q. And you stayed.
A. I wasn't in a fit state to go anywhere. I
was pretty out of it.

Q. Why was that?

A. I had had too much to drink.

Q. Had you taken anything else that might have intoxicated you?

A. Not to my knowledge at the time but afterwards I wondered if someone had spiked my drink. I didn't remember everything that happened that night and it was the first time I'd ever experienced that.

Q. Did you have any other symptoms?

A. Yes, I found it hard to walk. That was why I didn't leave with my friends.

Q. Did you stay the night?

A. Yes.

Q. Did you sleep?

A. Yes.

Q. Where did you sleep?

A. In Guy's — the defendant's bedroom. He had flatmates and I didn't want to sleep on the sofa in their sitting room.

Q. So who was in the flat at this stage?

A. Me and Guy and two other men. I think one was called Nolan and the other was Wilf. I don't know if those are nicknames, sorry.

Q. That's all right. So were Wilf and Nolan with you?

A. They were, like, chilling in the kitchen and waiting for us to get out of the way. So then Guy and I went to his room.

Q. And can we talk about the layout of the flat for a moment. I wonder if you could look at a floorplan from the exhibit bundle you've got.

This is in your jury bundle, members of the jury, behind divider two.

So just give yourself a minute to get your bearings. This is the flat at Pollock Road where Mr Lanesbury lived. Can you show us where the sitting room was?

A. Yes, here.

Q. And the kitchen was beside it?

A. Yes. With a gap in the wall. Like a serving hatch. We could see the guys in the kitchen from the waist to mid-chest and they could see us if they bent down.

Q. And can you indicate Mr Lanesbury's bedroom?

A. Right at the end of the corridor on the other side.

Q. So quite far from the common areas of the flat.

A. Yes. The bathroom was opposite him. There was a storage cupboard next to his room and

247

then Wilf's room and then Nolan's. That's on one side of the hall. The other side is the kitchen, living room and bathroom.

Q. Thank you. So once you went to Mr Lanesbury's room you were further away from the others.
A. Yes.

Q. It was more private.
A. Yes.

Q. Who suggested you should move to the bedroom?
A. I don't recall.

Q. And did Mr Lanesbury come with you?
A. Yes. He carried me.

Q. Carried you?
A. I was very sleepy and my legs weren't working properly.

Q. Did you want to go to his room?
A. I — I didn't mind.

Q. Did he sleep in the same room?
A. Yes.

Q. And where were you sleeping?
A. In his bed.

Q. With him?

A. He got in beside me after I got in.

Q. Did you undress?

A. I took off my dress and my tights. I had a
    hole in my tights and it was cutting into
    my big toe.

Q. Did he undress?

A. I don't know. I don't remember.

Q. And did you kiss?

A. Yes.

MR JUSTICE CANTERVILLE: I know this is diffi-
    cult but please speak clearly, Miss Muller,
    and speak up. The audio on the video link
    is not as clear as I would wish and the jury
    need to be able to hear you.

A. Yes.

MISS ALLEN: Did you engage in any other
    sexual activity?

A. I don't think so. We kissed a little and
    talked. He smoked a cigarette. I fell asleep.

Q. What happened then?

A. The next thing I remember is waking up. I was
    on my front, face down. He was behind me.

Q. Was he lying down?

A. No. He was kneeling, I think. He had pulled
    me up so I was on my knees, folded over.

249

Q. What were you wearing at this point?

A. My bra and knickers, but he had pulled my knickers down to below my knees.

Q. And what was he doing?

A. He had put his penis in my vagina. He was raping me.

Q. Had you consented to sex?

A. No.

Q. Did you then consent to sex?

A. No.

Q. Did you react in any way?

A. I froze. I was terrified. He was on top of me, and he's a lot bigger than me. I was still groggy, and I was scared, and I just — I just wanted it to be over.

Q. Did you say anything?

A. I remember moaning. I wanted him to realise I was awake, so he would stop, but I was afraid to react in case I made him angry. He wasn't being rough, exactly, but I was afraid he would really hurt me if I tried to make him stop.

Q. Did he wear a condom?

A. Yes.

Q. What happened then?

A. He finished. He took the condom off and knotted it. I lay there for a while, keeping still. I couldn't say anything. He didn't say anything to me. Then he got up and went out of the room and I must have passed out again. The next thing I knew it was morning.

Q. Did you see him in the morning?

A. Yes. He was in the room when I woke up.

Q. What was he doing?

A. Getting ready to go out. He had a hockey match, I think. I got my things and I got dressed and left as quickly as I could.

Q. Did you talk to one another?

A. He asked me if I was okay. I said yes. I don't know why I said that. I just wanted to go.

Q. Take a moment, Miss Muller, if you need to.

A. I'm okay.

Q. Did you talk to him about the sexual activity that had taken place?

A. No. I was confused and scared. His flat-mates were awake — I could hear them talking and laughing. I just wanted to get out of there.

Q. Did you contact him after you left?

A. I sent him a message. I thought we should talk about it in a neutral space, somewhere in public. But then I spoke to my friends and a counsellor and I realised that what had happened wasn't okay. I blocked his number so he couldn't call or message me. I unfriended him and blocked him on all my social media accounts.

Q. So did he ever reply to your initial message?

A. Not to my knowledge.

Q. Did you speak to him again?

A. About three weeks later. I saw him in Russell Square, heading for the Underground, so I stopped him and asked him about it. I told him I hadn't given my consent and he'd raped me.

Q. How did he react?

A. He said that wasn't how he remembered it and he was sorry if I was upset.

Q. Take your time.

A. I'm all right. Just — it wasn't a real apology. He just wanted to get rid of me.

Q. Did you try to talk to him again?

A. I unblocked him on Facebook and sent him some messages but he didn't answer them.

Then I went to the police and they advised me not to try to contact him. I complained to the university about him and they suspended him so I didn't have to see him before this trial. Then I dropped out so I wasn't around anyway.

Q. Why did you drop out?
A. It was because of the rape. I couldn't get past it. I couldn't stop thinking about it. I got depressed. Some of my friends weren't that supportive or didn't understand what had happened to me and I lost contact with them. I felt lonely and sad and I couldn't be around people. I tried not to let it ruin my life — I really tried. But it did anyway.

Q. Thank you very much.
MR JUSTICE CANTERVILLE: (to Miss Grey) Unless there is something you would particularly like to ask before we have a break . . .
MISS GREY: No, thank you.
MR JUSTICE CANTERVILLE: So we will take a break there and resume at two o'clock.
A: Thank you.
MR JUSTICE CANTERVILLE: If you have any queries, please ask the witness service.
A: Thank you.
(The witness withdrew)
(Luncheon adjournment)

LISA MULLER
Cross-examined by MISS GREY

Q. Miss Muller, I have to ask you about a
number of things that you mentioned
today. If you find any of my questions
confusing, do ask me to explain further. I
don't want to confuse you.
A. Okay.

Q. We've heard your account of the evening,
of the birthday celebration and the
drinking and so forth, and quite under-
standably, because it was your birthday,
you were drinking quite a lot.
A. Yes.

Q. Was that unusual for you?
A. Um, not really. Maybe it was more than
usual. I don't know.

Q. But on a night out you would usually drink
alcohol.
A. Yes.

Q. Several drinks?
A. Yes.

Q. Until you were experiencing the physical
effects such as loss of balance, nausea,
dizziness, slurred speech, confusion.

254

A. I suppose. I would drink until I felt drunk, if that's what you mean.

Q. Thank you. In your evidence you said that on this particular night it was more than you would usually drink.

A. Yes. Because people were buying me drinks, so I had more than I probably would on an ordinary night.

Q. And as a result of that — or because your drink was spiked — you suffered some memory problems, you said.

A. I remember the main things that happened.

Q. It's the nature of memory loss that you don't know what you have forgotten, though, isn't it?

A. I suppose.

Q. Unless someone tells you what you don't recall.

A. Yes.

Q. Is that what happened on this occasion?

A. I don't remember a few things that happened. Walking back from the kebab shop to the flat. And the other flatmates coming back — I don't remember that. I remember them coming in and laughing at me.

Q. Did you know them, Miss Muller?

A. A bit.

Q. Had you been in a relationship with either of them?

A. N-no.

MISS ALLEN: My Lord, this relates to the alleged victim's sexual history. Do we really need to discuss that in a straight-forward allegation of rape? The issue at hand is consent, not the witness's past behaviour.

MR JUSTICE CANTERVILLE: I'm inclined to think that anything that might positively help the jury is admissible.

MISS GREY: If your Lordship thinks it is inappropriate, I will not pursue it.

MR JUSTICE CANTERVILLE: No, do go on.

MISS GREY: Perhaps I could rephrase the question. Had you been in the flat before?

A. Yes.

Q. With Mr Lanesbury or with one of the other flatmates?

A. One of the others. Nolan.

Q. And did you spend the night there on that occasion?

A. Yes.

Q. And did you sleep in Nolan's bedroom?
A. Yes.

Q. And did you engage in sexual activity with Nolan on that occasion?
A. Yes.

Q. So when he returned to the flat on the night of your birthday, what happened?
A. He made some remarks. I was embarrassed.

Q. Did you want to get away from him?
A. Yes.

Q. Is it correct that Mr Lanesbury suggested calling you a taxi so you could go home?
A. Yes.

Q. And is it correct that you suggested to Mr Lanesbury that you would prefer to stay?
A. Yes. I was tired.

Q. You asked him to take you to his bedroom.
A. Yes, but that was to get away from Nolan and Wilf. They kept whispering and sniggering in the kitchen and making weird remarks that I couldn't understand. I thought Guy was embarrassed, and then I was embarrassed.

Q. I understand. So is it fair to say you wanted to be alone with Mr Lanesbury?

A. At the time.

Q. What about earlier in the evening?

A. I don't know what you mean.

Q. If I can draw your attention to the bundle you have in front of you. This is bundle 4233, my Lord. After the third divider there is a printout of a text message recovered from your phone.

A. Yes.

Q. As you can see, it's dated 18 October 2015 and it was sent at 02.33.

A. Yes.

Q. Could you read out what it says?

A. 'You two can go. I'm staying.'

Q. Who did you send that message to?

A. My friend Tess.

Q. And if I can read out her reply, she said: 'Are you sure?' Can you read out what you replied?

A. 'No cock blocking.'

Q. What did that mean?

A. That I didn't want her to get in my way.

Q. Cock blocking usually means stopping someone from having sex, doesn't it?
A. Yes.

Q. And on this occasion.
A. (inaudible)

MR JUSTICE CANTERVILLE: I'm going to remind you to speak clearly, Miss Muller.
A. It was just a joke.

MISS GREY: It was just a joke between you and Tess.
A. Yes.

Q. But the effect of the messages was that Tess and Umi left you in the flat with Mr Lanesbury, as you wished.
A. Yes.

Q. One other thing that I wanted to raise. You said that Mr Lanesbury wore a condom.
A. Yes. I could feel it and I heard him take it off afterwards.

Q. Where did he get the condom?
A. I — it was actually mine.

Q. Yours.
A. I had it in my bag.

Q. How did Mr Lanesbury know that?

A. I had given it to him when we went into his room.

Q. Given it to him so he could use it during sexual activity with you?

A. I — I don't know. We were talking about it and he said we couldn't have sex because he didn't have a condom and I was messing around and said, I do. I got it out and showed it to him.

Q. And what did he do with it?

A. He put it on the bedside table.

Q. How did you feel?

A. I don't know.

Q. Were you disappointed that he wasn't intending to engage in sexual activity?

A. At that time, maybe.

Q. Did you say something to him of that sort?

A. I think so. I don't remember.

Q. Please refer to the bundle again. After the fourth divider, there's another text message from your phone, sent at 04.12 to your friend Tess. Could you read it out?

A. (inaudible)

Q. Do you want me to read it out?
A. (inaudible)

MR JUSTICE CANTERVILLE: Could you read it, please, Miss Muller.
A. It's hard to read. There are mistakes. Um. 'Nooooo lmp dickkkk. Fuckkkkkk.'

MISS GREY: And what did that mean, Miss Muller?
A. I don't know.

Q. That he wasn't able to sustain an erection?
A. Yes.

Q. Was that the case?
A. That's what he told me.

Q. How did you react?
A. I was upset.

Q. Were you vocally upset?
A. I said something to him. I don't know. I just wanted to go to sleep. (weeping) The whole night was ruined. I just wanted a good night for my birthday.

Q. How long were you asleep before you woke up to find Mr Lanesbury engaging in sexual activity with you?
A. I don't know.

261

Q. Could it have been an hour?
A. I don't know.

Q. Could it have been ten minutes?
A. I don't know. Yes.

MR JUSTICE CANTERVILLE: This isn't a quiz, Miss Grey.

MISS GREY: No, of course not, my Lord. But I think it is relevant to consent if the time that passed was short.

MR JUSTICE CANTERVILLE: In point of fact there is no way for Miss Muller to answer this question. She does not know. Mr Lanesbury may be able to supply further information about the timing if he chooses to give evidence.

MISS GREY: Thank you, my Lord.

MISS GREY: I have almost finished, Miss Muller. I do wish to ask you about one more detail from your evidence. You said that Mr Lanesbury was not rough during the sexual act.

A. He wasn't rough, no.

Q. Did you feel discomfort afterwards?
A. No.

Q. Were you aware of any unusual bleeding?
A. No.

Q. Bruising?
A. No.

Q. Was there a forensic examination of you, physically?
A. No. By the time I spoke to the rape counsellor, too much time had passed.

Q. Why did you talk to the rape counsellor?
A. A friend suggested I should.

Q. Is it the case that you hadn't thought of it as rape until someone told you you should think of it in those terms?
A. Yes.

Q. You were upset about it, though.
A. Yes.

Q. Not because you were sexually assaulted, but because it didn't lead to a proper relationship.
A. No.

Q. My client avoided you, afterwards. Not the act of a gentleman, but not illegal.
A. He wouldn't talk to me at all. He was ashamed of what he'd done.

Q. Did you threaten him when you saw him?
A. I said there would be consequences to his actions.

Q. And that wasn't a threat.

A. No.

Q. But he could have taken it as a threat.

A. I don't know how he took it and actually I don't care. You can't just do what he did to me and walk away as if nothing happened. I wanted him to talk to me afterwards to prove it was all right. I wanted it to be a normal thing that had happened. I wanted it to be the start of something so it wasn't the worst thing that had ever happened to me. I wanted it to be funny, not awful, but the more I talked about it the more I realised it was wrong. It was wrong, and he didn't care.

Q. Thank you.

Miss Allen: I have no further questions.

(The witness withdrew)

28

It was always risky to make any arrangements during the week, even if I was scheduled to be finished in court by mid-morning. Anything could go wrong, from being bumped down the list so your case didn't get on until the afternoon to a brief hearing developing into something far more complicated, as had happened with Ronnie Gilmore. The only reason I agreed to meet Adele for lunch was because I was desperate to see her; I missed her. I felt trapped between John Webster and Adam Nash, both of them vying for control over me and how I thought and what I did. Adele was a voice of sanity on the phone, familiar and blissfully cheerful.

'I just thought because my boss is on holidays we could sneak in a proper lunch, for once. I mean, I don't want to take the piss, but if she's in Bali on a sun lounger she won't mind me having an extra half hour. Work is dead anyway. No one wants to recruit new members of staff in the run-up to Christmas.'

'I'd really like that,' I'd said. 'It's been ages since I've seen you. How's Paul?'

'That's one of the things I need to talk to you about.' All of the good cheer had evaporated from her tone. I bit my lip. Up to his old tricks, I guessed.

'He hasn't proposed, has he?'

'Not exactly. He wants us to start trying for a baby.'

'*What?*'

'He's decided he's broody.' She perked up. 'I mean, it's quite sweet, really. But I've had to go back on the pill because I just don't trust him not to sabotage the condoms.'

'Well, if you don't trust him and he'd lie to you, he definitely sounds like good babyfather material.'

She snort-laughed. 'You see? This is why we need to have lunch.'

The place she picked was a little French restaurant in a back street of Knightsbridge, not too far from her office. I searched for it on the internet: small, intimate, quiet and reverently reviewed for its food.

Good choice, I texted her. **Not our usual kind of place though.**

No – the reason I picked them is because they don't do Christmas lunches. Every other restaurant around here is packed with miserable office workers in party hats, choking down the set menu. It would put you off your goat's cheese and cranberry roulade.

I grinned. Adele often reminded me how lucky I was to be self-employed, enjoying the loose camaraderie of chambers rather than an office with all of its routines and codes.

For once, everything went smoothly in court (Southwark today, by the river) and I had time to drop my work things in chambers before I headed to Knightsbridge. It was a cold, clear day, and I hopped off the bus a few stops early so I could walk there. I arrived with my face flushed from the chill air and the exertion, and the warmth of the restaurant made my skin tingle.

'It's a reservation in the name of Adele Phipps—' I broke off. I had been scanning the small room over the maître d's shoulder in case Adele was there, so I saw Mark getting to his feet, slowly.

'Ah yes, your companion is here already.' The maître d' led me to the small round table in the corner where Mark was standing, and I thanked him automatically as he pulled out the chair for me and slid a menu in front of me. I hadn't taken my eyes off Mark, who sat down opposite me and cleared his throat.

'Now, I know you weren't expecting me—'

'You can say that again.'

'—and I know you don't like surprises, but I wanted to talk to you.'

'That makes a change.'

He winced. 'I didn't handle our last meeting particularly well. It's been bothering me.'

'So you decided to persuade my best friend to lie to me rather than just asking me if I wanted to have lunch.'

'Yes.' He looked down at the table. 'I didn't think you'd say yes.'

'I'd have liked to have a choice about it.' I looked around. 'Really, I should have known. This place is much more your speed than Adele's.'

'I like it here. It's quiet. And no one can see in. That seemed like something you would find reassuring.'

I turned to look and he was right; the window was

267

screened with a half-curtain so passers-by couldn't gawp at us.

'Thank you.'

He shook his head, dismissing it. 'Do you want to order before we talk?'

'I – yes.' I studied the menu, not taking in a word of it. I was still reeling from the shock of finding him there. My first instinct had been to walk out of the restaurant without a backwards glance, but it was not the sort of restaurant where people made scenes.

'Have you decided, Ingrid?'

The waiter was standing next to me, I realised with a start. 'I – no. Yes. Yes, I have.' More or less at random I picked a starter and a main course.

'Will you have wine?' Mark was frowning over the list. 'White?'

'Yes.'

'A bottle?'

'I think we need it.'

He glanced at me with a quick flash of amusement in his eyes that was like the old Mark and I felt myself blush: how easily he could slide past my defences. I watched him as he talked to the waiter about the wine, both of them taking it as seriously as if it was life or death rather than Sancerre or Meursault. When they had reached an agreement, the waiter disappeared.

'This reminds me of the little restaurant we found near the Rialto Bridge,' Mark said. 'I hope the food is good.'

'I'm sure it will be.' I leaned across the table. 'One question. How did you persuade Adele to lie for you?'

'I talked her into it.'

'What did you say?'

He took a moment before he replied.

'That I'm worried about you.'

Oh. I looked down at my hands and took a tiny breath, which was as much as I could manage.

'Adele is on your side, you know. She wants you to be happy.'

'With you?'

'Ingrid, I—' He cleared his throat, embarrassed. 'I just wanted you to know, that's why she lied. She would never do anything to hurt you.'

'No. I know.' I drank some water, concentrating on keeping my hand steady as I lifted the glass. 'What were you planning to talk about that we didn't get to discuss the last time we met?'

'Lots of things.' Mark hesitated. 'How are you getting on with John Webster?'

'Fine.'

'Fine?'

I relented. 'He's on his best behaviour. He's being weirdly helpful actually. He came round to the flat and searched it for me.'

'You let him go through your things?'

'I know. I struggled with it too. But I wasn't on my own with him, and it was worth it. Webster found this bracelet – which I'd managed to lose, incidentally – and three hidden recording devices which the police had somehow missed when they were searching the place after Vicki was killed. It's no wonder they've hit a dead end with the investigation, honestly.'

'Recording devices?' Mark's eyebrows had shot up.

'Yep. He thought they were used to put together the voicemail he played to me.'

'The one you accused me of making.'

I wriggled. 'I asked. I didn't *accuse* you.'

'Go on.'

'I made a couple of phone calls when things had happened, like finding the blood in my bed or the scaffolding accident. I was in a bit of a state, begging for help. I suppose it was easy enough to take out Adam's name and make it look as if I was saying those things to Webster.'

Mark had gone very still. 'Who's Adam?'

'Adam Nash. He's a police officer.'

'Is he investigating Vicki's murder?'

'No. No, he was around before that.'

I stopped talking so the waiter could pour our wine. It was very tempting to knock back the whole glass in one go. 'He was involved in prosecuting Webster the time I represented him. He understands John Webster and what he does. He's been amazingly supportive since all of this started up again.'

Mark turned his wine glass around through ninety degrees, apparently concentrating on it. 'Are you involved with him?'

'N-no. Not exactly. Nothing has happened between us,' I added quickly.

A flick of a glance. 'But it might.'

If I was being honest there had been a handful of moments that made me think something could happen between me and Adam, interspersed with a lot of serious advice and doom-laden warnings. I remembered staring at his mouth on the Underground as we swayed in time to the movement of the train, and the way he had held my arms, and how I felt when I was with him: safe. He was the opposite of Mark in every way, and maybe that was what I needed.

'Mark—'

'You don't need to tell me about it. You're free to see whoever you like. You certainly don't need my permission.' He had withdrawn though, the easy warmth evaporating.

'As I said, nothing has happened. I don't know if it will. He's very professional. I'm work, as far as he's concerned.'

We paused as the waiter set down the starters with a flourish. I had completely forgotten what I ordered. It smelled delicious and I couldn't bring myself to eat any of it.

'So you have this Adam, and you have John Webster, and both of them want to save you.' He gave it an ironic inflection that made me flinch.

'Basically.'

'Both of them want to sleep with you.'

'Well, that's certainly not true.' I lifted something on my fork – a scallop, I thought. 'You can't judge Webster by ordinary standards. That's not what motivates him. Sex is a tool for him, and he uses it to persuade people to do what he wants. I don't think he takes any particular pleasure in it. And he's not capable of being in love. What he wants from me is for me to break my own rules and trample all over my moral code. He wants to see me compromise my own principles.' I put the scallop in my mouth and chewed while I thought. 'And he really enjoys telling me what to do.'

'What does Adam think about you letting John into your flat?'

'He was there.'

Mark's jaw tightened as he took that on board.

271

'But he hates John Webster even more than you do. He thinks Webster is the one who's been harassing me. He wants me to get enough evidence to send him to prison. Beyond that he doesn't want me to spend any time with him.'

'And how do you feel about Webster?'

'It's . . . difficult. I'm still terrified of him. But he's being helpful – more helpful than I expected.'

'To manipulate you.'

'I'm manipulating him.' The wine was delicate and perfectly chilled. 'I know what I'm doing, Mark.'

'I know you do.' He shifted in his seat. 'Look, Ingrid, you're incredibly clever and brave and resourceful. I don't really see why you need this police officer or John Webster to help you find out what's going on when your entire working life is about examining the facts and working out their significance. You can figure this out for yourself. If you need someone to protect you from physical harm, you've always got me. No strings attached. No obligations.'

'That's . . . kind,' I said warily. *The last time you saw me you more or less accused me of arson and murder, and I think you lied to me about your affair with Flora, and I don't know why you want to involve yourself in this, so I'm not altogether convinced, lunch or no lunch.*

He put his hand out and covered mine; I jumped away, rattled by the physical effect he had on me. My skin tingled where he had touched me.

'I don't want you to take risks so you can trap John Webster for me,' Mark said evenly, 'and I don't have an agenda to break you to my will. I just want to make sure you're safe. And you know you can trust me.'

The trouble was, I wasn't sure I could. I watched a bubble climb the side of my water glass, bumping its way to the top, and I didn't answer him one way or the other, then or later.

But some of what he had said stayed with me. Neither Adam nor Webster saw me as capable of working things out on my own. Mark knew me better than either of them.

I thought about it long into the night, and all the next day, and then I made some phone calls.

29

I remembered DC Tara Jones the minute I saw her hurry into the reception at the police station to retrieve me. She was a stunning black woman, tall and elegant, and she favoured bright red lipstick. We had been on opposite sides the last time I'd met her, but she was warm in her greeting.

'It's been a long time, hasn't it?'

'Four years.'

'That's gone quickly.'

She led me into a small meeting room, an anonymous, blue-painted space that vibrated with trauma for me: it was in just such a room that I had stumbled through the terrible things that John Webster had done to me, to just as sympathetic a detective, and where I had tried to help DS Gold work out who killed Vicki.

I snapped back to the present to find Tara waiting patiently.

'Sorry. What did you ask me?'

'I was wondering what I could do for you.' A frown

creased her forehead. 'I was going to ask if you were all right, but it seems like a silly question when I can see you're not.'

'I'm okay.' I tried to smile. 'I'm sorry for bothering you about this. I know it was a long time ago and you might not remember the case particularly.'

'No, I remember it very well.' She grimaced. 'It was a tough case. We had to push the CPS to get it charged in the first place, and then the trial didn't go our way.'

'Juries do tend to give defendants the benefit of the doubt in a case like that.'

'That's what I told Lisa. But it's hard to know that twelve strangers listened to your version of events and decided you were lying. That's why they say it can be more traumatic to go through the court case than to experience the original rape.'

'Why do you think she was so determined to get him charged?'

'It was a fixation for her. I was worried about what would happen to her if we didn't end up getting it to court, I remember that. And then, of course, he was acquitted, which was horrendous. But why do you want to know about that?'

'I'm trying to work out if there's any connection between Lisa and a series of violent attacks on people who were involved in the trial.' I counted them off on my fingers, explaining to a silent and shocked DC Jones about what had happened in the previous couple of months. 'The only thing I can think is that she hasn't got over the case and she's looking for revenge.'

'Well, she definitely hasn't got over the case. She didn't have time. She killed herself six months later.'

275

'She did *what*?'

There was just a hint of satisfaction in the police officer's eyes; my reaction was everything she had wanted. 'When I knew you were coming in to talk to me about this case, I wondered if it was to do with Lisa. She jumped off a motorway bridge on the M4. Got run over by a lorry. It was instant, I gather.'

'Oh my God.' I was genuinely shocked. 'But was it connected to the trial? Or—'

'I can't say it was directly connected – she didn't leave a note or anything – but there's got to be a link. After the trial ended she was in a right state. She did have counselling but she also made a couple of attempts to kill herself. She ended up going into residential care at a private hospital in Windsor. The day they discharged her, she packed up her room, said goodbye to the staff and her friends, left her bags and belongings in an alley behind a café in Windsor and made her way to the motorway. She found a bridge. That was it.'

'How *awful*.'

'She didn't waste any time about it – she was determined. Usually someone spots potential suicides before they can put their plans into action, and they call us. You get people standing on the bridges, watching the cars, trying to talk themselves into jumping. She didn't give anyone a chance to save her.'

'Her poor family. Her dad—'

'Well, he wasn't talking to her at that stage.' Tara Jones leaned back and folded her arms. 'They'd had a big falling out which could have been a factor too.'

'What was that about?'

'He didn't feel that she was trying hard enough to get

better. In fairness to him, he'd remortgaged the family home to pay the fees at the Halliday Hospital. Her family couldn't have done more to support her in practical terms. Maybe the emotional support was a bit lacking here and there.'

'How do you know all of this?'

'I went to the inquest. Her mother asked me to come along. I always got on well with Mrs Muller.'

'That was kind of you.'

She shook her head, dismissing it. 'It was a morning out of my life. But it meant a lot to them. After the inquest they actually sued the hospital for negligence. I thought it was risky but they ended up getting a settlement out of them, so it worked out. I suppose the hospital didn't want word to get out that they'd kicked Lisa out as soon as her parents' money ran out. They didn't tell them she needed to be in a proper mental health facility either. Funny how she was suddenly cured as soon as they'd got everything they could out of the Mullers.'

'Was it a big payout?' I asked.

'I don't know how much it was but it was enough for them to be able to emigrate.'

'Where did they go?'

'Cape Town. He was South African. They'd moved to the UK to bring Lisa up because they thought her life would be better here. They sank everything into her, one way or another, so I was glad they had the money to start a new life for themselves.'

'And are they still there?'

'Yes. They sent me a Christmas card the other day – they always do, and they always invite me to stay with them, but I've never been. They bought a little guesthouse somewhere touristy. You can do whale-watching there. It looks nice.'

'Do they ever mention Lisa? Or coming back to the UK?'

'Lisa was their only child. From what they said, they wanted to get the hell away from the UK and put the whole thing behind them.'

After I'd finished with Tara Jones, I went home and spent some time searching the internet for any reports of Lisa's death. I found a report on the inquest (verdict: suicide) that contained both the date it had happened and the location. Armed with that information I searched again. The single report I found was brutal in its bald statement of the facts.

Woman Dies after Hospital Release

A young woman has died in an incident on the M4 hours after being discharged from hospital in Windsor. The woman, who was 20, had a history of mental illness and self-harm. The incident happened at 5 p.m. on Saturday between junctions 6 and 7 of the M4. Police confirmed her family has been informed, though she hasn't yet been named officially.

A spokesman for the Halliday Hospital said they couldn't comment on individual cases but that it will cooperate fully with any investigation. The Halliday is a private hospital that specialises in mental health problems, eating disorders and addiction. It has been involved in controversy over treatments likened to 'torture' by ex-patients.

Traffic restrictions as a

result of the incident caused travel chaos, with two-mile tailbacks on the M25 near Heathrow and major delays on the M4 until the road was fully reopened around 9 p.m.

Because of course the traffic was the most important aspect of a young woman taking her life. The tone was very much *how dare she inconvenience so many people*.

Poor Lisa, I thought. Poor, poor Lisa. The consequences of her brush with the criminal justice system had been catastrophic. If the outcome of the trial had been different, that might have helped, but it was no guarantee. The trauma was built in to the process.

And I couldn't deny that I had played my part in it too.

30

'Adam. What are you doing here?'

It was halfway through Wednesday afternoon. Of all the people who could have been knocking on my door unexpectedly at that time, Adam was just about the best option, but I was still surprised to find him there.

Are you involved with him? I'd said no, when Mark asked me that, but seeing Adam now made my heart flutter. His hands were shoved in his pockets and his eyes looked troubled.

'I thought I'd come and see you.'

'Okay,' I said slowly. 'Why?'

'I wanted to see how you were.'

'That's kind.'

'You're letting all the warm air out,' Adam observed after a pause.

'If there was any to let out, I would be.'

His gaze slid past me. 'Have I come at a bad time? Have you got company?'

'Not really and no. But . . . well . . .' I gave up on

keeping him out and stepped back. 'Come in and have a look.'

He came in and stopped to survey the table. It was covered in sheets of paper. 'What's all this?'

'I've got some free time because a trial moved. I've been doing some research. Trying to sort out what I know about the Lisa Muller trial.'

'This is basically a wall of mad, isn't it? Except that you haven't stuck it up yet.'

'I don't have enough spare wall to put it anywhere,' I admitted. 'I was just about to start again on the floor.'

'Talk me through it.' He was looking grim. 'Tell me about this rape trial.'

'Guy Lanesbury was our client. He was accused of raping a fellow student, Lisa Muller. She was nineteen and tiny. He was athletic, six foot, handsome, articulate – your classic public-school boy. He looked like an adult but in many ways he was young for his age. They had a night out to celebrate her birthday, along with a group of friends. They wound up back at his flat, in his bed, and at some point during the night there was sexual activity. He said she was fully consenting, she said he raped her. The jury decided there wasn't enough evidence to prove rape, and he was acquitted, which was the right decision. It was impossible to prove.' I paced up and down, circling the table. 'But it took a terrible toll on Lisa. I spoke to the OIC and she told me Lisa killed herself six months later.'

Adam whistled. 'Because of the trial?'

'You'd have to assume that was part of it.'

'And you think this is connected with your present difficulties? I'm not sure it is.' Cold water, incoming. I braced myself. 'The conviction rate is staggeringly low for rape. What you're suggesting is an extreme reaction, to say the least. Why would anyone spend what – four years? – planning revenge? Wouldn't they want to put it all behind them? Especially since she killed herself?'

'You'd think. I read the transcript of her evidence again, and Belinda's cross-examination. It was brutal, Adam. Belinda took her apart, question by question. It wasn't just that she was able to prove she had lied in her initial statements. At the start of her evidence, Lisa looked vulnerable and sweet, and Belinda proved she was no innocent. She had slept with half of their friendship group – girls and boys, as it happened, though that didn't come out at the trial.'

'Not a crime, unless they weren't consenting.'

'No, of course not, but it did play a part in what happened that night. In the beginning, Guy wouldn't tell us much about what went on. It took a long time for him to trust us enough to give us the details. Well, me. He trusted me.'

'Did he?'

'I suppose I was the youngest person on his team. The least threatening.' I paused, remembering him sobbing in the conference room in Garter Buildings, a room that was significantly grander than the one in my chambers. He had sat with his elbows on the table, his hands covering his face, racked with pain and humiliation. It had taken him over an hour to give me his version of events, brief though it was. 'He was a virgin. She wasn't. They were both very drunk and she had her heart set on getting him to have sex with her. I think, for what it's worth, she wanted a real relationship with him, and she'd decided this was the best way to persuade him to go out with her. Between the drunkenness and nerves, he couldn't perform, and she was furious. She said he was weak and pathetic and she was going to tell everyone that he hadn't been able to do it. He was devastated by it, at the time and afterwards. She sent a text message to a friend complaining about him not being able to get it up, so we were able to avoid putting Guy in the box to get that evidence in front of the jury. That was something that probably helped him deal with the trauma of the trial, but it was bad. We were seriously worried about him.'

'So you worried about him. What about Lisa? There are two sides to the story, I should think.'

'Of course, and if I had been putting her side of the case to you I would be telling you about how the events of that night traumatised her. She was genuinely devastated. She had been humiliated in every way. Their peers took sides, as they always do, and because Guy was popular, once she got him suspended from their university she became an outcast. People judged her hard for her behaviour that night and for reporting him to the police. I wonder if she thought about walking away without going through with the trial. I think she thought if he got convicted then everyone would have to accept that she'd done the right thing in getting him suspended. But it broke her.'

'She's still sounding like the victim to me.'

'She was. No one came out of the trial unscathed, believe me. Her dad sat through the whole trial, every day. The evidence was hard for him to hear, but the verdict was worse. He collapsed.' I remembered him, grey and panting as the first-aid-trained police officers hurried to his side and the judge ordered the court to be cleared. 'We won, but I haven't done a rape trial since.'

'I don't know how any of you can.'

'They all deserve a defence.'

'If you say so. But some people need to be locked up.' Adam sighed. 'You've told me this whole story about how he was traumatised and she was mean to him, but the facts of the case are that she was asleep, or passed out, and he screwed her. She simply could not have given consent to that, and you know it.'

'The jury felt—'

'Oh, the *jury*. I bet they didn't know left from right by the time you'd finished confusing them.'

'It wasn't me for the most part, it was Belinda, and all she did was challenge the evidence. I just found the messages that made our defence. And I cross-examined a couple of the witnesses. There wasn't enough evidence for the jury to convict him. It must have felt as if he won and she lost. I felt sorry for her then and I feel sorry for her now. But the trial, and how we handled it – that's irrelevant. The key thing is that it has to be this, Adam. It just has to be. It's the only connection between all of us who have been targeted – Belinda, the judge, me. And the reason no one has put it together before now is because I'm the only person who's aware of all of these things. We have separate investigations into Belinda's death, and the judge's, and poor Vicki. No one would ever connect the three investigations unless they were standing in the centre, like me.'

'You're right.' His face softened. He stepped forward and put his arms around me, drawing me against him. I resisted at first and then relaxed against him. He was whippy rather than muscular, and I could wrap my arms around him, holding him close. He smelled of cold winter air. 'You're not on your own in the centre, though. I'm here with you.'

'Do you think I'm right about this?'

'You might be. Or it could be John Webster trying to make you think it's about this case. Either way, we need to keep you safe.' He was tall enough to rest his chin on top of my head. I felt a sigh stir my hair. 'I can follow it up for you. Would that help?'

I stepped back so I could see his face. 'What would be helpful is if you could find out if the Lanesburys are still at the same address so that I can warn them about what's been going on. And you could contact the Mullers to find out if they're still angry.'

'Absolutely not.'

'But—'

'No, Ingrid, listen to me. I don't know what your plan is, but you can't bother them about their daughter. This was the worst thing that ever happened to them and you mustn't drag it up again. You could get in serious trouble, which I think is Webster's plan. You know he's quite capable of taking a trial and working his way through the people who were on your side, just to make you panic. He would set this kind of thing up in a heartbeat. They are real people with real feelings, and you are not going to blunder into their world with your own issues. You'll upset them, or you'll put yourself in danger and either is unacceptable.'

'So what, then? Will you do anything?'

'I'll make some calls behind the scenes to find the Lanesburys. Warning them might actually be helpful.'

'What else can I do?'

285

'What else have you got?' He was looking at the table.

'This is a list of the court staff who were there – which is a long shot, because most of them are far more cynical than you or I could ever be, and I don't think they would have got fussed about a particular rape trial. Whatever the evidence is, they've always heard worse.'

'Right. Who else?'

'Police.' I tapped the sheaf of paper. 'I spoke to Tara Jones who was the officer in the case. She told me about Lisa's death. I could imagine that the court case and the fallout from it might have upset her.'

His eyebrows drew together. 'And you think she's involved in all of this? A police officer? In *murder*?'

'If she is, she's some actress. I didn't sense any kind of hostility from her. Human nature being what it is, I think she took a certain amount of satisfaction out of being able to tell me what had happened to Lisa, but it didn't feel personal. Anyway, she was in court so she's on the list for now.'

'Okay. And?'

'The witnesses. Lisa had two friends, Tess and Umi. Tess was the one I cross-examined. She'd had text messages from Lisa during the evening and night that helped prove Lisa had intended to sleep with Guy.'

'Anyone else?'

'The CPS lawyer. The opposing barrister who is now Susie Allen QC, so I can't say that losing this trial held her back in any meaningful way. She didn't have a junior. The jury . . .'

'You can't have tracked them down.'

'I haven't and I won't be able to. But they were there.' I pushed my hair back, noticing that it was escaping from

286

its ponytail. 'It wasn't a unanimous verdict, I remembered. It was eleven to one in the end. One of them held out.'

'But you'll never know which one it was.'

'No. It's just a possibility, that's all. I'm putting all the possibilities together and seeing what comes of it.'

'You should do my job.'

It was a joke but I didn't feel like laughing. 'I'm scared, Adam. Someone is trying to kill me – maybe someone on this table, maybe someone I haven't even thought of yet. You can't blame me for doing whatever I can to stay alive, including asking John Webster for help.'

'Okay. Let me help you instead.' He shuffled through the piles of paper. 'You need to cut down on your collection of suspects. This is unmanageable. Get rid of the cops' – Tara went on the floor – 'and the court staff, and the jury, and the legal professionals. Leave the family, I suppose. Add in John Webster. I'd drop the friends – you have no way of tracing them and they'd hardly be able to find you and carry out this kind of sustained harassment and murder.'

'You never know,' I said, watching my stack of suspects dwindle. 'You'd better leave me *someone*.'

'I'm going to add one. You realise you've left someone else out.'

'Who?'

'Your ex.'

'Mark? I don't think . . .' I trailed off. Did he know I'd met Mark for lunch?

Had Mark met me for lunch to find out what I knew?

'You said yourself he was angry with you when you saw him. He had the ability to bug your flat and fake the phone call that brought Webster back to you. He hasn't ever forgiven you for how his life fell apart.'

'But none of that was my fault,' I said. 'It was John Webster who ruined everything.'

'Was it?' Adam had been leaning over the table, looking at my notes. He straightened up and looked at me, reluctance written all over his face. 'I didn't want to say this but after I heard John Webster's account of what happened to your cat I realised I couldn't take what you said at face value. Your version of events was almost true – maybe you even convinced yourself that it was accurate – but it cast him in the worst possible light and it made you look like a victim. He says he helped you and for once I believe him.'

'Really? You believe John Webster and not me?'

'I've been making some calls myself, Ingrid, and I know you've been lying to me. I keep wondering if this is just a huge con and I'm the one being fooled.'

The shock of it hit me like a vast, icy wave, knocking me off balance. 'What do you mean?'

'Why didn't you tell me about Flora Pole?'

'You knew about Flora Pole,' I managed to say.

'I knew she *died*.'

'What else is there to know?'

His mouth tightened. 'What about the little detail that you were arrested for killing her?'

31

Extract from an interview with Ingrid Lewis (IL) conducted by DS Kyle Cooper and DC Phil Roberts. Audio only. No visual. No solicitor present. Miss Lewis is under arrest and under caution.

KC: Right, so you've been arrested because we have some new information that unfortunately puts you in the frame as a suspect.

IL: I find that hard to believe.

KC: And you've waived your right to free and independent legal advice.

IL: I am a lawyer. What is this new information? I must say, I'm looking forward to hearing it.

KC: Let me just take you back to the night of the fire, three nights ago. Can you remember what you were doing that day?'

IL: I've told you this before.

KC: Tell me again.

IL: I was waiting for a jury to come back in Kingston

Crown Court. I was there from nine in the morning until just after four. Then I came back to the house. I got changed. I put a load of washing on. I called my best friend. I think – yes, I booked the car in for a service because I'd driven to Kingston and it was making a weird noise on the way back. A grinding sound. I thought there was something wrong. I rang Mark to ask him if he needed the car later in the week or if I could book it into the garage. He had a dinner to go to – a work thing. That's why I was on my own. Then I had something to eat – beans on toast, if you're wondering – and went out to the local cinema. It must have been half past seven when I left the house.

KC: Did you put the alarm on?'

IL: Yes.

KC: Did you lock the door?

IL: Of course. I checked all the doors. I'm very careful. You know that. I've told you about John Webster and what he's been doing—

KC: Let's just focus on the night in question. What film did you see?

IL: *North by Northwest.* They have a Hitchcock season at the moment.

KC: And what time did you leave?'

IL: I left at twenty to ten.

KC: Did you go straight home?

IL: Yes. I walked.

KC: You weren't scared to walk around late at night.

IL: No, I was. But I don't like taxis or buses either. I'd rather be on the street. That way I can run away.

PR: [inaudible]

KC: Did you want to say something, Robbie?'

PR: No. Sorry. Carry on.

IL: I went back to the house. I saw a fire engine turning into our road just before I got there and I thought, I hope that's nothing to do with us. You know how you always think that . . .

KC: I do.

IL: Well, this time I was dead wrong. I came round the corner and I saw the house.

KC: Did you know it was your house?

IL: I thought it was, but I hoped it wasn't. [crying]

KC: Do you want a minute? Because—

IL: No, but a tissue . . .

KC: Are you okay to keep talking?

IL: Yes.

KC: Let's get back to it. So you saw the house. What else?

IL: Um, the street was busy. There was a cordon. Everyone had come out to look at the fire and the firefighters. The police were keeping the crowd back. I said it was my house and they didn't believe me at first, and then the ones on the cordon let me through and sent me to another police officer. I've forgotten his name.

KC: It's okay, I've got it.

IL: Yes, you would. Sorry. I'm trying to remember.

KC: Take your time.

IL: They asked if there was anyone in the house and I said no, because I thought Mark was out. I told them Mark had a dinner. But then they said that he was there, and that he'd been in the house. I thought – I thought he'd been in the house when it caught fire. I didn't know he'd gone in.

KC: Did you talk to him about why he went in?

IL: Not – not exactly. He said – he was worried. He wanted to see if – if I was there. Or the cat. I think he just – he could see the way the fire was burning, that we would need to get whatever valuables we had. Um. Passports, computers. That kind of thing. My work things. My wig and gown – but actually they were in the car. You can ask him about why he went into the house.

KC: I have.

IL: Oh. Well, I'm just telling you what he told me. And I didn't know where he was. [inaudible] I was – well, I was—

PR: Of course.

IL: And it was a police officer who took me to the ambulance where he was. He had been in the house. He had inhaled smoke. They took him to hospital after that. But he was released a few hours later.

KC: What did he say when he saw you?'

IL: He cried. They'd told him there was a body in the house. He thought it was me.

KC: What did you think?

IL: I thought it might be John Webster. I hoped.

KC: You hoped he burned to death?'

IL: Look, you don't understand.

KC: Explain it to me.

IL: Forget it.

KC: I'd like you to tell me more though.

IL: I just thought if he was burning down our house and he got caught in the fire that would be fair.

KC: Fair?

IL: You have a full account of what John Webster has

been doing. I know you do. That was my initial feeling about the body. And then they said it was a woman and I was upset, as you might imagine.

KC: Why were you upset?

IL: It's an awful way to die.

KC: It is. She was trapped in your bedroom.

IL: [inaudible]

KC: They found her under the bed.

IL: I don't want—

KC: No, I'm sure.

IL: —to think about it. I can imagine it. I knew her. I liked her.

KC: Did you?

IL: I didn't know her very well. She seemed sweet. Young.

KC: How did you meet her?

IL: She's the receptionist at Mark's recording studio.

KC: And what was she doing in your house?

IL: I have no idea. None.

KC: Flora Pole was your husband's employee, wasn't she?

IL: Yes.

KC: She was twenty-three.

IL: Something like that.

KC: Exactly that. Very young.

IL: I don't know how she got into the house. I've been wondering about that.

KC: She let herself in.

IL: How? She couldn't have. She'd never even been in our house before.

KC: I'm going to show you some messages now and I'd like you to read them out loud.

IL: What kind of messages?

KC: Emails.

IL: Okay. This one is addressed to Flora at her company email address and it says 'Please don't wear that skirt to work any more. It's distracting. I want to put my hand up it.' It's not signed. Who sent it?

KC: The messages were from an anonymous email account, but the account comes back to Mark.

IL: Mark? My Mark?

KC: Yes.

IL: That's not possible.

KC: Can you read the next one, please?

IL: It says, 'When I saw you this morning I wanted to bend you over the desk and have you. Do you know how hard it is to behave normally around you? Do you know how hard I was?'

KC: And then read her reply.

IL: Hold on . . .

KC: Okay?

IL: I just – that's a bit— right, I'm okay. This one says 'I wish we could be together. This is driving me insane. I know we can't take the risk of getting caught at work, but I'd do anything to be with you.'

KC: There were other messages from a mobile phone number. We were able to look at both sides of the conversation. I'm going to show you a printout of some of the messages.

IL: Was she sending him pictures?

KC: Yes.

IL: Naked pictures?

KC: For the most part. Very graphic images.

IL: Do you have them?

KC: Yes.

IL: Can I see?

KC: I don't think that's appropriate.

IL: What if it's not her?

KC: It's her. Here's another conversation from four days ago. As you can see, Mark is asking her to come to your house. He gives her the alarm code and tells her he'll leave her a key. Did you buy a ticket to the film that night or earlier in the week?

IL: Earlier in the week.

KC: Did you discuss it with Mark?

IL: Yes.

KC: So he knew you were going out.

IL: Yes.

KC: And he told you he was going to be out.

IL: Yes.

KC: But he arranged to meet Flora in your house.

IL: I – yes. I don't know.

KC: You had no idea about Flora and Mark being in a relationship.

IL: A – no. But I don't call this a relationship. A flirtation, maybe.

KC: It was clearly sexual. The pictures – arranging to meet . . .

IL: What did Mark say about this?

KC: You'll have to ask him.

IL: I don't really want to speak to him.

KC: Are you all right, Miss Lewis?

IL: Yes. No. I'm going to be sick.

KC: Interview suspended at 5.14 p.m.

KC: Interview resumed at 5.29 p.m.

KC: Did you know he was planning to leave you for her?

IL: No comment.
KC: Did you confront her about it?
IL: No comment.
KC: Did you threaten her?
IL: No comment.
KC: Did you know she was going to be at your house that evening?
IL: No comment.
KC: Did you tell her you were going to be out?
IL: No comment.
KC: Did you start the fire?
IL: No comment.
KC: Did you kill Flora Pole?
IL: No comment.

32

The café at the V&A was crowded, as usual at lunchtime during a popular exhibition, and it was with some difficulty that I had managed to get a table for two in the corner of the Morris Room. Having got it, I had to keep it, which was a challenge when all I had was an almost empty cup of coffee and a do-not-fuck-with-me expression on my face. There was no sign of John Webster, half an hour after we had been supposed to meet. It wasn't like him to be late, except that it *was* like him; he would love the idea that I was waiting.

An elderly woman carrying a tray loaded with teapot, cup and saucer and a vast, oozing cream bun stopped beside my table, breathing heavily. 'Could I?' Without waiting for an answer, she began to slide her tray onto the table.

'I'm so sorry,' I said quickly. 'I'm waiting for someone.'

She gave me a filthy look, lifted the tray, and swung away, and everything – the cup, the saucer, the teapot, teaspoon and fork and even the blessed bun – slid a few inches sideways. For a breathless moment I thought they were all going to fall off the tray. There would be a mess, and a fuss, and an endless cleaning-up process involving the staff and reams of absorbent paper . . .

I stood so I could steady the tray, and took it from her.

'Please. Let me help. There's a free table over there, if you don't mind a few crumbs on it.'

'No, that's fine. Or you could find someone to clean it for me.'

Humbly, I accepted that sorting it out to her satisfaction was going to be my job now. But she was elderly, and hot, and probably exhausted by her morning of looking at the exhibition. I should be kind.

I cleaned the table myself, and made sure she had a napkin before I left her to her bun. When I turned to go back to my own table, there was a man in a dark coat sitting in my seat, smiling faintly. He had moved my half-empty cup to one side to make room for the tiny, inky espresso in front of him.

'You're late.' With very bad grace I sat down in the red leather chair opposite Webster, and discovered that it wobbled, because of course it did. 'Where have you been?'

'That's not a very nice way to say hello.'

'Let's not do that.'

'Oh dear. Don't you look glum.' He stuck out his bottom lip in mock sympathy. 'What's happened to you?'

'Nothing,' I snapped. I knew I looked terrible. I hadn't slept the night before, and I hadn't been able to eat anything that day. Seeing Webster made me nervous at the best of times but that wasn't why I had shadows under my eyes and a pallor that was making me look as consumptive as any Victorian artist's model against the ornate backdrop of the Morris Room.

'All right, let's start with an easier question. What's wrong with this beautiful, historic place? Most people love the café at the V&A. They did a whole advertising campaign about it. Are you still keeping to your practice of meeting me in places you don't like or have you forgotten about that?'

'No, I hate it. It's over-crowded and they never have what I want.'

'Which is what?'

'Come on, John. You should know this. Don't tell me you have a gap in your big book of Ingrid facts.'

He beamed, delighted. 'Apparently I do. This is why you're so much fun. There's always something new to learn.'

I shuddered. 'Can we please talk about why I wanted to meet?'

'Of course.'

I told him about the trial and what I had found out about Lisa Muller.

'So what do you want me to do?'

'Find the friends, Umi and Tess. I don't have any information about them, so you might struggle. I don't even have pictures of them. I can describe them to you but it's a long time since I saw them.'

Webster smirked. 'That really won't be a problem.'

'How do you do it? How do you find out anything you want to know?'

He laughed outright. 'Psychology, mainly, and common sense. People are drawn to places they know. I'll find them somewhere they studied, or somewhere they have or had family.'

'It's like witchcraft,' I said.

'People shed information about themselves all the time.

Pick someone in this café and I'll tell you the colour of their front door within twenty-four hours. It's even easier with someone you know. People never change. You can predict what they'll do and how they'll behave. You can use that against them.' He looked smug. 'You think you're making free choices but really the decisions you make are about what you know, and what you find comforting.'

'Are we talking about me now?'

He grinned. 'I'm always thinking about you, Ingrid. Makes sense that you came to mind. I bet you've been looking at the cost of flights to Copenhagen.'

'I— what? How did you know?' I felt my face get hot. 'Have you been spying on me again?'

'No. You want to go and see your dad, don't you, because he makes you feel safe. Not your mum – you don't need her. You need a man. You need someone to make you feel better about the fact that you had a row with Adam Nash.'

I was blushing and I hated it. 'Stop pretending you can work all that out from whether I'm wearing mascara, or pink, or something. You're not Sherlock Holmes – you're a con artist. You are definitely spying on me.'

'Really, I'm not.' He was watching me closely. 'You haven't mentioned him once, you realise. I know he's not helping you because you wouldn't be sitting here with me if he was doing what you wanted.'

I didn't want to admit he was right. I sighed. 'All right. There's one other thing I wanted to ask you to do, but I don't think psychology is going to help. I need to find someone and I don't know anything about him except that he was at Ludgate Circus when Belinda died.'

'What can you tell me about him?'

'He was homeless.' I corrected myself. 'He looked as if he was homeless.'

'What else?'

'He had a limp but it didn't stop him from moving pretty fast when he needed to. He disappeared after Belinda went under the truck. No one saw him go and the police couldn't find him on CCTV or anywhere else. He basically disappeared.'

Webster rolled his eyes which I took as a comment on the shortcomings of the police rather than anything else.

'I was sure he was the one who shoved Belinda under the lorry, but the police were looking for reasons to call it an accident. They didn't see what I saw when they watched the CCTV.'

'What makes you think you're right and they're wrong?'

'I don't know.' I shifted in my seat, restless. 'I just want to find him. I want to know what he knows.'

'Height?'

'About the same as you.'

'Age?'

'I don't know. Twenties or thirties.'

'Build?'

'The same as you.' I chewed my lower lip. Well, he seemed to like that I was being honest with him. I would see how this went down. 'He looked like you. I thought it *was* you when I watched the CCTV first.'

I'd expected him to make some crack about me being on his mind but he frowned. 'That's interesting.'

'Is it?'

Webster considered it for a moment, and it wasn't like him to take time to think. He was usually two steps ahead of me at the very least. At last, he announced, 'I'll find him if you tell me something.'

I fidgeted, hating it. 'Depends on what it is.'

'It's a simple question. What was the row about?'

'What row?'

Webster clicked his tongue. He was genuinely irritated. 'Don't be annoying, Ingrid. Naivety doesn't suit you. The argument you had with DC Nash.'

I took a deep breath. 'Okay. It was your fault.'

'Good. Go on.'

'Adam found out that I was arrested for murdering Flora Pole.'

Webster started to laugh. 'Oh, that's funny. That's really hilarious.'

'I'm glad you're amused.' I leaned across the table and hissed, 'It would really be very helpful if you would just admit that you set fire to my house.'

'And get arrested for arson? Not to mention a little charge of murder?'

'I promise to defend you if you get charged.'

'Oh, that's tempting, but this so much more fun, don't you think.' He sipped his coffee. 'Don't tell me the policeman was shocked.'

'Of course he was. Even though I was only a suspect for a day or so, the fact is that I was arrested, and interviewed, and held in a fucking cell, John. You might be used to that but I certainly wasn't.'

The big detective, bald and hearty, friendly and considerate from the moment he arrested me to the moment he accused me of murder.

'I can imagine. Poor Ingrid. But you talked your way out of it.'

'With difficulty.' I could add that to the long list of things I had never wanted to think about again.

'Well, you shouldn't have killed her.' Webster sipped his espresso again, his expression just short of demure.

'That's not funny, John,' I said. 'Not even a little bit.'

'What's it like for the man of your dreams to think you might have killed someone?'

'Adam isn't the man of my dreams.'

'I was talking about myself.'

I stood up. 'You're sitting on my coat.'

'Oh, come on. Sit down. You're capable of killing if you need to. That's a compliment.'

'But I'm not. Sometimes I wish I could, especially when I'm around you, but I'd never be able to. And you know that.' I sat down again, exhausted.

Webster looked at me fondly. 'She was a stupid girl. Worthless, in comparison to you.'

'I didn't start the fire. I didn't kill her. I was sorry she was dead.'

He leaned across the table. 'You were furious about Mark betraying you.'

'According to him, he's the one who should get all the sympathy. His life was ruined, you realise.'

Webster snorted. 'What a ridiculous man.'

'Yes.' I was fiddling with the teaspoon on my saucer, turning it over and over so I didn't have to look at him. 'It's strange, seeing him again. He's changed. Or I have.'

'Is that so?'

I didn't want to talk to Webster about Mark. I shrugged. 'Anyway, Flora died. Nothing will bring her back. It's not the sort of thing you can forget about.'

'If you'd known she was there, and you'd known there was going to be a fire, would you have warned her?'

'Of course.' I blinked at him, shocked. 'She didn't deserve what happened to her.'

'If you say so.' Webster said it absently though, and I had the sense that his quick mind had moved on to consider something else. He was frowning to himself.

'What is it?'

'You'll find out,' he said. 'In the end.'

It wasn't the most comforting reply he could have given me.

33

From: Durbs@mailmeforfree.com
To: 4102, IATL

Should we be worried?

From: IATL@internetforyou.com
To: Durbs, 4102

No. She thinks she's worked the whole thing out but
she's as lost as ever.

From: Durbs@mailmeforfree.com
To: 4102, IATL

Are you sure about that?

From: IATL@internetforyou.com
To: Durbs, 4102

I was concerned for a while that we were going to lose

control of this but she's come round nicely. She's pathetically easy to fool. And so are the others. They get close to the truth but they never quite get there.

From: Durbs@mailmeforfree.com
To: 4102, IATL

I don't know how you keep a straight face.

From: IATL@internetforyou.com
To: Durbs, 4102

Neither do I. She's got the idea that she can crack this case if she just thinks hard enough.

From: Durbs@mailmeforfree.com
To: 4102, IATL

Stupid bitch.

From: 4102@freeinternetmail.com
To: Durbs, IATL

I don't think we should assume that she's going to stay confused. She's clever. Clever enough to talk her way out of trouble

From: IATL@internetforyou.com
To: Durbs, 4102

No one is assuming anything. She's playing right into our hands.

34

Even though I had told John Webster that Adam and I hadn't argued, and even though that was technically true, somehow I felt tense when I saw him next. He seemed completely normal though when he picked me up outside the main gate of the flat complex on Monday at lunchtime. He was driving a nippy little Golf GTI that snarled and groused through the traffic in central London, then ate up the miles to our destination in Guildford. It didn't surprise me that Adam was a good driver. He was remarkably calm, relaxed to the point of torpor even when he was pushing the speed limit.

'Don't you ever get edgy about driving so fast?' I was clinging to the door handle for dear life.

'I go as fast as I'm allowed to, when it's safe. What is there to be nervous about?'

'Crashing. Dying.'

'Not today. Today I'm being good.'

I sneaked a look at him. It was strange how there were people who were instantly attractive, and others who grew on you over time: Adam was definitely in the latter category. If Adele had been in the car she would have been kicking the back of my seat. *Go on, Ingrid. Don't let this one get away.*

He had sounded excited on the phone when he called to tell me he had found the Lanesburys, and had spoken to them, and had got permission to bring me to see them.

'Thank you for sorting this out,' I said now.

'That's all right.'

'I thought you didn't approve of me contacting the families.'

'The family of the victim.' He tilted his head sideways, anticipating what I was going to say. 'I know. The court decided she wasn't a victim. Anyway, I don't mind you talking to the defendant's family. I'm interested to hear what they have to say about him and what he did.'

'Don't go in there with the wrong attitude,' I warned him. 'We'll get thrown out. He was acquitted.'

'I won't say anything.'

'It's not just about what you say. It's how you look.'

'How I look,' he repeated. 'How do I look?'

I did my best attempt at an Adam Nash glower and he took his eyes off the road to glance at me, then laughed.

'Wow. That's terrifying.'

'I have a lot to put up with,' I said sedately. He looked at me again.

'Ingrid . . .'

'Ingrid what?' I prompted him after a few seconds.

He sighed. 'Nothing. Nothing at all.' With a flick of his thumb he turned the radio up, and we passed the remainder of the journey with music that was loud enough to vibrate my seat, instead of conversation. I wondered what he had been going to say, and why he hadn't said it, all the way to Guildford.

Guy Lanesbury's parents lived in a small house in a modest housing estate on the outskirts of the town. I leaned forward to look at it as we pulled up outside.

'Are you sure this is the right address?'

'Yeah, why?'

'They must have come down a bit in the world. Four years ago, Mrs Lanesbury was all diamonds and designer handbags. Guy went to a very expensive school. They were proper three-holidays-a-year types, which is how they could afford to pay for his private defence.'

Adam shrugged. 'My heart bleeds for them.'

'Well, clearly it doesn't. I'm just wondering how they went from that to this. Something must have gone wrong for them. They were nice people, even if they were loaded.'

'Nice people who brought up a nice sort of boy.'

I glared at him. 'Do I have to leave you in the car?'

'You can't,' Adam said with a certain degree of smugness. 'They're expecting me.'

I wouldn't have recognised Mrs Lanesbury when she opened the door. Gone were the expensive highlights and the diamonds. She was thinner and paler, but her smile was warm when Adam introduced himself, and me.

'We spoke on the phone,' she purred, blinking at him. 'Call me Roberta.'

'Hi, Roberta,' I said, and waved awkwardly.

'Ingrid! It's lovely to see you.' She kissed me on the cheek and drew me into the house, leading me to a small living room where Jack Lanesbury was standing.

'Come in, come in. Please do excuse the house. It's on the small side but we make do. Things have changed here, let me tell you.'

Jack was leaning on a stick and there was a grey tinge to his skin. He looked dreadful, I thought, and tried to cover my shock with a smile. 'Mr Lanesbury.'

'Jack, please.' He gave me a wavering smile. 'I've been in poor health since we saw each other last.'

'Jack's had to shut down his business. He hasn't been able to work. We had to downsize.' Roberta shrugged. 'I couldn't care less about it. The house, the car – none of that matters. Jack being all right is what matters.'

'Ah well. We have to make the best of what we have.' Jack lowered himself carefully into his chair and I sat near him as Adam deftly fended off Roberta's efforts to feed us and make us drinks.

'We were surprised to get a phone call from the police,' Jack said. 'Especially to do with Guy. We thought that was all behind us now.'

'It's not because he's in trouble again,' I said. 'Or not directly, anyway. He hasn't done anything wrong, as far as I know.'

'I do hope you're right.' Roberta was chewing her lip anxiously. 'We haven't seen him for – oh, it must be eighteen months.'

'Twenty-two,' her husband said, and gave a deep, rattling cough.

'Where is he?' I asked.

'We think he's in Australia. Well, not Australia,' Roberta said. 'He went to volunteer in one of those offshore migrant camps they have in Papua New Guinea. Manus is the name of the island.'

'Couldn't be further away,' Jack commented. 'And don't think that's a coincidence. He ran away.'

'What did he need to run from?' Adam asked.

'We don't know exactly.' Jack coughed again, dragging a tissue out of his sleeve with shaking hands.

'It was the court case,' Roberta said. 'No offence to you and the others, Ingrid, because I know you did your best to look after him, but he never got over it.'

'But he was acquitted,' Adam said.

'The jury believed he was telling the truth – and he was. You know that, don't you, Ingrid? He was completely honest about what happened that night. He made a terrible mistake, don't get me wrong, but he was young. He didn't know what he was doing or how to handle it afterwards. If he'd just talked to me – but then, no young man is going to want to talk to their mother about sex, are they? Would you?'

'Er, no.' Adam had been the target of that remark. He was blushing, I was fascinated to see. 'I can understand why he didn't want to discuss it.'

'Well, me too.' She sighed. 'But we could have helped him. Instead he got into such a muddle.'

She made it sound as if he'd got into a harmless scrape, as if he'd stolen a traffic cone or something equally trivial. I was afraid to look at Adam; I assumed he was fuming silently and hoped it wouldn't show on his face.

Jack cleared his throat. 'The thing is, we did take it seriously. We were worried about his future if he was sent to prison. We knew things hadn't happened that night as they should, but we knew our son, and we believed him when he said it was a mistake. We thought that if he could just get through the court case and be acquitted then he

311

could put it all behind him and move on with his life. But we didn't reckon with how he felt about it – afterwards, you know. Because he *felt* guilty, even if the jury didn't think he was. He knew he'd upset the girl. He knew he'd hurt her very badly. That affected him much more than going to prison would have, I think. Now, looking back on it, I almost wish he had been convicted. He would have been out by now, with no guilt about getting away with anything he shouldn't have. I don't think he should feel guilty, but he does. There it is.'

I swallowed, hard. Well done us for getting him acquitted. Before I could say anything – before I could think of anything to answer – Roberta chimed in.

'I think he would have got over it in time, if it hadn't been for the messages.'

'What messages?' I asked.

'Anonymous ones. Emails. Messages telling him he'd get his comeuppance for what he did, that it wouldn't be forgotten.'

'Did he report this to the police?' Adam was sitting up straighter now.

'He didn't want to. He didn't want to talk about what had happened, and the trial and everything. He thought everyone would judge him just as harshly as he judged himself.' A fat tear slid down Roberta's cheek. 'They would have helped him, obviously. That's their job. Well, you know, it's your job.'

'We would take it seriously,' Adam said. 'Do you have any of these messages?'

Roberta shook her head. 'He deleted them as soon as he got them. We only found out about them by chance.'

'He left his phone behind when he took our old dog

out for a walk. I happened to need to check something and I knew his password. The email was on the screen when I unlocked it.' Jack grimaced. 'I tried to get him to open up to me about it but he wouldn't. He did admit that he'd been getting messages for a few months and he said it wasn't going to stop.'

'Were there any actual threats?' I asked.

'Nothing specific that he mentioned, but he was scared.' Roberta swallowed. 'He was worried that someone would take it out on us, too, you see. He wanted to get away from us because he was the target, not us. I told him we didn't care about that – we only cared about him. But he left home and cut off contact with us.'

'He came to see us before he went to Manus,' Jack said. 'To say goodbye. And that was it.'

'Are you in touch with him?' Adam asked. 'Email? Phone? Skype?'

Roberta shook her head. 'I wish we were, but he cut us off completely. He doesn't have a mobile phone or anything. We don't even know for sure that he's in Manus. It's the end of the world, really it is. There's no way we could go and visit him with Jack's lungs – he's not allowed to do long-haul travel any more.'

'Any kind of travel,' Jack corrected her. 'I need oxygen a lot of the time. Better to stay in one place in case I get caught out.'

'He told us not to tell anyone where he was.' Roberta looked from Adam to me. 'But you don't count, do you? He wouldn't mind us telling you.'

'We'll keep it to ourselves,' Adam said. 'And if you don't mind me giving you some advice, you should avoid talking about him and where he is from now on, especially if someone you don't know asks you about him – someone who says they're a friend of his, even. Unless you know them personally, say nothing. The reason we're here is because there might be a threat to your safety, and to him. It's vitally important that you don't trust anyone else who tries to talk to you about Guy.'

Roberta nodded, her eyes wide. Jack shifted uneasily in his chair.

'Do you think the messages were genuine, then? Actual threats? I thought it was just a load of rubbish. Anonymous messages usually are.'

'I don't know if there's a connection,' I said carefully, 'but I do think you should take care. The main thing is to keep you all safe, even if we're worrying about nothing.'

'Are you going to try to track him down?' Jack asked Adam, who nodded.

'I'll do my best.'

Jack paused to master his emotions, but when he spoke his voice was steady. 'If you find him, tell him we miss him.'

We left the Lanesburys and drove away in silence. The radio stayed off this time; jaunty music didn't seem appropriate. After a few minutes, Adam pulled off the A3 and took a smaller road that struck off to the east.

'Where are we going?'

'I don't know.'

Okay then. I stayed quiet and watched the wintry scenery pass by in a blur. The road ran through the Surrey Hills, an area so ravishingly beautiful that it was like a perfect postcard of England at every turn in the road. The sky was a clear, bright blue, making the most of the brief

314

period of daylight before the night came down again. The trees and fields were muted in colour, despite the low, slanting sunlight: washed-out browns and greens with patches of white frost clinging here and there where the sun hadn't reached them throughout the whole short day. Adam drove through it as if he couldn't see anything but the road that dipped and swung beneath our wheels, through tunnels made by bare-branched trees and into the open again.

At last we came to a signpost for Box Hill and Adam took the narrow road that climbed up the side of the hill, twisting and turning, slowing for Lycra-clad cyclists who favoured it as a test for their stamina. I could sense his frustration building as he crawled along behind them, waiting for a chance to overtake. Near the top of the hill he gave up and pulled off the road, stopping at a viewing point. Miles and miles of low, rolling farmland stretched out in front of us, crosshatched with the long shadows of hedges and trees. The sun was already slipping towards the horizon, burning out in a blaze of red. He turned off the engine and sat for a few seconds, silent. He was staring out at the scene in front of us as if he needed to memorise it for a test.

'Adam,' I said tentatively.

He got out of the car and slammed the door, hard. I watched him walk a few paces away, the cold air turning his breath to clouds.

I got out of the car too and turned the collar of my coat up – no scarf, not since Webster had tried to strangle me with it on the bus, but God I regretted it at that moment. The air was icy on the hillside, stinging my cheeks, turning them as red as the sunset.

Adam had his back to me. I walked slowly towards him, stopping a short distance away.

'Nice view.'

No response.

'Worth the drive.'

Still nothing.

'Adam.'

He turned and looked at me. Then he closed the distance between us with a single stride. He slid his hand inside the collar of my coat, and turned my face up to his, and he kissed me.

35

If you're going to kiss someone for the first time, and then drop them as if they are red hot, it's a kindness to have some sort of exit strategy planned so they can recover their equilibrium in peace. Instead of that, Adam and I were standing on a hillside together, in what might as well have been the middle of nowhere. Once the kissing stopped, all we could do was return to the car and pretend it hadn't happened at all.

I was not good at pretending. I sat beside him with my fingers pressed to my mouth, and he concentrated on driving. He swore quietly a few times at other cars but otherwise he was silent all the way back, until we reached the outskirts of London itself and I broke.

'I think we might need to talk.'

His hands tightened on the wheel. His shoulders were up around his ears: so much for the calm and easy driving I'd admired on the way out. 'I'm sorry.'

'Why are you sorry? It wasn't as if it was a bad kiss. Believe me, I've had worse.'

He winced. 'That's not the point. It shouldn't have happened.'

'Why not?'

'It's complicated. There's a very important rule about not getting involved with witnesses and victims during a case. It's massively inappropriate.' He glanced at me and immediately looked away. 'There's the power imbalance. They're vulnerable and you represent safety. You can't take advantage of that.'

I cleared my throat. 'You're not really taking advantage of me, though. I'm not the kind of person who goes starry-eyed around police officers, as you might have noticed. And this isn't official police business, is it? So you're not going to get disciplined for getting involved with me.'

'Not the point. I should have more self-control.'

'Adam, it was one kiss. Stop torturing yourself.'

The traffic had bunched up in front of us without me noticing, and we slid to a stop, so Adam had to look at me.

'Is that all you want? One kiss?'

'I don't know,' I said, truthfully, thinking of Mark. I wasn't over him; I wasn't ready to be with anyone else. But I'd never given myself a chance to get over Mark. I'd never allowed anyone else to try to be with me. 'It's complicated.'

'Right.' He said it under his breath and turned back to stare out of the windscreen.

I balled my hands into fists from pure frustration. 'I'm not trying to put you off, but I don't know what you want me to say. I wasn't expecting it.'

'You didn't see it coming?'

'Not really. I mean, I didn't know you were attracted to me, even though I—' I broke off.

318

'You?' he asked politely.

'I had thought about it.'

'Oh, really.' A sideways glance that made my catch my breath; my God, when he dropped his grim policeman façade there was something seriously hot about DC Nash.

'But I didn't think you felt the same way.'

'I've been wanting to do that,' Adam said, 'since I saw you in the café that first day.'

'Really?'

'Really.' He looked at me and whatever he saw in my face made him smile. 'But I did try very hard not to show it. I wasn't going to say anything until all of this was over.'

'You still haven't actually said anything except that you wish it hadn't happened,' I pointed out. 'And a lot of guff about taking advantage of me.'

'I think I've made myself clear.'

'Do you? Because I'm still confused.'

'Maybe I should show you how I feel.' He sounded matter-of-fact, and that in itself made my stomach do a slow somersault.

'Maybe you should.'

The car in front began to move again and Adam returned his attention to the road, and that was the end of our conversation for the remainder of the journey. The silence had a different quality now, though. It was charged with a strange kind of energy – anticipation and yearning and doubt, humming at a level below sound. I could feel it, all the time. I hadn't felt this way since Mark.

But I didn't want to think about Mark now. I pushed him out of my mind with an effort that was almost physical. This was nothing to do with him. He'd said as much himself.

It was dark by the time we reached the flat. For once there was a parking space on the road near the gate. Adam pulled into it and turned off the engine, taking the key out of the ignition. I guessed he was making some fairly reasonable assumptions about what was going to happen next.

Not now. Not yet.

That was pure instinct talking; I wanted him, but I wasn't ready.

'Adam, it's not that I don't want you to come in,' I said slowly. 'I just – I need some time to get used to it. I have a lot to think about.'

'Of course.'

'Is it okay, though? I don't want to upset you. It's not really about you, or us, or whatever this is. I just need to get my head straight.'

He reached over and touched my face tenderly. 'Take as long as you need to. There's no hurry.'

'Thank you.'

'Come here.'

I leaned across the gap between the seats and he kissed me again, for longer this time but without the bruising intensity of the kiss on the hillside. It was strange and different and exciting, and I felt myself start to waver. I pulled back.

'Adam.'

'Mm.'

'You *could* come in.'

He sighed. 'No. You were right the first time. It's better if we take our time.'

'Is it?'

'Get out of my car, Ingrid,' he said softly, and leaned

closer to me, which I interpreted as being a move to kiss me again but in fact was him reaching for the door latch. The door swung open behind me. 'I'll see you tomorrow,' he said.

'Okay. But—'

'Goodbye.'

'Bye.' I got out of the car, my nerves humming as if someone was drawing a bow across them with exquisite control and patience. I shut the car door. Adam started the engine, but sat with it idling while he waited for me to go inside. I found myself smiling to myself as I walked across to unlock the gate, and I waved at him as he drove away.

The courtyard was deserted, most of the lights off in the flats around it. No sign of Helen. Thoughtfully, I went up the steps to my front door. I could still feel Adam's hands on me, and his mouth on mine. I closed my eyes for an instant, then bent to tackle the new lock, which was annoyingly stiff. I started with calm tinkering, then frowning concentration, and had got all the way to swearing and threats by the time the door finally came open. I stamped in and slammed it, fed up beyond words by the whole situation.

The flat was in darkness and I stopped, overwhelmed by the memory of coming home to find poor Vicki's body in the corner. *Stupid, Ingrid.* I switched the light on and looked around to reassure myself that there was no pool of blood this time, no smears of it on the floor, no signs of a struggle.

Everything was exactly as neat and tidy as I had left it.

Everything was the same, except for John Webster, who had been sitting on my sofa in the dark, waiting for me to come home.

321

36

I screamed, of course, and of course the sound came out thin and reedy. *When you're afraid, your vocal cords tighten up*, Kate's voice said in my head and I tried very hard to relax, to take a proper breath and let myself go, but nothing happened.

On the sofa, Webster rolled his eyes. 'Really, there's no need for that.'

'What – what are you doing? Why are you here?' Fear first, then anger, predictable as the seasons. The very fact that it was predictable made me even more furious. 'You broke in.'

'No. Nothing is broken.' He smiled. 'I haven't committed an offence.'

'Try burglary,' I snapped, fumbling in my bag for my phone, to call the police on him once and for all.

The smile widened. 'Now, Ingrid, you should know better than that. Unless I have the intent on entering the building of committing theft, grievous bodily harm or damaging property, it's not burglary.'

'But—'

'Entering a house and sitting in it is trespass, which is a civil matter. You're welcome to sue me.' He leaned forward to rest his elbows on his thighs, his face alight with mischief. 'Anyway, don't you want to know why I'm here?'

'First I want to know why you were sitting here in the dark,' I said tightly. 'I presume it was because you knew it would scare me.'

'No, it was because your neighbour was on the prowl.'

'Which neighbour?'

'The dumpy little girl from downstairs.'

'Helen?' I let my phone slide back into my bag, distracted. 'What do you mean by on the prowl?'

'She came up the steps and looked in through the window. She spent quite a lot of time doing that, actually.' Webster frowned. 'I don't like her. I assume she heard me moving around. I wasn't very keen to attract her attention.'

I had started to shiver, shock kicking in now. 'You really scared me, John.'

'Not my intention.'

'Just an unexpected bonus, maybe.'

'How can you say that?' He leaned back and stretched his arms out along the back of the sofa, luxuriating in the moment. 'I'm only here because you wanted my help. I'm doing my best to be discreet. Have you forgotten that someone is trying to hurt you, Ingrid?'

'No. I haven't.'

'So we need to take care about who sees us coming and going. That's just common sense.'

It seemed completely insane that John Webster was lecturing me on my personal safety. 'Why are you here?'

'I've got some good news and I wanted to share it with you in person.'

'What you think of as good news isn't necessarily what I think of as good news.'

'You'll like this. I've found your homeless man.'

'Really?' I pulled out a chair from the table and sat down, interested now in spite of myself. 'How did you manage that?'

'Bit of shoe leather, bit of imagination, a little bit of tailoring the truth to suit my purposes – which are, of course, your purposes. I spoke to a lot of people who are involved in providing services to the homeless, and I spoke to a lot of homeless people. Eventually I found someone who had given him a hot meal at Lincoln's Inn Fields.'

I knew that park was a regular haunt of the homeless; there was nothing remarkable about that part of his story. It was all too close to me, though: Lincoln's Inn Fields was behind the Royal Courts of Justice, abutting Lincoln's Inn where many barristers' chambers were based, halfway between where I lived and the Temple. I walked through it from time to time. London was vast and some-times it felt like a village.

'How did you get them to trust you?'

'I told everyone he was my brother.'

'But you didn't have a name for him. And the police couldn't find him. I'm sure they looked in places like Lincoln's Inn Fields.'

'I had two great advantages over the police. One, according to you, I look like him. Two, I was prepared to lie. In the family, we always called him Jason but, how sad, he stopped using that name when he left us behind.' Webster brushed an imaginary tear away. 'It would break my mother's heart if she knew.'

It was a mark of how rattled I was that I said the first thing that came into my head. 'Do you actually have a mother or was there some sort of egg-hatching involved in how you came into the world?'

'I did have a mother once.'

'What happened to her?'

He looked perplexed. 'I have no idea. She wasn't very interesting.'

If I had thought he was saying it to impress me, I wouldn't have found it particularly shocking, but he wasn't. He had dismissed her from the brief list of things he cared about. It was typical Webster: icy, calculating, unsentimental, utterly contrary to everything that most people held to be a basic truth. I wondered if she missed him, or if she was relieved that he wasn't in touch with her any more. I wondered if she had ever known what he was. It was hard to imagine Webster as a baby, or even a small boy. I pictured a miniature version of him setting fires and torturing animals, wearing the sharp tailoring and expensive cashmere overcoat he was sporting on my sofa, and it almost made me laugh.

Webster looked suspicious. 'What have you been up to, anyway? You look different.'

'Different?' I managed not to put a hand up to my mouth, though my lips still tingled.

'Where have you been?'

'I went to speak to Guy Lanesbury's family.'

'Alone?'

'Adam came with me.' I felt the colour rising in my cheeks and cursed silently: there was no way that Webster would miss that . . .

'So you kissed and made up.'

'*What?*'

He looked as close to puzzled as he ever allowed himself to appear. 'The last time I saw you, we discussed the argument that you'd had with him. You were on no speaks, if I recall correctly.'

'That's not true.'

'Well, we both know it is, but we also both remember you lied about it.' Webster smiled, not pleasantly. 'Did you talk about Flora?'

'No.'

'Why not?' The question cracked through the room like a lasso that tightened around me.

'Because we were having a pleasant time and I didn't want to ruin it.'

'And you thought talking about Flora would ruin things? You don't have a lot of faith in DC Nash, do you?'

'No, that's not—'

'There's something so beautifully stupid about the way you conduct yourself, Ingrid. You're bristling with hostility towards me, even though I just want to help you. And here you are, hanging around with Nash, afraid to even ask him what he really thinks of you.' He was pale, his eyes glittering with anger. 'I can't understand why you don't expect more from him, and your moronic fiancé. You're so willing to be judged by them and found wanting. It's almost as if you know you don't deserve anything more.'

'I know what I deserve and I don't want your advice.'

326

I said it quietly, as a statement of fact. 'But I do want your help. You came to tell me you'd found the homeless man, and I'm grateful. Who is he?'

Webster shut his eyes and took two or three deep breaths, getting himself under control again. When he opened his eyes, he was back to what passed for normal.

'His name is George Reese.'

'I don't know that name.'

'I didn't say you would.'

'Okay,' I said slowly. 'So why did he push Belinda under a lorry?'

'That I can't tell you.'

'John, I—'

'I said I'd found him. I didn't say I'd talked to him.'

'Why not?'

'He was in no fit state to have a conversation, I'm afraid. Poor George is a heavy drinker.'

'Right.'

'And someone gave him a very generous present of a litre of vodka.'

'Someone. You.'

Webster smiled.

I felt heat rush into my face again, but it was anger this time. 'You could have killed him.'

'He can take it. Besides, it made him much easier to handle.'

'What have you done?'

'Nothing. I just put him in a safe place. I didn't want him to wander off. You know what the homeless are like – you can never lay your hands on them when you need to.'

'Where is he?'

'It's very hard to describe.'

'Try,' I said.

'I think it would be easier if I showed you. But that means you're going to have to come with me.' He stood up and I found myself shoving the chair back as I got to my feet too, poised to run. 'Ingrid, really, don't annoy me. Do you want to speak to this man or not?'

'I do, but I don't want to go anywhere with you.' I was trembling.

'You can't expect me to bring him here.'

'Let me call Adam. He can come with us.'

'No, I don't think so.'

'Please.'

'It would be a little inconvenient for him to do that. I might get in trouble. It's not strictly legal to keep someone locked up, you know, even though I did it with the best of intentions.' He was closing the gap between us slowly, almost imperceptibly: if I hadn't been so aware of the danger he represented I might not even have noticed. 'No, Ingrid, you're the one who wants to speak to George. If you want to talk to him, you need to come with me.'

'You can't make me.'

'Well that's not true.'

The fear swelled and rose within me like water on the verge of boiling over.

'But I don't have to force you,' Webster went on. 'All I have to do is point out that no one else knows where George is. No one is looking for him except you. If he never resurfaces, who will raise the alarm?'

'I could.'

'But you wouldn't.' He looked amused. 'You don't even know if I've given you his real name or not. I could have lied about that too. But here's something that's not a lie. At the moment, George is fast asleep. When he wakes up, he's going to think all his dreams have come true, because a kind benefactor has left him several bottles of vodka within easy reach. Now, I imagine his tolerance is higher than yours or mine might be, but everyone has their limit. If you want to get to George before he drinks himself to death, I suggest you stop wasting time and come with me.'

37

One thing about having endured John Webster's attentions for so long was that I knew there was no point in calling his bluff. If he was lying about how he'd left George Reese, he would make sure he made it happen now, just to teach me a lesson. I walked behind him as if I was going to the scaffold, every step dragging. In contrast he swept down the steps and across the courtyard in high good humour. He held the gate open for me with mock courtesy.

'Where are we going?'

'Just down the road.'

My relief evaporated when our destination turned out to be a large off-white van.

'I'm not getting in that.'

'You are. I'm even giving you a choice between sitting up front with me, or in the back. The ride is bumpier in the back, for what it's worth. No seats. No windows. No light.'

'But on the other hand there's no need to make conversation with a sociopath.'

'I really dislike that word. Don't use it again.' He stalked to the driver's side. 'Get in. Front or back.'

'How long is the journey?'

'Not long.'

Keep listening to your instincts, Kate murmured in my head. *They'll tell you who to trust and who to avoid.*

I shook my head at my own folly and opened the passenger door anyway.

Webster's definition of 'not long' didn't correspond too well with mine. We headed south of the river, cruising past Waterloo and Lambeth and Clapham. I spent my time imagining all the lives that were being led in the hundreds of thousands of homes we were passing. My own life had slipped sideways in a terrifying way since Belinda's death, I thought. Everything I had taken for granted, and everything I had worked so hard to create for myself was being turned on its head. And now I was in a van with the man I feared most in the world, speeding into the darkness as road signs with half-familiar names flashed by.

'Where are we going?'

'Have patience. All will be revealed.'

He was enjoying this, I thought. He liked that I was doing what he wanted, and he was all the happier that I was miserable about it. Was it worth it?

Yes, came the answer. I needed to know what George knew about what had happened to Belinda. I needed to know if all of this had started with Guy Lanesbury's trial, and if so, who was responsible.

'Where are we?' I peered out at the houses we were passing, desperate to see something I recognised.

'This is a bit of Croydon.'

'Which bit?' Croydon was enormous, a second city on the southern outskirts of London. It had absorbed many small towns, filling up the green spaces between them with houses and characterless shopping areas. I was aware of where you could get to from the main train stations, and I'd worked in Croydon Crown Court, but otherwise the place was a mystery to me.

'Who cares? It's a convenient place to speak to George, that's all. Don't worry about it.'

'But I—' I broke off with a gasp as the van lurched across the oncoming traffic and barrelled down a road between two industrial areas. On one side, cement piping was stacked up in vast quantities. The other side was a depot of some kind, with lorries backed up to a huge warehouse. The headlights illuminated an area of empty wasteland ahead of us. There were no cars in front of us or following behind. The businesses were shuttered and dark aside from their security lighting; there was no one at all around to see us. I didn't like it one bit. 'Where are we going?'

'Don't panic. This is a short cut.' He glanced at me. 'Why would I bring you all the way out here to kill you? I could have saved myself the petrol and done it in your flat.'

'I don't know, but I'm sure you'd have your reasons.' My hand was on the door handle; there was some part of my brain preparing for fast movement if the van ever slowed enough to risk jumping out . . .

'It's locked,' Webster observed. 'So you might as well relax.'

'Why is it locked?'

'Because I locked it. For security,' he added smoothly. 'We drove through some dodgy areas back there.'

'For God's sake,' I began, furious, and he swerved

towards the kerb, parked and switched the engine off, all in the space of a couple of seconds. Without the van's lights everything seemed much more threatening. The night pressed against the van's windows. We had stopped beside a row of terraced cottages that overlooked the waste ground, but they were empty. Graffiti-scrawls decorated the metal shutters that blocked the windows and doors, and there were no signs of life. 'Why have we stopped?'

'We're here.'

'Here?' I looked at the houses again. 'Here.'

'These houses are marked for demolition. Actually, they've been scheduled to be knocked down for almost five years. They were workers' cottages at one time and some of the local community feel they're of historical importance, so the developers can't get permission to demolish them.' Webster leaned on the steering wheel to look at them. 'They have absolutely no importance, architecturally or historically. These were horrible little slums with no proper plumbing and the people who lived in them led small, shabby lives. They're worthless. But for my purposes, they're perfect. No neighbours, no one to see us coming or going, no alarm system or security guards. It's in the developers' interests to see them fall into disrepair so they aren't very assiduous in making sure they're secure.'

'And this is where you brought George Reese?'

Webster nodded. 'I found him in Oxford, in a homeless shelter run by one of the churches.'

'How did you persuade him to stay here?'

He raised one eyebrow and said nothing.

'So you weren't joking when you said you kidnapped him.'

'That's a very harsh way of putting it. He was getting ready to come back to London in any case. I gave him a lift.' He hesitated. 'There's one thing you should know about George. He's a bit . . . simple.'

'What does that mean?'

'It's either the booze and drugs or he's got learning difficulties. Or both, I suppose. Anyway, he's been a bit hazy on the details. Hopefully he'll be more focused now after he's had a sleep.'

I followed Webster to the last house in the little terrace. There was something nightmarish about this row of desolate homes. He unlocked a shiny padlock on a battered side gate.

'Your addition, I take it.'

'As I said, the security left something to be desired.' He had a torch which he shone on the weed-blighted path so I could follow him. Of course he didn't need it; he had a cat-like ability to see in the dark.

The back door was nailed shut with a metal screen that looked solid enough, but Webster went to the kitchen window instead. A minute of tinkering with the top right screw and the whole thing swung down, pivoting on the point where it was still attached to the house. Behind it, I saw a smudgy window with a single pane missing. Webster reached in and unlatched it.

'Want a leg up?'

'I can manage, thank you,' I said, and watched as he levered himself up and disappeared through the narrow opening with ease. He reappeared for an instant.

'Watch out for the sink. It's right under the window.'

'Thanks.'

Then he was gone again, something that I was profoundly

grateful for as I hauled myself over the splintering window frame and slithered into a deep ceramic sink. It felt gritty yet slimy to the touch and I heaved at what I could see of the staining on it. A strong smell of dead mice hung in the air.

'All right?'

Webster's voice came from far too close at hand, and I fell off the edge of the sink instead of jumping down gracefully as I'd intended.

'Fuck's sake.'

'I warned you.'

I didn't say anything. I was confronting the reality that the window was high up and my only exit from a property I didn't know at all, and that no one knew where I was, and even if John Webster was right in saying he could have killed me at any point up to now, there was no reason to think he wouldn't trick me into trusting him and *then* kill me.

'This way.'

He led me through the room that had been the kitchen (aside from the sink, only the outlines of cupboards remained on the walls), into a tiny, freezing hall. I didn't want to go up the narrow stairs and it was a relief when he turned into the living room instead. The torch sent shadows racing up the walls and reflected off the window with dazzling brightness, so it took me a second to get my bearings. It wasn't a large space even without furniture, but it was warm: a small battery-powered heater on the floor whirred busily. A body lay on the floor, wrapped in a couple of sleeping bags. I had done Webster something of an injustice: there were several bottles of vodka standing an easy arm's length from the sleeping bags. It wouldn't even be necessary to get out of bed for George to begin the process of killing himself. They were all still sealed though.

'George. Wake up.' Webster kicked the centre of the sleeping bags and I cried out.

'What are you doing? You'll hurt him.'

'George.' He kicked him again, as if I hadn't said anything, and the figure within the bags stirred. A flap slipped back and a face appeared, squinting against the torch light. He was youngish, with a fair beard, and absolutely filthy. He was finding it hard to focus, groggy from sleep or something else.

'How did he get that black eye?' I asked sharply.

'Oh – no idea.' Webster crouched in front of him, whipping his coat up so it didn't trail on the grimy floor. 'George. Come on, buddy.'

'It looks recent.'

'Forget about it,' Webster threw over his shoulder. 'George, we've come to see you. This is Ingrid, the woman I told you about.'

The homeless man blinked up at me. He was cringing away from Webster, which was entirely reasonable. The injured eye was bloodshot and blue-red bruising stained the skin around it. He looked like John Webster and he didn't; there was something missing from his face. It was a kind of blankness.

'L-leave me alone,' he slurred.

'Now, now, George. I explained this to you.' Webster reached out and took a handful of the man's hair, then bounced his head off the floor. He dragged him back up to a sitting position. 'Answer her questions and then you can go.'

I had put my hands to my face involuntarily, from shock. 'John, no. Don't hurt him.'

'Shut up, Ingrid.' Webster shook George's head from side to side. 'I'm waiting.'

'Okay, okay.' Tears were standing in his eyes. 'Just stop, all right?'

'Tell her about the road accident. Why were you there?'

He blinked. 'They gave me money and drink. Told me to come to London. Told me where to sit during the days, by that road. I was off the booze then but I went straight back on to it. Can't stop when I've got it.'

'How long did you wait there?'

'A couple of days. I didn't know. There was a guy. Told me to stand next to the road when she went into it.' He whistled and tipped his hand forward. 'One minute there. Then gone.'

'Who was the man?' I asked, and he shook his head.

'How old was he? What do you remember about him?' Webster gave George a short, sharp dig in the shoulder. 'How did he find you?'

'I don't know. Leave me alone.' George curled into a ball like a hedgehog, spikes out.

'You're not being very helpful.'

'Don't hurt him.'

Webster grinned up at me. 'Now is not the time to lose your nerve.'

He looked more alive than I'd ever seen him, his eyes bright. With a squirm of revulsion I realised this wasn't just useful; it was fun for him. There was no point in trying to appeal to his better nature when he didn't have one.

'I haven't lost my nerve. But the more you torture him, the less likely he is to tell you anything useful. He's just going to try to guess what you want to hear.' I knelt beside George's head. 'George, listen to me. You can trust me. I won't let anyone hurt you. Did you push the lady into the road?'

'No.' The response was instant and strong, even if it was muffled by his sleeping bag.

'On the CCTV, it looks as if you did.'

'It was him.'

'Who?'

'A man. Old. He was holding on to me. I thought he wanted me to fall too.'

'The same man who told you to wait at the junction?'

'Didn't see him again.'

'Did anyone else give you instructions or money while you were in London?'

'A woman.'

'What sort of woman?'

'Just a woman. Younger than you.'

'Tall?'

A shrug.

'How did the first man find you, George?'

'He came looking for me. Asking around.' He was shivering and I thought the flush on his face was a sign of a fever. He needed to be in hospital, not lying on the floor of a derelict house.

'He asked for you by name? Are you sure you didn't know him?'

'Never seen him before. He had a photo of me. A mugshot. He knew my name but he didn't know anything else about me.'

'Why did he want you there?'

He shrugged and shut his eyes. 'Tired.'

'Just two more questions,' I said quickly, hating myself. 'Did he threaten you?'

Another headshake.

'Then why did you do what he said?'

George opened his eyes at that, looking at me as if I was insane. 'Because I was scared.'

38

I don't like to think about what might have happened to George if I had left it up to Webster to decide what to do with him. George had withdrawn completely after my last question and nothing – begging and coaxing on my part, bored threats on Webster's – would persuade him to talk again. He looked very ill, his condition deteriorating by the minute. It might have been reluctance to talk that was making him silent, or else he was just too weak to answer any more questions. Eventually, Webster lost patience. He dragged me to my feet and into the hallway.

'This is pointless.'

'I know.'

He was standing in front of me, a little too close. 'What do you make of what he told you so far?'

'He hasn't said much.'

'He said the man who found him had his mugshot. Makes me think it might have been a police officer.'

And you're a little too keen to make me notice that, I thought. I shouldn't have been surprised that he wanted to make me wary of the police. He wanted me dependent on him, and him only.

'You could be right. But why did they want him?'

'Because he looks like me,' Webster said, as if it was obvious. 'If you want to frame me, you have to put me at the scene of the crime. They found someone in the files who matched my description and they went and got him.'

'That's assuming they had access to the Met's files.'

'Yeah. It is.'

'Do you have access to those files?'

I know Webster thought about lying to me, but in the end he couldn't stop the smile from spreading across his face. 'Maybe.'

'So there's no reason to think it was a police officer. It could have been someone like you. George would have spotted a cop a mile away.' George started coughing and I winced. 'We really need to take him to hospital.'

'Not keen, sorry.'

'*John.*'

'I can't take him to hospital. I'll get arrested.'

'Well, you can't leave him here! He'll die.'

'Of course I won't leave him here.' Webster hit exactly the right note of wounded outrage, which was how I knew he was lying.

'I'm not going anywhere until I know he's safe.' I folded my arms, as if that would make a difference. 'We need to get him out of here. We can take him to a public place and call an ambulance if you really won't take him into the hospital yourself.'

He groaned. 'That just seems like a lot of hassle and risk, Ingrid. Why don't you leave it up to me to sort it out?'

'Because I don't trust you. Obviously.' I jerked a thumb in the direction of the kitchen. 'Is that window really the only way in and out?'

'I could probably unlock the back door.' He sounded sulky.

'You could have done that all along, couldn't you? There was no reason to make me climb in through the window.'

'It was more secure that way,' Webster protested. 'And I didn't want George to get any ideas about leaving without my permission. Watching you fall off the sink was just a little bonus.'

Prising the metal screen off the back door proved to be the easy part of getting George out. I tried to wake him but he was lost in his own misery, muttering to himself with his eyes rolled so far back in his head that the whites were showing. He smelled dreadful and careful investigation revealed that the source was his foot. It was bound with a filthy bandage. The limp I'd noticed on the CCTV had an actual physical cause, it seemed.

'How are we doing?'

'He's unconscious.' I looked up at Webster who was looming over us. 'I'm really worried about him.'

'Fine.' Webster bent and picked him up, sleeping bags and all. 'You bring the heater and the vodka. Remember the torch. We don't want to leave any trace of ourselves behind.'

He carried George out of the room with very little effort although the other man was the same height as him and should have had the same build if he had been properly nourished. It was a useful reminder to me that John Webster was stronger than he looked – strong enough to do more or less whatever he liked. Trusting him was like keeping a great white shark as a pet.

I got on with clearing away the evidence that we'd been there, playing the torch over the bare floorboards. I was complicit now in the kidnapping, even if I hadn't been before. I might not have wanted or asked Webster to imprison George, I thought unhappily, but I hadn't stopped him. I hadn't refused to question the homeless man. I had taken advantage of the situation he created for me. I thought of myself as a good person, but when it came down to it, I had gone along with Webster's plan while it suited me to do so.

'All right?' Webster met me in the kitchen and relieved me of the shopping bag that was clanking with bottles.

'Yes.'

'You don't seem all right.'

I turned my face away from him. He was the last person I wanted to talk to about what I had done, and what I was doing now. If I wasn't careful I would end up just like him. 'What's the plan?'

'He's bedded down in the back of the van.'

'The back,' I repeated. 'But—'

'I don't want him in the front because one, he stinks and two, he's not well enough to sit upright, okay? It's not up for discussion.'

'Right.'

'I'm going to take you to East Croydon train station. You can catch a million trains from there. One of them will get you home.'

My first reaction was that there wouldn't be any trains in the middle of the night, but when I checked my watch I realised it wasn't actually that late. There would be trains, and people. I would need to act normally, which meant I needed to pull myself together.

'Okay. Where are you taking George?'

'Somewhere a long way from here.' Then he relented: 'I'll make sure he's looked after, all right? I need to take him far enough that no one traces him back to here, and to us.'

Us. Webster and I were bracketed together now. I shivered, but he didn't notice.

'I'll find a CCTV blackspot and drop him off. Then I'll call him an ambulance. I'll make sure they come and look after him but I'm not going to get directly involved.'

'Fair enough.'

'Don't worry.' He dragged me into his arms and held me for a moment, burying his nose in my hair and inhaling deeply. I fought, silently and desperately, but I couldn't get free. He behaved as if he hadn't even noticed, loosening his grip in his own sweet time and smiling at me. 'I'll make sure none of this comes back to you. I'm here to help you, not harm you.'

'Let go of me.'

'Can't you be nice, for once?' Webster looked hurt. 'A little civility isn't too much to ask, is it?'

'I don't like it when you maul me.'

'A small price to pay for my help, I'd have thought,' he said evenly. 'But we'll see. You might have a reason to be more grateful soon.'

'What does that mean?'

Something like sympathy softened his face and it was unsettling; I knew he didn't have the capacity for it. 'You'll understand eventually. Now go and get in the van. We've been here for long enough and I need to lock up.'

*

Once I got out of the van, in a dark access road five minutes' walk from East Croydon station, it seemed impossible that the previous couple of hours had really happened. I walked to the station and bought a ticket with cash, on Webster's instructions. He had given me a hat to wear – a black woollen hat with a ridiculous furry pompom on the top – and watched while I tugged it down over my hair.

'There. Now you look completely unlike yourself. You'll probably change at Victoria – you can go straight up to King's Cross on the Victoria line. Leave the hat at Victoria somewhere. Take it off before you get to the main station concourse. Go straight to the Underground – don't hang around.'

'I hate the Underground,' I had said, all of my attention focused on the jolts and bumps of the journey. I hadn't seen George since the house but Webster had promised me he was all right – but then a promise from Webster was worthless, and I knew that . . . and he hadn't made a sound so far, but then again he had been unconscious, more or less . . . my thoughts squirrelled around and around unhappily.

'On this occasion, take the Tube.' Webster had gripped my jaw hard, twisting my face around so I had to look at him. 'Act as if you have a perfect right to be there. Behave normally. If you usually stand, stand. Don't make eye contact with anyone but don't avoid it either. Forget what you've been doing this evening.'

Impossible, I had thought and hadn't said. But as the train slid into place in front of me and the doors opened, it felt like an ordinary journey after all. On autopilot I sat in a rear-facing seat, ignoring the other passengers who were scattered through the carriage. At Victoria I followed

Webster's instructions exactly, pausing by a bench and putting my hat down as if I needed free hands to get out my phone. Then I wandered away, apparently lost in what was on the screen in front of me. No one called me back. No one came after me.

No one even noticed I was there.

Because I had been told to, I went down to the Underground and used my bank card to tap through the barriers instead of buying a ticket, flagging up where I was and where I was going if anyone cared to check. Being in Victoria station, Webster had explained, was not a crime. It was a positive help to be traceable, if anyone came looking to see where I had been and what I'd been doing. Along with hundreds of others I moved through the tiled tunnels, not hurrying, not walking too slowly. I got on the first Victoria Line train that came and stood in the centre of the carriage, eyes fixed on the ground, listening to the announcements so I knew where I was. Green Park first, then Oxford Circus where half the carriage got off and the same number of passengers got on. Warren Street. Euston. King's Cross, where I stepped off the train and walked along the featureless passages for what felt like hours before I finally made it to the ticket hall of the station itself, and then up the escalators to the open air.

Emerging from the darkness, I realised that I was tired and absolutely starving. I stopped at a stall and bought a massive burger. Ordinarily I would have waited to get home before I ate it but there was no question of that: I stood near the stall and took huge, inelegant bites of it until it was gone.

The walk back to the flat was a lot easier having

refuelled. I went quickly, chilled by the wind and tiredness. My bones were aching. What I wanted was a hot shower, my favourite pyjamas and an early night, I decided.

What I got was nothing of the kind.

I turned the corner to walk towards the gate and stopped. A police car was drawn up just outside the gate, with an officer leaning against the side of it, his head bent to listen to his radio. A second officer stepped through the gate holding a notebook. She glanced left and right casually, saw me and stiffened.

'Ingrid? Ingrid Lewis?' She started walking towards me at a brisk pace, as fast as you can go without actually jogging. Her colleague straightened up and fell into step behind her.

Run, a voice in my head said.

Too late. I was always too late.

I walked forward to meet them on legs that felt detached from the rest of me. 'What's wrong?'

'We need to talk to you, Ingrid. We need to bring you to a police station for an interview.'

Incredible that they knew about George Reese already, I thought, and that they knew where to find me. I dragged a word out in response.

'Why?'

'There's been an incident.'

'What kind of incident?' I felt a bolt of pure terror run through me. 'What's happened?'

'A friend of yours has been involved in an altercation of some kind. I don't know the details, I'm sorry.' She had a confident manner, and a clear voice, as if she was used to people not listening because they were lost in shock. 'His name is Mark Orpen.'

'*Mark?* But what's actually happened to him? Is he okay?'

It was the big male policeman who answered. 'Someone beat him up. He's in hospital.' And as if I wasn't looking sufficiently upset for his liking, he added, 'In a coma.'

39

The police delivered me to an interview room in Islington police station where I stared at the dingy walls while the detectives prepared to speak to me. I knew what would be going on behind the scenes: a frantic attempt to pull together enough facts to give them a theory about what had happened to Mark. They would probably know about Webster and our house burning down, I guessed. That would be why I was there. I didn't need to worry about being a suspect this time.

I did need to worry about Mark, though.

Was it because of me? Had someone decided he was a legitimate target in their campaign of terror against me?

Or was it much simpler than that?

I remembered sitting on a wobbly chair in the V&A café, telling John Webster – in passing, to make a point – about Mark, and how he'd changed.

I remembered standing in the draughty, dark kitchen of the house in Croydon, with the torchlight catching Webster's cheekbones and eyelashes and glittering in his irises.

You might have a reason to be more grateful soon.
What does that mean?
You'll understand eventually.

Webster would have enjoyed teaching him a lesson. He was strong enough to overpower Mark, it would present no moral difficulties to him and I assumed he knew where Mark lived. Motive, means, opportunity: he had all three.

But if I reported him to the police for anything he did from now on, he could drag me into a court case. I could end up in the dock beside him, both of us charged with offences relating to the kidnap of George Reese.

I was leaping ahead of myself, I thought, biting the inside of my cheek to bring myself back to the present, to the reality of a cold cup of tea sitting in front of me and the clock on the wall ticking towards midnight. Panic was not going to help.

When they came, the detectives were professional and pleasant. One was male, the other female. There was no news on Mark, the woman told me. He had a skull fracture. No news until tomorrow at the earliest.

'Are you treating this as a potential murder inquiry?'

They both reacted, going still for a second. I knew the degree of police involvement was a way to gauge how bad it was.

'We are staffing this as a possible murder, yes.'

A wave of dizziness came over me. I bent forward and put my head on top of my hands, on the table. 'Sorry.'

'No, it's fine.' A chair scraped and the door clicked. After a minute I lifted my head to see a plastic cup of water sitting in front of me. 'That might help.'

'Thank you.' I gulped at it, my hand shaking. The two

detectives watched me and drew whatever conclusions they wanted.

'What happened to him?'

'He was attacked outside his flat, early this morning.' The male detective twisted in his seat to check the time and discovered it was just past midnight now. 'Yesterday morning,' he amended.

'On his way home?'

'Putting out the bins, we think,' the woman said. 'Around six o'clock. He was found lying near the bins and there was a full bin bag on the ground beside him. His front door was open.'

'Was it a fight?'

'He was hit over the back of the head. There were no defence injuries to his hands. He didn't even put them out to break his fall.'

He would never have turned his back on Webster, and Webster would never have lost the chance to taunt him before he attacked. Whatever Webster had been talking about, it couldn't have been this.

'Was his flat burgled?'

'Nothing seems to have been disturbed. As far as we can see, Mark's valuables were all there – computer, phone, bike, car keys, quite a quantity of cash.'

I could picture it. He kept everything fully charged, ready to be scooped up in a single swoop on his way out the door. There would have been a handful of change and a wad of notes beside his keys and cards.

'Are you looking for a mugger?'

'He was wearing a very expensive watch which they didn't take.' The woman half-smiled. 'We did consider that.'

'I'm sure you did.' I knew the watch: a present from his godfather. Any decent mugger would have spotted it. I shook my head. 'I don't know who would do this.' Webster would have toyed with Mark, and taken his time about it.

The two detectives exchanged a look that I couldn't interpret, but some decision was made without words.

'When Mark was found he was barely conscious. While his neighbour was waiting for the ambulance to come, he kept saying the same thing. Two words. "Tell Ingrid". Over and over again.' The female detective folded her hands in front of her, prim as a Victorian miss. 'So what we want to know is why he said that. We thought you could tell us what he meant.'

The detectives let me go eventually, after a long and repetitive interview where I really tried to help but couldn't.

'Could "tell Ingrid" have been him trying to say "tell Ingrid I'm sorry"?' the female detective had suggested.

'It could have been, but I don't know why he'd say that now.' Tears were sliding down my face and I didn't seem to be able to stop them. I had wanted him back, I admitted to myself now. That was what had kept me from sleeping with Adam. After everything we'd been through, and the terrible things we'd said to one another, I still longed for Mark to come back.

Why would you want him? He left you. You should have more backbone, Webster's voice said in my mind. *You should be less pathetic, Ingrid.*

When I came out of the police station, I jumped in a taxi and went straight to the hospital. I couldn't just go home. Besides, his parents would be so worried, and I felt I should check whether they needed anything. That was what Mark would have done if the situation had been reversed.

Really, Diana and Julius were a convenient excuse; what I needed was to be near him. The possibility of him dying was unthinkable.

It was the dead time of night when the only people in hospital are the drunks, the seriously unwell, police officers with prisoners, and the staff. I walked through echoing, shadowy corridors on tiptoe. The nurses' station in the intensive care unit was busy with three members of staff talking in hushed tones, their heads bent together. One glanced up as I approached.

'Can I help you?'

'I'm Mark Orpen's . . . fiancée,' I said, pushing my ring-less hand into my pocket. 'How is he?'

'He's stable, my love. He's resting. We're happy with him.' She tilted her head to one side, sympathetic now. 'Do you want to see him?'

'Yes please.' I did, desperately.

'If you wait a few minutes, you can come in with his mum. She's in the relatives' room at the moment.' The nurse came out from behind her desk and pointed. 'She's been here all day.'

'Does she need to stay?'

'No. We did tell her to go home, but she wouldn't listen to us.' The nurse eyed me speculatively. 'You could persuade her, maybe.'

'I'll try.' I walked down the hall, aware that they were watching me go.

The lighting was dim in the relatives' room and it took me a moment to pick out Diana, a huddled shape on a small sofa. I wouldn't have woken her but she raised her head as I stood in the doorway.

'Oh, Ingrid, *darling*, I knew you would come.'

I put my arms around her, noticing with a pang that she had become frailer. Time and worry had worn her away. She was still a strikingly attractive woman though her hair was threaded with grey. 'How are you?'

'Worried.' She sniffed and tried to smile. 'I couldn't believe it when they called me. We're his next of kin. I rushed here – I left Julius at home because I thought he would get so tired waiting around. And then it didn't seem right to leave Mark here on his own.' Her voice broke on the last word and she bit her lip, hard.

'The nurse said he was doing well.'

'Did she? Oh, that's wonderful.' Diana held my hand. 'You're so good to come.'

'I wanted to help.' I hesitated. 'Diana, I really think Mark wouldn't want you to stay here all night. It's terribly late and Julius will be worried. What if we went in to see Mark and say goodnight?'

'Maybe . . . but I don't want to drive home on my own.' Diana's lower lip wobbled. 'If you could come with me . . .'

Home was a tiny, perfectly furnished house in Barnes, nowhere near my flat. 'Of course I will.'

'You can stay with us for breakfast and then come back to the hospital with me.' Her grip tightened. 'Mark will be so touched you came. This could be a blessing in disguise.'

Alarm bells began to ring, faintly.

'I've always thought the two of you would get together again if you just gave yourselves a chance. We always adored you, Ingrid.'

'Let's not get too far ahead of ourselves,' I suggested brightly. Mark was unlikely to be pleased if I encouraged her to think we were getting back together. 'I'll go and talk to the nurses now.'

There was something completely unreal about standing at Mark's bedside, opposite his mother, looking down at him. He was unconscious, unmoving, his body hooked up to the machines that beeped and flashed around the bed. The good news was that he was breathing unaided. All of his test results were encouraging.

'All we need to do is wait.' The nurse who was monitoring him all the time had smiled, full of kindness but with professional detachment that I envied. Diana wept, her eyes fixed on his face.

I felt dreadful. Would Mark have wanted me to be there? Would he have wanted me to see him like that – bare-chested, vulnerable, with grazes on his knuckles from where he fell? I touched the back of his hand gently, stroking it with one finger. His skin was warm.

'Ingrid is here, darling. She was worried about you too.'

No reaction.

'I wish you were awake so we could all talk together.' A tear slid down her cheek. 'Poor darling. My poor, poor little boy.'

Her poor little boy was six foot two, I thought. His eyelashes were fanned against his cheeks. His breathing was slow and regular. I wanted to put my head against his and breathe in the smell of him one more time.

I still loved him, and he wasn't mine any more.

That was why I had held back with Adam, I realised. I liked him, but while there was still the slightest chance of Mark coming back to me, I couldn't allow myself to fall in love with anyone else.

What had Mark meant when he said my name? *Tell Ingrid. Tell her this has happened. Tell her she was right. Tell her she was wrong.* No one knew, including me, and no one would know until Mark woke up.

If Mark woke up.

You can figure this out for yourself, he had said.

'Tomorrow,' the nurse said as she escorted us to the lift. 'Come back tomorrow and see how he is. Maybe he'll be awake tomorrow.'

But I wouldn't be back. I knew that already. I helped Diana to find her car and kept an eye out for red lights and wavering mopeds as she drove through the quiet streets.

The house in Barnes was as lovely as ever, and lovelier still was the look on Julius's face when he opened the door and saw his wife.

'You should have gone to bed,' she scolded and he nodded.

'I was worried about you.'

'Ingrid came and found me.'

'Good girl.' He kissed my cheek. Julius was such a gentleman. He was fragile these days, hobbling slowly through the hallway as Diana chivvied him to bed. Mark had timed his return from Canada well.

'You can sleep in the guestroom, Ingrid. It's all ready for a visitor – my sister was coming next week but I'm going to tell her to cancel it. I can't possibly have anyone to stay now, with Mark being in hospital. I don't

356

mean you, of course, Ingrid, but you're not like a *guest*. You're *family*.'

Oh God. I should have known she would assume – but then, if I hadn't gone, could I have lived with myself?

Diana and Julius disappeared. I followed more slowly, taking the time to look at the familiar paintings on the walls and the well-chosen, well-loved furniture as I turned out the lights. The last time I had been there was before the fire, when I had been about to marry Mark and become part of the family. I felt as if that life had belonged to a different person, a person who had no reason to doubt herself or her future happiness.

I made my way up to the pale blue guest room and discovered that Diana had found time to leave a long-sleeved nightdress and a new toothbrush on the bed for me. With a longing look at the plump white pillows on the bed, I forced myself to detour to the bathroom next door. I washed slowly, layers of dirt lifting off my skin. The day had been endless, and traumatic, and I was exhausted. I pulled the nightdress on and looked at myself: it was fussy, frilled with broderie anglaise and absolutely not my style. Diana would have worn it well. I could just imagine what Mark would have made of that particular Freudian nightmare: his fiancée in his mother's nightie. The smile faded from my face. I hoped I might get to tell him about it when he was well again.

I woke to Diana sliding a cup of tea onto the bedside table.

'I thought you'd like to know that I phoned the hospital and he's improving.'

'Is he awake?' I struggled to my elbows, still dazed.

'Not yet. They said it might not be today. But we can go and see him.'

'Diana, I don't think—'

'I'll see you downstairs for breakfast in half an hour,' she said firmly and left the room before I could say anything else.

I drank my tea and thought about what I should do, and what I shouldn't. When I came downstairs I was dressed and ready to leave.

'That was quick,' Diana said approvingly, pouring cereal. 'We should be able to get away soon after breakfast.'

'I'm not staying for breakfast,' I said. 'And I'm not going to come to the hospital.'

'But—'

'Please listen to me. I don't know what happened to Mark yesterday, but it might be connected with me. If that's the case, I don't think it's safe for him if I go to the hospital. When I saw him recently, I told him I was worried about my safety because a few strange things had happened – it doesn't matter what. I think he was trying to tell me that I was right to be worried.' I swallowed. 'I don't know why Mark was attacked but I really need to find out who was behind it, and I can't do that sitting in the hospital.'

'But—' Diana began again, but her husband put out a hand and touched her arm gently.

'Diana. She's right.' To me, he said, 'What are you going to do?'

'I don't know yet. Something.' I pulled my coat around me. 'I'm not in court for the next few days, so I have some time to think.'

'Then go and do that.' Julius smiled. 'You're capable of anything, my dear, once you set your mind to it.'

I turned to Diana. 'Will you tell me how he is?'

'Yes, of course.'

'I'll send you my number.'

'I'm sure I have it. Or Mark does. Or your mother would.'

That phone was switched off in the bottom of my handbag, the SIM card in an envelope I'd acquired at Islington police station and addressed to my own flat. At that very moment it was probably passing through the sorting office.

'I've changed numbers,' I said. 'I'll make sure you have the new one.'

'All right.' Diana's voice wavered a little.

I bent and kissed her cheek, then did the same to Julius. 'This is all going to be all right, you know. Mark is tough. He'll be fine. But whoever did this to him made a big mistake and I'm going to make sure they regret it.'

40

I walked towards the river, heading for Barnes Bridge station, and I was as sure as I could be that I wasn't being followed. It was almost nine in the morning and the train station was busy with silent commuters muffled in enormous coats. I squashed myself onto a train, pressed against a woman with a bulging handbag and a man who was determined to read his hardback book, despite the crush and the fact that he elbowed me in the head every time he turned the page. At Clapham Junction I got off and went up the steps to the footbridge that ran across the many tracks: seventeen platforms, two thousand trains a day, tens of thousands of passengers. I walked as far as the painted board that showed which platforms served which destinations, stood on the other side of the footbridge and considered it. Webster's words ran through my mind.

People go back to places they know . . . People shed information about themselves all the time. You think you're making free choices but really you're just going back to what you find comforting . . .

To avoid a hunter, think like a hunter.

I carried my passport in my bag, a lesson learned the hard way when the house burned down, and I always had a couple of hundred pounds in cash on me for the same reason. I'd taken more money out that morning on my way to the station. I wasn't going to use my cards again if I could help it. I could get to Gatwick Airport in half an hour. A few hours after that, I could be in Copenhagen, in my father's flat, where I would be welcome. My impatient, funny father, who still clung on to the rebel image he'd adopted in his youth in the shape of two piercings in one ear and the battered moped he loved to ride around town. I wanted to be folded in his arms and reassured and taken out for drinks and dinner in a nice restaurant, or spirited away to the lakeside holiday home that had been in our family for generations. No one could find me there, I thought, knowing from the ache in my heart that they could, and would, and if I went to him I would only put him at risk.

My eyes tracked down the list of place names again, looking for the unfamiliar, the unknown. The criteria: nowhere too small, nowhere too distant.

'What time,' said a querulous woman who was walking past, 'do we get to Brighton? Because if they won't let us check in to our rooms, I just don't see the point in getting there early. I don't want to have to walk around for hours with my bag, Andrea.'

I joined the flow of passengers heading in the opposite direction, towards the ticket office.

I had been to Brighton before, but not for a long time – not since a school trip that had taken in the Royal Pavilion and the pier. It had been summer on my last visit and I remembered sitting on the pebbled beach eating ice cream. I didn't recall a lot more, unfortunately. As I walked out of the train station and set off down the hill I recognised absolutely nothing. It was a cold day with low cloud grazing the rooftops and a sea mist blurring the outlines of buildings in the distance. I walked quickly, cutting down random side streets, wanting to get away from the station. I had nothing to carry but my handbag. At Clapham Junction I'd bought a pay-as-you-go SIM card. I'd texted Diana the number and had an acknowledgement from her, so that was all right. She had promised to tell me how Mark was, and I trusted her.

All roads downhill led towards the seafront and I arrived there eventually, to find a sea that was dark and violent and full of white horses. The wind scoured the promenade. Shivering, I retreated a couple of streets back to the shelter of the Lanes where I wandered for a while. I found myself staring into windows without seeing anything but my own reflection and the street behind me, so I could check I was alone. Leaving the antique shops and jewellers and narrow alleys behind, I found a Marks & Spencer where I bought pyjamas and underwear and an extra jumper. The shop assistant told me where to find a pharmacy, helpfully pointing out an enormous shopping centre opposite Marks. I bought some snacks and moisturiser and another new toothbrush and toothpaste and a hairbrush and anything else I could think I might need, within reason. My cash needed to last me a couple of days. Last of all I bought a notebook and pen. I had lunch in a tiny café with foggy windows, and sitting there felt almost like normal life had resumed. It was an illusion and I knew it, but I let myself go along with it for an hour or two. I stayed there nursing a cup of coffee until after three, when I tore myself away from eavesdropping on the conversations around me and walked back to the seafront with my purchases. The sea was churning and the wind had strengthened, blowing spray through the air. I put my head down and battled along the front to a small, faded hotel where I was able to negotiate a double room with a sea view for three nights. It took most of the money I had left but that was fine. I wasn't planning to go out.

The room was on the fifth floor. It was decorated in brown and cream and in ordinary circumstances I might have wrinkled my nose at the worn carpet, and the stained grout between the bathroom tiles, and the grey net curtains. It felt like a haven to me though as I shut the door behind me and locked it. There was a bed, and a desk, and even a lumpy armchair. The main thing I liked was the view from the window: the seafront, and beyond it the sea. There was something about being able to see the horizon that soothed me. I unpacked my few things, turned the armchair around to face the window and settled down to watch the waves until the last light faded from the sky.

I didn't go out much in the next few days. I sat and thought, turning the few facts I knew around in my mind, rearranging them to see if I could force them to make sense. The harassed chambermaid was happy to skip my room and I had enough to eat so I didn't need to brave the hotel breakfast. The weather was so terrible that I didn't feel guilty about not walking by the sea – the few dogwalkers and runners I saw were kitted out in full wet-weather gear and still looked miserable. Rain and sleet blasted the window at regular intervals, as gale-force winds whipped across the south of England. The television news was full of dire warnings about flood risks and structural damage; it all seemed incredibly remote. The hotel room was now the extent of my world.

On the second day, around noon, my phone hummed with a text message.

Mark awake!! Improving but v confused & doesnt remember wt happened. Out of ICU tmw. He sends love to you bt he has no idea why he said yr name!!! D xxx

I felt a rush of affection for her and the stupid abbreviations that probably took longer to type than the actual word would have. Tears stood in my eyes: Mark was awake and would soon be out of the ICU. I almost couldn't bear the relief of it. He wasn't going to die. *He sends to you* – but that was a commonplace, words chosen by his mother who was always effusive. If I'd been in any doubt about my feelings for Mark, the fact that I read the text message over and over again might have given me a clue.

It was frustrating that he didn't remember anything, but I had been braced for that. A bang on the back of the head hard enough to fracture his skull would have made him a very shaky witness. Saying my name could just have been a kind of mental short circuit instead of a warning to me.

I sent back a brief message of thanks and good wishes, after dithering over whether I should send love or not. I thought of them sitting in the ICU, reading it out, and what Mark would say about it, if anything.

There was one other thing about Mark's situation that gave me pause. The staff in the ICU had been so matter-of-fact, even though they clearly cared about what they did. It was their job, just as the law was mine. What seemed extraordinary to me was routine to them. I frowned, thinking about it. I'd thought my knowledge of the criminal justice system, and my experience in organising facts into a narrative would help, but what if it was part of the problem? I was coming at it from the wrong angle.

What I needed was an ordinary member of the public, and fortunately I knew where to find one.

'Hello?' Adele sounded wary when she answered her phone.

'It's Ingrid.'

'Ingrid? Why are you calling me from an unknown number? Did you lose your phone?'

'No. I'm just using this one temporarily.'

'Okay.' She sounded baffled.

'What are you up to?'

'Finishing up at work. Do you want to meet up?'

'I'm not in London,' I said. 'But if I can borrow you for a while, I'd appreciate your help with something.'

'Anything.'

She meant it, too, I thought, and I loved her for it. 'I know it sounds weird, but I want to tell you a story.'

'Okay.'

'And I want you to be honest about what you think.'

'Is it a love story?' She sounded hopeful.

'It's a story about a rape trial.'

'I should have known better.' She sighed. 'Okay. I'm listening.'

I told her what I remembered about Guy Lanesbury's trial, and how it had played out. 'She lied and we proved that she lied. Guy didn't do anything wrong. The jury believed him.'

'Ye-es.' She didn't sound convinced. 'But Lisa was upset by what he did.'

'That doesn't make it illegal.'

'I don't think that's the point, Ingrid. She was heartbroken and embarrassed and – and guilty, really, because it was her fault that he was acquitted.'

'You feel sorry for her.'

'Yeah, of course. Don't you?'

'I do, but that doesn't mean I think Guy should have gone to prison.'

'Well, no. They're both victims in a way – victims of bad judgement and being young and stupid. She hurt his feelings, but then he didn't do the right thing either. He couldn't have had consent for what he did to her. And she didn't deserve to be a social outcast. She didn't deserve to be humiliated in front of her dad. She was entitled to be unhappy about what he did but even if he'd been convicted she would still have lost all her friends and her privacy. You're just looking at it from the point of view of winning and losing and the law. Life isn't like that. Emotions aren't tidy and logical and *legal*.' She paused. 'How do you feel about what you did during the trial?'

'Me?'

'You sound defensive when you talk about it. What part did you play?'

'I didn't do much. I talked to Guy about what actually

happened. I went through a million printouts of phone records. Oh, and I did cross-examine someone. A witness.'

'Which one?'

'The best friend, Tess.' I remembered her: pale, round-faced, earnest, pushing her glasses up her nose every few seconds. 'She admitted that Lisa had been intending to sleep with Guy that night. It was her idea that Lisa should report the incident to the police. She basically convinced Lisa that what had happened to her was rape rather than—'

'Rather than what, exactly?'

I leaned back, staring out at the sea. 'An unpleasant incident.'

'You can say that again,' Adele said. 'You know, if that happened to you, and I talked you into going to the police, and this was the outcome, I would be pretty upset with myself. I'd hate to let you down.'

'She didn't really let Lisa down,' I said absently. 'There were lots of other people who didn't cover themselves in glory.'

'Like you?'

I had been out to impress Belinda and Hugh Hardwick, the solicitor. I didn't recall exactly what I'd said to her, though I remembered the judge gently reining me in once or twice, with a twinkle. Over-keen young barristers needed a steady judicial hand, but he had been kind to me all the same. It might even have looked as if he was taking my side, if you hadn't known what he was saying, and why.

I hadn't thought about the young woman in front of me, except as a challenge. I hadn't thought about how she might feel.

'I was younger then. Less experienced.'

'I suppose you get used to that kind of thing.'

'You do, but I didn't.' I hadn't wanted to get pigeonholed into only doing sex cases, as many women at the bar did. I wanted to do big frauds and robberies and murders – the complicated, demanding, high-stakes trials that were so much more satisfying than the impossible evidence-free rape trials that came down to one person's word against another. My career had taken a different direction. But it wasn't just a career decision, I admitted to myself. I hadn't liked the experience of winning when it came at such a cost.

Belinda had laughed at me when I tried to talk to her about it, and not kindly. 'Do you think men have to justify defending rapists? Do you think they're expected to identify with the victim? It's a trial like any other and it's your professional duty to do the best you can for your client, no matter what they're accused of doing.'

'Are you still there?' Adele sounded worried.

'Yes.'

'I know you were only doing your job. But I can see how someone who doesn't know you might think it wasn't a very good job to do.'

After I'd talked to Adele, I switched my phone off altogether. The SIM went into a bin near the big shopping centre. The weather was bad enough that no one was around and anyway I doubted whether anyone would have recognised me scuttling along the deserted streets with my hood pulled down over my face. I circled back to the hotel nonetheless, dodging down side streets and waiting to make sure no one was after me. It made me feel mildly insane to take precautions like that, but I had gone to a lot of trouble to disappear off the face of the earth and walking an extra kilometre or two couldn't hurt.

Back in the safety of my dingy room I settled down and spread out the notes I'd made over the past few days. I'd done the emotional side. Now I needed to think of this as if it was a brief and I was writing a case summary, spinning a clear and coherent story out of the facts that I knew for certain and the likeliest answers to the questions I had. There were still gaps – things I didn't quite understand yet, things I only suspected, things I wished I was wrong about.

I needed to fill in the gaps before someone else I loved got hurt.

41

From: IATL@internetforyou.com
To: Durbs, 4102

Where is she? Anyone know?

From: Durbs@mailmeforfree.com
To: 4102, IATL

You've lost her?

From: IATL@internetforyou.com
To: Durbs, 4102

I don't know exactly where she is, no. But you were supposed to be shadowing her too.

From: Durbs@mailmeforfree.com
To: 4102, IATL

Now and then, when I can. I've literally spoken to her. What if she gets suspicious?

From: 4102@freeinternetmail.com
To: Durbs, IATL

She's bound to be suspicious, isn't she? Strangers, turning up more than once, being all friendly?

From: IATL@internetforyou.com
To: Durbs, 4102

Can I just point out you've been absolutely no practical help so far in keeping an eye on her.

From: Durbs@mailmeforfree.com
To: 4102, IATL

Exactly. We've done loads. IATL has taken most of the risks but I've been there too. What exactly have you done?

From: 4102@freeinternetmail.com
To: Durbs, IATL

You know what I did. It sickened me, to be honest. I'm ready to do what I need to do next but I'm not going to trail around after her. I don't want to get to know her. I want to deal with her when the time comes and then forget about it.

From: IATL@internetforyou.com
To: Durbs, 4102

Okay, calm down. This is pointless. Until we find her, no one can do anything.

From: Durbs@mailmeforfree.com
To: 4102, IATL

But where is she?

From: IATL@internetforyou.com
To: Durbs, 4102

I'll work it out. I know her.

She's not going to get away.

42

The next day I went in search of an internet café, a dying breed in the era of smartphones and free WIFI. There was one on a side street not far from the train station, the hotel receptionist told me. I walked a long and twisting route to get there, checking behind myself frequently. I didn't really know who I was looking for, or what. If I'd learned anything it was that evil didn't come trailing obvious menace. Kind smiles could hide a lot.

In the café, I took out my notebook and worked my way through the list I'd made, with a hollow feeling in the pit of my stomach. It wasn't a long list, and it didn't take much time. I felt like John Webster, prowling the internet, paying for information when I couldn't find it any other way. It was surprisingly straightforward to track people. There were companies who made a fortune from gathering up personal information and sharing it, packaging us neatly as consumers with measurable value. For curiosity, I searched for my own name, and found every address I'd lived at in the last five years filling the screen. I sat back in dismay. Given that I was someone who had learned the hard way to be cautious about my security, I was far too easy to find.

Like Webster before me, I couldn't find any trace of Ben Sampson that matched what I knew about him, but I found two of the other people I wanted to locate. Lisa Muller's name prompted a thousand suggestions that were not her. But when I searched my own name and Lisa Muller's name together, I got a very different result. The search engine gave me a website – Justice Is Blind UK – and an abstract quote from the relevant material.

> . . . *there can be no doubt that the other barrister Ingrid Lewis also has blood on her hands for how she handled her part in Lisa Muller's trial, with ruthless disregard for . . . amounts to professional misconduct although we know that never gets . . .*

I closed my eyes as a wave of dizziness swept over me. It was like overhearing someone criticising you, except on a global scale. Anyone in the world could click the link and find out about my alleged professional misconduct, and I had no right to reply or defend myself.

The Justice Is Blind UK website loaded quickly, probably because it had been designed with minimal attention to how it looked. A glaring yellow banner topped the page, promising 'Attention for Every Miscarriage of Justice Until Our Voices Are Heard'. The rest of the page was a forum, the landing page for the discussion about Lisa Muller's case.

Welcome guest, please log in or register.

You may browse the forums without logging in but you may not post material. Please see FAQs for more.

Media reports provided on this forum are provided for information only Anything posted on this forum is the responsibility of the individual member

Endorsement of such material is neither intended nor implied.

Posters are asked to keep to thread topics Libellous or defamatory material will be removed immediately Abuse will not be tolerated

Listen to the moderators and read the rules!

Justice Is Blind UK forum >> Alleged Miscarriages of Justice >> Guy Lanesbury, Lisa Muller and a Sex Crime that Went Unpunished

Subject/Started by	Replies/Views	Last Post
Guy Lanesbury, Lisa Muller: An Overview of the Case

Started by Durbs
<<1 2>> | 48 replies

209 views | March 03, 2019, 03:08:41 AM by IAmTheLaw |

Prejudice in Court: Judge Ron Canterville and his history of bias Started by Durbs <<1 2 3>>	121 replies 1409 views	September 30, 2019, 22:42:39 PM by Durbs
Evidence against Guy Lanesbury Started by Durbs <<1 2 . . . 6>>	98 replies 249 views	January 14, 2019, 08:31:06 AM by Durbs
Lisa Muller and what happened next Started by Durbs <<1 2 . . . 4>>	66 replies 340 views	February 22, 2019, 13:48:12 by Felicity Brumhill
Lies, Bullying and Misconduct: the Defence of Guy Lanesbury Started by Durbs <<1 2 3>>	51 replies 218 views	January 14, 2019, 08:31:06 AM by Justice Moderator

I hopped back a page to discover that this was not one of the more popular subject threads on the forum. Big, notorious cases such as Jeremy Bamber's campaign for release attracted tens of thousands of posts and views. I went back to the Guy Lanesbury thread and started clicking through the sub-threads, skim-reading the first and last posts in most cases. The user 'Durbs' was the main poster, replying to themselves frequently to keep the conversation going. The forum was organised so that updated threads appeared on page one – if you wanted to attract attention from casual browsers, you needed to keep adding material.

Durbs clearly had close knowledge of the case and the individuals involved in it. I read through the posts with a feeling of foreboding that sharpened to actual fear. It was a powerful collection of accusations: that the witnesses had been intimidated and harangued, that key evidence had been ruled inadmissible by a biased judge, that the lawyers had laughed and joked among themselves even though they were on opposite sides, that Lisa had no lawyer to represent her . . . on and on it went, a cloud of doubt and anger that was shocking – appalling, even, if you didn't understand how the criminal justice system worked. Lisa hadn't had a lawyer because the case was the Crown's prosecution. She was the alleged victim, but that made her a witness. She hadn't needed legal representation because she wasn't on trial.

But at times, she had effectively been on trial. She had been held up and examined, judged for her past behaviour, filleted for dishonesty and thrown away once she had no further use for the prosecution or the defence.

Most of the responses were from random users commenting to say they had had no idea how the system worked, and that it was very unfair, and that their hearts broke for Lisa and everyone who knew her. Trigger warnings abounded before people shared their own stories of unsympathetic police, brutal charging decisions and trials that had left them with PTSD. For those who hadn't gone the legal route there was a litany of trauma too: schools or colleges that had taken the side of the accused rather than the accuser and led to interrupted education, or pressure from HR to drop suggestions of sexual harassment in the workplace. Job opportunities failed to materialise. References were tepid in their enthusiasm. Lives took different paths, while the alleged perpetrators sailed on to their destiny, unharmed. There was nothing to be done except bear witness. Something was fundamentally wrong in society, an imbalance of power so familiar that it was almost invisible. I felt outraged too, and I was part of the machinery that was chewing these women up instead of helping them. Adele was right: the law didn't cover everything. Right and wrong weren't just legal terms, subject to legal decisions. There were grey areas all over the place.

The sub-thread about Judge Canterville was popular with users who had their own stories to tell about him. It ended, to my shock, with a link to a brief obituary of him. Durbs had added a comment:

One down ha ha

No one had replied. Maybe that was too dark even for the users of Justice Is Blind UK.

In the thread about the defence, I found Belinda being eviscerated for internalised misogyny, anorexia and class privilege. Hugh Hardwick was there too, with a few choice quotes from the proceedings in his divorces. I found the discussion where I was mentioned, a series of posts that described in searing, furious detail how I had

378

cross-examined one of Lisa's friends. My demeanour was at fault ('smirking, smug, playing to the jury, arrogant') and my appearance ('cheap mascara and bottle blonde highlights') and the way I spoke ('posh, snooty bitch') and what I had said. In among the torrent of posts from Durbs was one from User4102, who simply replied:

Not surprised at all knowing what I know

Durbs had replied with a smiley face and

Check your DMs

So the discussion had continued, out of sight. I wished I knew what they had said to one another.

User4102 hadn't posted anything else on the forum, and a search for the name across the internet brought me nothing but pages of junk. A throwaway username to raise a flag: *I am here and I feel as you do*. A connection had been made. Interested, I started to look at the dynamics of the discussion – the replies from other users. A long account of Lisa Muller's life before and after the trial ended with a comment from a user who hadn't tried to disguise her identity – Felicity Brumhill.

I found this forum by accident and I've been reading it for hours. I am really shocked by what I've read here. I was a friend of Lisa's in school and I'm horrified by what happened to her but I'm also horrified that you're sharing it like this! Doesn't her family deserve some privacy? It's their tragedy. You seem to mean well but I think you should take it down.

Durbs hadn't replied. The forum had stayed up, but they hadn't posted again in the thread about Lisa. An attack of conscience, maybe.

There was one other post that caught my attention, an old one from a user named IAmTheLaw. It was short and to the point.

Meet me in the other place

What was the other place, I wondered, and why had this person wanted to meet Durbs there? It was frustrating, only hearing part of the conversation. IAmTheLaw had posted in some other parts of the forum, I discovered, clicking through to their history. It amounted to twenty or thirty posts, most of them brief, many with links to other websites where photographs or legal documents were available to look at. The posts were made over three or four years; this wasn't an obsessive, like Durbs. This was something else.

This was someone with a plan.

Luckily, I had one too.

43

I had been away for four nights by the time I came back to my flat – not even a week – but I felt as if I'd been gone for months as I walked through the courtyard in the quiet mid-morning. I had collected a handful of post that included the SIM card I'd posted to myself after my police interview. Everything looked strange to me, even the fairy lights Helen had strung in her window. The flat was exactly as I'd left it with John Webster. The place smelled wrong, though, and I went through the kitchen cupboards and the fridge, throwing out bread that had taken the opportunity to sprout green fluff and a sad pair of bananas that were too far gone even for baking. Four nights: I lived my domestic life close to the edge when it came to shopping and use-by dates. A load of laundry was still sitting in the washing machine so I threw in another dose of detergent and put it on again, hoping that the dank smell would dissipate.

Once I was quite ready, I put the SIM card back into my phone and switched it on. Instantly the handset began to vibrate with messages. Notifications flashed up on the screen faster than I could read them: voicemails, texts, emails, most of them concerned with one thing only.

Where are you.

Where are you.

Where are you.

I replied to the work ones first, easing into it. Friends next. My mother after that (with an actual phone call because I wasn't stupid enough to think a text message would be enough). I found her surprisingly easy to placate but that was thanks to Diana, who had called her the same day she texted me.

'Julius told her to tell me that you had business to attend to, and not to worry about you.'

'So you didn't?'

'Well, of course I worried, darling. I worry all the time. That's what mothers do.'

'Of course.'

'It was very nice of you to go and check on Mark.'

'The wedding's still not happening, Mother. Put your hat back in its box.'

'I did just wonder.'

'Please don't.'

'Diana thought—'

'That sounds unlikely.'

We both laughed. Then she turned serious. 'I trust Julius, but look after yourself, Ingrid.'

'I will.'

'Promise me.'

'I promise,' I said, and meant it, although we probably had different ideas of what that entailed.

*

London was the sort of place where you could be completely unfamiliar with a whole area, even if it was close to where you lived. I walked across the canal and into Camden. My destination was a grubby little townhouse on a side street near Camden Town Tube station, an office building carved out of a Victorian home. Three small businesses operated out of it: a wedding-dress designer in the basement, an architect's firm on the ground and first floor, and a small logistics company on the top floor. I had timed my arrival for the close of business and discovered that the architect had moved premises since I'd researched the address. The office was empty, with whitewashed windows. The wedding-dress designer was closed to customers except on Wednesdays and Saturdays, which left the top of the building as the only place where people were actually working. The lights were on, I could see from my position on the street. I leaned against a wall and did my best to look unobtrusive.

About ten minutes after I arrived, at half past five on the dot, a middle-aged man in a bike helmet emerged from the building carrying his bike. He spent some time fussing over the bike and adjusting the bag he wore across his torso before he set off, wobbling alarmingly, to join the traffic on the main road. A woman in a gorgeous red coat was the next to leave, walking away quickly in flat ballet shoes that didn't make a sound on the pavement. Finally, a youngish guy in trainers skipped down the steps. He was wearing giant headphones and a Doctor Who T-shirt and might as well have had IT SUPPORT tattooed across his forehead. I waited for him to go, then crossed the road and pressed the buzzer for RTW Logistics Enterprises. It was an old-fashioned intercom with no video camera, which was a help.

There was a crackle. 'Yeah?'

'Hi, is Martin there?'

'You just missed him.'

'Damn,' I said. Martin was the name of the IT expert, I knew from trawling the company website. 'Look, I told him I would drop something off for him. It's too big to go through the letterbox and I don't want to leave it on the step. Is there any way you could buzz me in?'

Silence. Then the door hummed and I pushed it open. I found myself in a bare hallway, in the area outside the architect's office. There wasn't a sound in the building as I walked up the stairs except for the drone of fluorescent bulbs overhead. The doors were all closed on the tiny first-floor landing. I went up the next flight of stairs, wary now. On the second floor, both doors stood ajar. One was labelled RECEPTION, so I went and tapped on it lightly.

'You can just leave whatever it is on the desk near the door. I'll make sure he gets it.' Her voice was light but metallic and it raised the hairs on the back of my neck: I recognised it. I pushed open the door slowly and peered into the room, to see that she was sitting at a desk on the other side of it, her back to me. It wasn't a large room but there were two other desks crammed into it, both stacked with box files and folders. The computers looked antique and the carpet was ripped. RTW Logistics (Specialists in Office Moves and International Shipping) didn't waste any glamour on the back office.

'Thanks so much for this.'

She half-turned but didn't make eye contact. 'It's fine. Really. I'll tell him you came by.'

I put the box down on the desk, as directed. 'Tess, isn't it?'

Most people would have looked around if someone said their name. She didn't. She looked straight ahead at the greying, dented plaster in front of her and said nothing.

'I'm not here to leave something for Martin. I'm here to see you.'

She put her hands flat on the desk, on either side of the keyboard. 'I'm sorry. I don't understand. I don't think I know you and I would like you to leave.'

'You do know me.' I perched on the edge of the desk near me and folded my arms. 'You have some quite strong opinions about me, in fact. I'm Ingrid Lewis.'

Her fingernails went white as she pressed them into the desk. 'You need to go.'

'Can you look at me, Tess?'

She turned slowly, dragging her eyes up to meet mine with an obvious effort. I saw a small, thin woman, her hair scraped back into a ponytail. Her skin was colourless, from shock or because that was how she looked most of the time. A motorbike roared up the street outside, the sound of its engine bouncing off the buildings, loud thanks to the single glazing in the old windows. I waited until it was gone to speak.

'You were at the self-defence class in the parish hall.'

'Well done.'

I called her to mind, smiling timidly, wearing pink lipstick on that occasion in a shade too blue to suit her. Her hair had hung down around her face.

I'm here to get more confidence.

'You said your name was Laura.'

'I lied.' She said it flatly.

'You followed me there.'

'I've been following you for weeks.'

385

'Why?' I tilted my head. 'And why risk being caught? You must have known it was dangerous.'

A shrug. 'I wanted to see you, I suppose. To test you.'

'You wanted to look me in the eye and see if I remembered cross-examining you during Guy Lanesbury's trial.'

She flinched. 'I'd have known you anywhere but you didn't remember me at all. I was shaking in case you recognised me. But I didn't ring any bells.'

'In fairness, you've changed,' I said. 'You had glasses then, and you were . . .'

'Fat. You can say fat.'

Nowadays she was so skinny she looked ill. I had to outweigh her, I thought, and I was taller than her. Plus I was closer to the door. There was no reason to feel scared even though Tess Ivors was looking at me with absolute loathing.

Her emotion was a weapon I could use, in the same way I often provoked a defendant's temper in cross-examination. People gave themselves away when they forgot to be on their guard. I looked sympathetic.

'You must have been so disappointed that I didn't know you.'

'I shouldn't have been surprised. I'd have known you anywhere. I suppose you're used to destroying people. One more here or there wouldn't stand out.'

'I don't make a habit of it.'

'No, you make a career out of it. Do you remember what you did when I was on the stand? What you implied? You suggested that I was in love with Lisa.'

'I never actually said that.'

'Oh no. You were too clever for that. You made me

386

look like a fool. You implied I was jealous of Guy. You made the jury think I'd made the whole thing up to get back at him.'

'I'm sorry about that. It must have been hard to take. I was tough on you.'

'Lisa deserved to be listened to in court. She deserved to be believed.'

'Lisa lied about what happened. The jury couldn't find Guy guilty when she had lied.'

'You twisted her words. She was drunk and he took advantage of her. She didn't know what she was doing.'

'She didn't think it was rape until you told her it was.'

'Fuck you,' she snapped. 'I don't want to listen to you justifying yourself.'

'What do you want?'

'Justice.' She said it simply. 'Lisa never got it.'

'Is that why you started posting on the Justice Is Blind forum?'

She stared at me. 'I— what?'

'Durbs, isn't it? I like that nickname. I'm guessing you studied Thomas Hardy at some stage. Tess of the D'Urbervilles. Grim book, but hey, that fits.'

'It wasn't – I didn't study it.'

'Did Lisa? Was that her nickname for you?' I knew I'd hit on the right answer from the expression on her face. 'Okay. I see now why you chose it.'

'Don't say her name. Don't even say it.' Tess jumped off her chair and stood with her hands balled at her sides. She was shaking. 'You don't get to talk about her. Not after what you did.'

'What happened to Lisa was a tragedy,' I said slowly. 'But I wasn't the reason she died.'

'Oh, of course not. You didn't do anything wrong. You were just doing your job.'

'I didn't even know she was dead,' I protested. 'It happened months later.'

'You didn't bother to find out, though, did you? You never thought about her again. Or me.' Her eyes were full of unshed tears and her face was quivering with the effort of holding them back. 'Look, what do you want?'

'I'm not here to threaten you with anything. I just want to understand what you've been doing and why. And I want to know who IAmTheLaw is, and what they wanted with you.'

She caught her breath. 'You shouldn't ask about him.'

'Him? Have you met him? What's his real name?'

She shifted her weight and almost overbalanced. Without looking, she reached out to steady herself on the desk, or so I thought. Instead, her hand went unerringly to the stationery-holder on her desk, and she grabbed something: a box cutter with a sharp, sharp blade.

'What are you doing?' It was a stupid question, I thought; I could see very well what she was doing.

'You shouldn't have come here.'

It felt very unfair that I should be held to account for something I'd done at the start of my career, I thought, with a wave of utter exhaustion. 'We all make mistakes, Tess. I'm sorry for mine. Don't make this into another one of yours. If you hurt or kill me in your actual office what do you think is going to happen to you? How are you going to explain that away? Where are you going to go if you have to run away?'

'Fuck you.' She looked past me and smiled. 'Well, look who it is.'

My heart thumped painfully as I turned to look at the doorway, because if she was happy that couldn't be good news for me.

I hadn't expected it, but I probably should have, given what I knew and what I feared.

It was John Webster who was standing there, tall and lean with his hands in the pockets of his long overcoat. His expression was utterly blank.

'You wanted to know who IAmTheLaw is,' Tess said. 'Now you can see for yourself.'

And that was the point when I began to despair.

44

'What the hell are you talking about?' John hadn't taken his eyes off her. 'Don't listen to her, Ingrid. She's messing with you.'

'How does she know who you are, John?'

'I don't know.'

'And how did you know I was here?'

He shrugged. 'You put your phone back on. You must have known I'd find you.'

I didn't know who to believe. All I knew for certain was that Tess was standing far closer to me than John, and I knew I should be scared of her.

Tess rolled her eyes. 'You should just admit it. There's no point in trying to trick her any longer.' To me, she said, 'John has been helping us.'

'She's lying.' His voice was toneless, but when I looked at him his eyes were bright with anger. 'I know who she is but only because I've been following the same trail as you. You wanted me to find Tess for you, Ingrid. We got to the same place at the same time by different routes.'

'You're not going to believe him, are you? He's been part of this from the start.' Tess was blazing with triumph. This was what she had wanted all along – what she had waited for. It wasn't just that she wanted me dead. She wanted me to know I had been comprehensively tricked first. 'He told us he could make you do whatever he wanted. I'll admit, I was sceptical, knowing what he did to you in the past – what he did to your life. I thought you'd never fall for what he was proposing. But you really are that stupid, aren't you?'

'Don't listen to her. Listen to me.' His voice was urgent. 'You have to trust me, Ingrid, so I can get you out of here.'

'He won't help you. He's going to kill you.' She grinned. 'Or I will, if he lets me.'

'No one is going to hurt anyone,' John said levelly. 'You're going to put your stupid little knife down, and Ingrid and I are going to walk out of here.'

'Changed your mind?' She took a step closer to me. 'I haven't. Even if you can stop me before I kill her, I should get to do some damage to her pretty face. Let's see if he still likes you when you've got scars, Ingrid. Let's see if juries still listen to you then.'

'Move towards me, Ingrid.'

I couldn't bring myself to do it.

Tess smiled. 'Bit late, but you're finally seeing sense. That's what I've never been able to understand, Ingrid. Even if you were desperate, why would you trust him?'

'You know better than to believe her.' John sounded irritated now.

'Yes, Ingrid, ignore me. Trust him one more time.' She laughed. 'See how that pans out.'

He made as if he was going to step towards her and she faltered for the first time, edging backwards with the knife pointed at him, not me. I could do something, I thought, watching her. If she was focused on him, maybe I could grab something from the desk and hit her with it. The lamp looked good and heavy, though the cord would limit how far I could swing it.

It's your only chance, I thought, but it was a crap chance. There had to be another way.

What I was mainly thinking was: *it can't end like this. I don't want to die like this.*

Because if she was telling the truth, I had to get past John Webster before I could get away.

He sighed. 'I don't know what game you're playing, but I'm not joining in. Now, you can tell the truth because I ask you nicely, or you can scream it because I'm hurting you. I really don't care which option you choose, but I suspect you might have a preference.'

'He means it,' I said.

Tess rolled her eyes. 'He wouldn't do that to me. He wouldn't dare.'

He had been leaning against the door frame and there was no warning before he moved to grab her. Tess jumped away instinctively and her heel snagged in the ripped carpet. For an endless moment she swayed backwards, off balance for real this time. Her body was curved, her arms outstretched, but there was nothing for her to hold on to.

It was an accident. I swear it was an accident.

She collided with the tall window behind her and the thin glass shattered, the glazing bars old and rotten, and she reached out to grab the window frame but her hands slipped off it. I had time to take two steps towards her before she disappeared from view, momentum and gravity dragging her into space. She didn't make a sound as she fell through the air. I heard the sound of a catastrophic impact and I wished to God I hadn't.

Someone screamed, far below, and I tried to go to the shattered window but Webster caught hold of me.

'No you don't. Stay well back, please. You don't need to be seen here. We need them to think this office was empty when she fell. There'll be a back way – you can get out, and walk away.'

'Tess—'

'Is very fucking dead indeed.' He shrugged. 'Who cares? You're not. Now get your things and disappear. I'm going to wipe the place down.'

'We killed her.' I couldn't seem to get enough air.

'Hardly. She fell out of the window, Ingrid. No one pushed her. No one made her jump.'

'If we hadn't been here . . .'

'I don't see why you're getting upset,' Webster said flatly. 'She was a problem and now she's not.'

'She was a problem for you. Especially if she was going to tell me the truth about you being on her side.'

She had known exactly who he was. She hadn't been surprised to see him.

I knew I couldn't trust John Webster.

'Come on, Ingrid. Pull yourself together.' Her death hadn't bothered him in the slightest, I realised. 'It's not important. Move on.'

'I think you wanted to stop her talking,' I said softly. 'I think you were terrified I'd listen to her and not you.'

He rolled his eyes, irritated. 'Look, we can discuss this at length some other time. Right now, we need to make tracks. They'll think it was an accident – or suicide. Maybe I'll leave a note. God knows this place is depressing enough that you'd want to kill yourself if you worked here. You'll need to tell me what you touched and which way you got here so we can come up with a cover story for you.'

'I don't want your help.' I turned and ran from him, rattling down the stairs, petrified that he would follow me – but he let me go. He didn't need to chase me then. He would track me down whenever he felt like it.

I managed to compose myself as I stepped out of the building into a tiny grey yard littered with cigarette butts. A gate led me to a narrow alley that ran back to the street. I walked out of it at my usual pace and glanced back casually in the direction of Tess's office. A crowd of people had gathered in front of it. A bundle of something was lodged on the railings outside: she hadn't even made the pavement, I realised with an uneasy lurch from my gut.

I walked away, passing through the Underground station with unhurried focus, as if I was on my way home from work like everyone else instead of fleeing from a monster.

45

It had started to rain while I was watching Tess Ivors die, and I was soaked to the skin by the time I got to Adele's flat. My throat ached from unshed tears; I was still devastated but I couldn't cry about it yet. I was too angry, and too scared.

'Ingrid, what happened to you?' It was surreal how normal Adele looked in her jogging bottoms and big jumper, her hair greasy with some sort of leave-in mask, ready for a night of snuggling on the sofa watching a box set. That life – that normal, untroubled, tranquil existence – seemed as out of my reach as the far side of the moon. I couldn't imagine how I looked, but her eyes were wide with shock as she looked me up and down. 'Come on. You can't stand out there all night. Come in and get warm. You look terrible.'

'I can't stay here. He'll know I'm here. He'll look for me here.' My teeth were chattering.

'Who? Webster?'

I nodded.

'Is he chasing you again?'

'He never really stopped.' I leaned against the wall, exhausted. 'He'll come here when he doesn't find me at home. I feel like such a fool.'

'What did he do?'

'A woman died in front of me. She was trying to tell me he was working with her to punish me for what I did in that rape trial. He scared her and she fell out of a window.'

'Oh my God.' Adele covered her mouth. 'And you saw it?'

'He was glad she was dead. And I'm sure he attacked Mark.'

'You think that was him too?'

'Who else?'

She put her arms around me and I closed my eyes, breathing in the coconut smell from her hair. 'I'm so tired, Adele, but I can't stay here. I don't want to put you in danger.'

'So what are we going to do?' She stepped back and folded her arms, my fierce defender in fluffy slippers.

'You're not going to do anything except lock your door after I leave. Don't open it for any reason. Lock all the windows too. Keep your phone with you in case you need to call 999.'

Adele swallowed: this had all become real for her, all of a sudden, and I felt nothing but guilt about it. But she rallied. 'What about you? What are you going to do?'

'I'm going to call the police.'

The police turned up about forty-five minutes later, in the Golf, alone. Adam had a thunderous expression on his face as he pulled in beside the bus shelter where I'd been waiting for him.

I opened the passenger door and got in.

'Thanks for coming.'

'What's going on?' He was at maximum grimness. 'Why wouldn't you tell me on the phone? And where the hell have you been for the last few days?'

'Away.' I couldn't bear to look at him; I knew he was right to be annoyed. 'Getting my head together.'

'Away? What does that mean? Where did you go? I thought – well, I thought all kinds of things.'

'It doesn't matter where I was. I just needed to get away.'

He controlled his temper with an obvious effort. 'Okay. You don't have to tell me everything. Here's a question you might like to answer though – why didn't you tell me you were disappearing? I've been going out of my mind.'

'I'm sorry. I thought it was best not to talk to anyone about it. I hadn't been in touch with anyone at all until this morning when I came back.'

'So I wasn't first on your list to contact.'

I bit my lip. 'I wasn't ready to talk to you.'

'I thought something had happened. I couldn't think of any other reason you wouldn't call me.'

There was a question implied in that: *don't you care about me?* I chose to ignore it for the time being. 'If anyone was looking for me, they'd start with you. I couldn't take the risk. It wasn't a planned thing. I just went.'

'Okay.' He looked out through the windscreen, collecting himself. 'What's the problem now?'

'I need to get away from here.'

'Why?'

'John Webster is looking for me.'

That actually made him laugh. 'What else is new?'

'I know.' I shoved my hands between my knees, shivering. 'I'll tell you everything if you just take me away from here.'

The amusement faded from his eyes. 'You're really scared, aren't you?'

'Yes.'

'Are we going somewhere just for tonight, or—'

'I don't know. I don't know.'

'My flat?'

'No.' I said it before I thought about it. 'He would look for me there. I'd assume he knows where you live.'

It wasn't just that. I couldn't be alone with Adam Nash, not without explaining to him that I was still in love with my ex-fiancé, and after I explained that to him we would be stuck in a small flat together for an indefinite amount of time. I'd experienced more than my fair share of awkward situations, especially lately, but that one was off the scale. I liked Adam, but when I tried to remember kissing him it felt like something from another life.

'I could take you somewhere out of London. A safe house. I was thinking about this anyway.' He paused. 'I've been waiting to get the full picture before I talked to you, but you know there's an ongoing police investigation into Vicki's death. They've been doing a lot of work to confirm that there is a real and credible threat to your life. It looks as if there's a group of people behind this, from what they've told me, but until they're all in custody, you're in danger.'

'Well, as of this evening you can cross one of them off your list.'

'What? What happened?'

'I'll tell you. I'll tell you everything. But can we just go?'

'I'll need to make a phone call.' He was staring at me, concerned. 'And you probably need to pack a bag. Clothes, toiletries—'

'No way. Neither of us is going back to the flat. I can manage without my things.'

'Let me make this call,' he said slowly, 'and then we can hit the road. On the way you can tell me everything.'

'The person who died was a woman named Tess Ivors.'

He listened, concentrating on what I was saying. We were crawling through London in traffic that was unexpectedly heavy. Red taillights snaked into the distance in front of us.

'It happened in the office where she worked, this evening. I'd gone there to talk to her. To confront her, I suppose.' I swallowed, hard. 'While I was away, I did some thinking about the trial that we're all connected with – me, Belinda, Ron Canterville. I found an internet forum concerned with miscarriages of justice – Justice Is Blind UK, it's called. Tess Ivors was Lisa Muller's best friend. She was the one who encouraged her to go to the police about what happened that night. I cross-examined her. I wasn't particularly nice about it.' I hesitated. 'I would do it differently now. Anyway, Tess never got over it. She felt guilty and humiliated. I think she was still depressed about what happened to her friend. When people feel that way, they lash out. And she lashed out at me. You were right about a group of people being involved. I think one was Ben Sampson, the man I told you I saw after the scaffolding accident and in the Temple and at the self-defence class, but I still haven't been able to trace him and I didn't get the chance to ask Tess. She told me John was one of them. That's why he killed her. She was going to give the game away.'

'John Webster was part of the conspiracy against you,' Adam said. 'And so was this Ben.'

'That's what she said, and what I've worked out. I found Webster on the forum. His username was IAmTheLaw, which I presume was ironic. I think Ben was User4102 And I don't think they knew each other in real life. Tess followed me to that self-defence class but Ben had no idea she was there, or that I would be one of the participants. If they had a conspiracy it was all online.'

'IAmTheLaw. Cheeky fucker.' Adam was shaking his head. 'I told you not to trust Webster.'

'Don't rub it in.'

'I'm just glad you didn't get hurt.' He looked away from me, thinking about it. 'We still haven't traced the homeless guy on the CCTV when Belinda died, have we? I think that was John Webster. You recognised him immediately when you saw it.'

I was about to say we had located George but in a split second I thought better of it. Webster had found George, and presented him to me as if I could trust what the poor lad said. I didn't know if he was actually telling the truth. John could have convinced him to say anything. And when I'd tried to push George further on what he knew, he had gone silent.

John Webster was quite capable of finding himself a double, if he needed one. He was quite capable of hurting George to give him a limp to match the vagrant on the CCTV of Belinda's murder. And he was quite capable of killing.

He had primed George to give me a set of random suspects that I could chase forever, and I had fallen for it – fallen so far and so hard that I hadn't dared tell Adam or anyone else about George, and how I had been complicit in questioning him.

My main problem was that I still wasn't sure how Adam would feel about George and the part I had played in kidnapping him, so I decided to keep on saying nothing. Whether it was John at the roadside or not, it didn't matter at all.

Adam looked across at me. 'Are you sure this Tess was dead?'

'Very. She fell out of a window.'

He took that on board, his lips pursed in a silent whistle. 'Did you call the police?'

'No. And I didn't stay. I just ran.'

'Are you prepared to give evidence against Webster?'

'Yes. And he knows it too. He lost his temper with her. She was threatening me with a box cutter—' I broke off because Adam was swearing under his breath. 'I could have talked my way out of it.'

'I'm sure you could. Not the first time you've had to deal with that kind of thing, is it?'

'No.' I was silent for a moment, and so was he. I suppose we were both thinking of Emma Seaton in that grim bathroom, John Webster's first victim. 'Anyway, Tess, John and Ben were involved in this conspiracy. I think you might be able to find out Ben's real identity quite easily if I give you the link to their discussion on the website.'

'Good thinking,' he said. 'You've done an amazing job, Ingrid. I can't believe how much you've managed to find out on your own.'

'I was highly motivated,' I said drily.

He drove on in silence for the next few miles, then pulled off the road at a petrol station and bought some food, and coffee. I would have said I wasn't hungry but I ate it anyway, barely tasting it. I felt fractionally better afterwards, and the coffee helped to prop open my eyes which had been threatening to close.

The weather was even worse on the motorway. The windscreen wipers were operating at full speed and still they couldn't quite keep up with the rain. The wind tugged at the car when the road was exposed.

'Where are we actually going?'

'Hampshire.'

'That's a big county. Do you want to narrow it down a little?'

'You don't need to know where it is. I know and that's what matters.' He gave me an affectionate smile, though. 'It's a lot nicer than our official safe houses. It's also more secure. I don't trust John Webster not to know where every police property is, but he shouldn't have any idea about this one.'

'Good.'

'I'm glad we're doing this. Until they're all in custody, you're in danger. We can't take any risks with you.'

I drifted a bit as the road disappeared under our wheels, soothed by the thud of the wipers. I actually dozed off for a while, despite the coffee, and woke up to discover we were on a country road.

'Where are we?'

'Ten minutes to go.'

Apart from the whirling rain and the tree branches that

glanced past, silver-white in the headlights, there was nothing much to see. The road we were on was narrow and made narrower by the hedges on either side.

'All right?'

'Fine.' It came out as a whisper.

The car slowed and he leaned forward, looking for something. Two granite gateposts loomed on the left and he drove between them, then stopped.

'I have to close the gates.'

He jumped out and I heard the metal squeal as he dragged them closed. I leaned forward so I could see him in the side mirror. He had stopped to look at his phone, tapping out a short message. When he got back into the car, I raised my eyebrows.

'Should that be on?'

'What?'

'Your phone.' He had taken mine, back in London, and removed the SIM.

'Don't worry.' He reached out to trace the curve of my cheek with his thumb. I moved away a couple of inches, uncomfortable. His hand dropped and his eyebrows drew together, but he didn't comment except to say, 'It's a throwaway one. I'm not taking any risks.'

I would need to talk to him about Mark, I thought. I needed to be honest with Adam. He deserved that.

'John Webster—'

'—is probably in custody even as we speak.'

He set off again, the car making heavy weather of the rutted track that led down the other side of the hill. Woods stretched away on either side of the road and dead leaves danced in front of us. The road improved as it swept down to the bottom of the valley – a river valley,

I realised as a narrow humpbacked bridge came into view. The bridge wasn't much longer than the car, but Adam took it slowly, inching forward and swearing under his breath. I looked over the side to see white foam as the water forced its way downstream, and remembered the weather alerts I'd watched in Brighton.

'They did say there would be flooding.'

'What?'

'Never mind.' I drew my knees up and hugged them for comfort as the car left the bridge and accelerated around a bend. A foursquare Georgian house stood there, not large but immaculate, with a lawn in front and a straggling collection of outbuildings behind it. In the darkness the white-painted house seemed to glow against the black backdrop of a wooded slope.

'Beautiful.'

'Isn't it?' Adam glanced at me and smiled. 'Not such a bad place to wait this out.'

He drove carefully along the side of the house, pulling into the big empty courtyard to the rear of the property. I must have been looking apprehensive because Adam patted my knee.

'It's going to be fine.' Without waiting for me to reply, he got out of the car and went to the boot, lifted my bag out and carried it across the yard. The back door opened before he had a chance to knock. A silver-haired man stood on the threshold, nodding to Adam. He said something and both of them turned to look at the car where I was still sitting.

There was no reason not to get out of the car except that I didn't want to, and I couldn't work out why.

Adam handed the silver-haired man my bag and he turned away to put it down in the hallway behind him.

I was afraid, and there was no reason to be.

Adam was making his way back to the car at a jog, frowning as the rain stung his face. 'Come on,' he mouthed at me, puzzled, and I heard a car engine roaring behind me. Headlights lit up the interior of the Golf, and Adam's horrified face beyond it. The car wasn't slowing as it approached.

Get away from here, a voice said in my head, and I obeyed it without thinking.

I shot across to the driver's seat where the keys still hung from the ignition, and started the car, and swung the wheel to the right as I accelerated, trying to make a quick turn, and I was too late. The vehicle behind me ploughed into the back of the Golf, spinning it off course and off balance. The car slid across the yard as I braked uselessly, and the thick stone wall of an outbuilding filled the windscreen, with Adam right in front of it. He had no time to react. I think he tried to jump clear once he realised what was happening, but he was too slow.

The car ploughed into the wall with a horrible metallic screech, the airbag exploded, and I blacked out.

46

I blinked back into a dazed kind of consciousness after a few seconds, no more than that, but my world had changed fundamentally. The deflated airbag filled the car and a chemical smell stung my nose. My ears were ringing and I tasted blood. Putting a hand to my face, I found that it came away red. I couldn't complain about a nosebleed, though, when the airbag had stopped me from smashing every bone in my face on the steering wheel. My neck and arms tingled with the promise of pain later. Moving as if I was underwater, I tried to shove the airbag out of my way. The windscreen had shattered, turning to frost. Through a fist-sized gap in front of me I could see the headlights were still working. Fuzzily I leaned to my left to check whether I could see anything except the wall in front of me, and I saw, and I remembered.

'Adam!' I fought to reach the door handle and shoved the door open, slithering out onto the cobbles of the yard. I stumbled around the door and stopped, horrified, hanging on to it for support.

He had fallen but not all the way to the ground. The Golf had pinned him against the wall, the bonnet pressing into his chest. For a moment I thought he was dead, because he was completely still and his face was white. He had braced his hands against the bonnet and his head was tipped back, his eyes closed. Even as I stood there, his eyelids fluttered, and he groaned.

'Get out of the car.'

I looked around to see the silver-haired man who had greeted Adam. He was holding a shotgun, pointing it at the car behind the Golf. It was a big, black Mercedes SUV – no wonder the Golf hadn't stood a chance against the heavier, fast-moving vehicle. And I hadn't stood a chance when the driver I was trying to outmanoeuvre was John Webster.

Webster looked comparatively unruffled, despite the fact that he was sitting in a write-off with drifts of broken glass from the windscreen sitting on all the surfaces.

'Sorry about that, Ingrid. I hope you're not hurt. I thought it was Adam who was driving, not you. If I'd known it was you I'd have let you get away.'

'Don't talk to her. Get out of the car.' The man moved closer. He held the gun with what looked like a high degree of competence, and I could see the calculation in John's eyes.

'Watch his hands,' I said to the silver-haired man, who nodded.

To John, he said, 'Get out of the car slowly. Keep your hands where I can see them. I will shoot you if you don't do what I say. I'm going to count to three. One. Two.'

He was showing every sign of being prepared to get to

three, I thought, and John must have reached the same conclusion.

'All right. But I have to take off my seatbelt.' He lowered one hand and undid it, then eased himself out until he was standing beside the cars. 'Poor old Adam. That was a bit of bad luck, wasn't it?'

Adam winced instead of replying and my heart twisted. He needed help, and soon.

'Turn around and put your hands on the roof of the car. Spread your arms and legs.' The silver-haired man glanced at me as Webster did what he was told. 'You'll have to search him.'

I stepped forward. John was wearing his usual uniform: a long black coat and jeans and a soft cashmere jumper. I checked every pocket, then patted down his arms and legs and back while he kept up a stream of encouraging advice. I really didn't want to touch him, but I had no choice.

'You should check my shoes. People often hide weapons in there. Don't hold back. You don't want to miss something because you're embarrassed. Get right in there between my legs.'

'I'm not embarrassed,' I said through clenched teeth. 'I am furious.'

'I'm here to help you.'

'I can do without it.'

'You really can't.'

'How did you even get here?'

He looked bored. 'I followed you. Really not that difficult or interesting. I had to hang well back so PC Plod didn't spot me. You've made a big mistake, Ingrid. This is a trap. You need to get out of here.'

'It's a trap for you.'

'I knew that before I got here.' He lowered his voice. 'You can't trust them. And you shouldn't have listened to Tess. I'm a little hurt that you took a stranger's word over mine.'

'Ignore him,' the silver-haired man said.

I stepped back. 'I haven't found anything.'

'Okay.' He started issuing orders, waiting for Webster to cooperate between each one. I wondered if he was a police officer – retired, maybe. Or ex-military. 'Hands on top of your head. Turn around and face me. Not too fast. Okay. Walk towards me. Stop. That's far enough.' The man backed away, maintaining the distance between himself and John. 'Now walk towards that building.'

He was indicating a stone-built barn on the left of the courtyard. John looked at it, frowning.

'You know, I don't think I want to go in there. And I don't think you're going to kill me if I refuse.'

'You're right. I won't. I want to hand you over to the police so they can deal with you.' The man shrugged. 'I don't mind shooting you if you insist on it. But it won't be fatal, assuming you get treatment in time.'

John's mouth tightened, but he nodded. There was something utterly believable about the way the man had said it.

'Ingrid,' the man said, 'there's a light switch on the right of the door. Can you run ahead and put it on, please?'

The open door looked as inviting and safe as a black hole. I slipped through it, smelling dust and the ghost of horses long gone. Something moved in the darkness, a small and scurrying creature. I shuddered as I searched for the switch, touching cobwebs and cold stone before my fingers made contact with it.

The lights came on, all the way along the building. It was a stable block: ten stalls with stone partitions between them.

'Keep going,' the man said from outside, and Webster walked in. He was being too docile, I thought. Too obedient. It wasn't like him.

'Move.'

'Where do you want me to go?'

'Into the stall straight in front of you.'

I was standing well back, out of John's reach. He smiled at me before he disappeared from view.

'I imagine you're going to wish you'd listened to me in about half an hour. Maybe less.'

'All the way to the back, please,' the man said. His voice was harsh. 'Face the wall. Don't turn around until I say you can.'

I heard John sigh. 'This is unnecessary.'

'Shut up.' The man slammed the stall door closed, bolting it. The doors were in two halves, and once the upper door was closed and bolted, John was trapped. There were no windows in the block, but the partitions didn't go all the way to the ceiling. I pointed up.

'Can't he get out over the top of the stall?'

'It's a ten-foot wall. Plus there's only one door to the stable block. Even if he gets out of the stall he'll be stuck like a spider under a glass until we can come back and deal with him.' The man smiled at me. 'I'm not worried. He just needs to stay in there until the police arrive. Now let's get on with helping your friend.'

He double-checked that the bolts had gone all the way

home before ushering me out, flicking off the lights as we went. The darkness was absolute. It wouldn't help John to escape, if that was his plan.

In the cold, damp courtyard the Golf's headlights still blazed: Adam still hung limply, pinned to the wall. Nothing had changed, except that he looked worse.

He was running out of time.

I turned to the silver-haired man. 'What's the plan? Sorry, I don't know your name.'

'I'm Christopher.' Surreally, he held out his hand and I shook it. The habits of polite society were hard to shake. 'I'm going to call the police, and an ambulance for Adam.'

'I don't think we can wait for the emergency services to come. We need to move the cars, now.'

Christopher looked dubious. 'We might do more harm than good. Let me call them—'

'There's no time. He can't breathe. He's suffocating. If your ribs can't expand, your lungs can't fill properly. It's a horrible way to die.'

'All right. But if the Merc won't start, we're going to have problems. I might be able to tow it away with the Land Rover but there isn't a lot of room to line it up.'

'Just do your best.'

Christopher set off for the Mercedes and I ran to Adam.

Up close, I could see the sweat soaking his hair, and the fear in his eyes. His skin was waxy. His lips looked blue. There just wasn't enough oxygen making its way into his body, I thought, and tried to smile at him. 'We're doing our best. We'll have you out of there in a minute.'

'Ingrid . . .'

I bent my head to hear him better as the Mercedes engine hummed into life. 'What was that?'

411

He rolled his head against the wall, from left to right. He was frighteningly weak, I thought, putting my hand over his. He didn't have long.

With a grinding noise and clouds of blue exhaust smoke, the Mercedes dragged itself free of the Golf. The car juddered and Adam caught his lower lip between his teeth. He made a low sound deep in his chest and I swallowed, horrified. We were hurting him but there was no alternative; he needed to be able to breathe.

Christopher reversed four or five feet and switched the engine off. He got out of the car.

'Please hurry up.' The words tore themselves out of my mouth in spite of myself, making a mockery of the reassurance I'd offered Adam. Christopher nodded.

'It's all right. Nearly there.'

He inserted himself into the Golf with some difficulty. Methodically, he punched out the remaining glass in the windscreen, clearing his view. He turned the key in the ignition and the car sat there, inert. He tried again and this time the engine made a coughing sound before it shut down.

'We could push it back,' I said, trying to keep my voice steady. 'If you take the handbrake off, we can push it together. We only need to move it a bit.'

Adam groaned. Christopher ignored me. He tried one last time, and it didn't work, and it wasn't going to work, and then, just as I despaired, the engine started. It sounded dreadful but it didn't need to run sweetly; it just needed to be able to move the car.

The gears ground and then, at last, the shattered, twisted bonnet inched away from us. I was holding Adam up which was a good thing because he buckled as soon as the support of the car was gone, sliding down the wall. I couldn't keep him upright but I was able to slow his progress as he folded into the space the car had left.

'Adam?'

Breath sawed in and out of his chest and he winced, holding on to his ribs. They were bruised for sure and probably fractured down one side of his body, I thought, given that the full weight of the cars had crushed him. He could have internal injuries. He needed to be in a hospital.

'Take it easy,' I said to Adam, trying to sound confident. 'You're going to be fine. Everything is going to be fine.'

There was a thumping sound from the stable block, steady, rhythmical, maddening.

'Are you sure . . . he's locked away?' Adam asked.

'Positive.' Christopher sounded almost cheerful. 'He's not going anywhere. Now let's get you inside.'

47

Oxygen was a hell of a chemical, when you thought about it. In the fifteen minutes after the pressure on his chest was removed, so he could breathe properly again, Adam was transformed into a different person. We had helped him into the house with his arms draped over our shoulders, moving through a space that smelled of ancient wellington boots and the waxed jackets that hung on a row of hooks. I stopped in the kitchen and looked around. An Aga threw off vast amounts of heat. It was a big room; the table in the middle was surrounded by nine or ten shabby chairs. The walls were dark yellow and lumpy with old plaster. The room was cluttered with the sort of junk that accrues over decades rather than months: pots and pans, newspapers and magazines, an old radio, jelly moulds, dressers full of mismatched china, a stopped clock, letters and cards, dried flowers, bruised windfall apples and a cat bed felted with white hair. It was cosy and domestic and a world away from the horror in the courtyard.

'Should we stay here?' I said hopefully.

'I think he needs to lie down. There's a sofa in the sitting room,' Christopher said.

He guided us down a narrow, dark passageway that led to the front of the house and a square, stone-flagged hallway with a round table in the middle of it. The main staircase was at the back of the hall, facing the unused front door.

'It's the door on the right,' Christopher said with an effort. He was taking most of Adam's weight.

I pushed open the door and found a chintzy sitting room, furnished with deep couches and antique furniture marked with smoky water-rings. The room smelled sour and brackish, like an unemptied ashtray, and it was cold.

'I can light the fire,' Christopher said as Adam collapsed on to a battered green velvet sofa.

'That sounds like a plan.' I was shivering now.

'Get yourself a drink. There's a tray in the corner. Brandy is the usual spirit of choice on these occasions and I'm sure Adam would appreciate one.'

'Do you want something?'

'I'll have a whisky.' He grinned at me. 'We've earned it, don't you think?'

I did think. I went and poured the drinks, not really sure how much to slosh into each heavy cut-glass tumbler. There were no mixers. *In this house, we drink our spirits neat*, I thought, and tried not to giggle. That was the after-effect of shock, hysteria bubbling up to the surface.

Out in the courtyard, John Webster was locked in a dark, unheated stable.

'We need to call the police,' I said.

'I'll do that now.' Christopher was crouching at the fire,

moving logs around with his bare hands as the flames began to build, with the insouciance that comes from lighting fires every day. 'This will take a little while to get going but it should be okay now.'

'Thank you.'

'Don't worry.' He stood with his back to the fire. 'You did well. I'm impressed.'

'Don't underestimate her,' Adam said, and reached out to take my hand.

'Wouldn't dream of it.' Christopher looked from him to me and back again, but whatever conclusions he drew, he kept them to himself. 'Back in a minute.'

I knelt beside Adam. 'Are you okay?'

'Feeling better every second.' He drew me down and kissed me as if to prove it. His mouth tasted of alcohol. His hand was tangled in my hair, and at that moment I wished more than anything that Mark had stayed in Canada so I could have given Adam a fair chance. As it was, I was going to have to let him down gently, but now didn't seem like the right moment.

'Okay, I accept you're feeling better,' I said when I could speak again.

He gulped some brandy and winced. 'That's the stuff.'

'If you say so. It's not my drink of choice. I'd rather have a cup of tea.'

'Get it down you.'

I got up and started wandering around the room, looking at the paintings on the walls. They were murky with dirt but good. A collection of tiny snuffboxes filled one table. The whole house had the feeling of somewhere people had lived for generations.

'Does Christopher live here on his own?'

416

'Think so.'

'That's a shame. It's a big place for one person. Isn't he married?'

'No idea. You can ask him yourself.' Adam eased himself upright with a wince. 'Can you sit down? You're making me dizzy.'

I had stopped at a table covered with photograph frames. Dust felted the table between them, as if no one had bothered to clean properly in a while. Couples gazed out of silver frames in sepia, from generations that seemed impossibly remote. There was a younger Christopher in a wedding picture, handsome in colour despite a dated haircut. His wife was small, delicate, and looked very young. At the front there was a photograph in a silver horseshoe frame: a teenage girl, round-faced and pretty, leaning against a chestnut pony with perky ears. There was something about it that caught my attention. I picked it up to have a closer look, and heard Christopher coming back.

'I've called them and they're on their way. I've asked for an ambulance too, to get you checked out, Adam.'

'I don't need it. I'm fine.'

Christopher grunted as if he didn't agree. 'Don't expect an instant response. We're off the beaten track here.' He looked at me. 'Are you okay?'

'Yes, very.' I lifted the glass. 'This is really helping.'

'Take a seat,' he said, smiling, the kind and gracious host, as if everything was completely normal.

I sat in an armchair with high sides and looked at the fire. Flames were beginning to lick up the chimney and the first hint of heat reached me. The air in the room was so chilled it was practically solid, and I thought it would take me hours to get properly warm, if I ever did.

'Is he secure?' Adam asked Christopher again, who nodded.

'I wasn't going to get close enough to him to tie him up, but I'm pretty confident he can't get away.'

'How much do you know about what's been going on?' I asked Christopher. 'Do you know who John Webster is?'

Christopher looked at Adam. 'I knew you were coming because Adam had told me. I knew that other bloke wasn't invited. He seemed like a dangerous sort of chap to be knocking about so I wanted to get him squared away.'

'He's one of the people who's been targeting Ingrid and the other lawyers who worked on a rape trial a few years ago,' Adam said. 'Ingrid discovered a connection to a website where people were discussing miscarriages of justice. Justice Is Blind.'

Christopher shrugged. 'Never heard of it.'

'The guy in your stable block seems to have manipulated some people with a grievance in order to terrorise Ingrid.'

'What does he get out of that?'

'Fear,' I said. 'He wanted me afraid. That's how he gets his kicks. He's not like a normal person – he wants to be able to manipulate me. He wants to find my breaking point and push me beyond it.'

'Sounds like a charmer.'

'He's a killer,' Adam said grimly. 'You can't trust him. You can't turn your back on him for a second. He murdered one of the people he was working with – a woman named Tess.'

Christopher blinked. It seemed to take him a moment to find a response. 'Even though they were working together?'

'He had no further use for her.'

'He didn't murder her.' I was reluctant to defend John Webster, but in fairness I had to. 'She fell. It was an accident.'

Adam went on as if I hadn't spoken. 'And he killed one of Ingrid's colleagues. Shoved her into a road under a truck. He made it look as if it was a homeless guy called George, but it was actually him all along.'

'Okay,' Christopher said.

'You've got to hand it to him – he's clever. He's been pulling Ingrid's strings – and mine, if I'm honest – for weeks.'

'And he followed you here. Why was that?'

'He's obsessed with Ingrid. He wants to kill her.'

'No. He wanted to save me,' I said slowly, turning my glass in my hands, 'and I didn't listen to him. I seem to make a habit of trusting the wrong people.'

There was a short silence before Adam leaned forward with a wince and a hand to his chest. 'Ingrid, my love, I don't know what you're talking about.'

'When we got here, I didn't want to get out of the car,' I said. 'I was scared. I didn't really know why – nothing had happened. Every instinct I had was telling me I was in danger, and it took me a while to realise why.'

'Any chance it could have been the psychopath who was right behind us?' Adam's eyes were troubled. 'Look, you've had a bad day. A shocking day. Of course you're jittery. But you're safe now.'

He was absolutely sincere, honest to the bone, and if we had been on our own I might have been reassured.

'It was when I saw Christopher that I got scared. I didn't *know* him but I knew I'd seen him somewhere before.' I turned back to Christopher. 'You're on CCTV. You were the man holding your mobile phone up to film Belinda's body after she died.'

419

'I think it's understandable that you're upset,' Christopher said, 'but that's insane.'

I looked again at the shape of his head, the distance between his nose and mouth, the weak chin that slipped into a sagging neck. Unmistakable.

Impossible.

'Ingrid,' Adam said, 'Christopher is helping us. He's a friend. You can trust him.'

'I wasn't sure. And then I wasn't sure if you knew, Adam. I thought you might be genuinely on my side. But I've just been listening to you telling Christopher what I know so he doesn't put his foot in it – all that detail that he shouldn't care about, like the name of the website, and that Tess is dead, and that I believed she'd been working with John. You must have been very worried Christopher would let something slip if I talked to him about it. So much so, that you let something slip yourself.'

He had gone very still. 'What are you talking about?'

'How did you know George's name?'

Adam opened his mouth to answer me, and closed it again.

'You shouldn't even know he exists. The police never tracked him down. I know *I* didn't tell you I'd met him, and John definitely wouldn't have told you he'd located George, so how did you know it?'

He shook his head. 'I – I probably heard you say it.'

'No.' I half-smiled. 'I know I never mentioned his name to you, because I was worried about what you'd think of me for letting Webster kidnap him.'

Adam was looking bewildered.

'Your trouble is that you've always gone a bit too far,' I went on. 'You didn't want to leave anything to chance. You put George by the side of the road because you weren't absolutely sure that I would connect what happened to Belinda with John Webster, and you needed him to be a suspect. I don't know how you were planning to make sure I saw the CCTV – you were lucky that I gave her my umbrella, so I was one step ahead of your plans at that point. I suppose the scaffolding incident was supposed to ram home the idea that I had been the real target. I played right into your hands, every time. When I felt threatened, I called you, which was what you wanted – you used that to create the phone message that brought John Webster back. Every time you thought things were moving too slowly you raised the stakes again.'

'No.' Adam leaned back. 'This is ridiculous.'

'The blood in my bed was clever. You needed to get rid of Alison Buswell because you wanted to be the only police officer I called. You set me up to look like a fantasist and a fake. And of course it made me more scared than before, more needy. You were always there when I needed pointing in the wrong direction. I involved you in my life and I invited John Webster into my home at exactly the moment you wanted him there. I'm not surprised you think you can convince me I'm wrong. I've been sitting here thinking about what an idiot I've been, all along.'

'What do you mean?' The hurt was audible in his voice.

'You couldn't wait to go and see Guy Lanesbury's parents because I was useful cover for you. You wanted to know where Guy was, because he was on your list of targets but he'd disappeared – you couldn't track him down. And then afterwards you were livid that he was out of reach. You couldn't disguise that you were upset, so you pretended you were struggling to control your feelings for me. That did confuse me, I'll admit.'

'Ingrid, this is madness.' He looked devastated. 'I thought you and I – I thought this was real. I know you're scared but how can you be so cruel? I would never, ever hurt you.'

'It's very convincing, Adam, but don't bother. It's not just a suspicion, or a feeling, or a man who looks like someone I saw in a half-second of video. You shouldn't know about George, and you do. There's no explanation for that. It's a cold, hard fact.'

His face changed from one moment to the next, the hurt and sincerity switched off. In its place came a kind of calculating anger. He looked nothing like the man I had trusted and liked, and thought about loving. 'So? From here, it looks as if you've rather run out of options. What are you going to do about it?'

I stared at the floor as if I didn't have any idea, my shoulders slumped like someone who had given up hope. Then I threw the contents of my glass straight into Christopher's face. He wasn't expecting it and from the noise he made, and the way his hands went to his face, most of the brandy had hit him in the eyes. I ran past him, heading for the door. I was in the middle of nowhere with no car and no phone but I did have the best weapon available that I could think of – if I could only make it to the stable block to let John Webster out. He had promised me I would beg for his help, and he had been right; I was absolutely prepared to beg if that was what he wanted me to do.

A perfect plan, if I'd made it to the door, but Adam had recovered just a little too well from the crash, and for the second time that evening I was just a little too slow. He came off the sofa in a low dive and caught me around the knees as I reached out for the door handle. I pitched forward and hit my head on the door, and by the time I'd recovered from that, he was kneeling on my back.

'I . . . can't breathe . . .'

'Too bad,' he said, and leaned on me some more, and blackness slid across my field of vision as I struggled to stay alive, somehow, until I couldn't fight any more.

As I said, oxygen is a hell of a chemical, but you only really realise that when you're running out of it.

48

I blinked back to awareness in the back of a car – the
Land Rover Christopher had mentioned, I guessed, from
the heavy growl of the engine and the stiff suspension. My
hands were tied together and there was something rough
covering my head. It smelled indescribably foul, as if pota-
toes had rotted in it. When I moved to test how tightly
bound my hands were, someone pushed my head down
between my knees.

'Don't move.' It was Adam's voice but he sounded cold,
unfeeling, like a stranger.

'Is she awake?' That was from further away, I thought,
and it had to be Christopher. I presumed he was driving.

'Yeah.'

There was a pause. Then Christopher said, 'Good.'

'Where are we going?' I asked.

The hand on the back of my neck got heavier. 'Shut up.'

I did as I was told and listened instead as the engine
laboured. We were on an unpaved road, I thought. Five
minutes from the house? Ten? It was hard to tell how

long I had been semi-conscious, and what had happened during that time.

The car took a turn to the right and bounced down a track, picking up speed. I presumed Christopher was driving and that he knew the road, because he pushed through the bends like a rally driver. I was starting to feel sick. It was almost a relief when the car slewed to a stop.

Christopher switched the engine off and in the sudden silence I could hear the rush of floodwater close by.

'Where are we? What are you doing?'

Instead of answering me, Adam opened the door and hauled me out. I stood beside him, shivering, feeling rough gravel under the soles of my boots. The wind carried spray from the river, dampening my clothes.

'Come on.' Adam took my arm and guided me, quite gently, down a path. I could hear the scrape of a key in a lock, and a grunt of satisfaction as a door creaked open. He pushed me inside and pulled the covering off my head so I could look around.

At first I could see nothing except the beams from the men's torches. The air was full of dust and I coughed, holding my hands to my mouth. It was an old building, empty of furniture, and it stank of rodents and the birds that had roosted in the roof and dappled everything with pale shit. The wind whistled through gaps in the wood and I could feel the force of the river rushing below my feet. A huge circular stone lay in one corner along with some rusted machinery.

'What is this place? A water mill?'

'Used to be. Hasn't worked for a long time.' Christopher's face was grim. 'Do you even know why you're here?'

'Not entirely,' I said. 'I have some idea, though.'

'Go on.'

'I think you did spend time on the Justice Is Blind website, even though you said you'd never heard of it. I think you made contact with Tess Ivors when you read the threads about her friend, Lisa Muller. You were searching for my name and you found someone else who hated me just as much as you do.'

'Why would I hate you?'

'Because you blame me for the death of your daughter.' I took a deep breath. 'You are Flora Pole's father. And this is where she grew up.'

He looked dumbfounded. 'How did you know that?'

'I saw her picture on the table in the sitting room. It took me a while to recognise her. She looked . . . different when I knew her.' The photo dated from before she had contracted sophistication like a virus and lost weight and started sleeping with my fiancé.

'When you killed her.' He said it through clenched teeth.

'I did not kill her.'

'The police were hopeless. They couldn't find enough evidence to prove what you did, and they were never going to be able to get you to confess.'

'I wouldn't confess because I didn't do it.'

'That's not true, my dear. I know you did.' He took a step closer to me, his eyes bright with pain. 'I'd like the truth now. This is your last chance.'

'I didn't do it,' I said stubbornly. 'And I don't know why you're so convinced that I did.'

He jerked a thumb at Adam. 'He told me the truth. He told me all about you. How you harmed people. That girl, Lisa. Other people. He told me you had burned down the house to teach your fiancé a lesson.'

'Adam, you know that's not true. You even told PC Buswell that John Webster burned the house down.'

Adam shrugged. 'I was hardly going to accuse you then and there, was I? It helped to convince her that Webster was a threat and you were in danger, which was what I wanted. When you died or disappeared, Webster would be the obvious suspect.'

'I am not going to take the blame for what he did.' My voice was wavering. I turned to Christopher. 'You have to believe me. It was Webster who started the fire.'

'John Webster had an alibi for Flora's death,' Christopher said dully. 'A proper one. Unshakeable.'

'He could have faked that alibi. He's good at faking alibis.'

Christopher shook his head. 'He got himself arrested. He made a nuisance of himself in a pub and tried to hit a police officer when they came to sort him out. I'm sure it was deliberate, but it was effective – he was locked up from mid-afternoon until the following day when he'd sobered up enough to go home. He couldn't have started the fire. Once they knew that, they looked at you as a suspect. You had a motive, and access to the house.'

'But I didn't do it – I would never have done it. I *liked* Flora. I wasn't pleased to find out that she was having an affair with Mark but I only found out after she died, and if I'd been going to take it out on anyone it would have been Mark. She was silly to get involved with him when she knew he was engaged to someone else – that was only going to break her heart, whatever happened – but he was the one who encouraged her. He was older and he should have been wiser.'

'He has to bear some responsibility too.'

'Did you try to kill him? Mark?'

427

Slowly, Flora's father nodded. 'At least, I asked for it to happen.'

'I did it.' Adam's mouth was tight. 'That's how we organised ourselves, you see. We shared out the jobs between us. That way we could each arrange an alibi, just like John Webster.'

It was starting to make sense. 'There were no connections between the three of you, except that you had me in common. Christopher didn't care about Belinda but Tess did. That's why you filmed her death. So Tess could see it.'

Christopher looked nauseated. 'It was her request.'

'It was a horrible thing to do. And if you hadn't filmed her, I would never have noticed you among the crowd of pedestrians who were standing there. I would never have recognised you when I came to the house earlier.'

'Then we'd have saved ourselves a bit of trouble,' Adam said coldly. 'But you'd still be here.'

'You are a police officer,' I said, struggling to stay calm. 'You can't do this.'

'No, I *was* a police officer. John Webster took that away from me too.'

'You got fired? How? What did you do?'

'Emma Seaton and I had a relationship for a while.'

'*During* the trial?'

He looked defiant. 'It just happened. Not for long.'

'I always wondered why you came looking for her in that bathroom,' I said slowly. 'She hadn't even screamed. You must have been worried about her.'

'I was. I loved her.' His face hardened. 'She was in love with Webster, though, not me, even though I was kind to her. And my boss – well, she didn't approve. After Emma broke up with me, Delia Singh made it very clear that I wasn't welcome on her team any more, even though the relationship was over. I had to move to a different bit of the Met. Then I was too far away from Webster to keep track of him unless I broke the rules.' He looked pained. 'It's not fair that someone like Webster can do what he wants, and we can't do anything to stop him. I may have crossed the line a couple of times but it was for a good reason. They should have understood it.'

'So when I met you near your office . . .'

'My old office. I spend a lot of time there. I still have friends – favours I can call in. I can find out what I need to know.' He sounded defensive. 'People like me. They want to help me.'

'You ended your career over Webster.'

'It was a misunderstanding.' He moved restlessly. 'If Webster gets convicted of murder, everything will change. I'll be exonerated. I can rejoin the Met, or go to a different force. I can get my life back.'

'By destroying mine?'

'You are a means to an end.' His eyes were entirely dead; there was no human emotion there, no pity. 'I learned a lot from Webster.'

'You can't keep me here for long. People will be looking for me.'

'Let them look. They'll never find you.'

'What if they trace your car? You drove out of London with me in the car. There are cameras everywhere.'

'Stolen plates.' He smirked. 'Nothing will come back to me. No one will ever see you sitting in my car. They won't even know where to start looking.'

'This building is basically invisible,' Christopher added.

'You can't see it from anywhere that's not my land. No one will ever know you were here.'

'So you're just going to lock me up?' I was trembling.

'No. That's not what I have in mind,' he said. He was bending over something in the corner, behind the mill-stone, and straightened up holding it. A petrol can. 'It won't be pleasant, but it will be over eventually.'

I swallowed. 'Belinda never knew what hit her, and the judge got a quick death too. Why the special treatment for me?'

'Two reasons,' Adam said. 'One, I agreed that Christopher could do whatever he liked. Your punishment fits your crime, and that's the deal I made with him. Two, John Webster would want to take pleasure in killing you. A shove into the road or off a steep cliff would never do for him. Webster will get the blame if they ever find your body, and even if they don't. I'm happy, Christopher's happy.' He paused. 'Tess was supposed to be happy, but I doubt she would have been. She didn't really have much capacity for joy.'

'I understand why she wanted to get back at me. And I understand why Christopher blames me for his daughter's death.' I felt tears sting my eyes and blinked them away; I would not cry, not now. 'But I can't believe you said you would help me when you were planning to use me.'

'Do you feel betrayed? Let down?' He laughed. 'That's what happens to all of Webster's victims. You're feeling what they felt. You set him free to do that – to lie, and cheat, and manipulate other people. I loved every second of tricking you into thinking I cared about you, that I wanted you. You were so easy to fool.'

He thought I was going to be heartbroken, I realised,

and instead of making me feel even sorrier for myself, it made me laugh. 'Well, you certainly got full value out of pretending to have feelings for me. I haven't been mauled like that since I was a teenager.'

'You loved it.'

'No. I talked myself into going out with you because you seemed like a nice guy, but I couldn't quite make it work. I spent the whole drive down here trying to think of a way to tell you to back off.'

His face darkened; that had got under his skin, I saw with some satisfaction. 'Fuck off, Ingrid.'

There was one more thing I needed to know. 'Did Tess lie, when she said John Webster was part of your conspiracy?'

I saw Adam hesitate, deciding whether I deserved the truth or another lie, or maybe trying to decide which would hurt me more. 'Yes,' he said finally. 'She was lying. We didn't want you to know you should trust him. You should have listened to him that time, but you said it yourself – you got it wrong again.'

'I'm ready,' Christopher said from the other corner. The stink of petrol reached me at the same moment and I caught my breath, genuinely afraid.

'You can't do this.'

'It's only fair,' Christopher said, beginning to pour the petrol onto the wooden floor. 'You should suffer the way Flora did. You need to be scared. You need to know what it's like to scream for help and not be heard.'

He was backing towards the door, sloshing petrol as he went. Adam had reached the door already. He looked completely unmoved by what was happening. There was no point in trying to appeal to him again, I knew, and I fixed my eyes on Christopher instead. Maybe he would change his mind, even now. He wasn't *evil*.

Even as I thought that, he straightened up. 'It's all round the outside of the building too. I soaked the ground earlier, when I knew you were coming. You've got nowhere to go. But it will be quick. This place won't take long to catch.' He paused, his face full of grief. 'And then you will burn.'

49

After the two men had left me alone in the dark, locking the door behind them, there was a very short pause before I heard scrabbling outside. I imagined Christopher lighting the fuel, and the soft *whomp* as it caught. I didn't have to imagine the smell of smoke. The old mill building was largely wooden, a ramshackle structure perched on the edge of the river. In the old days the water would have turned a wheel on the side of the building, to grind the wheat grown on the estate, though it must have fallen into disrepair many decades before. I looked up, trying to see if I could climb up to the next storey and find a way out, but the darkness was complete.

The smoke was beginning to build, thickening the air around me. I coughed, and coughed again.

If I was lucky, the smoke would kill me before the fire did.

That didn't sound like my idea of luck. I started working my hands to loosen the rope that tied them together. I didn't know which of them had tied me up, but they had done a thorough job of it; the rope twisted around my wrists five or six times. It wasn't soft, friable hemp rope either but some kind of woven nylon climbing rope that had an amount of give in it, so it was impossible to pull it completely taut. All that I achieved by wriggling was to rub some skin off my wrists.

Tongues of flame were starting to appear between the wooden slats of the mill, seeking more fuel as they climbed higher. It made it possible for me to see, which was good, but what it showed me was not all that helpful. I searched for a sharp edge, a bit of broken glass – anything that would let me cut through the rope – but the pile of junk didn't offer me anything useful beyond splintered wood and rusty nails. And even if I did free my arms, the cold little voice of reason said in my head, what exactly was my plan? The fire was currently on all sides of the mill except the one where the river thundered past. If the fire burned enough of the walls, then maybe I could make a run for it and break out, but that assumed that Christopher wasn't waiting outside to make sure I didn't escape.

I was wasting time thinking about it. I didn't have long, I thought, and as if to confirm it flames crept across the trail of petrol Christopher had made on the floor. I backed away, trying to shield my face from the heat. It was getting harder to breathe.

Think, I told myself. Think about the mill. How did it work?

The answer came back instantly. It used the river. There would have been machinery inside and outside the building, and a way for the power of the water to reach the stones inside.

I knelt beside the back wall of the mill, the only part

that wasn't yet burning. Cold air was coming in from somewhere near the ground. I started to pull the pile of junk away from it until I could see a substantial hole where the mechanism of gears would have been, when the wheel had been in the river. There had been a half-hearted attempt to board up the gap when the machinery was removed. With the strength of pure desperation, and the help of a short and rusty metal bar I found among the rubble, I dragged the planks away from the gap until it was large enough to fit my head and shoulders through it. I peered out cautiously. In ordinary circumstances, the river would have been several feet below the hole, contained within the banks. Now, though, the water was high enough that I could reach out and touch it. The river looked dirty and full of debris from further upstream: large branches swung and spun as the water swept them past. Only someone who was actually insane would consider jumping into it.

Unless they had no other choice. While I had been working on the hole, the heat behind me had intensified. My skin shrank from it. I looked over my shoulder and couldn't suppress a gasp at the sight of the fire. It had climbed up to the next floor of the mill, wrapping around the old wood. The whole building was creaking. If the fire and smoke didn't get me, the collapse of the structure would.

Flora must have been so scared.

The thought hit me hard, exactly as Christopher had intended. But I hadn't set that fire, and I didn't want to die the way his daughter had. The truth was that I knew it was suicidal to jump into the river, but at least it was my choice.

A clatter made me look up: three floorboards overhead had given way as the fire ate through their supporting beam. They sagged down and a collection of stones and other debris cascaded onto the floor near me.

Now or never.

I took my boots off, then wriggled through the gap, not listening to the panicky little voice in my head that told me to wait, that some other way out would have to appear, that this was stupid and dangerous . . .

There was no point in easing into the water. I jumped off the edge, into the flood.

I had been expecting it to be cold, and I had expected it to be fast-moving. What I hadn't anticipated was that the cold would rob my lungs of all their air and freeze my muscles in a spasm. Swimming was out of the question, hands or no hands. I struggled to keep my head above the water as I gasped for breath, and the river rushed me away from the burning mill. I wasn't exactly better off, though if this was how I died I could bear it, I thought. The river might kill me, but at least it had no malice. It was simply pouring itself towards the sea, bloated with rainwater and mud and the damage it had done upstream.

A ripple of water slapped me in the face and something collided with my legs and I sank under the surface for a few unbearable seconds. The bottom was clogged with obstacles and I couldn't stand because of the force of the water. The current pushed me down towards the mud as my lungs burned.

'Swim, Ingrid, swim.' I saw my oma smiling at me, holding her arms out so I could plough through the water towards her, and safety. But she was dead now, and the water wasn't the still clear blue of the lake near our house in Denmark, and dry land was an impossible thing to wish for, and my hands were tied. I couldn't swim, or float. It was over.

As I thought that, the water flung me against something solid and floating. Instinct made me grab on to it: a huge tree branch, I realised, that was buoyant enough for me to pull my head above water and keep it there long enough to drag some air into my body, and I found I still had some determination to survive after all.

I clung to the branch while I waited for the cold-water shock to release its grip on me, and for the panic to ease. The tree branch was about nine feet long and substantial. Maybe, I thought, I could use it as a brake. If I could wedge it against the bank, I might be able to grab on to something more solid. I turned in the water to see what lay ahead and realised with a shock that I was just about to pass under the bridge by the house. The branch caught the current and spun sideways, wedging itself across one of the arches of the bridge instead of going through it. I had time to look for – and fail to find – a handhold on the stonework before the pressure of the water pushed me away from my branch and forced me out the other side of the bridge.

It was an absolute disaster – and then it wasn't. The landscape below the bridge was different, with shallower, sloping banks that let the river spread out and flow more slowly instead of barrelling down a narrow channel. Trees and shrubs, half-drowned, showed me where the banks were when the river wasn't in flood, and that meant I knew where the water was shallower. I half floated, half kicked my way to the left side of the river and started to make a more determined effort to get my feet under me.

The water was far too strong. The riverbed caught at my feet, bruising them. Standing – even stopping my wild progress – seemed impossible. Branches slashed at my hair and face, and I ducked under the surface again, then rose up in clear space for an instant under a tree with branches that were just above the water. I could see nothing at all, but I reached my hands up and felt a branch slide between them. This time, the rope around my wrists was a help. The knotted rope was stronger than my grip would have been, and when the water dragged at me it just pushed me along the branch. I hung there, too exhausted and too cold to think of making any further effort. I would wait, I thought hazily, until I could move more easily, or until daylight came and I could see.

Or until hypothermia got me. That was another possibility.

Oh God, you have to try, I scolded myself, despairing. Otherwise you should have stayed in the mill and burned the way they wanted you to.

It didn't matter that I knew I should try to get out of the water. I couldn't do it. Eventually I found a hollow in the bank beside me where I could wedge one foot, and keep myself upright in the water that was pummelling me, and that was a big improvement. Things unseen buffeted me under the surface and I turned to face downstream, hunching my shoulders against the things that were bruising me. I closed my eyes. I just needed to rest, to get my strength back, and then I could try to move again, when I was ready. All I had to do was not fall asleep . . .

It was light that made me come back to myself: not

438

daylight, but a bright, artificial light from above. I squinted up and could see nothing, and then the light went off again. I had imagined it, I thought, and felt utterly desolate. My whole body was numb and heavy, like lead. I couldn't unhook myself from the branch. I was stuck, in every way.

A shout made my head come up again. Lights were bobbing towards me, nearer the ground now: someone running. Even as I thought it, there was a splash nearby and the sound of feet wading through water, and then there were arms around me, lifting me up.

'I've got you. It's all right. You can let go.'

I had been expecting John Webster to come to my rescue, I realised, but this wasn't him.

'I – I can't.'

He yelled over my head. 'Stewie, over here.'

The bobbing lights turned towards us, and came closer, and resolved themselves into torches held by serious-looking people in black jackets with POLICE written all over them. One of the men leaned out over the water, holding on to the tree that had been doing such a good job of keeping me in one place.

'She's tied up,' the man behind me said, and his teeth were already chattering from the cold. 'Can you cut her free, mate?'

'Not a problem.'

It was a problem, though, as it turned out, and it took a lot of steady sawing and swearing while I shivered, and let them loop a rope over my shoulders, and did exactly what they told me to.

'Come on, sweetheart. Let's get you out of here.' The officers on the bank began to haul on the rope, and the man behind me guided me towards them, staying close so that his body shielded me from the worst of the debris in the water. The ground began to rise under my feet and two men came forward to take hold of me, pulling me out of the water with cheerful determination. I stumbled up the muddy grass and collapsed, every part of me aching. I had never felt anything as wonderful as the solid ground under me.

After a moment I became aware that someone was leaning over me, dripping water everywhere.

'Ingrid? Are you okay? Sorry it took so long to come to the rescue, but we had a hell of a job trying to find you. We had to put the drone up.'

It was the man who had been in the river with me – a man that I recognised straight away, now that I could see him properly, as Ben from the self-defence class. Ben, who I'd asked Webster and Adam to find – the man who didn't exist. Ben, who was now wearing a stab vest labelled with POLICE over his soaking wet clothes. My eyes tracked across to the woman next to him in a heavy high vis jacket, who was clutching a police radio and smiling apologetically.

'Helen?'

'It's all right,' my over-friendly neighbour said, sounding competent and professional. 'You're safe now. We've got you.'

Priorities. I could marvel at how they'd tricked me later.

'There's a man – John Webster,' I managed to say. 'He's – he's in the stables—'

Helen was shaking her head. 'No. He's not.'

'He's the reason we're here,' Ben said. 'He called me to tell me you were in danger, about an hour ago. On my *personal* mobile.' He said it as if it was incredible, but that was John Webster all over, I thought, shivering.

'And Adam—'

'He and his pal were in the farmhouse when we got here,' Helen said, and I imagined the pair of them drinking brandy by the fire, congratulating themselves on a job well done. Helen's next words made me rethink the scene. 'Your friend Webster left them for us.'

'Did he hurt them?'

The two police officers nodded in unison.

'They've gone to hospital,' Ben said. 'Then they'll be taken to the nearest custody.'

'G-good.'

'That he hurt them or that they've been arrested?'

'Just that everything is all right. Where is John? D-did you arrest him too?'

'We don't actually know where he is,' Ben said.

'But we'll find him.' Helen sounded quietly confident.

I was just as confident that she was wrong.

50

The courtroom was packed, which I had expected, even though it was a routine hearing. There was nothing routine about the case, or the defendants. An ex-police officer, in disgrace: that would be of interest to the media without the addition of a father driven mad by grief for his daughter. We were back in the Old Bailey, where it had all begun for me with Belinda's death, to hear the two men plead guilty to her murder.

Helen was minding a place for me in the public gallery so I lingered outside the court with DS Jennifer Gold. I knew what would be happening inside: the usual pre-hearing discussions between the prosecutor and the defence barristers who would have been down in the cells taking their final instructions from their clients. And I knew what to expect: guilty pleas to most of the charges, but not all.

The two men would be in the dock, side by side, with the dock officers flanking them. Defence counsel and the prosecution would be counting up witnesses and calcu-lating the likely length of the trial, sorting out the basic admin before they had to fix a trial date. With the current backlog of cases running through the courts, it would be months before Vicki's murder came up for trial. I shivered.

It was nice of DS Gold to stay with me. The various murders in the case had come under the control of the team who had been investigating Judge Canterville's death. That had been set up to look like an accident but the police had quietly gone about investigating it as a murder, and Adam's car had been seen in the area, complete with false plates. He had parked on the edge of the woodland, well away from the official car parks, and it was his bad luck that a dog walker had been irritated by the way he'd left his vehicle and took the number down. It was even worse luck that the police went to the trouble of tracing the car that was supposed to have those plates, and that a neighbour had excellent security cameras that had caught not only Adam stealing them, but his car driving away. That meant they could put him near the scene of the crime but they couldn't begin to guess why he had murdered Ron Canterville. While they watched him, trying to find out what connected him to that killing, they had become concerned that I was at risk. That had triggered the surveillance operation involving Helen and Ben and the listening devices. Everyone had known he was impersonating a police officer, from PC Buswell to DS Gold – everyone except me. The investigation had eventually absorbed Belinda's case, and the attack on Mark. But DS Gold had insisted on keeping Vicki's murder file on her desk.

'You want her to get justice too, don't you?' I said now, and Jennifer nodded, not needing to ask who I meant.

Helen pushed open the door and leaned into the hall. 'The usher has gone to get the judge.'

'Shall we go in?' Jennifer asked me and I followed her through the doors. I took my seat next to Helen, who nudged me reassuringly.

'It's going to be all right. The prosecutor wanted a word to tell you what's going to happen.'

'No need,' I said with a smile. 'I know the routine.'

'That's what I told her.'

I made myself look across at the dock, where Adam was sitting beside Christopher, his arms folded. He looked unsure of himself for the first time. They had both co-operated fully from the moment they'd found out I wasn't dead after all, but alive, and prepared to give evidence against both of them.

Adam turned his head and I caught my breath at the livid scar that ran up one side of his face and the eye patch that covered an empty socket, the legacy of John Webster.

'Webster thought you were dead,' Helen had told me. 'He took his feelings out on the two of them. But especially Adam, which you'd understand.'

I didn't like feeling grateful to John Webster. I wouldn't have wanted Adam to be harmed like that. But without Webster summoning the police, I would have died in the river, hooked on my branch as the cold water chilled my blood.

'Court rise.'

We got to our feet and the judge came in to take his place on the bench: a judge I didn't know, with a ruddy complexion and shrewd eyes.

'Would the defendants please stand,' the clerk intoned, and they did.

'Is your name Adam Nash?'

444

'Yes.'

'Is your name Christopher Pole?'

'Yes.'

'Sit down, please.'

The prosecutor rose, shaking out the folds of her gown. She had a carrying voice and I listened as she introduced herself and her opponents for the judge's benefit.

'Can the defendants be arraigned?' The judge peered at the defence over his glasses, as they stood to agree that yes, they could.

Adam was as white as paper.

The clerk stood up. This was the ritual that had been followed for centuries and when the charges included murder the words still carried a chill of dawn in the prison yard, a rough noose and a long drop.

'Defendants, please stand.'

They stood.

'Adam Nash, on count one, you are charged with murder and the particulars of that offence are that on the twenty-ninth of September 2019 you murdered Ronald Canterville. Do you plead guilty or not guilty?'

'Guilty.' No hesitation. There was an intake of breath in the court even though it was what we had expected. My palms were wet.

'Guilty,' the clerk repeated and noted it in the court record. 'Christopher Pole, on the same count, do you plead guilty or not guilty?'

'Guilty,' Christopher said with a gulp.

The clerk went through the indictment, reading out the charges. The prosecutor had elected not to charge them with any minor offences; this was all-or-nothing murder and conspiracy to murder.

As the details of Vicki's murder were read out to the court I bowed my head.

'Not guilty.' Adam's voice was strong and definite, with no possibility of doubt.

'Not guilty,' Christopher said in his turn.

Beside me, Jennifer Gold sighed. It was a tiny noise that was almost lost in the hum of interest across the courtroom.

At the end of the arraignment the prosecutor stood. 'Notwithstanding the pleas to the other counts, we do intend to seek a trial on count three against both defendants.'

'Of course,' the judge said pleasantly.

'I've spoken with my learned friends and we estimate the trial would take two weeks.'

The high drama of the pleas modulated into gentle bickering with the List Office over trial dates, and I followed with half an ear while I thought about what had just happened.

'Could the defendants please stand,' the judge said at last, and they stood. Adam was taller than Christopher but both had lost weight in custody, and both looked as if the strain of proceedings was taking a toll on them. 'As you've heard, your trial will take place on the thirteenth of April 2020, at this court. You are remanded in custody. You will be sentenced for the crimes you've admitted at the conclusion of that trial. Go with the officers, please.'

Before they went down to the cells, Adam turned and looked straight at me. He had known I was there all along, I realised. I could see nothing in his face but hatred. The dock officer nudged him and he started down the steps, his head bowed. He looked defeated. Prison would be hard for him.

'Please don't wait. Thank you,' the judge said, and there was a general upheaval as the barristers and police officers and public made for the exits, to be replaced by their counterparts in the next hearing. The business of the court rolled on. This tragedy was one of thousands, all different, all devastating in their own way.

'Why do you think they won't admit to Vicki's murder?' I asked Jennifer once we were outside court. 'It won't make any difference to their sentence. It just means we have to have a trial.'

'Adam has an alibi, thanks to you, and Christopher denies all knowledge of it. I suppose it could have been the third conspirator who did it.'

'Tess,' I said, thinking of the way she had threatened me with the box cutter. She had been prepared to be violent, and she had been so angry with me. Webster had said the murder looked personal. 'Maybe she came round on her own initiative and was frustrated that I wasn't there. I know she wanted to see me. She followed me to the self-defence class later.'

'Is that the class Ben Jones was at?'

'That's the one.'

Jennifer Gold laughed. 'I knew him in his first job, you know. This is why I could never do undercover work. He must have shat himself when he realised you were there.'

'I think he probably did,' I said ruefully. It was a complete coincidence that he'd been there, helping out Kate, who was also a police officer but not connected to my case in any way. It was too late for Ben to make a dignified exit once I saw him there, but he'd done his best to cover his tracks, giving a false name to the church and priming Kate to reassure me if I followed it up. And then

447

he had been relegated to the office, leaving Helen to keep an eye on me, and an ear. 'Nothing about their surveillance went right, you know. Webster found their listening devices. That must have been very frustrating for them.'

Jennifer nodded. 'They'd tipped me off after the murder, so I knew the devices were there. It's just a shame no one was listening or recording the day Vicki died.'

More than a shame, I thought. A disaster. But I hadn't been there, and the rules for surveillance were strict to protect people's privacy. They had been watching Adam and trying to protect me, and no one had thought Vicki was at risk too.

The DS went to speak to the prosecutor, to find out what work she wanted them to do before the trial date, and I tried to feel positive. Adam would go to prison for a long time, whether he was found guilty at his trial or not.

And that was that.

51

Except, of course, it wasn't.

To begin with, I was worried about John Webster. The police had promised to warn me if he reappeared, but I knew he wasn't going to walk back into his old life and pick up where he'd left off. I saw him in crowds and on public transport and in court, and every time it proved to be a stranger. I heard his voice in my head, mocking me. I couldn't accept that he was gone, and I knew he would return when I wasn't expecting it.

I don't want to give the impression that I was thinking about him all the time. In fact, he would have been disappointed to learn how little of my mind he was occupying. I was far more concerned with someone else. I had been to Barnes to visit Mark, who was recuperating at his parents' house. They had all been pleased to see me and we had talked like old friends.

Friends. No more than that.

He'd stopped at the front door when we were saying goodbye.

'Is it over now?'

'I hope so,' I'd said. But I wasn't sure I was right. I felt as if something was about to happen, something terrible. I was on edge, and still confused.

I could do nothing about any of it.

I could wait for it all to go away.

I could hide.

After wrestling with myself for a week, I picked up the phone instead.

'Ingrid?' Mark sounded cheerful. 'What can I do for you?'

'How are you feeling now?'

'Back to normal, pretty much. No lasting ill effects.'

'Good. I'm so glad.'

'Was that all? A health check?' He sounded amused. 'Did my mother put you up to it?'

'Absolutely not. Do you remember offering to help if I needed someone to act as a bodyguard?'

'Vividly.'

'Well, I think I might need you.'

'Any time you like.'

'How about this afternoon?'

The drive down to Croydon was slow but I didn't mind. I'd borrowed Adele's Fiat 500 and picked Mark up on the way. He pushed the passenger seat back as far as it would go to accommodate his legs.

'We could have gone in my car.'

'But you don't know where we're going.'

'That's very true. You could have told me.'

'Well, in the first place I'm not sure of the address – I'll know it when I see it. And secondly, I wanted to drive.' I looked sideways at him. 'This is my fight, Mark. I just want you here for back-up.'

'I get the picture. You're in charge.' A minute passed. 'Where are we off to?'

'A house.'

'To buy?'

I laughed. 'No. Definitely not.'

'I'm intrigued.'

'You'll find out what's going on soon enough.' I glanced at him again. 'Thank you for coming. I appreciate it.'

'Genuinely, it's my pleasure.' He cleared his throat. 'Mum told me about the hospital. About you turning up and making her go home. When I saw you the other day, I didn't know. She hadn't told me. She didn't want to upset me by talking about the hospital, she said.'

I grinned. 'She's so protective of you. It's sweet.'

'It's maddening.' He paused. 'But thank you for being kind to her.'

'You don't need to thank me.'

'Why did you come to the hospital?'

I felt the heat rise in my face and hoped he wouldn't notice if I didn't look at him. 'I don't know. I couldn't just go home after I left the police station. I needed to make sure you were all right.'

'The nurses congratulated me on my lovely fiancée.'

'Ah.' I bit my lip. 'I had to tell them that to persuade them to let me see you.'

'Of course. And it must have been method acting when you cried all over me.'

'I didn't!'

'I got it from two different sources.'

'Your mother is hardly a reliable source,' I said tartly.

'She didn't say anything about you crying. It was the police, and a nurse. The exact word that came up both times was "distraught".'

'Well, I was upset. I hated that you were hurt. I thought it was all my fault.'

'Was that the only reason you were upset? That you thought it was your fault?'

We were stopped in a queue of traffic so I could look at him properly. He was watching me. Neither of us spoke, or looked away, until the car behind erupted in a volley of furious beeps and I remembered I was supposed to be driving. He didn't push me for an answer, but the question lay between us.

I remembered quite a bit of the route I'd driven with Webster in the van, but not all of it. There was a frustrating period when I drove around aimlessly, hunting for anything I recognised.

'This is charming,' Mark commented as I did a three-point turn in a particularly bleak dead end between a tile wholesaler and a lumber yard.

'Shut up. I'm looking for something. Keep your eyes peeled for cement piping stacked up.'

It was Mark who spotted the piles of pipe, in the end, while I was looking the other way.

'Is that what you want?'

'The very place. I knew there was a reason I wanted you to come along.'

He laughed, but there was the faintest hesitation first that made me wonder what I'd said wrong.

The houses were exactly as they had been the last time I'd seen them, although daylight showed just how dilapidated they were: sodden with damp and missing hundreds of roof tiles. I parked and looked around. There was no one passing. No cars were parked anywhere nearby. We were on our own.

'This is the place?'

'This is it.'

'Have you been here before?'

'Once.'

If Mark had other questions, he kept them to himself. We walked down to the end of the row and I tried the gate. Webster had taken the padlock with him when we left with George, so it swung open as soon as I touched it. The garden at the back of the house was covered in weeds and full of junk, now that I saw it in daylight: an old bath turned upside down, a cupboard with the door hanging off it, a ladder with grass growing through it. The metal screen on the back door still hung loose, as it had been when John eventually unscrewed it, so I didn't have to brave the window and the sink.

'Christ. What a shit hole.'

'Come on.' I took a deep breath and slid inside.

Immediately, I knew there was someone else in the house. There was a presence that announced itself in the silence, and the weight of the air. I raised my hand to warn Mark, then moved through the kitchen. The sink was dry and there were no crumbs or used plates or signs that anyone had been there at all; I almost doubted myself. I stood in the hallway to listen, and heard nothing except Mark's breathing behind me, slow and reassuring.

The door to the front room was ajar. Light leaked in around the edges of the metal grilles that covered the window, enough to show me the bare boards where George had lain.

Slowly, carefully, I pushed open the door, so I could see the rest of the room.

He was standing with his hands in his pockets, his coat on and a bag at his feet. There was a smile on his face that didn't reach his eyes. He was affecting to be calm but every part of him was tensed to run.

'How did you know I was here?'

'People are predictable. They go to places they know.'

He laughed. 'I taught you that.'

'You taught me a lot of things.'

'If you had been five minutes slower, you would have missed me.' Behind me, Mark moved into view and Webster raised his eyebrows. 'So you're back on the scene, are you? Ingrid, you are full of surprises today. Don't tell me I can expect the police to turn up next.'

Casually said, but he was worried and I knew it.

'I owe you for helping me. Consider me not tipping off the police as my way of paying that debt.'

'Noted.'

'But there's one condition. You need to leave me alone from now on. I mean it. If you come back to bother me in any way – a phone call, a postcard, a *wink*, even – I will contact the police and I will tell them what I know about you.' I balled my hands in my pockets for courage. 'You don't live in the same universe as the rest of us. Even when you have a good reason for what you do, the way you behave is completely lacking in ordinary human feeling. Prison would teach you nothing. It wouldn't change you at all. But you wouldn't like it – I know that about you. So I think you'll do what I'm suggesting.'

He shrugged. 'Maybe.'

'You need to stay out of trouble. Stop committing crimes.

454

Take a lesson from all of this and go somewhere far, far away. Use your charm and your talents for good, not bad, and see what happens.'

'I like my life,' John Webster said.

'I really doubt that.' I looked at him with all the emotion of a butcher deciding where to make the first cut in a carcass. 'This image – the cashmere jumpers, the expensive coat, the attitude – that's all fake. You probably nicked everything you're wearing. You make your living by conning vulnerable people out of money and love. You've always taken what you wanted without ever thinking about the consequences for anyone else, but the consequences for you haven't been great, have they? Here you are, squatting in a derelict house. You own nothing. You have a criminal record, so every time your name comes up in a fraud investigation they will know you're the one they're looking for and look no further. You'll scrape a living by preying on vulnerable people until you get too old and too slow to play your usual games, but what happens after that? No savings, no pension, no career, no house, no assets, no one to love you—'

'That's enough. You've made your point.'

He made a move as if he was going to step towards me and Mark spoke from behind me.

'Don't.'

'I'm not afraid of you any more,' I said evenly. 'I know you too well. I'm just sorry for you.'

It was the most annoying thing I could have said to him. He tilted his head back in pure frustration. 'Oh my God, spare me.'

'That's all I wanted to say. You know what to do. Disappear. You're good at that.'

I should have known Webster wouldn't give in that easily. His eyes narrowed. 'Did they ever find out who killed your little friend? Vicki, wasn't it?'

'What do you know about it?'

'Oh, it wasn't me. But I don't think it was Nash either. You should devote some time to finding out who killed her, and why.'

'Tess was more than capable of murder. You said so yourself.'

'Ah, but Tess didn't hate her. And it was full of hate, the way she died.'

'What if it was someone who hated me?'

'Who could hate you, Ingrid?' Webster leaned sideways to look past me. 'What about you, Mark? All of that time being miserable and blaming Ingrid for poor little Flora's death. It must have come as a huge relief to take your feelings out on someone. Shame that it couldn't be Ingrid, but Vicki made a decent stand-in.'

I sighed. 'You never stop, do you? It wasn't Mark.'

'How do you know?'

Because I know him. Because I should never have doubted him. 'I just do,' I said. 'He's the opposite of you. He's honest, and direct. If he was that angry with me, he'd never be able to hide it. I mean, he wasn't able to hide the fact that he blamed me for Flora's death. That's why we split up.'

'Actually,' Mark said from behind me, 'we split up because you wouldn't believe me when I said I hadn't been sleeping with her.'

I turned to look at him. 'I just wanted you to admit it, that's all. You were always honest with me.'

'I couldn't admit to what I hadn't done.'

'The police showed me the messages you sent her—' I broke off and shook my head. 'Look, it doesn't matter. It never mattered. I'm not going to argue about her any more. You were under so much pressure. We were going through hell. I thought I was losing my mind, and I'm sure I was horrible to live with—'

'I never sent her any messages.' Mark was completely focused on me, as if Webster wasn't even there. 'Never. I didn't talk to her about anything except work. She was my employee, nothing more.'

People never change. You can predict what they'll do and how they'll behave, once you know them. You can use that against them.

John Webster had known I would hate Mark for lying to me. He had known that, above all other things, would be unforgivable.

I turned back to look at John, and he started to laugh.

'Oh Ingrid. I wish you could see your face. How long has it taken you to realise you were wrong?'

'Too long,' I said tightly. 'What did you do?'

Webster was still smiling; he was enjoying this. 'I never liked you, Mark. I never thought you were right for Ingrid. I tried everything to get rid of you. Nothing worked. Nothing made you give up on her. One day I noticed that dizzy little receptionist and how she watched you when no one was looking. I started sending her messages. Nothing creepy, nothing too pushy. Emails and text messages.'

'You did *what*?' Mark's calm demeanour had evaporated.

'Things escalated. She was very keen. Quite forward with photographs and so forth. Tasteful and discreet, at first – then less so, with a little encouragement from me.

Or you, should I say. I'm afraid I arranged for her to come to your house that night. I told her to take off her clothes and wait in bed. I had a key that I sent her so she could let herself in, and of course I had your alarm code. I used to pop round quite often.'

I must have made a noise because Mark reached out and held on to my wrist. 'Let him finish.'

'I thought that you would come home and find her, Ingrid, or that your fiancé would come home and fuck her. She was a pretty girl – who could resist? Either way, you would have broken up.' He sighed. 'There was never supposed to be a fire. I think the stupid little cow lit a few candles and one of them caught the blinds in the bedroom. The whole house went up. I wasn't there, as you know, but I did think it was a little bit my fault.'

'Do you think so?' Mark was white, and there was something in his voice that would have made me run.

Webster held out his hands and then brought them together. 'You two can live happily ever after now. There's no need to thank me but I hope you remember that if I hadn't chosen to tell you the truth, you would have had no future together.'

'That's not true,' I said, suddenly realising he was playing one last game. 'Nothing you've said changed anything. You aren't controlling us – it's not your choice to bring us together. I love Mark, and I never stopped. I didn't trust him when I should have. That was my mistake. But I've learned my lesson and it has nothing to do with you.'

He hated losing, I could see that. His face was tight with rage as he considered what he could say to hurt me. Mark moved to stand beside me, to support me or threaten Webster or both.

'You deserve each other,' John sneered. 'I thought you were better than him, Ingrid, but I was wrong.'

'Get out,' I said. 'Right now. This is over.'

Webster picked up his bag and slung it over his shoulder. He looked from me to Mark, glowering, shook his head and stalked out. The back door banged. More like a teenage tantrum than the dramatic exit he might have wanted, but it didn't matter, I thought. He was gone, and we were alone.

Mark recovered first. 'So where does that leave us?'

'I . . . don't know.' I didn't dare look at him.

'Ingrid. Forget about him.' He turned me to face him and his eyes were as soft as I'd ever seen them. 'I'm so sorry. I'm sorry I accused you of hurting Flora. I'm sorry I didn't hold my nerve and stay with you. I let you down, and I knew it the second I left. I was just too proud to admit it.'

'You couldn't have done anything else.'

'Nor could you.' He closed his eyes for an instant. 'The *arrogance* of me to say that you should just have trusted me, when I knew what you'd been going through. I went to live thousands of miles away and I thought about you every day. I came back and I didn't know if I should try to get in touch with you or not. When you invited me round to your flat, the minute I saw you I felt as if I'd been kicked in the heart. I decided I was going to do whatever I could to get you back. Even if it killed me.' He grinned. 'But look, I survived. Just about.'

'Mark—'

I didn't get to say anything else, because he was kissing me with a fierce kind of joy and determination and hope that took my breath away.

459

It was quite a while before we remembered we were standing in a derelict house on a derelict street in the unfashionable end of Croydon, and dusted ourselves down, and went outside, hand in hand, to discover John Webster had stolen the car.

52

You can't have a happy ending unless everyone is happy, and I wasn't happy.

Let me be clear: I was blissfully content to be with Mark again. For the first time since John Webster had begun to disrupt our lives, we were able to be together without a shadow chilling the air around us. John had disappeared, apparently for good. I knew him well enough to believe he would regret the way he'd appeared at our last meeting. I had twitched the curtain back and surprised him before he was ready for the spotlight. He could cope with anger and fear, but never ridicule. I thought he'd meant it when he said he wasn't coming back.

And even if he did, I wasn't afraid of him any more.

No, the bar to my happiness was that every so often I would find myself thinking of Vicki and how she had died in my home, and what John had said about her murder. Her ghost seemed to trail around after me when I was in the flat, silently trying to get my attention, standing at my elbow waiting for me to acknowledge that she was there.

There was nothing new to report, Jennifer Gold told me in an apologetic way when I called her.

'We've been putting everything together for the court case. The prosecutor thinks it's worth a try but she's not holding out too much hope if the defence are on their game. We didn't get anything off the forensics, as you know. There was a mixture of third-party DNA on her skin and clothing, but nothing that was significant enough to test.'

'What if it wasn't them?'

Silence on the phone. Then, 'What do you know that you're not telling me?'

'Nothing. Really, nothing. I was just wondering about her personal life.' *What about my old friend Harry?*

'I looked into it.' She hesitated, weighing up whether she could tell me more. 'I had full cooperation from anyone I spoke to.'

I tried to read something into the DS's tone – a suggestion that she wasn't convinced by Harry's story, a hint that she was interested in finding out more – but there was nothing to hear.

The memory of Vicki's sweet, hopeful little face made me lie awake at night staring at the ceiling while Mark sprawled beside me, snoring on two-thirds of the mattress. I turned it over and over in my mind, remembering what had happened before Vicki died, and after, and that day.

'You need to work it out,' Mark said one evening, out of nowhere.

'What?'

'Vicki.' He was adding vegetables to a stir-fry and the sound of hissing oil meant it was impossible to talk for a moment. When it died down, he said, 'You won't be able to move on until you know what happened, and I like this place, but I'd like to live somewhere warmer at some stage in my life.'

'Mark—'

'You need to know, don't you?' He crossed the room and put his arms around me. 'So find out.'

I leaned against him and thought about it. He was right. I had to know.

A day or two later, I went to see Jennifer Gold. She looked tired, her hair scraped back in a ponytail, her shirt crumpled and creased from long hours at work.

'I still don't have any news,' was how she greeted me.

'I know. Look, I know this is a strange question but did you keep a record of the search of my flat and the things you took away?'

'Of course.'

'Could I have a look at it?'

She left me sitting by her desk while she went to get it. I saw her scanning through it before she brought it back, trying to work out what I wanted to know. This case bothered her as much as it upset me, I thought.

Once she gave the booklet to me, I read through it with care. They had done their best to list everything, including a pizza box that had been propped up beside the bin and the receipts from the items Vicki had bought.

'What are you looking for?' Jennifer had been watching me read with barely suppressed impatience.

'Could they have missed out on mentioning something else?'

'Like what?'

'Like a note I left Vicki before I went to work. I didn't want to wake her.'

463

'Handwritten? Definitely not. We would have paid close attention to it.'

'Maybe she put it in the bin.'

'We took the contents of the bin too.'

'Oh.'

'What did the note say?'

'Nothing much,' I said, and got the look I deserved. 'I promise I'll tell you when I can. I need to get a couple of things straight first.'

I had written something about Harry, I half-remembered, and I didn't want to think about what that might mean.

But of course, I had to.

One Saturday afternoon in February, I went around to a neat little house in a back street of Clapham and knocked on the door. The window was full of stacked boxes: the occupants were moving out. When the door opened, I smiled.

'Lucky I caught you. I didn't know you were moving.'

Vicky ran a hand over her stomach. 'Well, we decided it was a good idea once I found out I was pregnant.'

'Pregnant? My goodness. That was fast.' I looked again and saw that her body was very slightly rounded. If she hadn't drawn my attention to it, I would never have suspected a thing.

'Thank you,' Vicky cooed. 'It was a honeymoon baby.'

'There wasn't much else to do,' Harry said from behind her, and she rolled her eyes as if she'd heard that one before.

'How are you?' I asked him.

'Not bad, not bad.' He looked tired, though, and he'd lost weight. His hair had thinned dramatically. He looked ten years older than when I'd seen him at the engagement party at the end of October. 'This was good timing. We're moving on Monday.'

'Where are you off to?'

'The most gorgeous house in Norfolk.' Vicky was glowing with pride. 'Huge. So much space for the baby to run around when he's old enough. Or she. We decided not to find out what we were having.'

'The main thing is that it's not twins,' Harry said, with a little too much feeling.

'The main thing is that he or she is healthy,' Vicky said, and smiled to take the sting out of her words. She had mellowed, I thought, but she hadn't mellowed that much.

'Anyway, why did you want to come round, Ingrid?'

'I just wanted a quick word with Harry,' I said. 'In private, if that's possible.'

'Very mysterious.' She turned and went into the tiny sitting room where she started putting cushions into packing crates, singing under her breath.

'Come in, come in. Let me make you a cup of tea.' Harry ushered me into the kitchen where every surface was covered in stacks of plates or packing boxes or bubble wrap.

'I won't stay long.'

'What can I do for you?'

I went over and closed the kitchen door softly. There was no point in being vague. 'Did you tell the police that you were having an affair with your neighbour Vicki?'

'Yes. I contacted them straight away when I heard she was d-dead. They were able to keep it p-private.' He was trembling, I noticed, and stumbling over his words. 'How – how did you know?'

'She told me.'

'When?'

'Your engagement party. The night before she died.' I took pity on him. 'It wasn't common knowledge. I don't think she had told anyone else.'

'Right.' He leaned back against the kitchen counter. 'Okay. I don't want to complicate my life. Especially now.'

'No. That would be awful.'

My tone made his head snap up, but he had enough control of himself to keep his voice low. 'Do you think I don't miss her? Do you think I'm not devastated that she's gone? I can't even mourn for her in case Vicky notices something is wrong.'

'You haven't told Vicky.'

'Of course not.'

'Why wouldn't you tell her now?'

He looked baffled. 'Why would I? There's nothing to be gained by telling her.'

'You'd rather keep lying to her.'

'I don't like lying. But you do what you have to do.'

I nodded slowly. 'I thought that might be how you felt about it. It must have been very important to you to keep the affair a secret.'

Harry's eyes narrowed. 'What do you mean by that?'

'Do you recognise this?' I showed him the bracelet I was wearing, the silver one that I had lost and Webster had found.

He shrugged. 'Not really.'

'I rang the bar where you had your party. They found it when they were cleaning up. The barman remembered because you took it and said you would get it back to me yourself, and Vicky wasn't pleased, and you ended up arguing. He thought it was a sad way to end your evening.'

'I remember that.' He was frowning. 'I had forgotten though, genuinely.'

'I think you meant to give it back to me. I think you came to my flat – because you knew where I lived, and it wasn't far from your office at the time – and you meant to leave it there for me, but you found Vicki was there instead of me.'

'No.'

'I think you were surprised to find her there when you were expecting me to come to the door.'

He looked as if he was going to be sick, then and there.

'I think you argued,' I went on. 'Maybe she said she was going to tell Vicky that you'd been sleeping with her, or maybe she wanted to continue the relationship when you wanted to end it, or you wanted to keep seeing her even though you were getting married. You had a disagreement, anyway. Things became heated. One of you picked up a knife – one of my kitchen knives. I think it was probably you, because you dropped the bracelet as you reached for it. The bracelet fell into the toaster. The police missed it when they were searching the flat, and so did I for a few weeks, so I never made the connection with you, or the engagement party, or even Vicki's death.'

He stared at me in mute misery. His eyes were dark and empty.

'You struggled. It was more of an accident than anything . . . even though she was stabbed forty-two times and crawled across the living room to get away from you. That's the story, isn't it? Am I right?'

Harry swallowed. 'Almost.'

467

'What did I get wrong?'

'I was in a meeting all day. In Paris. I got back at ten o'clock that night, on the Eurostar. The police checked my tickets, and the CCTV. I wasn't here.'

'So who—'

Harry raised a finger to his lips, which were bloodless. 'I gave the bracelet . . . to her. She said she would put it through your letterbox. She said she was happy to do it. That was how we ended the argument. With me saying she could deliver it.'

I imagined Vicky coming to my flat, buzzed into the courtyard by one of my neighbours. Maybe she had seen Vicki through the window, or maybe she had knocked on the door and discovered her when she opened it.

What on earth are you doing here? Did you have a good night?

And then she had walked in and sat down on the sofa – maybe to talk about the party and her ring and the honeymoon – and the note I had left for Vicki had been right in front of her. I thought of my black handwriting, all too legible:

And do not ring Harry! He doesn't deserve you.

Vicky would have noticed her fiancé's name, in the circumstances. I knew she was jealous, with good reason. I knew she had a temper.

What does that mean? Explain it to me? What do you mean, you can't? Why are you crying?

Or maybe she had come there primed for a fight with me, ready to unleash the hostility that had been bubbling under the surface the previous night, and found her worst fears realised in a different way.

Tell me what I want to know. Has he been cheating on me with you?

The bracelet tight in her fist. Pacing the flat. *How could you. How could you.*

Reaching for the knife that was hanging in the kitchen, ready to be used.

Killing the woman who threatened her beautiful perfect marriage, and her beautiful perfect life.

'What are you going to do?' Harry's voice was a whisper. 'Are you going to tell the police?'

I hesitated. There was no physical evidence. She had covered her tracks well, removing the knife and not leaving a usable fingerprint or a hair behind. I was the only person who could say that the bracelet had been in the toaster. Adam was hardly going to be a star witness, even if he was prepared to give evidence, and John was gone. It would be my word against hers. There was no guarantee the CPS would take a case on that basis.

But I would be a reliable witness, and there was the evidence of the bar staff who remembered the engagement party and the bracelet and the argument. Harry might even give evidence against her, if the police could talk him round.

I thought he had loved poor little Vicki very much.

'The baby . . .' Harry faltered. 'What about the baby?'

'What if she harms the baby, Harry? Can you take that risk?'

His eyes filled with tears, but he didn't respond.

'I can't, you see,' I said softly. 'I have to try to keep you

469

and the baby safe. I can't pretend Vicki isn't dead. Her injuries were catastrophic—'

'Stop.' He turned away from me sharply. 'Vick's been so much better lately.'

'She's happy at the moment, because she got what she wanted. It's not safe for you or the baby, Harry. And it's not right.'

'She has to live with herself. Don't you think that's enough of a punishment?'

I didn't answer him, because I could only have said no.

I walked out of the kitchen, and found Vicky standing in the doorway of the sitting room. She looked down at the bracelet on my wrist, and back at my face.

'Did you get what you wanted?' She asked the question in a pleasant tone, and I knew she was guilty.

'I think so.'

She nodded slowly. I let myself out of the house without saying anything else, and the knot in my stomach got tighter and tighter as I pulled out my phone and called DS Gold.

I believed Vicky had committed a terrible, evil crime and it wasn't up to me to decide what her punishment should be.

I would place my trust in justice, unlike Adam Nash and his fellow conspirators. I would tell the police what I knew and what I suspected. I would let them investigate Vicky. I would give them a chance to find the evidence that would put her behind bars for life.

470

I think about death a lot, and the truth. I think about evidence.

Evidence is more important than the truth.

Evidence is everything.

I put my faith in the law and in evidence, because when it comes down to it, evidence is all that matters.

Acknowledgements

The Killing Kind simply would not be the book it is now without the help, guidance and support of many people, some of whom I can thank here by name. There are many others who helped along the way and I am immensely grateful to them all. One name goes on the title page of a book but it takes a lot more than one person to make it all happen.

My thanks to:

The incredible team at HarperCollins, especially super-editor Julia Wisdom who steered me through several drafts and many narrative hazards to bring my idea to life, Kathryn Cheshire, Hannah O'Brien, Fliss Denham, Katy Blott, Phoebe Morgan, Claire Ward, Kate Elton and Charlie Redmayne, as well as the devoted, hardworking team in the Dublin office.

Anne O'Brien for her excellent copy editing, as ever – she is very kind about my inability to keep track of the days of the week – and Linda Joyce.

Everyone at United Agents, but in particular Ariella Feiner (the best agent imaginable) and Molly Jamieson (her equally talented sidekick). Nothing would happen without the dedication and hard work of United Agents and I still get a thrill from saying they represent me.

My husband James, who has given me a particular insight over the years into the dramatic, hilarious, strange, demanding, underpaid, overworked and utterly vocational world that barristers inhabit. I would also like to thank lovely Rhiannon Crimmins for a chance conversation outside the Old Bailey that was exactly what I needed to make Ingrid feel real to me. Dolphins for life . . .

Soren and Claudia, who bid very generously at a charity auction for the right to name a character in this book and made Ingrid become real for me. My version of Jens Villemand is undoubtedly not the same as the real Jens Villemand, but I think of him very fondly and I hope the real Jens approves.

My fellow crime writers who have shown me such kindness and support, especially Liz Nugent, Sinéad Crowley, Catherine Ryan Howard, Erin Kelly, Sarah Hilary and Elizabeth Haynes. (There are literally hundreds of other authors I could thank here, if I had the space – crime writers are the best of people in every way. They know who they are.)

I'd also like to thank my family in what has been a particularly difficult year – Edward and Patrick, Philippa, my brave and wonderful father Frank Casey, and Kerry Holland, who is one of the best people I know. The extended family in Dublin and Devon and everywhere else were equally important, in particular Mary and Fergus Brennan who have done so much for us. My other family of friends in London brought me through a dark time, especially Claire, Sarah and Alison. This book is dedicated to Alison who is a joy to know, and kindness personified.

There are two absences in this list, and in my life. One is Fred, the best companion, much missed. The other is my mother, Alison Casey, who died at the very end of the worst year most of us can remember. She was my first reader, my toughest critic, my biggest cheerleader. She read everything I ever wrote, except this book. Every story has an ending, but some of them come too soon.

Turn the page for a sneak peek at the
brand new novel from Jane Casey, featuring
DS Maeve Kerrigan and DI Josh Derwent,
coming soon . . .

1

All murder investigations were different and yet all of them began the same way, at least for me: standing in silence near a body, trying to catch the faintest echo of what had happened to bring them to my attention. Sometimes the air still vibrated with violence and high emotion, and sometimes the silence was empty. It was a habit that I kept to myself, but one that reminded me of the fundamental truth: this was more than a job. Someone's life had been ended too soon, and finding out who had done it, and why, was my duty.

Silence could be hard to come by, however, depending on the crime scene and who else was there. Currently, I was battling to hear anything at all over the hum of conversation from uniformed officers and scene-of-crime specialists and, inevitably, my colleague, Detective Constable Georgia Shaw, who talked as if she was paid by the word. I tuned back in time to hear, 'So he was in the driver's seat but I mean, clearly, he didn't drive here, did he? Because he was already dead from what Dr Early said. With the rigor, and everything.'

The body was slumped, half inside a cyan BMW sportscar, though opening the door had caused the torso to slide sideways. One arm dangled. Dr Early, bright-eyed and brisk, had demonstrated with a quick swing that it hung loose.

'He would have been in full rigor when they moved him to the driver's seat. You can see he's not in the correct position to have been driving. The angle of his legs is all wrong and his feet wouldn't have been near the pedals. I'd guess he was curled up and they were able to slide him into the seat all right but they must have needed to move his arm to close the door.' She had straightened up with a shrug. 'You can break rigor, but you can't make it come back again.'

'So we were supposed to think he was killed in the car?' I said. 'And assume it happened here?'

'Your guess is as good as mine.' Dr Early had returned to her examination, probing the bloody mess on the top of the victim's head, where someone had hit him with enough force to smash his skull.

The victim: one Hassan Dawoud, a doctor, aged thirty-four. And where we stood was the car park of the big, sprawling London hospital where he had worked. It was just after five on a clear June morning, the light delicate but with the promise of some heat later on. The nearest hospital building was a triumph of sixties brutalism in stained concrete and aluminium-framed windows that flared brightly as the first rays of the sun caught them. Behind them, hundreds of onlookers, potentially, attracted by the fuss of a murder investigation in full swing. We had taped off half of the car park, which had sent the hospital authorities into a tizzy: people would be coming to appointments and to visit their loved ones and to visit A&E and the car park was already inadequate. Without access to parking, the hospital simply could not function. The sooner we could take our dead body and go, the better, they had strongly implied.

'Do you want to talk to Liz St John? She's keen to get home,' Georgia said.

'Who is that? Oh – the woman who found the body?' My first instinct was to tell Georgia to do it. I spent a lot of time trying to find work to give her that she couldn't get wrong. I had seen the woman already, sitting in the back of a police car with the door open, a blanket around her shoulders, her eyes wide with the kind of stare that saw nothing. Make an effort, I told myself, and nodded. 'I'll speak to her. They're ready to move the body, if you don't mind looking after that.'

'Of course.' Georgia sounded keen and competent, and at

least one of those things was true. She was getting a lot better, I reminded myself. I still found myself checking up on her, but nine times out of ten she'd got everything right. It was really just the thought of the tenth time that kept me on edge.

And speaking of being on edge, Liz St John was doing a fair impression of someone who had reached that state some time ago. She was holding an inevitable cup of tea, probably not the first one she'd been given. Her other hand was heavily bandaged.

'Mrs St John?' I introduced myself. 'I understand you found the body.'

She nodded. 'I didn't know – I said to the police when they came, I had no idea. I would never have opened the door if I'd known.'

'You opened the car door?'

A convulsive nod. She was thin and pretty usually, I guessed, though tiredness had put bags under her eyes and dulled her skin. Fair hair, fat diamond stud earrings, another few carats on her fingers and a Mulberry bag at her feet. A well-off woman who had blundered into her worst nightmare. She was staring at me with matching interest, seeing, I supposed, someone whose life was nothing like her own. I was wearing a dark trouser suit with a plain white top underneath, minimal jewellery, minimal make-up. I was tall and striking enough to attract attention but I tried to look neutral when I was at work, and some of the time I got away with that. What was shocking to her was routine to me, and I reminded myself to be gentle with her.

'Go back to the start. Why were you at the hospital?'

'I was chopping carrots for the children's tea. Batons.' She half-laughed. 'They don't even like carrots, you know. They wouldn't have eaten them.'

'And you cut your hand,' I prompted. I wanted to get her out of there before the body was moved. It was behind screens but there were things you didn't need to hear, never mind see.

'We have these knives – they're Japanese. Very expensive. They're far too sharp. I must have been distracted and I sliced into my hand.' She grimaced. 'I had to wait for Hughie – my husband – to come home before I could go to the hospital. To mind the children. So I was quite late getting here, and then it was a four-hour wait. They made me have an x-ray – anyway, they were nice to me. I was worried that I was wasting everyone's time by coming here, but—' she trailed off, lifting her hand as if to show me the bandages.

'What time did you leave the emergency department?'

'Coming up on two in the morning. It was still busy.'

'It's always busy,' I said, with feeling.

'Yes. Anyway, I came out here and the parking machine was broken.' She gestured in that general direction. 'There was a notice on it. Coins only. No notes. I mean, who carries that much change? And the amount they charge for parking . . . well, I didn't have it. I was short two pounds. Everything was closed and there was no one around. I was stuck and Hughie was at home with the kids so I couldn't get him to come and rescue me. I knew the receptionists wouldn't be able to give me change but I thought I might find someone to help. I was just about to go back into the building when I saw the car.'

'Hassan Dawoud's car.'

She nodded.

'Why did you go over to it? Was there something about it that attracted your attention?'

'I know – knew him. He's my next-door neighbour.'

I blinked. 'Wow.'

'Quite a coincidence.' She frowned. 'Except, not really. Lots of doctors live around where we are, and it's the closest A&E to us. It wasn't a surprise to see someone I knew. I just didn't think anything of it except, "oh good, Hassan will help me". The windows are tinted but I could see him in the driver's seat.'

'So you went over.'

'And knocked on the window. When he didn't look up, I opened the door. And he fell out.' She swallowed convulsively. 'I thought he was ill. I thought – well, I don't know. But then his cap fell off and I saw his head.'

'It must have been a shock.'

'A total shock. I was almost sick.' She shut her eyes, and I saw a glint of sweat across her forehead as if the nausea had returned. 'Hassan means handsome, did you know that? Someone at playgroup told me. He was terrifically handsome. Beautiful, really. Seeing him like that was *horrendous*.'

'Did you touch him?'

'I sort of caught him when he flopped out. I checked for a pulse, but he was cold.' She shuddered. 'Maybe I shouldn't have touched him, but I didn't know.'

'We'll need to get a sample of your DNA, if that's all right.'

'Of course. Anything.'

'Was Hassan married?' I had noticed a platinum ring on his hand.

'Yes. Last year. They seemed happy.' She bit her lip. 'Most of the time, anyway.'

'What do you mean?'

'There were arguments now and then. Breaking china. Shouting.' Her eyes slid up to mine. 'It's not that I'm nosy. I couldn't help hearing, when we had the back doors open. It gets so hot in the kitchen. Late at night – when they'd been partying – there were rows.'

'Violent ones?'

'I don't know. I can't say.' Instant regret, common to witnesses who felt they had said too much. She looked down at the tea. 'This is cold and disgusting. Could you take it away?'

I took the cup out of her hand and put it on the roof of the car. 'Go back to Mr Dawoud's marriage. Tell me about his wife.'

'His – oh, no. No. Sorry. I've misled you. Hassan didn't have a wife. He had a husband. Cameron. But he's away.'

She shivered. 'So it couldn't have been him who did this. Could it?'

'I told you all of this before. We had a good marriage.' Cameron Grant Dawoud sat with his hands clasped in front of him on the table, pressed tightly together. A tremor ran through his body every few moments: a physical manifestation of the grief that had left him red-eyed and puffy-faced. He was big, his muscles well-defined, his shoulders straining the cotton of his t-shirt. He was thirty-six, I knew, but his sandy hair was thinning across the back of his head already. The sun had burned him pink across the bridge of his nose and the upper part of his arms. He had come straight to meet us when he got back to London, pausing only to get his solicitor to join him.

I was reserving my opinion of Cameron Dawoud.

'Did you ever argue?' Beside me, Georgia was taking a confident lead with questioning him.

'Of course.'

'Of course?' she repeated, her eyebrows raised as if she was surprised. *Don't overplay it, Georgia.*

He shrugged. 'I'm not going to try to tell you we didn't fight now and then. That would be unrealistic.'

It would have been a lie, too, I thought.

'Was it physical?' Georgia said. 'When you argued?'

'No.'

'Was there damage to property?'

'No.'

'Neither of you ever got angry enough to throw things?'

'I said no.' His jaw was clenched.

'That's not what we've heard,' Georgia said cheerfully and I saw his eyelids flicker as he thought about who might have come up with a different version of events.

'You must be talking about Liz.'

'What makes you say that?' Georgia hopped on what he'd said as if it was evidence of wrongdoing and he sighed.

'I know she found him – you told me that much – so I suppose you've been talking to her.' He rubbed his eyes. 'You can't have had time to talk to anyone else, really. What is it – twelve hours since he was found? Less than that? And I presume you want to start with me since I'm his husband.'

He was no idiot, I thought, and he was easily out-thinking my junior colleague.

'What difference does it make if Liz told us?' My voice was quiet. It was almost the first thing I'd said in the whole interview and Georgia looked around as if she had forgotten I was there. She was enjoying herself, and I was not. I wished I was somewhere else, and glanced down at my notebook, worried that it showed on my face.

'None, really. Except that she was mistaken.' He shrugged. 'I don't know why she would say that we fought. She seems like a perfectly nice woman but I can't say I know her well enough to judge her as a witness.'

'Did you ever call the police? Either of you?'

'During an argument? Absolutely not. And you can check that quite easily, can't you?' He glared at me, his brow furrowed. 'Why are you wasting your time on this? Acting as if it's a big deal that we argued. That's what adults do from time to time, kids. Life isn't one long honeymoon no matter how much you love each other.'

'But you hadn't been married very long,' Georgia pointed out. 'Still in the honeymoon period.'

'It was almost a year.' His voice broke and he hung his head for a moment. 'We'd been together for four years before that.'

'Why did you decide to get married after all that time?'

'Because we could,' he snapped. Then, in a gentler tone, 'Because we wanted to make a permanent commitment to one another, I suppose. We both felt marriage was for life. We didn't have anything to prove – everyone who knew us knew we were completely devoted to one another.'

'What did you argue about?' I asked. Cameron turned his attention to me, his forehead furrowed.

'All kinds of things. Who hadn't loaded the dishwasher properly. Who was supposed to pick up the meat from the butcher. Who didn't water the garden.'

'Was that all?'

'Sorry to disappoint you. Hassan liked to let off steam that way. He'd pick a fight over something small and we'd argue for ten minutes and then he'd make it up to me over a whole weekend.' He sounded more Scottish when he was upset, I thought, which was the sort of giveaway that could be useful. 'Were you hoping for some juicy details of infidelity? I presume you think that we weren't faithful to one another because we're gay. You're assuming we wouldn't play by heterosexual rules.'

'I'm not assuming anything,' I said. 'Some people have open marriages. Some people have affairs. Some people are faithful to one another. I'm sorry to ask about anything so personal but I have to.'

'Don't pretend you don't enjoy it.'

Cameron's solicitor shifted in his chair, a small but meaningful movement and Cameron pressed his clasped hands to his forehead, mastering himself.

'Of course I understand. You have to find out if I have a motive to kill him. Even though I couldn't have killed him because I was away. Which you know.'

Cameron Dawoud had been competing at a windsurfing competition in Pwllheli, in North Wales, when his husband had his head beaten in.

'I wasn't going to ask about your relationship and whether you were both faithful.' *Yet*. 'I was more interested in arguments about money.'

He gave a short huff of surprise. 'We weren't exactly short of cash, if that's what you mean. Hassan was a consultant which means he got paid a decent amount of money, even for his NHS work. He spent half the time working for the NHS and half of the time for Havenview Hospital, which is a private one. He was a kidney specialist. People respected him. He earned a lot and he spent money on things he liked. Same as me, if it comes to that.'

'What do you do?' Georgia asked.

'I'm an accountant.'

'Do you work for a particular company?'

'I'm self-employed. I have a decent client list.' He managed a grotesque kind of smile. 'You saw our house, right? You know we couldn't have afforded a five-bed house in a nice part of London if we weren't doing all right.'

'Appearances can be deceiving,' Georgia observed. 'You could have been managing a lot of debt.'

'Could have been. But we weren't. You're welcome to go through our financial records and I'm sure you will.' His eyes were steely. 'I was in charge of the financial side of things, as you'd expect. Hassan knew what he had to spend and he was careful about it. We didn't argue about it. We argued about stupid little things because that was how we were. And then we made up.'

'Did anyone wish him harm?' Georgia asked, and Cameron laughed, without humour.

'Well, clearly they did. But if you're asking if I was aware of someone wanting to kill him, then no.'

It was hard to tell whether Cameron despised us because we were women or because he thought we were asking all the wrong questions, but I could tell he hadn't formed a very good opinion of us. I tried to think of something to say that would cut through his defences and prove that we were on his side, really, assuming that he wasn't his husband's killer. My head remained stubbornly empty of anything useful. Beside me, Georgia cleared her throat.

'What I'm asking is if he had any enemies.'

'No. He was on good terms with his family. He didn't get on with all of his colleagues but we're not talking about anything disciplinary. He was just a very determined, focused person and he didn't like anyone saying no to him. If he couldn't get what he wanted by asking, or charming someone, then he shouted. That annoyed some people.' He blinked and pinched the bridge of his nose, fighting for composure. 'All I can think is that someone killed him because they hated what he was. I think someone killed him because he was married to a man and they loathed that. There are plenty of people who think that way, believe me. And some of them are prepared to act on it.'

I let Georgia scurry away after the interview on the pretext that I wanted to tidy up the interview room. The last thing I wanted was a full discussion of where we had both gone wrong in handling Cameron Dawoud. I should have played a bigger part when it became clear that she wasn't able to deal with him, and I had let her fail instead. To teach her a lesson, she had undoubtedly assumed, and I couldn't bring myself to put her right about that.

It's not that I didn't want to help you. I couldn't.

When I left the empty room I stood in the corridor and closed my eyes for a moment. There was work to do, and plenty of it, and conversations I needed to have, and all of that demanded energy. Unfortunately, I was all out.

The sound of a door opening brought me back to where I was and what I should be doing, a feeling that only intensified when I realised the tall figure sauntering towards me was Detective Inspector Josh Derwent at his most urbane, and therefore dangerous.

'That didn't go too well, did it?'

'You were watching?'

'On the monitor.' He brushed a thread from the sleeve of his jacket.

Of course he was completely entitled to watch any interviews I did; I was a DS and he was my DI. Supervision was part of his job. For anyone else, that would have been the whole story.

'Why?'

'Curious.'

'About what? The case?' I hesitated. 'How Georgia was doing?'

'No, angel. Not her.'

I rolled my eyes, not even attempting to hide my irritation as I set off down the corridor. I didn't know why I had expected anything different. Josh Derwent was a HR disaster, a walking liability who had done multiple training courses in professional behaviour. They had served only to arm him with awareness of when he was breaking the rules, and how, and exactly how much trouble he would be in if I complained.

I didn't complain. I had learned not to mind, mostly. Besides, if he was going to be unprofessional then at least that gave me permission to behave the same way. 'Give me a break.'

He fell into step beside me, with the kind of easy stride that told me I needn't bother trying to outpace him. 'What happened to you in there?'

My grip tightened on my notes. 'What do you mean?'

'You let him get away with not answering half your questions. He called you homophobic—'

'He did not.'

' —and so you let him avoid talking about whether they were faithful to one another. That's not like you.'

'It was a first interview and he's not officially a suspect.'

'Of course he's a suspect.'

'He wasn't even there.'

'Uh-huh. Pretty convenient for him to be five and a half hours away from where his husband was being murdered, don't you think?'

'I do,' I allowed. 'But I also think it would have made it quite difficult for him to bash his husband's skull in.'

'He could have hired someone. You heard him. Money wasn't an issue.'

I pressed the button for the lift with maximum force, as if that would make it come quicker. 'It's not easy to find someone to carry out a murder for you.'

'Not easy, but not impossible.' He turned to face me, leaning his shoulders against the wall, his hands in his pockets. 'What about the domestic violence angle?'

'What about it?'

'Did you ask him about it? Who was the aggressor? Did they ever call the police? Ever get counselling? What kind of injuries are we talking about?'

'I can find all of that out. In fact, he's not the best person to ask if he was the one who was handy with his fists. Hassan Dawoud was slightly built. Cameron is a tank. I'm not assuming he was the aggressor but if he was, we're more likely to hear about it from Hassan's friends or colleagues.'

He leaned towards me. 'You went somewhere else the second Georgia brought it up.'

'I don't know what you're talking about.'

'Yes, you do,' he said softly. 'And you know why I'm saying it.'

Without thinking I raised a hand to the collarbone that I had broken the previous summer, then let it fall when I realised what I was doing. The challenge in Derwent's eyes softened to pity, and that was almost worse. I felt my throat tighten.

'You're jumping to conclusions. I didn't know enough to take Cameron Dawoud on. He was pure granite and he wasn't going to give us anything unless he had to. All we had was a sketchy story from the neighbour. Once I've followed it up with her and confirmed it with their friends or relatives or anyone Hassan might have confided in, I'll go back to Cameron with it. At the moment I don't know enough to know when he's lying to me, but I will.'

'*You* didn't tell anyone when it happened to you.' Derwent's voice was silky. 'What makes you think Hassan did?'

I felt the colour wash into my face. 'This isn't about me and I don't know why you keep bringing it up. It's old news. I'm over it.'

'I wonder . . .'

'What?'

'I wonder if you really believe that.' Derwent straightened up, dropping the inquisition abruptly. 'And I wonder if now is the right time to ask you something.'

'What?'

'If you'd do something . . . unusual with me. It would involve going away. A complete change of scene.'

'For work?'

He looked affronted. 'Of course for work.'

No 'of course' about it, I thought. 'Going away – for how long?'

'Don't know.'

'Then no. I would say no.'

'Then I won't ask you.'

At that moment the lift doors slid open and I shot into it. He stood in the hallway, his hands in his pockets, his expression unreadable. He never took no for an answer if it was something he really wanted, I thought.

It was as if he'd heard me. 'I won't ask you *now*, anyway. Some other time.'

I had my hand on the button to keep the doors open. 'Are you getting in?'

'No. I'll take the stairs.'

The doors closed and I felt my shoulders drop, somewhere between relief and dismay. I knew Derwent well enough to be certain the conversation wasn't over.